Adrienne Chinn was born in G[...]
up in Quebec, and eventually m[...]
after a career as a journalist. In [...]
film researcher before embark[...]
designer, lecturer, and writer. [...]
computer, she can usually be found rummaging through flea
markets or haggling in the Marrakech souk.

www.adrienne-chinn.co.uk

𝕏 x.com/adriennechinn
f facebook.com/AdrienneChinnAuthor
⬚ instagram.com/adriennechinn

Also by Adrienne Chinn

The Lost Letter from Morocco

The English Wife

Love in a Time of War

The Paris Sister

In the Shadow of War

THE QUEEN'S NECKLACE

ADRIENNE CHINN

One More Chapter
a division of HarperCollins*Publishers*
1 London Bridge Street
London SE1 9GF
www.harpercollins.co.uk
HarperCollins*Publishers*
Macken House, 39/40 Mayor Street Upper,
Dublin 1, D01 C9W8, Ireland

This paperback edition 2025
1
First published in Great Britain in ebook format by
HarperCollins*Publishers* 2025

A catalogue record of this book is available from the British Library

ISBN: 978-0-00-864382-9

Printed and bound in the UK using 100% Renewable Electricity
by CPI Group (UK) Ltd

'My pride fell with my fortunes.'

William Shakespeare

Prologue

BRYHER

Los Angeles, California
October 2024

Bryher Finch swears under her breath at the throng of paparazzi clustered in front of the entrance to the parking lot of Long and Lean Pilates and beeps the horn of her Toyota Prius. Honestly, much as she appreciates her agent, Margot Chen, tipping off the paparazzi to her every movement, it would be nice, for once, to be able to hit the gym without full makeup on.

She pulls into a spot between a gleaming red Tesla and a Lamborghini in an unfortunate hue of lime green. She gives her face a quick once-over in the mirror as she sways to the latest Taylor Swift on her earbuds, slides on her oversized Tom Ford sunglasses and grabs her Birkin bag. Then, taking a deep breath, Bryher turns down the music on her phone, fixes her mouth into a rictus grin and opens the car door to a surge of photographers.

'Bryher! Bryher! Over here, babe!'

'Bryher, what have you gotta say for yourself? Is it true?'

Margot must have leaked her role as the second lead in the new Tarantino movie. Bryher flashes a smile of practised sincerity at the paps and taps her plumped lips. 'My lips are sealed, but listen out for more news.'

The cameras flash as she strikes a casual pose and tosses her long dark ponytail over her shoulder.

'Bryher, what's Jake say about all this?'

'Jake supports everything I do. I couldn't ask for a better husband.' She blows them a kiss. 'I've got to go, darlings. Watch this space.'

Pulling down the brim of her Prada baseball cap, she turns up the music in her ears and hurries to the gym's entrance, stopping for a moment in the doorway to grace the paps with a wave as the tune changes to 'Bad Romance'.

Bryher is on her sixty-eighth frog stretch on the reformer machine when her phone goes off in her Birkin, which she has left in view beside the machine.

'What did I say about phones, ladies?' the slender, hard-bodied Australian instructor says, an edge as sharp as a steel blade to her voice. 'Turn off the tone or leave it at home.'

Bryher scrambles off the machine. 'Sorry. Sorry.'

'I don't care if you're the Queen of Sheba, there's no special treatment here. You've thrown the class off its rhythm.'

Bryher glances at the text from Margot.

Sex tape! You and Jake's brother?! OMG. Call me! M.

Sex tape? What the f—?

She grabs her Birkin. 'Sorry, gotta take this. It's my agent.'

The instructor sweeps her sinewy arm towards the studio door. 'Be my guest. I can see where your priorities lie.'

Bryher mouths another *Sorry* as she shoves her baseball hat over her ponytail. She exits into the cool, white polished plaster hall and glances out the glass entrance door at the horde of paps outside. Her phone buzzes. Margot again.

Where are you? My phone's blowing up! Why didn't you tell me about this sex tape?

Bryher's stomach lurches. She taps Margot's number, who answers immediately.

'Bryher. Where are you?'

'At Pilates. What's going on? What's this about a sex tape?'

'Hon, it's all over the net. You and Nick Rogers having quite a good time with another woman in a very big bed.'

'What! That's crazy! A threesome? With Nick? Why would I sleep with my brother-in-law?'

'Darling, don't ask me to get inside your head—hold on a minute. Yes, Julian, what now? The *Cop Town* people are on the line and they're not happy? Right, okay, I'll be right with them. Bryher, sorry, hon. Just get here as soon as you can, and we'll talk.'

Bryher pushes open the door to her agent's office in one of Century City's premier addresses. She stops to scroll through the numerous social media posts pinging on her phone:

Fickle Finchy and Naughty Nick in Sexy Threesome!
Team Jake Bashes Cheating Bryher!
Bryjake Earthquake!
Jake Says 'Bye Bye Bry'!

She throws her bag onto one of a pair of white leather Barcelona chairs that sit on the plush silk-pile carpet like wings framing the striking figure of Margot Chen. One of the top agents at Pinnacle, Los Angeles's premier talent agency, Margot sits straight-backed and regal in a custom Chanel suit behind a vast black lacquer desk. She attempts a frown, but her forehead remains as smooth as a waxed wall.

Bryher flops into a chair and pulls off her baseball cap and sunglasses. 'It's a disaster, Margot! Me and Jake's brother in a threesome? I mean, what?!'

'Darling, what *are* you wearing?'

Bryher glances down at her purple lululemon tracksuit and her silver Nike Air Jordan hi-top trainers. 'I told you, I was at Pilates. I haven't even had a shower yet. I wish you'd stop tipping off the paps everywhere I go.'

'It's my job to keep you in the news, although you've done quite a good job of that yourself by the looks of it. That's quite a good cat's eye, by the way.'

Bryher rolls her dark eyes. 'Nothing happened with Nick! I swear it. He's married to the most jealous woman in Hollywood.'

Margot shrugs. 'Jodie has good reason. I mean, Nick's gorgeous. I've even taken up watching golf on TV because of him. Well, I record the games and fast forward to him. My heart rate goes up whenever he putts. It's better than cardio.'

Bryher grabs her bag and roots around in it. 'Honestly, Jodie scares me. I saw her in the gym once. I mean, two hundred squats while holding ten-pound weights? Come on. Totally excessive.'

'You're flushed, hon. Breathe. Let me get you a drink. I've been thinking about this … situation. It might not be such a bad thing after all.' Margot rises from her chair and crosses over to a marble-topped Saarinen table, where a selection of liquor bottles has been arranged by height beside a row of crystal glasses and a silver ice bucket.

'Not a bad thing?' Bryher grabs her phone and presses the screen frantically. She shoves it at her agent as Margot hands her a crystal glass. 'Have you seen this? I've become a meme!'

Margot glances at the phone screen. 'Well, it's very … creative. Don't worry. In the words of Oscar Wilde, "There is only one thing worse than being talked about, and that's not being talked about."'

Bryher takes a sip of the drink and sputters. 'What *is* this?'

'Carbonated green tea and ginseng. It's very good for you.'

Bryher wrinkles her nose. 'Thanks. I'll pass.' She sets the glass on the desk and scrolls through her phone. 'Oh, my God, it's on YouTube now. What am I going to do?' She looks over at her agent. 'You need to put out a press release, like now.'

'And say what, exactly? That you accidentally slipped and fell into Nick's bed?'

'Margot! I'm serious. It's obviously a set-up. Some AI deepfake thing. You've got to do something, or I'm finished.'

Her agent waves away Bryher's anxiety like it's an irritating fly. 'Darling, these sorts of things have been going on in Hollywood for a hundred years. It'll be forgotten by Monday. No one has an attention span anymore. We live in a TikTok world. Besides, you don't really need that cereal sponsorship, or that perfume deal you were about to sign.'

'They're cancelling my sponsorships?'

'Let's just say they're being parked for the moment. Give it a few months and I'll be able to milk this drama to our benefit. I mean, everybody will know who you are. Fame is everything. Trust me, darling. This sex tape is a gift.'

Margot sets Bryher's Birkin carefully onto the carpet and perches on the edge of a Barcelona chair, elegantly crossing her legs.

'Darling, I know this has been a difficult year for you,' she says, softening her tone, 'what with your marriage issues …'

Bryher huffs. 'Jake and Juno this, Jake and Juno that. What is it about women who have only one name? Every time I open my phone, there's a picture of her draped all over him, with those long, snaky arms of hers. She's an anaconda.'

'Juno's just using Jake for the publicity. I've seen it a hundred times. As soon as their movie is out, she'll drop him and be off with another actor or rock star. She's ambitious. You know how this town works.'

'Yeah, I know. It's just that it's made me look like a fool. And now all these allegations about me and Nick and this woman – who I've never seen in my life. Look, I might have flirted a bit with Nick in the past, sure. Who wouldn't? But, come on, Margot, I would never do the stuff they're saying. Not with that psychopath Jodie itching to take out any woman who goes near him.' She shifts agitatedly in the chair. 'You know what I think? I think Jake's framed me. He can't wait to dump me so he can jump into that basic barracuda Juno's bed.'

'I thought she was an anaconda.'

'Same thing.' Bryher shrugs. 'Or … wait. Maybe *she* framed me! That's it. Juno framed me to get Jake.'

'You're grasping at straws, hon. Calm down.'

Bryher exhales a puff of air. 'At least I've got *Cop Town*. That's been doing great in the ratings. And the Tarantino movie.'

'I'm still in talks about the Tarantino, darling, but yes, at least there's *Cop Town*. All's good. It's just as well it's on hiatus right now. Plenty of time for all this to blow over before the next series. I might even be able to get you a raise what with all this publicity.'

'Well, I *am* the star. They couldn't exactly kill me off, could they?'

'Kill you off? No, no, no. That would be crazy.'

Bryher eyes Margot who is surreptitiously glancing at her Cartier wristwatch. 'You don't believe any of this, do you? Margot?'

Margot shrugs. 'It doesn't matter what I believe. It's the optics. You cheating on the beloved Jake Rogers? People love Jake. Ever since *The Twin Universe*, they'll always think of him as Captain Tyro, the saviour of Planet Earth.'

Bryher presses her hands against her forehead. 'Oh, my God.' A sob wrenches from her mouth. 'I'm finished, Margot.'

Margot tugs a tissue out of the box on her desk and holds it out to Bryher. 'No, no, no. It's not all bad. I'll spin this. It's what I do. It just might be a bumpy ride for a while.' She pushes the glass of carbonated green tea towards Bryher. 'Drink your drink. It'll help.'

Bryher takes a gulp, grimacing as she dabs at her eyes with the tissue. 'I should look at this thing like it's a gift?'

'Exactly.'

'But people will think—'

'Don't worry about what people think. You'll be world famous.'

'You mean infamous. And my body's better than this AI woman's. I've spent a fortune on personal trainers and Pilates.'

Margot sits back in the chair and smiles, though the skill of her plastic surgeon has ensured that no crow's feet mar the smoothness of her mature skin. 'Darling, how do you feel about the UK?'

Bryher frowns. 'The UK?'

'The United Kingdom. England, Scotland, Northern Ireland—'

'Yeah, yeah, I know. What about the UK?'

'You have an offer to appear on *Do You Know Who I Am?* for the Comic Relief charity in the UK.'

Bryher wrinkles her nose. 'What would I want to go over there for? Doesn't it rain all the time?'

Margot's mouth twitches. 'I think it's best that you get out of town for a while.' She wiggles her fingers in the air. 'Let me spin my magic and I'll have Fallon's and Kimmel's people fighting over you for their shows by the time you come back. It's only for a day. They won't even miss you in your Pilates class.'

'Just a day?'

'They'll fly you out, do the filming and put you on the red-eye back to LA. You won't even feel like you've gone before you're back.'

'Couldn't they have put me up for one night in a nice hotel? I mean, seriously. That's brutal.'

'Hon, it's a job. They had a last-minute cancellation, and I jumped in and offered you. Bryher, with all these sponsorship cancellations …'

'Right, okay, I get it. What does it pay?'

'It's for charity. There isn't any pay, but the optics are great. You doing something selfless for charity will help neutralise this sex tape thing. Make you seem like less of a homewrecker.'

'A homewrecker?'

'Jodie's thrown Nick out of their house. It's on *TMZ*.'

'Oh, no,' Bryher groans. 'Jodie's going to come after me, too.'

Margot shrugs. 'You can't blame her, can you?'

'But I didn't do anything!'

'Hon, I've got to get back to them asap. What's it going to be?'

Bryher sits back against the white leather and folds her arms. What choice does she have? Maybe getting out of LA isn't the worst idea Margot's ever had. 'Fine, fine. When do they want me?'

'Monday.'

She wipes her nose with the tissue and nods. 'Okay. Let's do it. Now I have to go face Jake. Wish me luck.'

'Really, Margot? Can't you just give it a break for once?' Bryher mutters at the sight of paparazzi outside the gates to her estate in Calabasas, north of Los Angeles. She frantically presses the fob on her keyring as the photographers surge around her car like ants on a sandwich.

'Bryher! Give us a smile, babe! Hey, Bryher! Who's better in bed – Nick or Jake? Bryher! Hope ya got a big bed! We hear ya like a crowd!'

Bryher stomps on the gas pedal and screeches through the gates and up the driveway. She smiles as two of Jake's Dobermans chase after the half-dozen paparazzi who've snuck onto the property, and speeds up the driveway.

In front of the curved arches of the Italianate portico, Jake is leaning against a pillar watching her as she pulls up. A stack of suitcases sits behind him on the portico's stone slabs. He whistles in the direction of the driveway. 'Satan! Zeus! Come on! Job done, boys!'

Bryher presses herself against her car door as the two dogs gallop past her and up the steps into the house. 'I honestly don't know what you see in those beasts, Jake. Couldn't we have just gotten a nice little lap dog?'

'They're loyal, Bry. Which is more than I can say for you.'

Bryher eyes her husband's ruggedly handsome face, which a scruffy beard and short tousled hair seem only to enhance, as her stomach jolts. 'Why are you saying that? I don't know what you've heard, but it's all a lie. I'd never do anything to hurt you. I love you.'

'Is that right? Well, the sex tape that's all over social media paints an altogether different picture.'

Bryher rubs her forehead under her baseball cap. How can he believe she'd do such a thing? 'Nick and I never got together. In a threesome? Are you crazy? I'm your wife! What kind of woman do you think I am? What's Nick say about all this?'

'Why would I be talking to my brother when he's been sleeping with my wife behind my back? Jodie's just texted me. She's taking him back, which makes her a saint or a fool.'

'She is? Oh, good. That's good. That's great! Nick must have convinced her it's all a lie. Did she say anything else? What did Nick tell her?'

'I have no idea what Nick told her. Jodie said she has her reasons. She also said you're finally showing your true colours. Why would she say that, Bry? Huh? What does Jodie know about you that I don't?'

Bryher wraps her arms around herself and rubs them to calm

down the way her Havening practitioner has taught her. What's happening here? Everything was normal this morning, and suddenly it's like a bomb has gone off in the middle of her life.

'Jake, I've got nothing to hide. How can you believe anything she says? She's always had it in for me, ever since she lost the *Cop Town* part to me. How was that my fault? I'm just a better actress than she is, and she hates that.' Bryher begins pacing across the pavement as she taps at the lymph nodes above her collarbones. 'I'll tell you what else. Everyone knows that Nick has a wandering eye. Remember those pictures of him and that woman at the Australian Open before Covid? It's why Jodie follows him around to every tournament. She doesn't trust him. She's so possessive. It must drive him crazy. She's jealous of us.'

'Jealous of us? What are you talking about?'

'Because we're tight. We trust each other, right?' When he doesn't answer, Bryher's panic dissolves into desperation. 'Right?' She reaches out to touch his arm, but he jerks away.

Jake shrugs. 'All I know is that I saw you and Nick and this woman having a pretty good time.'

Bryher laughs nervously. 'It's totally made up. You can't possibly believe it. I'm your wife. I love you.'

'Is that right?'

'Jake, please. Believe me. It never happened! Why aren't you listening to me?'

Jake yanks his phone out of his jeans pocket and, after scrolling for a moment, thrusts the phone at Bryher. 'Here! Look! Tell me that's not you. She's even got your tattoo on your thigh.'

Bryher grabs the phone and watches the three bodies contorting on the screen. She swallows down a wave of nausea. She's watched the tape at least twenty times since Margot texted her, and each time she's felt her stomach drop and the blood drain from her face, just like the time she bungee-jumped off the Bridge to Nowhere.

'It's not me! I swear. I don't know how they've done it. AI

maybe? Someone's framed me. Maybe … maybe Jodie did this. Maybe she wants to test us. Or break us up.

'Really? Then why would she involve this AI Nick or whoever he is?'

'Because she'll look like a saint taking him back, and he'll be all contrite and even more under her control. And another thing, her social media profile will skyrocket. I'll bet her agent's phone is already ringing off the hook.'

Jake takes back the phone and shoves it into his pocket. He stares at Bryher, his jaw rigid. 'You're delusional.' He thrusts out his hand. 'Give them to me.'

'Give what to you?'

'The house keys and the fob for the gate.' He gestures impatiently. 'Give them to me. We're done.'

Bryher stares at the man who had once chartered a private plane to whisk her off to Venice for a surprise weekend at the Gritti Palace, who had bombarded her with hundreds of texts proclaiming his undying love. She'd never been happier than in those first few years together, after they'd met on the set of *The Twin Universe: Three*. She'd been just another jobbing actress with a bit part in a movie looking for a break. Then she'd met Jake Rogers and her life had changed almost overnight. Glamour. Publicity. Fame.

She's damned if she's going to let some trumped-up sex scandal tear it all away from her.

'You can't be serious. It's me, Bry. I'm your wife! You know me better than anyone. And I know you.'

'Do you? Really?'

'Yes, of course. I know … I know that you like peanut butter and bacon sandwiches – crunchy peanut butter, not the smooth stuff. I know you're a sucker for Hallmark movies at Christmas time, especially the ones where city girls end up with lumberjacks.'

She smiles when she sees Jake roll his eyes and his shoulders relax. She steps forward and lays a hand on his T-shirt. 'Look at us. Look at this amazing house. We're living the American dream. We're a team. Bryjake, aren't we? Hollywood's golden couple? We can't let something as stupid as this pull us apart.'

Jake runs his hand through his hair and shakes his head. 'I'm sorry. I can't.'

Bryher's stomach lurches and she steps back as if she's been punched. 'Why?'

Jake's face hardens. 'Well, you slept with my brother for a start. You've torn my family apart. *My* family.' He pauses. 'But then, you don't have a great track record with family, do you, Bry?'

Bryher gasps. 'What do you mean?

'Marnie.'

Bryher steps back as if she's been slapped. 'That's not the same.'

'You cut her out of your life, didn't you? Your own sister?'

Bryher swallows the lump forming in her throat. 'Don't go there. Marnie has nothing to do with this.'

Jake huffs out a loud sigh.

Bryher glares at him. 'Seriously. Don't go there, Jake.'

'Yeah, you don't go there, either, do you? You've never gone there once, have you? She's your *sister*, Bry.'

'Marnie has nothing to do with you.'

'Fine. Fine.' He holds up his hands. 'We've been together six years and married for four. I want kids. I told you that from the beginning.'

Bryher's jaw tenses. Is this what it's really about? Her failure to give him children?

'I tried. I tried for a year. The IVF was awful.'

'But it worked.'

She shuts her eyes at the memory of the blood on the sheets, Jake helping her to the bathroom, the empty cot. 'Stop it. Please.'

'You said you needed time after the miscarriage, and I get that. Totally. But that was four years ago. First, it was because your career was taking off. Then it was because you were too busy with *Cop Town*. But just last month, you told me you wanted to wait until *Cop Town* is over before we tried again. It's never going to happen, is it, Bry? Your career means more to you than having a family. Admit it. You get a buzz from the public adulation, even though it's not real. You always wanted fame more than I did. I mean, who was the first person you spoke to about the sex tape? Me or Margot?'

'That's not fair. She texted me first.'

'Margot. Your agent. Of course you spoke to her first.'

She rubs at the drops of perspiration on her forehead. 'I'm here now, aren't I?'

'After you went to see her. Am I right?'

Bryher looks down at her designer trainers and shrugs.

'Face it, Bry. You don't want a kid to get in the way of all that attention you crave. I'm sorry you had a crappy childhood. But, man, it's scarred you.'

'No, it's just … it's just not the right time—'

'Yeah. It's never going to be the right time. I'm done. We're done. This was the last straw.'

Bryher feels her knees shake and she clutches the car's wing mirror to steady herself. *What's happening?*

'Baby, you don't mean that. I know you don't. We just need some time and space—'

He holds out his hand again. He's not wearing his wedding ring. 'Give me the keys. I mean it.'

Bryher shuts her eyes as bile rises in her throat. 'I need some water.'

Watching her, Jake rolls his eyes. 'Don't be such a drama queen. You're so vain. Vain and shallow. I was an idiot. I thought you were different. I thought you really loved me.' He laughs mirthlessly. 'Jodie's right about you. You took me for a ride, didn't you? Man, I was a fool. I was obsessed with you. I loved you.'

She jerks her head up. He said he'd loved her. Maybe there's still a chance. 'I loved you, too. I still love you.'

'No,' Jake says. 'You don't. You saw a good thing when we met on the film set, didn't you? Hook up with Jake Rogers and you'd be set for life.' He shakes his head. 'You got me good, Bry, but you're two-faced, just like all the others. A total fake. You just want a piece of me because you want fame and adulation. Well, you've got that in spades, honey. You should be thanking me. Everybody knows your name now.' He laughs. 'Thanks to this sex tape, they know more about you then you ever imagined.'

'Jake, please—'

His blue eyes pierce her with contempt. 'I wonder, did *you* set this all up? If you did, congratulations. You've got everybody's attention now. Is this what happened to your sister? Destroyed by all the attention—'

'I said leave Marnie out of this!' Anger races up Bryher's spine and she swallows to regain her composure. 'If you really loved me, you'd know this is a set-up. Come on! Be serious. With your brother? I have everything to lose. My husband. My home. My reputation. My career.'

Jake regards her for a long moment. 'I just don't care anymore.'

'You can't just throw me out. It's my home too.'

'Is your name on the mortgage?'

Bryher frowns. 'No, but … where am I supposed to go?'

'Why don't you call Margot? Get her to sort you out. You're not my problem anymore.'

'Jake! Wait!'

But he's turned his back on her and slammed the door behind him.

Chapter One

BRYHER

Heathrow Airport, London, England
October 2024

One week later

Bryher yawns as she watches a suitcase trundle down the baggage slide and slam into the side of the carousel, narrowly missing a dented upside-down cardboard box marked FRAGILE. She hadn't been able to decide what to wear on the show, so she'd thrown a bunch of outfits into a suitcase along with all her makeup and skin lotions. She might be in the UK for only a day, but damned if she was going to look like she'd just hauled herself off an overnight flight from LA, even if she'd spent the whole time running the events of the past few days through her mind like bad music on a loop.

She's not going to let all this defeat her. She's tough. She'll save the emotion for the camera. She'll get through this. It's not the first time she's faced challenges.

Bryher glances at her Rolex. A two-hour delay, and a crying baby in first class the whole flight. Her head throbs and she yawns again and rubs her lower back. What she wouldn't give right now for a triple espresso with turmeric from Mad Lab in Hollywood. The mattress in Margot's guest bedroom was as hard as concrete and Margot's Siamese cats have brought her out in hives. She'll have to sort something else out as soon as she's back in LA.

She sighs and cranes her neck to peer into the shadowy mouth of the slide, hoping for a glimpse of her suitcase, but the conveyor belt suddenly jerks to a halt.

'No, no, no, no, no! For crying out loud.'

She pushes through the last of the LA passengers collecting their luggage and hurries around the carousel trying to spot her suitcase amongst the lonely baby carriers and cheap, plastic-wrapped suitcases. Spotting a luggage handler pulling the unclaimed bags off the carousel, she stomps towards him across the terrazzo floor.

'Excuse me! Sir!'

The luggage handler looks over his shoulder and squints at Bryher under his thick eyebrows. 'Yeah?'

'My suitcase hasn't arrived. I specifically told them to be careful with it when I checked in. It's Louis Vuitton.'

The man shrugs and waves in an obscure direction. 'Lost luggage. You'll need ta fill out a form.'

Bryher runs her hand across the top of her head, snagging her fingers in her loose chignon. She pulls her hand away, unaware of the clump of dark hair that straggles down her back. No, no, she can't deal with this. Not now.

'Seriously? Don't you know who I am? I'm on television!'

The luggage handler hauls a bright pink suitcase covered in BTS stickers off the carousel. He looks over at Bryher and jabs his thumb towards a crowd gathering at the far end of the luggage hall. 'Lost luggage. Tell 'em Tom Cruise sent ya.'

'Right. Well, thanks for nothing.'

The luggage handler laughs. 'Give my regards ta Madonna,'

he shouts after her. 'No wait! She probably doesn't know who ya are neither!'

Bryher, empty-handed except for her Chanel shoulder bag and a large soya milk vanilla iced coffee from Caffè Nero, exits the departures hall to find herself suddenly in the midst of a swarm of shouting paparazzi and flashing cameras. *For Pete's sake, Margot. Seriously?* She pulls down the brim of her designer baseball cap and turns abruptly, bumping into the couple with the baby from her flight.

'Sorry!' Bryher apologises as she tries to move by them.

'Watch where you're going!' the man says as he pats the baby's back on his shoulder. 'Can't you see I've got a baby here? Precious cargo.'

A soup of irritation and exhaustion boils over in Bryher. 'Hold on just one minute. What were you thinking bringing a baby into first class?' She jabs her coffee cup at the whimpering infant. 'That precious cargo kept me up all night with its screaming. Precious cargo? More like an implement of torture. I've got a throbbing headache and bloodshot eyes because of that thing.'

The woman pushes past her partner, her eyes wild, as the paparazzi fight each other for closer access to the altercation.

'Don't you dare speak to us like that! My baby isn't a thing! We have a right to travel with him in first class anywhere we want to.'

Bryher rolls her eyes. 'There we go. Total entitlement.'

The woman shoves Bryher aside, spilling coffee all over Bryher's Versace hoodie.

'Watch it!' Bryher shouts as the cameras flash. 'Look what you just did! It's Versace! I could sue you for this.'

'Just try it,' the woman says as she relieves the man of the whining baby. She cradles the baby on her shoulder and rubs its back.

'You know what,' Bryher says, her blood boiling. 'I just might!'

The baby lets out a huge burp and a spew of vomit splatters over Bryher's hoodie and yoga pants.

The paparazzi go crazy.

Bryher escapes into a women's toilet and calls her agent.

'Margot, I'm freaking out. They've lost my suitcase and I'm covered in baby sick and iced coffee.' She wipes at the mess with wet toilet paper. 'You've got to do something. I need my suitcase. It's got my life in there.'

'You took a suitcase? Darling, you're only there for a day.'

'Yeah, well, I needed a change of clothes and all my makeup, a hair dryer, a curling iron, hairspray, a travel iron, shoes, you know. And how am I supposed to fit all my cosmetics into one of those dinky little plastic bags? Honestly, airlines totally discriminate against women. We have so much more we have to bring than men when we travel.'

'You can buy cosmetics at the airport.'

'Not my brands! Duh!'

Margot sighs. 'All right, fine. Julian's a marvel. I'll get him right on to it and get your suitcase sent back to LA when they find it. Just wear whatever you're wearing now for the shoot.'

'Didn't you hear me? I'm covered in baby sick and coffee. I got assaulted by a crazy woman and her baby. The paps caught it all. It's probably on social media already.'

'Oh, Bryher,' Margot groans.

'Yeah, well, she ticked me off.' Bryher looks at herself in the mirror and sighs at the sight of her dishevelled reflection. Everything is crashing down around her. She lifts her chin defiantly and tucks the errant strands of hair behind her ears. 'You need to contact Wardrobe. Tell them to get me something in size two from Stella McCartney.'

The toilet in one of the cubicles flushes.

'Are you in a toilet?'

'Yeah, can't you tell by the cheap tiles behind my head? I came in here to escape the paps. Can you give it a rest about tipping them off? They're starting to drive me crazy.'

'No publicity is bad publicity, hon, although I'll have to spin the baby incident. I'll get Julian onto it. This sex tape scandal is just what your profile needs. You're all over the net. It's an agent's dream.

'And now I'll be all over the net with baby puke all over me. Any news from *Cop Town*?'

'I think we can park *Cop Town* for now. Listen, the production company has arranged for a car to pick you up. Look for someone holding up a sign that says "Dorothy Gale".'

'Good. I wasn't going to take a bus, was I?'

Margot sighs again. 'Look, hon, the flight delay's put the filming behind schedule. They're waiting to start the shoot as soon as you get to location.'

'You've got to be kidding. I haven't slept a wink. The lady with the baby was in first class and it screamed all the way over the Atlantic Ocean. I've got circles under my circles. I need coffee, a shower and a nap. I absolutely can't film anything today.'

'Bryher, listen to me,' Margot says, an edge to her normally calm voice. 'You need this job. Doing this charity thing will help me rehabilitate your image. You do want to save your career, don't you? Or should we just forget the whole thing and you can go back to opening boxes on game shows?'

Bryher bites her lip. 'No, it's okay. I get it. *Cop Town*'s still safe, right? They've sent you the script for the next show? We're supposed to start shooting the new series next month.'

'Still waiting for the script, hon. I'm sure I'll get it soon.'

'Good. That's good. Call them, okay?'

'Don't worry. Now put on a smiley face and do your job today, okay?'

Chapter Two

BRYHER

Hever Castle, Kent, England
October 2024

'My agent's going to owe me big time for this,' Bryher tells her driver as she scrolls through the social media sites on her phone. 'First the airline loses my luggage, then she tells me I have to go right into filming a show with some long-lost relative without a shower, a change of clothes or even a coffee.'

The driver nods sympathetically. 'Sounds grim. Maybe ya ortta sack 'er.'

'Sack her?'

'Yeah, ya know. Give 'er the old 'eave 'o.' The driver glances at Bryher's blank expression in the rear-view mirror. 'Give 'er the sack.' He expels an exasperated sigh. 'Fire 'er.'

'Fire her? Are you crazy? She's one of the best agents in the business.' She looks out of the rain-splattered car window as he pulls up in front of the grey stone bulk of a medieval castle sitting on a moated island.

'A castle? Why?'

The driver shrugs. 'Must reckon the show'll play better in the States if they tape it in a castle. Ya know, kings 'n queens 'n knights and princesses 'n all that. Like Disneyland, except real.'

'Right. I guess.' She groans at a video of the altercation at the airport showing the baby throwing up on her in slow motion. 'Oh, man.'

'Trouble in paradise?' the driver asks. 'Believe me, I 'ear it all in 'ere. Break-ups, makeups, cheating, divorces … drivin' a cab is like livin' in a blinkin' soap.'

She scrolls to the *TMZ* page.

Bye Bye, Birdie! Fickle Finch Flies the Coop!
Disgraced TV star flees US in fallout from racy threesome
sex tape!
Is this the end of Bryjake?

She stuffs the phone into her hoodie pocket and wrinkles her nose at the drizzle that has been cloaking the landscape in a dull grey since they left the airport.

'It's raining.'

'It's England.'

'I don't have a raincoat or an umbrella. How am I supposed to film if I look like a drowned rat?'

The driver grabs a tabloid newspaper and tosses it over the seat. ''Ere, use this over your 'ead. Keep the rain off ya till ya get inside.'

'Oh. Well, thanks.'

The driver glances at her in the rear-view mirror. 'If it's all the same to you, I'd like to get 'ome in time for the footie. Arsenal's playin' Liverpool.'

'What?'

''Urry it up, luv. We ain't got all day.'

Bryher sets her face into a winning smile and holds out her hand to the rake-thin, harried-looking young woman in jeans and an Arctic Monkeys sweatshirt who meets her in the wood-beamed entrance hall. She has a headset looped around her neck and carries a clipboard with a much-highlighted script.

'Finally!' she says, waving for Bryher to follow her. 'Come with me. Hurry, we're running out of daylight and it's gloomy as shit in here.'

Bryher follows the young woman, Arabella – 'Ari for short' – through a vast, wood-panelled inner hall where a fire roars in the stone fireplace, and into a large drawing room. Bryher glances around at the intricately inlaid panelling, the mahogany grand piano and the arrangement of overstuffed sofas and chairs upholstered in white silk damask. A camera has been set up facing a sofa, and newspaper clippings, an old photo album and various other items are heaped on top of a large ottoman. A small plump woman in a pleated skirt and a pink wool twinset rises from an armchair. Her short hair is a froth of white-streaked brown, and cat's eye tortoiseshell glasses are perched on the end of her pert nose.

'Oh, you must be Bryher,' she says, holding out her hand. 'I'm your cousin, Betty Pilcher. How lovely to meet you, dear. Here I thought I was all alone in the world, and now here you are! A long-lost relative!' She clasps Bryher's hand in both of hers and squeezes. 'I must say the world is a little less lonely knowing I have a cousin out in America. And, my, aren't you pretty? My mother had your colouring, you know. Lovely dark hair and eyes. She was quite a socialite in her day. Cecil Beaton took her picture on many occasions.'

'Sorry, ladies,' Ari says as she ushers them over to the sofa. 'We've got to hurry this along. Let me go find the crew and we'll get you both mic'd up.'

Bryher waves the damp newspaper. 'Wait a minute. I need makeup. My hair's a mess. Look at me. I need a change of clothes. The airline lost my luggage.'

Ari scans Bryher's stained electric-blue hoodie splashed with a pattern of fake jewels and the purple leggings. She swears incoherently under her breath. 'Okay.' She pulls off her sweatshirt and hands it to Bryher. 'Put this on backwards, so we don't see the logo.' She starts to unzip her jeans.

'What are you doing?'

Ari looks over at Bryher as she steps out of her jeans. 'We're switching clothes. A black top and jeans will look fine.'

'Those will never fit me. I mean, I'm not fat, but—'

Ari huffs impatiently. 'Just leave them unzipped and pull the sweatshirt over them. You'll be fine.'

Bryher nods as she unzips her hoodie. 'What about makeup?'

Ari laughs. 'This is for charity. We don't have that kind of budget.'

Betty pats Bryher's shoulder. 'Don't worry, dear. You look lovely. Very natural.'

'Natural? Oh, my God. Will somebody please pinch me and wake me up?'

Bryher shuffles through the old photographs, Girl Guide badges, a blue ribbon awarded to Betty for 'the neatest homework assignments' in Year 4, newspaper clippings of cake-baking awards, and photocopied records – school reports, marriage licences, birth and death certificates – which threaten to slide off the ottoman. *How much longer does this have to go on?* Bryher thinks as she feigns interest. *I hope there's time to hit duty free at the airport. I wonder if they have that new Mac gloss lipstick?*

Betty leans forward and pulls out a black and white photograph of a 1930s wedding party. 'This is my mother,

Barbara.' She points at a tall, dark-haired woman standing sombrely behind the bride. 'And this is Roberta, Barbara's half-sister. Your grandmother, Bryher.'

'Oh, right,' Bryher says as she glances at Roberta's sharp-chinned face. 'Interesting.' *I'll have to hit up the Versace store in Beverly Hills as soon as I get back. I can't show up in a stained sweatshirt at Long and Lean Pilates on Wednesday or I'll be laughed out of town.*

'This older woman here,' Betty taps the face of a heavyset woman in black sitting in a wicker chair, 'is Roberta and Barbara's mother, Beatrice, your great-grandmother. Beatrice's first husband, Barbara's father, died of the Spanish flu in 1918 and Beatrice remarried a Frederick Farnsworth, your grandfather, who'd unfortunately departed this world by the time this picture was taken. This man,' she taps the groom's unremarkable face, 'is Nigel Pilcher. A banker. He was my father.'

Bryher looks over at Betty, careful to show her better profile to the camera. 'This is fascinating, Betty. That means you are my …?'

'I'm your mother's half-first cousin. You're my half-first cousin once removed.'

Bryher laughs. 'Phew. Okay. It's a shame Mom never knew any of this. She didn't think she had any relatives. My dad was an only child. He died when I was only two.'

Setting her face into an of expression of wistfulness, Bryher picks up the photograph and looks into the camera. 'I didn't think I had any relatives.' She smiles at Betty and reaches for her hand. 'And now I do.'

That ought to do it. Tug at the heartstrings. No one but Jake knows about Marnie. I've worked hard to keep that a secret.

Betty grasps Bryher's hand. 'You do indeed, dear. You always have a home here in England.'

Bryher leans over and embraces Betty. 'Thank you, Betty. It's nice to know I'm not alone in the world.'

'And cut!' Ari claps her hands. Well done, ladies. That was perfect.'

'Great.' Bryher stands up and starts to unclip her mic. *Done and dusted. Get me home.*

'Hold on, Bryher,' Ari says. 'We're not finished. We've got one more location to shoot. It won't take long. It's just upstairs. We're just waiting for the Hever Castle tour guide … Ah, speak of the devil, here he is.'

For fuck's sake. Seriously?

Bryher glances at her watch. They've been filming for six hours, owing to Ari's perfectionism, and she's had nothing but four milky cups of tea and a candy bar to eat. She smiles wanly at the tour guide. 'Wonderful. Let's do this.'

Betty pats Bryher's hand. 'Isn't this fun?'

Bryher sucks in a deep breath. *Fun, my ass.*

'Watch your step there, ladies,' the castle's guide – Malcolm, according to his nametag – cautions, as Bryher and Betty climb the spiralling medieval stone staircase up into one of the castle's turrets. He rests in front of a small leaded window and wipes at his perspiring forehead with a handkerchief as he catches his breath. 'Some of the steps are lower than the others. It's easy to trip up. I've done it myself. I don't recommend it.'

Bryher steadies herself by pressing her hands against the cold stone walls. 'They should have hired better builders.'

'Oh, no, not at all,' Malcolm says as he stuffs the handkerchief into the back pocket of his corduroy trousers. 'The steps were designed especially this way. The family would know where the odd steps were so they could run up and down the steps without a care in the world, though it didn't do me any good, did it?' He chuckles at his own self-deprecating humour. 'The idea was that any invaders or unpleasant sorts would quite literally trip up, gaining the inhabitants more time to hide or escape down one of the hidden passageways.'

Betty follows Malcolm up the steps. 'Isn't this exciting, Bryher? Bryher's a famous Hollywood actress on the telly, you know.'

Malcolm glances over his shoulder at Bryher, a strand of brilliantined grey hair falling over his glasses. 'Is that right? What have you been in?'

'*Cop Town*. Do you know it?'

The guide shrugs, his shoulders sliding up and down within the confines of his argyle jumper. 'Can't say I've heard of it, but then I only watch the BBC. I'm partial to *Doctor Who* myself. And football, of course. Ah, here we are. The bedroom.'

Finally! Bryher thinks. *I was starting to get bed spins going up that staircase.*

She follows Malcolm and Betty into a small wood-panelled room with a large stone fireplace and a protruding lead-paned bay window. Other than a heavy oak chair and carved Tudor oak chest, the room is bare of furniture, though the walls have been hung with modest etchings and watercolours of Tudor life. Malcolm calls the women over from the window where they are gazing out at the drizzly green landscape below.

'Over here, ladies,' Ari says, beckoning them into the middle of the room with Malcolm. 'We'll just get you all mic'd up again and roll.'

When the sound has been tested, the cameraman focuses the camera on the three of them and gives Ari a thumbs-up. Ari calls out 'Roll camera!' and, after a brief bit to camera, Malcolm removes a scroll from behind a chair and slowly unrolls it.

He points to Bryher's name which has been handwritten in elegant calligraphy at the bottom. 'Here you are, Miss Finch.'

Bryher nods. *A castle AND a handwritten scroll. The American viewers will lap this up. The producers know what they're doing.* 'Yeah, I can see that.'

He unrolls the scroll a bit more. 'And here's your dear departed mother, Catherine Mary Farnsworth Finch.'

'Kitty. That's what everyone called her.'

He nods. 'Kitty.' He continues to unroll the scroll. 'Here's Roberta, your grandmother, and up here is your great-grandmother, Beatrice, with another line over here to her other daughter, Barbara, your mother's half-sister, and one down to Betty, your—'

'Half-first cousin once removed,' Betty interjects.

'Exactly.'

Bryher nods. 'Don't tell me I've got a murderer somewhere in my ancestry.'

'Well, that all depends at how you look at history.' Malcolm continues to unroll the scroll, tracing a line through generations as Bryher attempts to feign interest at the convoluted connections. 'Ah, here we go,' he says as he reveals a name near the top of the scroll. 'Lettice Knollys.'

'Lettuce?' *What kind of name is Lettuce?*

'Not lettuce like the vegetable. Lettice. A lovely girl's name, which appears to have fallen out of favour.'

Maybe because it sounds like a salad vegetable.

Betty nods, setting her permed curls quivering. 'Lettice. Oh, I like that. I'll remember that for my next cat.'

Bryher smiles in an attempt to hide a yawn. 'Okay, so I have an ancestor called Lettice. Nice.'

Malcolm unrolls the scroll further. 'Here's where things get interesting.'

It's about time.

'Lettice's father was Sir Francis Knollys. He was a courtier for Henry VIII, Edward VI and Elizabeth I as well as a member of parliament.'

'Oh,' Bryher says, smiling into the camera. 'An English courtier. How exciting.'

'Indeed. Now, Francis married this woman'—Malcolm taps a

name—'Catherine Carey. Catherine's mother was …' He unrolls the scroll further. A name has been written in large calligraphy.

Bryher frowns. 'Mary Boleyn?'

'Quite. Mary Boleyn was the elder sister of Anne Boleyn, Henry VIII's second wife.'

Bryher glances at Malcolm. 'I'm sorry. You're talking about the Tudors, right?' She remembers watching a mini-series once where she thought Jonathan Rhys Meyers' Henry VIII was pretty hot.

'That's correct. Anne Boleyn was the mother of our great Queen Elizabeth I.'

Now you're talking! I saw that movie! 'Oh, yes! Cate Blanchett was amazing in that movie—'

Malcolm holds up a finger. 'Wait a moment. There's more.'

'More?' *Oh, please God, no.*

'Mary Boleyn, while she was married to a man named William Carey, became the mistress of Henry VIII. She had two children during this time, the first of whom was very likely Henry's illegitimate child.'

Bryher's eyes widen. 'Wait a minute, hold on, hold on. So Henry VIII fooled around with both of the sisters?'

'I'm afraid so. It appears that once Mary became pregnant, Henry lost interest in her and turned his attentions to her sister, Anne.'

'Right, so Anne and Mary probably didn't get on?'

He nods. 'I expect their relationship was fairly glacial.'

Betty frowns like she is working out a maths problem. 'Does that mean that Mary's children and Queen Elizabeth I were both first cousins *and* half-siblings?'

Malcolm wipes perspiration drops off his forehead with his white handkerchief. 'Yes, well, yes. A little close for comfort we might all agree, but it wasn't unusual back then. When a noble's wife died in childbirth, he often married one of her sisters, particularly if they were of a good family. In this case, however, Mary went on to live many more years.'

Betty tuts. 'Poor Mary.'

'She cheated on her husband, Betty,' Bryher says. 'It takes two to tango.'

Malcolm stuffs the handkerchief in his trouser pocket and clears his throat. 'Yes, well, I don't imagine that Mary's husband, William, had much say in the matter. It didn't end well for those who opposed King Henry, as poor Anne Boleyn experienced several years later.'

Bryher huffs. 'Typical man. Once you're dumped, you're done.'

Malcolm shows her the scroll. Henry VIII's name is at the top. 'If all this is indeed the case, then you are directly descended from Henry VIII through Mary Boleyn's first child, Catherine Carey.'

Bryher scrutinises the names on the scroll.

'Hold on, are you saying I've got royal blood?'

'Me too, dear,' Betty interjects.

Malcolm smiles at Betty and turns back to Bryher. 'Possibly. There is no way to know for certain if Catherine Carey was Henry VIII's child, although at the time there was much speculation that she was. But you are most definitely descended from Mary Boleyn.' He glances at Betty. 'Both of you.'

Bryher smiles at the camera. 'That's pretty cool.'

Malcolm rolls up the scroll. 'I'm afraid there are plenty of Mary's descendants waltzing around, and they probably don't even know it. Mary's children, Catherine and Henry Carey, had over ten children each. If those children had children and then those children had children, well, I'd wager half of England is related to Mary Boleyn.'

Bryher face drops. 'Oh. So, being descended from Mary Boleyn isn't that special.'

'Well, it's a nice story, don't you think?' He hands Bryher the scroll and gestures to a small gilt-framed portrait on a wall. 'Come have a look at this. The famous portrait of Anne Boleyn wearing the Boleyn necklace.'

The women follow him to a painting of an attractive brunette in a pearled headdress and a black dress. Around her slender neck, a heavy gold 'B' pendant hangs from a pearl necklace.

'She's a nice-looking girl, isn't she?' Betty says. 'Not a beauty, though. You wouldn't have thought she'd catch the eye of a king.' Betty turns to Bryher. 'She looks quite like you, Bryher.'

Bryher grimaces and leans forward and squints at the painting. The same oval face, the same long nose and black eyes. It was like looking into a mirror. 'How weird.'

She pulls her phone out of her handbag and takes several selfies with the portrait. 'So, what happened to her? You said it didn't end well.'

Malcolm and Betty exchange glances. Malcolm clears his throat. 'Uh, well, she was famously executed for treason. Beheaded on the orders of her husband, King Henry VIII.'

'Right! I remember now. That's what happened in the mini-series!' Bryher rubs her neck. 'Poor Anne. That was brutal.'

Malcolm coughs. 'Quite.'

Betty leans forward and peers at the portrait through the bifocals. 'That really is a lovely necklace.'

Malcolm pushes his glasses back up his nose. 'In and of itself, it is nothing special. Initial necklaces were quite common back in Tudor times – as they still are today. Anne is known to have had an "A" necklace and an "AB" brooch, too, though this "B" necklace is the most famous.'

Bryher studies Anne's necklace 'What happened to it?'

Malcolm chuckles. 'If I had a penny for every time I've been asked that, I'd be a rich man. The fact is, no one knows. Most of Anne's jewellery was taken by King Henry VIII and destroyed after her execution, although a few of the items she owned prior to her marriage were either returned to her family or taken by loyalists and given to Anne's daughter, Elizabeth. Some say Elizabeth incorporated the pearls into new jewellery, or that some of the pearls are in the British Imperial State Crown. All we know, is that after Anne's death, the necklace was never seen in public again.'

'What if somebody were to find it?'

'Oh, well, I can't imagine that will happen. It's been lost for centuries. Very likely, the gold was melted down and the pearls re-used in some of Elizabeth I's jewellery. There are all sorts of copies of the necklace around. We sell them here in our own shop. They're very popular. Bestsellers, in fact.'

Bryher nods. 'If the real necklace showed up, would it be valuable?'

Malcolm chuckles, his thick grey eyebrows wiggling. 'Valuable? It would be priceless.' He presses his handkerchief to his mouth as he fights to control his laugher. 'Valuable? Oh, really, you've given me quite a laugh, now, haven't you? It's like asking if the *Mona Lisa* is valuable.'

He stuffs his handkerchief back into his pocket and gestures towards the door. 'Now, ladies, if you follow me, I have King Henry VIII's bedchamber to show you, where it is thought that the king stayed when he visited Hever Castle to court Anne. Then I'd highly recommend a nice cup of tea and a slice of Victoria sponge in our café.'

Chapter Three

THE BOLEYNS

Hever Castle, Kent, England
May 1513

Reginald Bacon, the Boleyn children's Latin tutor, taps with a willow pointer on the small slate he holds against his doublet, frowning at the absence, yet again, of the youngest child, George, who, he has been advised, has been taken by the groom on yet another riding lesson.

'Mary, Anne, in our lesson of yestermorn, you were taught that the largest group of second declension Latin nouns is masculine and ends in "us", "er" or "ir".' He focuses his gaze on the elder Boleyn girl, who twirls a strand of blonde hair that has escaped her linen coif as she stares out of the leaded window panes. 'Mary, what is the exception to these rules?'

At fourteen, Mary Boleyn is as plump and pretty as a spring lamb, and as she jerks her head around, her blue eyes widen. 'I most humbly beg your pardon, Master Bacon?'

Sitting beside her at the table, her sister Anne muffles a giggle.

'That will do, Anne,' the tutor says sharply. 'It is not meet to express glee at your sister's inattention to the lesson.'

Thirteen-year-old Anne Boleyn, her hair the colour of walnuts and worn loose about her shoulders, and her eyes as black as polished jet, bites her lip. 'My apologies, Master Bacon. Mary was intent on practising the galliard with poor George yestereve, and neglected her Latin study.' She glances at her sister. 'The exception are neuter nouns which end in "um",' she says smugly.

'Correct. I am gratified that my efforts of yestermorn were not altogether in vain. Now, Anne, recite the six singular cases for the noun "lord".'

Anne pushes away from the bench, almost unseating her sister, and stands perfectly poised behind the table. '*Dominus, domine, dominum, domini, domino, domino.*'

'Excellent, please sit. Mary, stand and recite the plural cases of dominus. Begin with the nominative case.'

Mary rises slowly to her feet, her face reddening. She clears her throat. 'Uh, *dominos*—'

The tutor taps the pointer on the table. 'Incorrect. Again.'

Mary glances at her sister, who has made an effort at composure by pressing her lips together though her shoulders shake with mirth.

'*D-dominis*—' Mary jumps as the pointer slaps on the table.

'Incorrect. Again.'

'*Domini, domini, dominos, dominorum, dominis, dominis,*' a man's voice chimes in from the doorway.

The tutor hastily sets down the pointer and bows his head to the visitor. 'Sir Thomas.'

Sir Thomas Boleyn's imposing frame, clad in a fine, forest-green silk doublet embroidered in silver thread, green velvet trunk hose and fine white stockings, fills the doorway as he removes his leather gloves. At thirty-five, he has the demeanour of a man who is master of his own destiny, having recently returned from the Continent where he had been sent by King Henry VIII on a diplomatic mission to shore up the Emperor Maximilian's support for an English invasion of northern France.

'I caution you to be patient with Mary, Master Bacon,' he addresses the tutor. 'She is our bright hope and her lack of an ability in Latin shall do her no harm.'

The tutor bows his head. 'Yes, Sir Thomas.'

Sir Thomas gestures to his younger daughter. 'Anne, I wish to speak to you on a matter of some import.'

Anne rises from the bench and inclines her head to the tutor. 'With your permission, Master Bacon, may I be excused?'

'Of course, as your father wishes.'

'Father, what of me?' Mary asks as she watches Anne join their father.

'Attend to your lessons, Mary, and then you may go help your mother gather flowers for the hall.' Sir Thomas looks over at the tutor. 'I shall send in George from his riding lesson to join you. He has need to practise his Latin if he is to progress to the court when he is of age.'

The tutor inclines his head. 'As you wish, Sir Thomas.'

'Oh, and one thing more, Master Bacon.' He glances at his eldest daughter. 'You are to spare the rod if Mary stumbles with her lessons. I will not have her pretty hands spoiled. With George or Anne, on the other hand, if lessons haven't been learned, the appropriate discipline is warranted.'

Anne follows her father into the family's private parlour, where the servants have laid out the long table for the mid-day dinner. Sir Thomas seats himself in the carved oak chair at the head of the table and gestures for Anne to sit.

'Anne, I have news from the Archduchess Margaret of Austria.'

'Oh, Father, she is not recalling you to her court already? You have barely returned.'

'No, I sail with my men to Calais this month coming to join King Henry's forces in France. This is another matter.'

A young serving woman enters the room with a basket of bread. Sir Thomas frowns at the intrusion and barks at the girl to leave.

'Anne, you have heard me tell of the archduchess, have you not?'

'Yes, Father. You stayed at her court this year past, as King Henry's ambassador.'

Sir Thomas nods. 'Indeed. The archduchess is a widow of uncommon intelligence who rules the Low Countries as regent owing to the youth of her nephew, Charles. She has a library such as I have never seen in England, and her palace at Mechelen is adorned with rich tapestries and paintings from the hands of the greatest artists on the Continent. I have seen with mine own eyes her collection of artifacts from the peoples of the New World. The kings and queens of Europe seek out her counsel, such is her reputation for sagacity. The archduchess is a woman whose qualities you would do well to emulate, Anne. You may not possess your sister Mary's beauty and sweet nature, which will doubtless secure her an excellent betrothal to the highest of nobles when she is of age, but your wit and education, if you work hard to hone them, should in due course grant you access to the English court. It is my great hope that you, too, will make an impressive match and contribute to the honour of the Boleyn name.'

Anne bites her lip, stung by her father's insinuation of her plainness. 'I wish that as well, Father.'

'Good.' He clears his throat. 'I have received a letter from the archduchess's own hand extending to you an invitation to join her court as one of her *filles d'honneur*. It is a great honour.'

Anne gasps, wishing she could throw herself into her father's arms the way that Mary does so easily. 'Oh, Father. This is the most marvellous news.'

'Yes. It took some strategic planning and much flattery, but I have managed to secure you this place, though you are yet but three and ten years. Mary, as the eldest, should be placed at court before you, but I plan to secure her a position in the great court of France where she has the best chance of polishing her charms to a high sheen, and this takes more effort than securing a place in the archduchess's more minor court. Now, we have little time to waste. The archduchess is sending over her equerry to accompany you to her court one month hence. There is but little time to accumulate appropriate gowns for you to wear. The archduchess's ladies are seen only in gowns of the highest fashion, and I won't have our English rose fading to a wallflower. And, Anne, I entreat you to perfect your French as this is the language of the archduchess's court. I will engage Monsieur Duwes of the king's court to tutor you and your sister.'

'Yes, Father. I shall study so well that I shall become as a French girl born.'

Sir Thomas smiles despite himself. 'That is very well, Anne. You must help Mary with her lessons, too. She will have just as much need of French if she is to make an impression in the French court.'

Anne nods, delighted to be charged with haranguing her sister with French verb conjugations. 'I shall ensure Mary speaks like a French girl born as well, Father. Shall I return to my Latin lesson now?'

'No, go and fetch your brother. I am well pleased with you, so after dinner go and enjoy the remainder of the day as you wish.'

Anne jumps up from the bench. 'Oh, Father! Thank you! If I may have your leave, sire, I shall ride my pony to Stone Castle to visit Bridget.'

Sir Thomas nods. 'Ensure the groom accompanies you and be

home well in time for supper, else your mother will be cross. Give my regards to Sir John and his good wife.'

Sir Thomas watches Anne hurry out of the parlour and disappear into the great hall. If only Mary exhibited a small amount of Anne's cleverness and vigour, he would be a happier man. Yet, his eldest daughter has been blessed with beauty and charm, and the fact is that these trump wit, spirit and cleverness such as Anne possesses. He has done well by Anne, placing her in the archduchess's court. Now it is time to turn his attention to Mary, his family's great hope.

Chapter Four

BRYHER

En Route to Heathrow Airport, England
October 2024

Bryher gazes out the taxi window at the blocks of rain-streaked concrete warehouses and the rows of 1960s pebbledash houses that whip by in a blur of murky greige under the lowering sky, like damp cardboard boxes fraying at the edges. She looks down at her phone and googles *Bryher Finch latest news*, tapping on the first site that comes up.

Is this the end for Hollywood's Golden Couple Bryjake?

Four years ago the world was treated to a Hello! magazine spread of the wedding of Hollywood heartthrob Jake Rogers and up and coming actress, Bryher Finch, at an exclusive private estate in Italy, after their meeting on the set of the third in The Twin Universe movie franchise. Since then, Bryher's career has been on an upward trajectory. After her tragic demise in The Twin Universe: Four she landed the lead in the top-rated TV show, Cop Town, as Jake continued conquering not just The Twin Universe, but our hearts, in his further on-screen forays as the stoic strongman, Captain Tyro. But is it all coming crashing down after the leak of Bryher's sex romp with pro golfer, Nick Rogers, Jake's brother?

Bryher winces just as Margot's name flashes onto her phone screen, and she adjusts her earbuds to take the call.

'Margot, it's all over the net, "the end of Bryjake",' she groans. 'What am I going to do?'

She hears her agent take a breath. 'Where are you?' Margot asks.

'On my way to Heathrow in a cab. Not a moment too soon if you ask me.' Bryher rubs at the condensation on the window and wipes her wet fingers on her stained Versace hoodie. 'Give me LA sun and decent coffee any d—'

'Hon,' Margot cuts her off. 'Nick's wife is pregnant. Twins.'

'What!'

'Yep. Four and a half months pregnant.'

'What? That means—'

'That Jodie was already pregnant when you allegedly had your threesome romp with her husband. Believe me, it was a surprise to me, too. It's obviously why she took him back so quickly. She's just given an exclusive interview to *Entertainment Tonight*.'

'What? Wait. Let me look.' Bryher taps *Jodie Rogers ET* on her phone. There she is in all her California blonde glory, her lithe-limbed body clad in pale rose cashmere loungewear, reclining on their white boucle Liaigre sofa cuddling her white Persian cat to her compact bump as she answers the reporter's questions.

'*… it was quite a shock, I mean, I thought Bryher and I were friends. To be stabbed in the back like this has been so upsetting. I shouldn't have been surprised. I mean, I'd been warned about her. How she's two-faced. I* *didn't want to believe it, I mean, she's my sister-in-law, right? Then to seduce her own brother-in-law when I'm … when I'm …'*

The reporter leans closer. *'Are you saying Bryher knew you were pregnant and still seduced your husband?'*

Jodie stifles a sob and accepts a tissue from the reporter. She dabs at her expensively straight nose. *'All I can say is that I have to honour my truth, which is that Nick and I are about to become parents, and I believe him when he says Bryher was the predator and caught him in a weak moment …'*

Bryher gasps. 'What? She's making that up. Nick knows it's fake.'

'… I mean, the first trimester isn't easy. Hormones and everything. Maybe I pushed him away, I don't know.' Jodie looks directly into the camera. *'I know all you mothers out there know what I mean. The mood swings. The hormones. I think Bryher saw a chance and took it.'* She looks back at the reporter. *'I feel so, so sorry for Jake, to have wasted so many years on someone who's nothing but a gold digger …'*

No, no, no, no, no. This can't be happening. 'She's lying, Margot.'

Her agent sighs. 'My phone's been ringing off the hook, Bryher. It's not good.'

Bryher shuts her eyes and shakes her head. 'What … what about *Cop Town*?'

Margot clears her throat. 'I'm just off a call with the producer. Hon, they're killing you off.'

'No! They can't do that!'

'I'm sorry. I know it's a shock.'

'A shock?' Bryher tosses her long ponytail over her shoulder and pounds her chest. 'I'm the Emmy-nominated star of *Cop Town*!'

'The Emmy-nominated former star of *Cop Town*.'

'But people love me.' Bryher swallows down a sob, oblivious to the glances from the taxi driver in the rear-view mirror. *'I'm* the one who was on the cover of *Us* in March. I've got a fan club!

Didn't you tell me a few weeks ago that Jimmy Fallon's people had been in touch?'

'Yes. But that was before—'

'Margot, they *can't* kill me off! Have you told them that? You're my agent. You need to protect my interests.'

'I'm afraid the advertisers haven't taken too well to all this. Especially Jodie's interview. Her people are swamping social media with her allegations against you. The network's not happy either. They've been on the phone, too. A Hollywood sex tape's one thing, but sleeping with a pregnant woman's husband who also happens to be your brother-in-law is something altogether different.'

Bryher wipes her tears on the back of her sleeve. 'Please tell me I get a good death scene.'

'They've killed you off in a plane crash, somewhere in northern Canada where you'd been sent to investigate illegal beaver poaching. They're covering it with a line or two when they tape the next show. They don't want you back.'

'No, no, oh God.'

The taxi driver slides open the window hatch separating his seat from the back and shoves a wad of tissues at her which she grabs gratefully.

'Bryher, hon, listen to me. This is major damage-limitation time. Have you heard the saying, "When one door closes, another one opens"?'

'Yeah,' Bryher says as she blows her nose.

'I've got you an offer on a TV mini-series.'

Bryher sits up against the leather upholstery. 'What?'

'I am very good at my job, darling. It turns out that the production company who filmed your *Do You Know Who I Am?* segment is making a mini-series about King Henry VIII and Anne Bovine.'

Bryher sniffs. 'You mean Anne Boleyn?'

'That's the one! Yes, Anne Boleyn. I didn't know you knew history.'

'We filmed in Anne Boleyn's family castle today. I'm related to her, you know,' she says, dabbing her nose. 'Kind of. Through her sister.'

'Ah, that explains it. The producers saw the footage. I've just got off the phone with them. They think you'll be great as Anne Boleyn in the mini-series. That, and the fact you're in England. They actually think your scandal will help them sell the series all over the world.'

'What? Really?'

'They were just about to start the shoot, but the actress who was going to play Anne pulled out. Rehab. There was an intervention. Anyway, they think you'll be perfect – you're an actress, you're in England and they're happy to overlook your current troubles … What do you say?'

'Uhhhh …' Bryher rubs her forehead.

'You say yes,' Margot says firmly. 'My sister's coming over from Hong Kong and I need the guest room back.'

Bryher sucks in her breath. She has no choice. This mini-series is probably the only lifeline she'll be thrown for a while. 'Yes, yes, okay. Sign me up.'

'I already did. You start filming on Thursday. I'll email you the contract and the details. It's a twelve-week shoot. You can do an English accent, can't you?'

Bryher grunts. 'I've watched every episode of *Downton Abbey* and *The Crown*. I'm an actress. How hard can it be?'

'Good. Keep a low profile and let this sex tape thing blow over. I suggest you find yourself a nice hotel and treat this as a holiday.'

'Uh, isn't the production company going to put me up in a hotel?'

Bryher hears Margot suck air through her teeth. 'That's the thing. The actress who's off in rehab is refusing to pay back the chunk of money she's already been paid. It's all going legal.'

'So?'

'So, they can't afford a hotel.'

'Are you kidding me? I'm supposed to pay for my own hotel? Don't they know who I am?'

Margot sighs down the phone. 'They're happy to pay for your travel expenses. I'm working on a refreshment budget. Give me some time, hon. I'll work on the hotel. In the meantime, I suggest you fill up on salads and sandwiches at the film studio. That'll be free.'

'What about clothes? I haven't got a suitcase, remember?'

'Go buy yourself some clothes on Bond Street. Consider it a shopping holiday.'

'I don't believe this.' Bryher huffs, her breath steaming up the window. 'What's the pay?'

'It's decent. Not A-list decent, but … Look, the only money you're bringing in right now is on residuals from *Cop Town*. You need to earn money while I do damage limitation. By the time you get back here, I'll have a stack of offers on my desk. Hold on, hon. Yes, Julian? Jennifer's here? Which one? Oh, right, that one. Definitely. Bryher, I've got to go, darling. One of my A-listers just arrived. Talk soon.'

Bryher switches off the call and knocks on the window hatch. The driver slides open the window.

'There's been a change of plan,' she tells him. 'Take me to the Savoy Hotel.'

The impeccably suited receptionist smiles apologetically and slides the credit card across the green leather inset into the mahogany desk. 'I'm terribly sorry, Ms Finch, but your card has been declined. Would you like to try another card?'

Bryher draws her dark eyebrows together. 'Declined? That's impossible. There's plenty of money on that card.' She roots around in her handbag and pulls out another from her wallet. 'Here, this one will definitely work.'

The man nods his head and takes the card. 'Certainly, madam.'

Bryher taps her trainer on the polished black and white marble floor tiles as she watches him tap the card details into his computer. He glances up and shakes his head.

'I'm afraid that one has been declined as well.'

Bryher takes back her credit cards. 'I don't understand it.' She digs out her bank card. 'Here, try this one.'

He tries the card, but shakes his head again. 'I'm very sorry, madam,' he says as he hands it back.

She taps the card on the green leather. *What's going on? There's definitely money in my account.*

She smiles her most winning smile. 'I'm an actress. Bryher Finch. From Hollywood? Maybe you've heard of me? I'm the star of *Cop Town*? On television?'

The receptionist shakes his head, not a strand of his precisely cut and styled hair falling out of place. 'I'm afraid I only watch BBC2. Documentaries and news programmes mostly.'

Bryher smiles tightly. *Of course he does. Doesn't anyone in this country watch real TV?*

She holds up a finger. 'Let me make a call. I'll be right back.'

'Certainly, madam.'

Bryher ducks behind a pillar and rings Jake's number, biting her lip as she waits for an answer. *This can't be happening. Pick up, pick up, pick up.*

'Bry. This is a surprise.'

'Jake, what have you done to my credit cards?'

'Hello to you, too.'

'Look, I'm at the Savoy in London and I'm trying to book a room, but all my credit cards are being declined. Even my bank card's been declined.'

'That's a shame.'

She looks over at the receptionist and catches him glancing at her surreptitiously. She smiles weakly and turns her back on him. 'What have you done to my cards? Why can't I access my bank account?'

Jake tuts. 'You mean *our* account, Bry. I took your name off our joint credit cards and transferred the money from our joint bank account into one of my accounts.'

Bryher's stomach lurches and she sways as the blood rushes from her head. 'That was *my* money. *My* money! You had no right.'

'I had no right? You humiliated me! Nick and I aren't speaking. My mom's in pieces. Jodie's all over the net saying I'm pathetic and you're a sociopathic gold digger. They're threatening to drop me from the next *Twin Universe* sequel. You disgust me.'

'Jake, listen to me, please. I told you already. It's all a set-up. None of it's true. Please, help me. I'm stranded here in London. I've got no way to pay for anything. I'll literally be out on the street.

'Yeah, it sucks to be you, doesn't it? If you've got a problem about this, you better have your lawyer take that up with mine. You do have a lawyer, don't you? Because you're going to need one.'

'Jake! Wait—'

The call goes dead.

Bryher leans her forehead against the cool marble of the pillar. *How can this be happening?* Just when she thought she'd hit rock bottom, the rock has turned to quicksand and she is sinking even lower. She bites her lip to stifle the tears that are threatening to spill down her cheeks. She takes a deep breath and wipes at her eyes. No, she's cried enough. She needs to pull herself together.

She taps Margot's number.

'Hon, can I call you back? I'm about to have my Botox injections.'

'This can't wait, Margot. Jake's cancelled all my credit cards and cleaned out our joint bank account. I'm stuck here in London with a *Hello!* magazine and a pack of Tic Tacs. What am I going to do? You've got to help me.'

'Breathe, darling. Where are you?'

'At the Savoy.'

Margot laughs. 'Of course you are.'

'This isn't funny.'

'I know. Sorry. Do you have any friends in London you can call?

'No. Why would I? The only person I know here is Betty Pilcher. I met her today on the shoot. She's some distant cousin seventeen times removed. She gave me her number, but that's not an option.'

'No, it's perfect! Why don't you call her and ask to stay until we can get this all sorted out.'

'Have you lost your mind? I don't know her. And she's at least seventy.'

'Look, if you stay with this lovely old lady, it would show your … human side. I mean, you've got some work to do that score …'

'What do you mean by that?'

Margot sighs heavily. 'Seriously, telling that journalist from *People* magazine: "I have more talent in my little finger than Meryl Streep has in her entire body"? Come on, Bryher. Meryl is a national treasure. That did not go down well. And now there's the baby thing with Jodie. Julian's working on getting you an interview in *Good Housekeeping* to rehabilitate your image, but there's been some push-back. The truth is there are a lot of people who are enjoying your current difficulties.'

'Really? Who?'

'Well … everybody. The opinion polls are a disaster. The perception is that you're an entitled, self-centred minor celeb who's gotten lucky. You're heading towards the F-list. A little humility would go a long way to helping revive your image. You staying with this Betty cousin, aunt, whatever, is perfect.'

The memory of Betty insisting on ordering them both endless cups of milky tea and two large wedges of sickly sweet Victoria sponge cake at the Hever Castle café flashes through Bryher's mind. *'No proper English person drinks coffee, Bryher. When in Rome!'*

'Entitled? Really?'

'That's what the polls say.'

Bryher frowns at her phone. 'You don't think I'm entitled, do you?'

'Well, hon, where there's smoke there's usually fire.'

'Wow. I had no idea.'

'Listen to me. Call this Betty person and take a train or a bus or whatever to her place.'

'I haven't got any cash.'

'So, take a taxi and ask this Betty person to pay for it when you get there. Tell her you'll pay her back.'

'This Puddleton place where she lives could be miles away. It could cost a fortune.'

'Hon, just get there. I'll wire you some money tomorrow by Western Union, then you can pay her back. Text me the town name. Just make sure you get to the studio on Thursday, and don't be late. Okay?'

Bryher sighs. 'Okay.'

'I have to go. I'm having a double Botox dose today and that's all because of you.'

Chapter Five

ANNE

Palace de Rihour, Lille, Flanders
September 1513

Anne sits as a table in front of the soaring leaded glass windows on the left of the palace's great hall with the Archduchess of Austria's other *filles d'honneur*, failing miserably to maintain a demure composure as she absorbs the vibrant tableaux unfolding before her. Everyone is in high spirits at the victory of King Henry VIII and the Holy Roman Emperor Maximilian over the French at Thérouanne. The thirty-three-year-old widowed Archduchess Margaret of Austria, resplendent in a gown of burgundy embroidered silk and a simple white linen widow's coif, is seated at the head of the table to the left of her father, the Holy Roman Emperor Maximilian.

A handsome and charismatic man of fifty-four, Maximilian is clapping enthusiastically as the masked male dancers, clad in garish red, yellow and green striped hose and doublets and feathered caps, jump and gyrate to a *moresca*. On Margaret's right, the seat where the tall, handsome, red-haired English King Henry had earlier been seated, is empty.

'Do be still, Anne,' the Countess of Hoogstraten chides in French as she helps herself to a cream-filled pastry. 'You are three and ten, not a child. The archduchess expects her *filles* to exhibit poise on every occasion. It is the mark of a true gentlewoman. It is well that you have come to her court at a young age. Another two years in the English countryside and you would be a fit wife for none but the third son of a landless knight.'

Anne juts out her chin. 'My sister, Mary, who is almost five and ten, is yet at our home in Kent.'

The countess flicks out her tongue and licks cream off her lower lip. 'Then she is past saving.'

Anne lowers her gaze so that the countess, the firm and humourless mistress of the nine young *filles d'honneur*, is not provoked into further derogatory comment. Though she and Mary have frequently had their differences, she will not brook anyone casting aspersions on her family. She will mix the countess's white lead face powder with vinegar in the morn rather than water and enjoy watching it dry into a white crust and flake off the countess's face like snow during dinner. A smile tugs at the corners of her mouth at the image.

What shall the Archduchess Margaret make of that, Countess?

The rollicking dance of jumps and twirls ends and one of the dancers whips off his mask to reveal his identity as the young English king. The hall explodes in shouts and clapping, and Henry doffs his cap and extends a flourished bow to the archduchess, who claps delightedly as her father, Maximilian, stands and holds out his gold cup of wine.

'*Bravo*, Henry! And here's to a victory at Tournai in the morn!'

The hall echoes with the riotous cheers of Henry and Maximilan's men, Margaret's *filles d'honneur* and the noblemen and noblewomen of Lille. 'More wine!' someone shouts and the minstrels in the gallery strike up the music of the Hungarian dance, the *alongaresca*. Several of Henry's men grab torches from the walls and rush onto the floor, throwing themselves around wildly while making lewd gestures with the torches as the noblemen and ladies join the melee. Standing a head taller than everyone else, Henry laughs as he dances with a beautiful, olive-skinned woman some years his elder.

Anne leans over to one of the other *filles*. 'Ursula, who is that dancing with King Henry?'

Ursula, a thin-faced girl of eighteen with an air of bored sophistication, looks over at the dancers. 'She is the bastard.'

Anne's eyes widen at the coarse word. 'Pardon me?'

Ursula shrugs her bony shoulders. 'She is the bastard daughter of a Portuguese laundress. She is no one. They call her Madame la Bâtarde.'

Anne observes the laughing woman who has the full attention of the king. 'She is very beautiful.'

Ursula laughs. 'A woman's beauty does the owner little service. It is a shiny thing to be pursued, possessed and then discarded by men. In my view, wit, charm and intelligence are better weapons for a woman in this world. Carry these, and a woman is a worthy adversary to any man.'

'You speak like we are at war with men.'

Ursula stares at Anne with eyes as pale as spring ice. 'We will be at war with men until they credit us as equals in this world and we are able to live a life as free as they. It is best that you learn to build your arsenal and fight for a life worth living, Anne.' She nods in the direction of the Archduchess Margaret. 'Why do you think the archduchess wears a widow's coif and refuses to marry though it has been nine years since her husband died? It is to show that she is owned by no man and is free to live life on her own terms. The best thing for a noblewoman in this life is to be widowed at a young age and left with an inheritance. This is what I wish above all.'

Anne looks back at King Henry and Madame la Bâtarde. She

cannot image that she will ever be graced with the fulsome figure, nor the comely face of such a woman. Anne's face is too sharp and her nose too long, and she will never be the plump blonde beauty so favoured in the courts – for no matter how much she eats, she remains as slender as a rail. Her hair is dark, her eyes almost black – and yet here is the king, held in thrall to a woman as dark as she.

Anne reassures herself that she is young yet, at only three and ten. There is time. She will read the manuscripts in the archduchess's extensive library and scrutinise every item of art in her collection; study French until she speaks it like a native; improve her courtly skills in dancing, singing and playing the clavichord and the lute. She will listen to the conversations of those more learned than she, to learn of the wars and politics of the day. She will pray to the Holy Mother to guide her way. She will not be pursued, possessed and cast aside like a tired toy. The Archduchess Margaret's court will be her university and she will be a willing and able student.

Chapter Six

BRYHER

Puddleton, England
October 2024

Bryher stands on the pavement in front of the taxi and examines the unprepossessing exterior of a post-war bungalow wedged between a hairdresser's called 'Do Yer Nut' and a car tyre dealership. The dullness of the grey pebble dash rendering is only marginally relieved by the faux Tudor woodwork and picket fence which shines bright yellow in the glare of a streetlight. An explosion of garishly coloured pansies froths over the tops of hanging baskets dripping from a recent rain shower.

The door yanks open and Betty emerges, neat in her pleated plaid skirt and wool twinset, a vibrant canary yellow this time.

'Bryher! How lovely to see you again! Your phone call was such a wonderful surprise.'

'I'm so sorry to show up on your doorstep in the middle of the night, Betty.'

Betty waves a hand. 'Don't be silly, dear. Let me fetch my purse for the taxi. He has turned off the meter, hasn't he? We don't want to be paying more than we need, do we?'

'Uh, yeah … no.'

Betty looks down at Bryher's damp and dirty silver trainers. 'Oh, dear, what's happened to you? Wait here a moment and let me get you a towel. Can't have you traipsing in all that dirt onto the carpet, can we?'

Bryher watches Betty disappear into the bungalow's hallway as she feels her stomach sink. This is a terrible idea. She's going to kill Margot for suggesting this. And Jake for being a jerk.

Betty emerges from the front door holding a black patent leather wallet and waving a peach hand towel. 'Here we are, dear. I'll let you clean up out here while I pay the taxi, then follow me into the lounge. I'm still ironing the sheets for the pull-out bed in my sewing room. Don't worry about putting me out. I can sew in the lounge, although the light isn't as good. I'm sewing squares for a peace quilt for the WI. Wait until I tell the girls that I've got a genuine Hollywood star staying with me. Marion Livesay, the club president, will just eat herself up with envy.

'I've just put the kettle to boil,' Betty continues as she picks dead flowers off the pansies. 'I'll make you a nice cup of tea and we can have a lovely catch-up. I ran out to the shop and bought Earl Grey and chocolate Hobnobs after you rang. You can't go wrong with chocolate Hobnobs and a good cup of tea, I say. You can tell me all about your little project here in England and then we can make up your bed.'

Bryher cleans her trainers and smiles tightly as she hands back the dirty towel.

Nope, nope. This definitely isn't going to work. Margot's got to get me out of this.

'I'll only be staying a couple of nights until my agent sorts me out a hotel roo—'

'Oh, I wouldn't hear of it,' Betty says as she counts out the money for the taxi driver. 'That's rather dear, isn't it? Did he bring you here via Scotland?'

'Uh—'

She waves her hand at Bryher and pays the driver. 'Not to worry in the least about putting me out, dear. You're family. Tell your agent you're all sorted out. You said on the phone you're filming at Elstree Studios, is that right? Well, that's just a hop, skip and a jump away on the train. Now, come in, dear. Take off your shoes and I'll put the towel in the sink to soak. I do hope this dirt comes out. The towels were a Christmas gift from Marion. Whatever happened to your clothes? Give me that top and I'll put it into soak as well.'

Bryher looks down at the stains on her hoodie. 'It needs drycleaning. It's Versace. A baby threw up on me and I spilled iced coffee all over myself. Do you think the stains will come out?'

'You don't need to be wasting money you don't have at the drycleaners, dear,' Betty says as she enters the house. 'Let me give it a soak and a handwash and it will be as good as new.'

'No, no, that's fine. I'll wait to take it to the drycleaners when Margot sends me some money. It's designer.' She wrinkles her nose as she smiles. 'You understand.'

Betty shrugs. 'Far be for me to keep you from needlessly spending money. Now, make yourself at home in the lounge while I fetch us some tea. I'll have to go to the bank tomorrow because the taxi fare has eaten up all my treat money. Except for my pound coins. I have jars of those. I keep meaning to bring them to the bank, but I never get around to it. Just as well, now, isn't it? But what better treat than to have you here, dear. I'll just have to wait on buying any more Hobnobs until you pay me back.'

Bryher follows Betty into a tiny peach-painted lounge crammed with three overstuffed armchairs in floral chintz slipcovers and tables laden with china birds and Hummel figurines. An ironing board and a sewing machine are set up in front of the small television, and a fat grey cat lies curled up in one of the chairs. Her nose begins to itch.

A cat. Of course there's a cat.

Betty smiles, the corners of her blue eyes wrinkling. 'Oh, Bijou, you naughty girl. I told you we were having company. Shoo Bijou off the chair, would you, dear? You don't mind cats, do you?'

Bryher sniffles and presses a finger against the base of her nose. 'Not at all,' she says as she stifles a grimace at the cat hair on the chintz slipcovers. She sits down in the armchair beside a tiled fireplace where an electric heater featuring fake coals glows a fierce red, sending an oppressive heat into the room.

Betty returns and sets the tea tray on the coffee table and pours out tea.

Bryher waves her hand when Betty is about to pour full-fat milk into her cup. 'Um, you don't happen to have coffee, do you? And soya milk? I'm not much of a tea drinker unless it's green tea with turmeric powder.'

Betty's eyebrows shoot up over the frame of her glasses. 'Green tea with … what did you say?'

'Turmeric. It's an anti-oxidant.'

'Is it now? Well, here in Britain we drink tea with good old-fashioned cow's milk. Don't you remember I insisted upon it when we had tea at Hever Castle?' She holds out the plate of the chocolate-covered biscuits. 'You will have a bickie, won't you? I like dipping mine in the tea. It's my little daily act of rebellion.'

Bryher pats her flat stomach. 'Watching my figure. The camera adds ten pounds.'

'Oh, now, you're as thin as a rake, dear.' Betty puts two Hobnobs onto the saucer and hands Bryher the teacup. 'Dunk them and eat. They're much better that way.' Betty dunks a Hobnob into her own tea and takes a bite of the soggy biscuit. She taps her lips with a paper napkin. 'When in Rome, I always say.'

After the tea trial and her introduction to soggy Hobnobs, Bryher pads down the green-carpeted hall behind Betty and Bijou and into Betty's spare room.

'Here we are,' Betty says as she sets the freshly ironed bedlinen on the fold-out mattress where a quilted peach nylon bedspread has been neatly folded. 'Your home away from home.'

Bryher surveys the room, taking in the rose-patterned wallpaper, the straw baskets spilling with sewing patterns, the frilly peach curtains, the green floral carpet and the pine dresser upon which stand a line of primly dressed dolls with disturbing glass eyes.

'Thanks, Betty. It's … uh … great.'

'It's a sweet little room, isn't it? Bijou just loves to curl up on the sofabed and snooze while I sew, don't you, Bijou?' She picks up the furry grey cat and cuddles it against her chin. 'It's really your room, isn't it, sweetie? You won't mind sharing it with our lovely guest, will you?'

Bryher grimaces as the cat squirms out of Betty's hold and jumps onto the pile of bedlinen where it proceeds to roll around.

I hope I can get reception on my phone because, Margot, you're going to get one helluva call from me.

'Here, dear,' Betty says as she tugs a pillowcase out from under Bijou. 'Help me make your bed.'

'Oh, no, no. I'll do that later. You've already done far too much for me.'

Betty folds the pillowcase and sets it neatly on the mattress. 'All right. That's very sweet of you.' She regards Bryher over the rim of her glasses. 'Now, what are we going to do about your clothes? I imagine you don't have a change of clothes in that tiny handbag of yours?'

Bryher looks down at her stained Versace hoodie and her purple leggings. 'Uh—'

'We can't have you traipsing around in dirty clothes, can we?' Betty opens the door to a wooden wardrobe, grabs an overstuffed green bin bag and dumps the contents onto the mattress. 'There we go. There are plenty of perfectly good clothes here for you to choose from.'

Bryher grimaces as Betty rummages through the knitted cardigans, tweed skirts and short-sleeved polyester blouses. Betty holds up a large brown and red plaid pleated skirt.

'This might fit.' She shoves it into Bryher's hands. 'Why don't you try it on? You can wear it to your script reading on Thursday.'

Bryher turns over the waistband and glances at the size tag, which is substantially larger than her own US size two. She hands the skirt back to her cousin. 'Thanks all the same, Betty, but I'll wear what I've got until Margot transfers me some money.'

Betty's forehead wrinkles as she frowns. 'Are you sure? It's a perfectly good skirt. Muriel Thornicroft had very good taste. I made sure to be the first one to get into her wardrobe after she passed away, poor dear. Still, eighty-nine is a good run, wouldn't you say? I couldn't let all of these lovely things go to charity.'

Bryher raises her eyebrows. 'These belonged to a dead woman?'

'Yes, such a shame,' Betty says as she holds the skirt up against herself and looks in the mirror over the dresser. 'Tripped over her dog at the top of her stairs. She was found by her cleaning lady two days later. Tumbled down the stairs and broke her neck. Muriel, that is, not the cleaner. Here one day, gone the next. We were meant to play bowls that very afternoon. Maurice Thwaite took poor Muriel's name in vain when she didn't show up, I can tell you. What do you think? Should I wear this to the WI meeting tomorrow? It's rather jolly, don't you think?'

Bryher eyes Betty's plump yet diminutive figure. 'It looks a little big.'

'Oh, that's not a bother. I'll just pin the waistband and wear my long orange cardie. No one will be the wiser.' Betty glances at Bryher in the mirror. 'Oh, dear! What am I thinking? You must want to freshen up. I'll get you a fresh pair of undies and you can have a good soak in the bath.'

Betty's underwear? Oh, my God, no!

'That's okay, Betty. I'll just wash out my panties. I'll be fine. Um, you don't mind if I take a shower instead?'

Betty raises an eyebrow. 'A shower? I'm afraid I don't have a shower, dear. There's nothing like a nice bath, I always say. Just like our dear, departed Queen Elizabeth II. She didn't believe in showers either. She had a nice bath every morning, and what's good enough for the queen, is good enough for Betty Pilcher and Bryher Finch.'

Two days later

'Margot, you've got to get me out of here. Betty's driving me crazy,' Bryher says into her phone as she shivers on the path outside Betty's house.

'Darling, calm down,' Margot says as she touches up her lipstick on the phone screen. Pretend you're Cameron Diaz in *The Holiday*, staying in a lovely cottage in the English countryside.'

Bryher holds up her phone and scans the front of Betty's bungalow where a green mildewy slime is slowly creeping up the pebbledash render.

'See that? If Cameron Diaz had found this at the end of her trek through the snow, she would have been straight back on the plane to LA. And I haven't seen anyone who looks remotely like Jude Law.'

'Hon, the last thing you need is getting tangled up with anyone just as your sex tape scandal is dying down.'

Bryher blinks. 'Are you saying I'm not in the news anymore? That was fast.'

'This industry is a revolving door of celebrity disasters. You can always rely on some pop star to fill the gap. Consider your time in England as a … sabbatical. Your *Do You Know Who I Am?* special will be aired in the US soon. You'll come back with a mini-series under your belt and everyone will be talking about how you're basically royalty. Then we'll hit the studios here with everything we've got. You're going to be huge, Bryher. Bigger than the Kardashians, even. I'll make sure your face is on billboards all over LA and Times Square, if it's the last thing I do.'

'Really? Bigger than Taylor Swift?'

'Let's be realistic, hon.'

Bryher scratches an itch on her scalp where she hasn't managed to properly rinse out Betty's shampoo in the bath water. 'What about Jodie, though? She's still posting horrible stuff about me.'

'I'm on it. I've been speaking to her agent. We're working on something for her once she's had her twins. My theory is that she's jealous of you. You've been able to keep your career going since you married Jake, but hers just shrivelled up and died after she married his brother. What can you expect? If you're following your husband around on the international golf circuit because you're paranoid about the golf groupies, who's going to hire you?'

'That's exactly what I told Jake, but he said I was delusional.'

'Why else would she have come after you so viciously?' Margot says. 'She wants what you have … or had. She wants her and Nick to be *Jonick*, Hollywood's new golden couple.'

'So you really think she set me up?'

'Well, somebody did. You've got to watch your back in this town, hon. Or hire me to do it for you.'

Bryher nods. 'Look, I need you to wire me that money, Margot. I'm getting desperate. Not just because Betty keeps asking when she's getting reimbursed for the taxi, but she tried to palm off on me some dead woman's clothes that were a million times too big for me. I'm walking around with a purse full of coins she's lent me. They weigh a ton. I'm getting a dent in my shoulder from my purse strap. I'm going to need extra visits to my chiropractor when I get back to LA.'

'She's just trying to be helpful.'

'And the tea. The tea! This house is a waterfall of milky tea. I spent half the night running to the bathroom. I don't know how long I can take this. Have you talked to the producers? There's got to be a decent hotel around here somewhere.'

'Darling, it's only for three months. Time will fly once you start filming. Why don't you start a vlog? Or go on TikTok? I told you, people need some relatability … your human side. Show everyone you're just like them. Let's turn this thing around, Bryher.'

'But … I'm not just like them. I'm *the* Bryher Finch.'

'Whatever that means.'

'What do you mean by that?'

'Sweetie, you're just another actress. I hate to break it to you, but you're not that special—sorry, I've got to go. Julian's waving at me from the door. Nicole's just arrived. It's looking like I might be getting Brad and Nicole into a movie together. Don't tell a soul.'

'The money, Margot—'

The call cuts off.

Bryher stares at her screen as Margot's words echo around her mind. *'You're not that special.'* The same words she'd heard from her mother and her sister growing up. The same words she's tried so hard to prove false. And now they're getting thrown back in her face.

Chapter Seven

MARY

Hever Castle, Kent, England
November 1513

Mary Boleyn is sitting in the parlour, intent on her embroidery, when her mother, Elizabeth, enters waving a sealed letter.

'Set down your needle, Mary. We have received a letter from Anne.'

Looking up, Mary watches her mother break the letter's seal then settle herself on the bench across from her at the table.

Anne this. Anne that. Always Anne, never me.

Nevertheless, Mary puts down the tablecloth she is embroidering and folds her hands in her lap as Elizabeth unfolds the letter.

'Listen well, Mary. You may well learn from your sister's experiences at the court of the archduchess.'

Mary smiles demurely in the manner she has learned pleases her parents, hiding her resentment.

I should be the one at court! I am the eldest daughter. Yet, I am sat here in Kent sewing and making potions while Anne enjoys the delights of the archduchess's court. It is not fair.

'I shall listen well, Mother,' she says.

'*Sir and Madam,*' Elizabeth reads. '*I thank you for your letter in which you desired me to be a worthy woman in the archduchess's court. I have endeavoured by every measure to be a credit to our family, and I rejoice that the archduchess has taken it upon her wise and worthy self to speak to me, her most humble Anne, in French, the study of which I am applying myself with diligence.*

'*I had happy cause to join the court ladies at the palace at Lille when the archduchess entertained our own King Henry and the Emperor Maximilian after their victory over the French at Thérouanne. King Henry exhibited a most lively manner and ensured that he danced with all of the archduchess's ladies through the evening, though there was a Portuguese lady he favoured above all. I will attest that His Grace is most handsome and is fair light of foot.*

'*Written by your very humble and very obedient daughter, Anne Boleyn.*'

Elizabeth sighs. 'Imagine, Mary. Anne has danced with the king.'

'How pleasant for her.'

'And the Archduchess Margaret speaks to our dear daughter, your sister!' Her mother regards her. 'Of course, Anne has always had the ability to charm and captivate with her wit, which is fortunate, since though she is middling fair, there is none so fair as you, my dear child.'

Mary forces a smile. *Always the same refrain. 'Anne is so clever. Anne is so witty. Anne is so captivating.' And me? Mary? I am fair. What is that but an accident of Nature? It nods at no personal attribute, no element of character. Beauty fades and withers. Is it my fate to fade and wither, too, as Anne grows and shines?*

Elizabeth folds the letter. 'I shall entreat your father to endeavour once again to secure you a place at the French court.

That your sister has had cause to be noted most favourably by the Archduchess Margaret may play well in your favour.'

'Thank you, Mother.'

Mary watches her mother leave the parlour and pass into the great hall. She picks up her embroidery and needle, but lets them fall back onto the table. What use is yet another tablecloth strewn with leaves and flowers? She rubs together the calluses on her thumb and forefinger, where the needle's pressure has hardened her once soft skin. She will be five and ten years old in the New Year, well of the age to attend court, and yet she is left to languish in the shadows of this ancient castle while her younger sister dances with the king.

Suddenly, Mary slams her hand on the table, overcome by a rare high temper. *It is not fair! I am Mary Boleyn, eldest child of Sir Thomas and Lady Elizabeth Boleyn. I shall make my own mark on this life, so help me God!*

She takes a deep breath to still the rapid beats of her heart and picks up the tablecloth and the needle again. Bending over the cloth, she calmly resumes stitching the fine linen.

I shall make my own mark on this life, so help me Anne.

Chapter Eight

BRYHER

Elstree Studios, Borehamwood, England
November 2024

'Ah, Bryher! Finally, darling. We thought you'd fallen into the Thames.'

Jeremy Burton, the director of *Henry and Anne*, adjusts the white silk scarf which hangs rakishly around his crepey neck and beckons for Bryher to join the others around the battered metal tables that have been pushed together into a semblance of a long boardroom table. The large room they are in is painted white, and fluorescent tubes cast a harsh yellow light over the motley collection of actors around the table.

Standing in the doorway, Bryher shivers at the chill in the unheated room, which is exacerbated by the grey-painted concrete floor. She pulls the over-large tweed coat Betty has lent her closer around her body and nods to the faces currently eyeing her with a mix of doubt, disdain and curiosity.

Suck it up, Bryher. You can do this. They're no better than you.

'Sorry I'm late. I thought a car was coming to pick me up. I had to take the train which was delayed because of "leaves on the line". I mean, leaves on the line?' She smiles at her new colleagues. 'Give me a break, right?'

'A car?' A handsome, red-bearded actor lets out a shout of laughter. 'Darling, you're not in Hollywood anymore. This is good ol' Blighty. We all fend for ourselves.'

'Except for you, Archie,' a round-faced woman of about forty with dark auburn hair says. 'I saw you get out of an executive limo this morning.'

'Well, what do you expect, Jennifer? I am the lead, the star of this production. You're just an actress off the telly. Have you ever been in a superhero movie?'

The woman, Jennifer, laughs. 'Darling, I've never even seen a superhero movie, and I don't intend to start now. I wouldn't be caught dead in one.'

'All right, children, behave,' Jeremy says as he slides out the chair beside him and waves for Bryher to join him. 'Let's all play nice with our new American friend, shall we? And no mention of *le scandale* everybody, am I clear?'

Bryher settles herself in the hard chair beside the director and sets her Chanel bag on the table; the freezer bags full of the pound coins Betty has loaned her clink loudly inside the quilted leather and she squirms under the dozen or so pairs of eyes boring into her. Jeremy goes around the table, introducing the other actors, including Archie Flanders, cast as the young Henry VIII, and Jennifer Foster, who is Katherine of Aragon, Henry's first wife.

'Now, darling, why don't you tell us about yourself and what inspired you to take on the role of the tragic Anne Boleyn.'

Bryher wets her lips. 'Sure. Yeah. Um, I'm Bryher Finch, star of *Cop Town* for the past three years.' She looks over at Jeremy. 'Do you get *Cop Town* over here?'

'I don't know, darling.' He looks over at the others. 'Do we get *Cop Town* in the UK?'

'Yes, it's on Channel 5 at midnight on Tuesdays,' says Cara Sweet, a blonde model-turned-actress who's been cast as Mary Boleyn. 'I've seen it a few times.' She smiles at Bryher. 'You're very good.'

Bryher smiles back. 'Thanks.'

'Nice, very nice,' Jeremy says. 'I only stream myself. I never watch terrestrial. What, from your research on Anne Boleyn, do you feel you can bring to the role of this iconic woman?'

Bryher stares at Jeremy. *Research? What research? Isn't this all about acting?*

'Uh, well, honestly, I haven't had much time. I only found out I'd got the role on Monday because the other actress playing Anne—'

'Yes, darling. We don't need to talk about Rowena. Of course, we all wish her well even though she's cocked up our filming schedule.' Jeremy cleans his throat. 'You do know who Anne Boleyn was, don' t you?'

Bryher glances around the room, conscious of the colour rising in her cheeks. Why does she feel like she's being auditioned for a role that everyone thinks is clearly out of her reach? She's got the job. It's just nerves and she can deal with nerves. She takes a deep breath and smiles her most winning Hollywood smile.

'Yes, sure, of course. She was one of Henry VIII's wives. I'm actually related to her … through her sister. She was the mother of Elizabeth I. She, uh, she had her head cut off. Anne, I mean, not Elizabeth.'

Someone chokes on their plastic cup of tea.

Jeremy smiles tightly. 'Yes, she did indeed.' He picks up a script and rolls over the pages to the first page of the scene. 'Right, let's have a bash at this, shall we? Henry's meeting Anne for the first time.' He looks over at Bryher. 'You can do an English accent, can't you?'

'Sure. I've watched every episode of *Downton Abbey*.'

Jeremy raises an eyebrow. 'Quite.'

'Oh, God,' Archie says. 'I'm going to sue my agent.'

Bryher scowls at her reflection in the costume department mirror.

'I look like a grand piano with a tablecloth over it,' she complains to the exasperated costume designer, Jo, who is trying to pin on the bodice. Bryher slaps the twig frame of the cone-like farthingale under her gown. 'How am I supposed to walk in this thing, let along sit in it?' She picks at the velvet of the tight bodice. 'Can you loosen this … what did you call it? It's crushing me.'

Jo takes the pins out of her mouth and sighs wearily. 'A placard. You have to wear it. It was the Tudor fashion.'

Bryher rolls her eyes as she runs her hands over the stiff velvet bodice. 'I didn't think I'd be breaking ribs on this job. It's torture.'

A quick rap at the door. 'It's Pieter,' a voice calls through the door. 'May I come in?'

Jo steps back from Bryher. 'Be my guest!'

A tall man with dark blond hair, a close-cropped beard and striking blue eyes enters the room, two paper coffee cups in his hands. 'Brought you a coffee,' he says to Jo in an accent touched with a European inflection. 'It's terrible, but it's hot.'

Jo takes the coffee gratefully. 'You didn't happen to put a double shot of vodka in it, did you? I could do with a drink.' She glances at Bryher. 'I'm taking a break. I may not return.'

The door slams behind her and the man offers the second cup of coffee to Bryher. She takes the coffee and sips at the watery brew as she scans the man's attire of jeans, a casual navy blazer and a fine ivory cashmere jumper.

'Thanks for the coffee. Sorry, but I've got to finish getting ready.' She jerks her head in the direction of the door. 'The men's dressing room's just down the hall.'

'Oh, I'm not an actor.' He holds out his hand. 'I'm Dr Pieter de

Beer. I'm an historian at the University of London. I'm advising on the mini-series.'

'Oh. Right. Sorry. I thought you were looking for an autograph or something.'

The corners of Pieter's blue eyes wrinkle in amusement. 'No. I'm here on business.' His gaze sweeps over Bryher's elaborate, burgundy-red velvet gown with its long fur-lined sleeves, and his blond eyebrows draw together.

'This is not correct. Farthingales weren't commonly worn in the English court until 1545. Katherine of Aragon was known to wear them before then, but the women of the English court wore gowns which sat over a petticoat and kirtle. Jo has quite correctly given Jennifer, as Katherine, a farthingale to wear in some of her scenes, but Anne most certainly wouldn't have worn one. I shall speak to Jo about it.'

Bryher expels a sigh of relief. 'Thank you.' She waves her hand in front of her bodice. 'How about this placard thing? I can barely breathe.'

Pieter sucks in his breath between his teeth. 'Tudor women wore placards, I'm afraid, to streamline their silhouette.'

Bryher huffs. 'Okay, no bread or pasta for the next three months, then.'

'If I may have your permission, I may be able to adjust the pins a little?'

'Be my guest. Anything to help me breathe. I haven't done a costume drama before. I'm used to running around on TV in jeans and a leather jacket, waving a gun at the baddies.'

Bryher waits for some acknowledgement of her career highlight so far, but Pieter appears unimpressed. He steps forward and carefully adjusts the brass pins that hold the stiff velvet placard in place over the bodice lacings of the silk kirtle underneath her gown.

'Such a shame that you won't experience the epicurean joy of *Orecchiette al Salmone e Asparagi* from Paolo's while you're here,' he says, with perfect Italian inflection. 'It's a local institution with the best Italian food this side of Rome.'

'Sounds great.' Bryher laughs off her pique at his lack of response to her TV comment. *He's obviously feeling me out for a date at Paolo's. He thinks he's pretty smooth. But, seriously, who says 'epicurean'? You may be tall, blond and handsome, but dream on, Dr de Beer. I'm not buying.* 'I'll just have to imagine it, otherwise I'll be bursting out of this thing.'

Pieter nods and stands back as he inspects his handiwork. 'How is that?'

Bryher runs her hand over the red velvet bodice, puzzled that Pieter isn't trying to change her mind and coax her out to dinner. 'Better. Thanks.'

He examines her bejewelled black velvet headdress. 'A French hood. That's good. Anne hated the English gable hood. She brought this hood style over from her time in the French court.'

'A fashionista,' she says, throwing Pieter a flirtatious smile. 'A woman after my own heart.'

Again, he doesn't react. Instead, he reaches into his jacket pocket. 'You need this to finish off the costume.' He holds up a necklace in the mirror. 'It's why I came by.'

'Oh. Right,' Bryher says, nonplussed by Pieter's demeanour. Then again, she's never hung out with a historian before. Maybe he doesn't care that she's a famous Hollywood actress? Is that even a thing? Doesn't everybody worship fame?

She eyes the necklace. 'I recognise it. It's the "B" necklace. Anne was wearing it in a picture I saw in Hever Castle.'

'Yes. It appears that it was one of her favourite pieces of jewellery. She wore it in several portraits.' He drapes it around Bryher's neck and fastens the clasp. 'There. Perfect.'

Bryher runs her fingers over the heavy gold 'B' as she stares at herself in the mirror. The same dark hair and coal-black eyes, the same long nose and sharp chin. She swallows. The same slender neck.

'You look the spitting image of Anne,' he says, as if he is reading her mind. 'It's quite remarkable.'

She shrugs. 'Hair, makeup and a costume. It's all smoke and mirrors. Although Anne was my great-great-great-great-great-great-auntie. I mighta missed a few greats.'

'Was she? How interesting.'

Bryher rubs the fake pearls. 'The guide at Hever Castle said no one knows what happened to the real necklace.'

'That's true. It was probably taken by Henry VIII after her death and its jewels used in other things, although no one knows for certain.'

Bryher nods. 'If the real necklace did show up, how would we know?'

'If it had been made by a decent craftsman, it would have a maker's mark on the back of the "B". If the jeweller could be traced to both the Boleyns and King Henry VIII, this would certainly aid in verifying its authenticity. It would be like finding a lost Da Vinci painting.'

'Our guide said it would be priceless.'

'Oh, yes. Not because of its materials, although the gold and pearls would have a decent value, but it's because of the necklace's history … its notoriety as Anne Boleyn's necklace.'

'Was it a gift from Henry VIII?'

'No. The "B" means it came from the Boleyn family. Once Anne married Henry, they intertwined their initials H and A on everything. It was probably originally her sister Mary's necklace. As her elder sister, Mary would have been Miss Boleyn and Anne would have been Miss Anne. How it came into Anne's possession is anyone's guess.'

'A mystery, then.'

'Yes,' Pieter says as he walks over to the door. 'One that is likely never to be solved.' He opens the door, then turns and smiles. 'It was a pleasure to meet you, Ms Finch.'

'It's Bryher.'

He nods and walks out of the room, shutting the door behind him.

Bryher stares at the door. *You're supposed to say, 'I'm Pieter. It's lovely to meet you. And, by the way, would you like to go out to the best Italian restaurant outside of Rome for dinner.'*

The door swings open. 'Call me Pieter, by the way. Try not to sit down too often in that gown or you will crush the velvet. I will see you on set.'

Chapter Nine

ANNE

Hof van Savoyen, Mechelen, The Low Countries
January 1514

Anne enters the Archduchess Margaret's vast library in the palace at Mechelen and makes her way past the roaring fire in the stone fireplace over to the shelves holding the archduchess's collection of bound manuscripts of the writings of the ancient Greeks and Romans. Anne has forged through the Latin translations of Homer's *Iliad* and *Odyssey* and was much entertained by the machinations and petty jealousies of the Greek gods and goddesses. She is now ready to tackle the Romans. The archduchess is out for an early morning ride with her nephew, twelve-year-old Charles, Lord of the Low Countries, for whom she acts as regent, and Anne had tired of practising the clavichord amongst the chatter of the other *filles d'honneur*. No one would miss her for an hour if she were to sneak away to read in the library.

She slides a black leather-bound copy of Ovid's *Heroides* off the shelf and flips through the parchment pages, pausing every now and again to run her fingers over the rich illustrations of the epic poems, written as letters by characters in Roman mythology. A letter written by Ariadne, the daughter of the King of Crete, to Theseus, the lover who has abandoned her on a desert island, catches Anne's eye.

> The words you now are reading, Theseus, I send to you from that shore from which the sails bore off your ship without me, the shore on which my slumber, and you, so wretchedly betrayed me – you, who wickedly plotted against me as I slept.

She wanders over to the bench by a large window, reading as she skirts around a table of masks, clay pots and the beaded jewellery that the archduchess collects from the New World. She settles down in the soft white light of the January morning and is just finishing the poem when she hears her name.

'Anne? This is where you've hidden yourself.'

Anne looks up. 'Your Royal Highness!' She shuts the book and jumps to her feet. 'Forgive me. I … I …'

The archduchess approaches, still wearing the boots and heavy black velvet overclothes of her riding attire. 'Sit, Anne. Far be it for me to disturb a girl reading. I wish only that more of my *filles d'honneur* were so inclined.' She takes the book from Anne and flips open the cover. 'Ah, Ovid. Excellent choice. Which of the poems were you reading when I came upon you?'

Anne clears her throat and runs her tongue nervously over her lips. 'That of Ariadne, ma'am.'

The archduchess gestures for Anne to sit and she joins her on the bench. 'A good choice. What lessons has it given you?'

Anne frowns. 'Lessons, ma'am? I read it simply for pleasure. And to improve my Latin.'

The archduchess smiles, her warm brown eyes lighting up with humour. 'It is good to read for pleasure, but it is best to read to expand one's understanding of the world as well.' She removes her gloves and taps the manuscript. 'What lessons have you learned from the esteemed poet?'

Anne wracks her brain. *Lessons?* There must have been lessons to be learned or the archduchess would not be querying her.

'Um …'

'Do not pollute the air with um's. Think through your thoughts and then express them clearly.'

Anne takes a breath and carefully plans her words. 'It seems to me that, by making Ariadne the narrator, Ovid gives Ariadne back her voice when she is at her weakest.'

'Very good. And why is this important?'

'She … she speaks her mind. She tells Theseus that she's angry at him for abandoning her after he has taken her as his bride.'

The archduchess nods. 'Indeed. It was the ancient Greeks who introduced the idea that a woman could narrate a story – that women were capable of their own thoughts and self-expression. At that time there were women poets, writers and playwrights. Why is this important?'

'Because … because women could tell their own stories.'

'Yes. Unfortunately, by the time Ovid wrote this, Roman women were confined to the household, with their purpose being to provide children and care for their husband. They were treated as their husband's property, and were thought incapable of holding a major role in society, nor did they have a voice in that society.' She smiles sadly and runs her fingers along Anne's smooth cheek. 'Does this sound familiar?'

Anne nods. 'It is the same now.'

'Yes, but there are ways around it, Anne. I am a woman, yet I have a voice. That was not always so. As a young girl, I was a pawn in two political marriages, both of which ended in my husbands' deaths. I now have no husband to rule me, nor do I wish for one. I rule the Low Countries, and I do it well by negotiating profitable trade agreements and keeping the peace by using foreign armies and funds to wage wars. I am the guardian and educator of the future Holy Roman Emperor, my nephew, Charles. And I open my court to the great thinkers of our day to enlighten me and my nephew on progressive ideas.'

'You are a very great lady, ma'am.'

She hands Anne back the book. 'I am a woman who has found her voice and uses it.' She surveys the large room, its shelves stacked with leather-bound books, and tables laden with maps and artifacts. 'I hope, one day, you will find and use your voice, too. Society will only flourish when women's voices are heard, Anne. Do not forget this.'

Chapter Ten

BRYHER

Puddleton, England
November 2024

Bryher sneezes awake. She raises her head from the pillow and squints across the bedcover at Bijou who is busy kneading her belly. She shoos the cat off the bed and flops back against the pillow.

Just what I need, a red nose and a swollen face for filming.

Bryher listens to the cat purr on the crocheted throw she had tossed onto the floor in the night and looks around the bedroom. The mismatched furniture and Betty's doll collection are shrouded in the dull grey morning light filtering in through the floral curtains. A soft rain patters against the window.

Bryher yawns and stretches as she debates getting up, before she pulls the cover up to her chin and snuggles into the pillows. For the first time in a long time, she allows her mind to drift back to her mother and Marnie. The pretty and talented Marnie Starr – the stage name chosen by their mother to highlight Marnie's obvious destiny. The sister whose shining star had cast such a glare upon Bryher's childhood. The sister who'd been her widowed mother's great hope.

'Marnie, sweetheart, we'll put you in that pale pink dress today for the *Annie* audition. Pink looks so lovely on you.'

Marnie had pouted prettily – with her strawberry blonde hair and turquoise eyes, she did everything prettily – and said, 'I hate pink, Mommy. I'm not a baby. I'm ten years old and I'm the Sugarmilk candy bar girl. I want to wear my yellow dress.'

So, Marnie had worn her yellow dress, and she'd gotten a part as one of the orphans in the Broadway revival of *Annie*. The commercials came and the magazine covers. But then, things started to go pear-shaped and, when Marnie was eighteen, everything came crashing down.

Their mother had been so proud of Marnie. Her 'princess' is what she'd call her golden girl. Bryher grunts and punches the pillow as she recalls trailing along after her sister on all her auditions, like the fading tail of a brilliant comet. Plain little Bryher Finch, hoping in vain for an affectionate glance from their mother, or some sisterly camaraderie from Marnie. But Marnie and their mother lived in their own little bubble, and Bryher could only look on, like a child yearning for a sweet that was forever out of reach.

She shuts her eyes and draws Marnie's face in her mind's eye. The heart-shaped face, the silky rose-gold curls, those mesmerising eyes fringed with thick black lashes. Their mother's cash cow. When she thinks back to those days now, Bryher realises how much Marnie had worked and the childhood she'd been deprived of.

'Here's another audition, Marnie. Another commercial. Another magazine cover. Don't eat that chocolate chip cookie, Marnie. Don't eat that Sugarmilk bar, Marnie, give it to your sister.'

But at least Marnie had their mom's attention. Their mother

had never had much time for mousy little Bryher. 'You're not that special, Bryher.' How often had she been told that? 'You don't have Marnie's gifts, so do your homework and keep out of the way.' She'd often wondered if the awful thing Marnie had told her once was true … if it had been the reason their mother couldn't seem to love her the way she loved Marnie. She rubs at the sleep in her eyes. No, she's not going to think about that now.

Marnie had worked and Bryher had trailed after her, schoolbooks in hand. She'd watched her sister. Learned from Marnie's mistakes. Watched the other actors and learned from them as well. No one had noticed the dull little brown-haired mouse in the corner, observing and absorbing everything, like a sponge sucking up an ink spill. Bryher knew her time would come one day. She'd show everyone that she was special, too. Then maybe her mother would notice her, would love her, too. Only it didn't work out that way.

When Bryher finally won the role on *Cop Town* it was too late. Her mother was already dead of a stroke, brought on by years of heavy drinking and smoking. Kitty Farnsworth Finch had gone to bed one night and never woken up.

And Marnie?

Bryher shakes her head to erase the image of her sister's face.

Funny how life turns out, isn't it, Marnie?

Chapter Eleven

CORNELIS

All-Hallows-the-Great, London
July 1514

Cornelis Hayes holds the faceted emerald he has just finished cutting and examines it under a magnifying glass. The cuts are sharp, the girdle thin, but not overly so, the facets and angles rendered so as to best exhibit the deep, rich green. He'd purchased the gem from a Spanish merchant in Paris who was known to import the jewels from 'las Indias Occidentales' – the New World discovered by Cristoforo Colombo twenty-two years previously. Cornelis blows on the stone, rubs it against the soft woollen sleeve of his doublet and sets it down on a chamois cloth. Picking up a slender needle file, he then bends over the wooden bench peg and proceeds to file a ring of fine gold. The bell on his door jangles as someone enters the shop.

'Just one minute,' he says without looking up, his English heavy with the accent of his native Antwerp. Ignoring the visitor, he files at the gold, running his finger over the shining metal from time to time until he is satisfied with its smoothness. He looks up from his worktable to see a man of some evident wealth, judging by the fashionable slashes in his embroidered woollen doublet, through which puffs of the fine white linen of his shirt have been pulled, and the opulent ostrich feather protruding from his velvet hat.

The jeweller rises from the stool and rubs the fine gold dust against the rough kersey cloth of his own doublet. 'How is it that I may be of service?'

'I am looking for Master Cornelis Hayes. I have been given to know that he is a jeweller of some good skill."

'I am he, Cornelis Hayes.'

The man nods, setting the ostrich feather waving. 'I imagined a man of more mature years.'

'I am of sufficient age and experience to undertake the work of a jeweller.'

The visitor glances around the shop, furnished modestly with a long oak table, heavily marked with gouges and scuffs, upon which the tools of the jeweller's trade lie arranged in a neat order: a stool upon which the jeweller sits; shelves containing lidded wooden boxes and jars; rows of hammers and files mounted upon the walls; two iron anvils – a large and a small; and, within a brick fireplace, an iron oven exuding an oppressive heat, adding to the discomfort of the humid July day. The man tugs a linen handkerchief from his sleeve and dabs at the perspiration on his forehead.

'Do you undertake your commissions by your own hand?'

Cornelis gestures around the empty room. 'Do you observe the bodies of any others within? I undertake all my commissions by my own hand.'

The visitor tucks the sodden handkerchief back into his sleeve. 'Good. I have seen it all too often, when men of skill become overly known their success requires them to entrust the work of an expert to the hands of an apprentice.'

The jeweller shrugs. 'When I become a jeweller of sufficient renown, I shall review the situation.'

The visitor smiles, amused at Cornelis's blunt honesty. 'As well you should.'

He retrieves a piece of folded paper from a leather pouch tied to his belt. 'I have sketched a rough design for a pendant for my eldest daughter, Mary. I have secured her a place at the Princess Mary Tudor's court upon her upcoming marriage to King Louis of France. I wish to mark the occasion with this gift.'

Cornelis scrutinises the rudimentary sketch of a fine chain, from which a large letter 'B' hangs. 'An initial pendant. Yes, I have made such on numerous occasions.'

'It is not simply a common initial pendant,' the visitor says with some pique. 'It is *our* initial. I am Sir Thomas Boleyn, Esquire of the Body of King Henry, and lately ambassador to the Low Countries. I charge you to fashion a necklace of both modesty and beauty for my daughter, who has reached the age of five and ten and is yet without a suitable match, much to the distress of my dear wife.'

The jeweller nods. A simple pendant for a simple girl. It is hardly a commission to challenge his skills, yet this gentleman's proximity to the king may play to a provident future.

'My wife, Elizabeth, is the daughter of the Earl of Surrey, of the noble bloodline Howard,' Sir Thomas says as Cornelis ponders the sketch. 'It was she who charged me with the task of this commission. The pendant is to remind Mary of her proud lineage during her time in the French court, and the familial expectations that reside therein in regard to her behaviour. My younger daughter, Anne, is a *fille d'honneur* in the court of the Archduchess Margaret of Austria, having had the invitation extended by the archduchess herself, whom I had the honour of meeting this year past.'

Cornelis nods politely at the man's posturing. Had he a penny for every self-important customer who had crossed his threshold—

'Mary is a great beauty,' Sir Thomas continues, warming to his subject at the prospect of a sympathetic ear. 'Both she and Anne are accomplished in the matters of French, music, singing and dancing, although it pains me to admit that Mary lacks the vivid intellect and lively spirit of her younger sister. Still, what need is there of these if one is blessed with a face which rivals that of fair Helen of Troy? It is my great desire that time spent in the court of the new Queen of France will polish Mary to a high sheen so that she may invite the attentions of a suitable English nobleman upon her return to England. The necklace is meant to serve as a reminder to Mary of her duties to her proud family name.'

Cornelis picks up a stick of charcoal. 'It is well you came to me, sir. I shall make a necklace of such elegant simplicity that it shall live in the memory of any who observe it, and render its wearer exceptional.'

'You are a gentleman of no small modesty.'

'I respect the skill I have acquired after years of diligent effort.' Cornelis turns over the visitor's drawing and sketches out a design. 'I suggest a rope of fine Persian pearls, from which I shall hang a large, yet elegant, golden "B".' His fair eyebrows draw together as he scrutinises the sketch and he adds three large oval pearls to the base of the 'B'. He hands the sketch to the visitor.

Sir Thomas examines it. 'I thank you, Master Hayes. This will do admirably. Naturally, this being an initial commission, I would expect a modest outlay of monies.'

Cornelis Hayes shrugs. *Of course. It is always thus. And now the cut and thrust of negotiation begins.*

'I am a jeweller of some considerable skill, Sir Thomas. I yet maintain premises in Antwerp where I serve the requirements of gentlemen of wealth and nobility. I have taken on this modest room in London to explore whether my skills may be of use to English patrons.' He shrugs again, a gesture he has long incorporated into his character. 'I may yet return to Antwerp should I not obtain the commissions and recompense my superior skills deserve.'

'Whether or not you return to Antwerp is none of my concern as long as you complete this pendant in good time, Master Hayes. My daughter departs for France with the princess's court two months hence. I require the necklace in my hands no later than St Bartholomew's Day.'

The jeweller sucks in air through his teeth. 'That day is nigh upon us, yet it is possible for an additional charge owing to its haste.'

Sir Thomas chuckles, though the humour fails to reach his grey eyes. 'My good man, though you come with a high recommendation from Sir Richard Wingfield, a neighbour of mine by my home at Hever Castle, you remain untested by myself. I would, therefore, expect to pay a preferential fee. I assure you that you shall be well-recompensed with further commissions from myself and others in the king's court should the pendant meet my wife's exacting standards.'

The jeweller shrugs again. 'In Antwerp I am assured of such commissions from the court of the Archduchess Margaret of Austria.'

Sir Thomas waves his hand dismissively. 'A woman yet. I speak of commissions of a superior nature.' He casts his gaze over the young jeweller's tall frame. 'King Henry is well fond of jewels. His fingers glitter like stars in the night sky so laden are they with rubies and sapphires.'

'Is that so?'

'It is so.' Sir Thomas removes the leather pouch from his belt. He unties the cord and counts out coins to the value of ten shillings onto the table.

Cornelis's mouth twitches. 'Ten shillings? I would not shame an apprentice with that amount.'

Sir Thomas inclines his head. 'Ten shillings now, and a further ten upon collection of the necklace.'

'One pound when I would have two pounds and ten shillings?' Cornelis turns his back on Sir Thomas and returns to his stool. He removes the ring from the bench peg and inserts another. Picking up the file, he commences filing the ring.

Sir Thomas frowns as he regards the money on the table. He looks over at the jeweller who is bent in concentration over the ring. He adds another ten shillings to the coins.

'One pound, with ten shillings more when the pendant is finished.'

The jeweller blows dust off the ring. He glances at Sir Thomas and returns to filing.

Sir Thomas's cheeks flush with irritation. He scoops up the coins and drops them into the leather pouch. 'If that is your demeanour, I shall secure the services of a more amenable jeweller.'

Cornelis looks up from the bench peg. 'As you wish.' He watches the man stomp out of the shop and shrugs. Twiddling the file between his fingers, he expels a heavy sigh. London is proving a disappointment, the beer too warm and the women too flat. He longs to speak his own tongue and enjoy a bowl of delicious *waterzooi* – the thick, creamy fish stew that makes him salivate at the thought.

The doorbell jangles again.

Sir Thomas enters and drops the leather pouch onto the table. 'Two pounds and not a penny more. One pound ten shillings now. Ten shillings upon completion.'

Cornelis Hayes nods. *Perhaps there is a reason to stay in London.*
'Agreed.'

Chapter Twelve

BRYHER

Elstree Studios, Borehamwood, England
November 2024

'And … cut!'

Bryher scratches her neck under the 'B' necklace. The itching is getting worse.

'Jeremy, this necklace is literally killing me,' she says as she stomps across the Tudor dining hall set towards the director and Archie Flanders who is in full Henry VIII mode.

Archie grunts. 'Will someone teach her the meaning of "literally", please? I can't take much more of this bastardisation of the English language.' He rolls his eyes at Jeremy. 'I won't even discuss the accent.'

Jeremy pats Archie on the padded shoulder of his velvet doublet. 'We'll dub it in post-production. Don't worry.' Jeremy turns and smiles broadly at Bryher. 'Yes, darling. Oh, dear, I see what you mean, but you've just got to soldier on. That necklace is

Anne's ID. It's iconic. Run off to makeup and get that rash touched up. If it gets any worse, I'll get it CGI'd in editing.'

Bryher scratches at a hive. 'Seriously?'

'Yes, darling. Get yourself sorted out while we set up for the next scene.'

Bryher addresses Jeremy over her shoulder as she flounces across the set. 'I'm calling my agent. I'm going to need major skin work done after this and I'm not paying for it.'

'Bloody telly actress,' Archie says.

'Just a couple more months, Archie, and we'll all be free,' Jeremy says.

'I heard that!' Bryher shouts back as she ducks under a sound boom.

———

In her dressing-room mirror, Bryher is examining the thick coat of concealer the makeup artist has stippled over her neck when there's a knock on her door, which swings open before Bryher can answer. Betty steps in, laden down with a large straw picnic basket.

'Knockedy knock knock knock,' Betty says as she marches over to Bryher's dressing table.

'Betty? What are you doing here?'

Betty sets the picnic basket down amongst the discarded lipsticks, eye shadows and powders. 'I brought you and your friends a little treat. The WI just had its Christmas bake sale and I bought out the cake stand. Marion Livesay was none too pleased, I can tell you. She said the cake stand was a major draw and who was I to decimate their baking triumphs. I slipped her an extra tenner and told her to pick up some goodies at Tesco's. Put them on some paper plates with some cling film, I said, and no one will notice the difference.'

'Betty, I—'

Another knock on the door and Oscar, the teenage runner, pops his head in. 'Ten minutes, Ms Finch. Oh, hello. Is that—?'

Betty hands Oscar a large brownie. 'A homemade brownie. I'm Bryher's cousin Betty. Enjoy, dear.'

'Cheers!' he says before he slams the door.

Betty pats the picnic basket. 'What would you like, dear? A brownie? A slice of millionaire's shortbread? Charlotte Fennell's carrot cake is quite delicious, too.'

'Betty, you know I'm on a diet. And I'm gluten intolerant. I can't have any of that stuff.' Bryher frowns. 'How did you get in? You don't have a pass.'

'Oh, I taught Stevie the security guard English literature and maths years ago. His mother's in the WI.' She leans over to Bryher and whispers, 'I slipped him a Bakewell tart and in I came.'

Another knock on the door.

'Oh, for crying out loud,' Bryher says. 'Yes? Who is it now?'

Oscar pokes his head into the room. 'Jeremy says to invite Betty onto the set. Show her around. And bring the picnic basket.'

'Oh, how exciting!' Betty shuts the lid on the basket. 'A private tour of a film set. My life has become so exciting since your visit, Bryher. Come along, dear,' she says as she grabs the basket's handle. 'We mustn't keep your colleagues waiting.'

As Betty exits into the corridor, her tweed coat swishing behind her, Bryher picks up the 'B' necklace and fastens it around her neck. She sighs as she rises from the chair, the heavy costume rustling around her.

Jeremy was only too right. Two and a half more months and she'll be free. She's tried, but she can't get a handle on this place, or these people. Every time she opens her mouth, she feels judged. Just like she used to feel as a child, when nothing she said or did impressed her mother. She hates this place, hates feeling so inadequate. And Betty's relentless passive aggressive kindness is doing her head in. Facing the wreck of her life in LA is beginning to look like the better option. This exile from sun and decent coffee had better be worth it.

Betty waves at the cast who are clustered around a dining table in their Tudor finery gobbling down her offerings.

'Top girl!' Archie shouts as he gives Betty a thumbs-up, oblivious to the brownie crumbs in his auburn beard.

'Stop by anytime, Betty,' Jennifer – regal as Queen Katherine of Aragon in her black velvet gown – says as she wipes carrot cake crumbs off her lips.

'Five minutes, everyone!' Jeremy shouts as he swallows a final bite of his millionaire's shortbread.

Betty joins Bryher where she is seated on a wooden bench along the dining room wall, her Chanel handbag beside her.

'My goodness, dear. You live such an exciting life,' Betty says as she surveys the Tudor room set. 'Mummy used to tread the boards herself, you know.'

Bryher smiles politely. 'Did she? What was she in?'

'Oh, lots of things. She was a friend of dear Noël Coward. Apparently, he always said she was his best Elvira in *Blithe Spirit*. She was quite the party girl in her day, you know, even after she and Daddy were married. They left me with a nanny mostly.' Betty adjusts her glasses. 'I was a plump, plain little thing. I think Mummy was shocked that she and Daddy had produced such an unremarkable child. She didn't quite know what to do with me.' She shrugs. 'They sent me off to boarding school and that was that.'

Bryher looks over at her cousin, shaken by an unfamiliar pang of empathy. 'I'm sorry. That must have been lonely.'

Betty smiles and pats Bryher's hand. 'I'm quite self-sufficient. I would read a lot. That's what led me to becoming a teacher. I enjoyed that very much.' She folds her hands in her lap and scrutinises Bryher. 'What about you, dear? What was your childhood like?'

'Uh … fine.'

'Fine? Is that all?'

Is that all? How can she tell Betty about her cold-hearted mother, about her mean, self-centred sister? About all the lonely days and nights she spent on her own when she wasn't trailing after them like neglected puppy, reading and watching old movies on TV while her mom was out with Marnie at auditions, dance classes and acting lessons. Maybe she and Betty aren't so different after all? Two lonely women in a hard-hearted world.

She is about to say something when her phone buzzes in her handbag.

'Sorry, Betty. I need to check this. I'm expecting a call from Margot.'

'You do keep that agent busy, don't you? You're always on the phone to her,' Betty remarks as she rises from the bench. 'I'll just go and say my goodbyes to everyone and be on my merry way.'

Bryher watches Betty head over to the others, then she slides out her phone.

Please contact us urgently re declined payment. Green Oaks Adult Residential Facility.

Chapter Thirteen

MARY

Montreuil, France
October 1514

Mary Boleyn adjusts her feet on the footplate of her padded side saddle, taking care not to scuff her new green velvet shoes. Her docile palfrey, like those of the other ladies-in-waiting to the new French queen, King Henry VIII's sister Mary, is draped with scarlet velvet, fringed with white silk. They file past colourful banners, bouncing acrobats and crowds of peasants and merchants alike who are cheering at the sight of the old French king, Louis XII's, beautiful eighteen-year-old English bride at the window of her carriage. Mary fiddles with her necklace, and its heavy 'B' pendant – her father's parting gift, given to her with the instruction to 'do the Boleyn name credit and shine like the star you are'. Mary is glad of the plodding gentleness of her mount, and shifts in the saddle to secure herself from sliding off.

'Take care, Mary, or you are likely to crush the velvet of your gown,' her thirty-seven-year-old step-grandmother, Agnes,

Duchess of Norfolk, admonishes. 'Your father has laid out a goodly sum for your wardrobe so that you may be worthy of the position he has secured you. It is fortunate that the new Queen of France rides ahead so as not to be disturbed by your fidgeting.'

Mary nods, which causes the starched linen lappets that hang from her gable hood to rub uncomfortably against her neck. 'I shall take care, madam.'

The procession slows as it approaches the walls of the old town, and the thump of hooves on the damp earth alerts the ladies to the approach of the welcoming delegation.

'Has the king come from Abbeville to greet his queen?' Mary asks.

'I would not doubt it,' Agnes says, 'though I confess I harbour concerns over her reception of a husband of such advanced years. I can scarce credit a handsome girl of eight and ten for expressing joy at the site of her husband's decaying expression, even if he does wear the crown of France.'

'Our mistress is none but a woman, such as we are, and a pawn in the games of men,' Jane Popincourt, a lady-in-waiting of long-standing in the English court – despite her French birth – says in softly accented English as she brushes a fallen leaf off the fox-fur cuffs of her hanging sleeves. 'I have heard King Louis offered King Henry one million crowns for her hand.'

'An easy decision to take after the Emperor Maximilian repudiated the new queen's engagement to his son, Charles,' Agnes says as she adjusts the tails of her gable hood. 'I have heard tell that King Henry was most enraged and has recalled all the English ladies and courtiers back from the Emperor's court in Mechelen.'

Mary turns abruptly in her saddle, almost unseating herself. 'Does that mean my sister will be returning to England? She is in the court of the Archduchess of Austria in Mechelen.'

Agnes nods. 'Without question. It is most likely that your

father will find her a place here in the French court, now that England and France are newly allied.'

'Won't that be a joy for you, *Marie*,' Jane says, her tongue sliding over the words with a silky sibilance. 'To have your own dear sister Anne at court with you.'

Mary smiles wanly. *Anne here? When I have finally secured a position of honour in the French court, the court all aspire to? Why must my own joy be compromised by Anne's wit and vivaciousness?*

'I shall await the day with anticipation,' she replies with a bland smile.

'It will be some months yet before she arrives,' Agnes says. 'She will need to visit England to be fitted with new gowns as she is yet a growing girl, and then there is the winter sea which shall no doubt delay her arrival. I venture we will not see Anne here till the New Year.'

Mary shifts on the uncomfortable saddle. *The New Year. Three months. I have three months to make my mark in the French court before Anne arrives and ruins everything for me.*

A group of finely dressed French horsemen rides up alongside the procession, slowing their pace as their leader pauses to address the new Queen of France. Mary regards the fine figure of the young man dressed in richly embroidered black velvet who sits astride a handsome white horse bedecked with red tassels.

'Who is that?'

Jane scrutinises the young noble. 'The Dauphin, François, Count de Angoulême. He is heir to the French throne – if the new queen does not provide King Louis with a son. François is not so pleased with developments—' She breaks off with a gasp. 'Oh, *mon Dieu*! The dauphin approaches.'

Mary casts her gaze down to the reins, which she worries between her fingers as the dauphin draws up alongside them. He sweeps off his feathered hat and bows his head in greeting.

'Welcome to my beautiful county, *mesdames et mesdemoiselles*,' he addresses them in excellent English.

'We are most gratified to have the honour of your welcome, Your Highness,' replies Agnes, who, by dint of her age and status, has taken on the role of head lady-in-waiting.

The dauphin smiles as his dark eyes scan the women. 'It is I who am most gratified, *madame*. We shall rest this night in the castle at Montreuil and then my dukes and I shall accompany you to Abbeville, where King Louis awaits the arrival of his bride.'

'We thank you must humbly for your solicitude to our welfare, Your Highness,' Agnes responds in the obsequious tone of one accustomed to the delicate task of engaging with royalty.

Mary steals a glance at the dauphin to see that he is regarding her. She looks down quickly.

The dauphin chuckles. 'I entreat you, *mademoiselle*, not to deny this humble prince the pleasure of admiring your beauty.'

Mary looks up at him. His face is long and lean under his neat black beard, and his prominent nose lends him an air of hawkish gravitas.

'May I have the honour of your name, *mademoiselle*?' He glances at her 'B' pendant. 'Ah, I shall venture a guess. Barbara? Bess?'

'Berthe!' one of his men calls out.

'Brigitte!' shouts another.

Mary feels the heat rise in her face. 'Mary. Mary Boleyn, Your Highness.' She touches the pendant. 'The "B" is for our family name, Boleyn.'

'*Marie*. The beautiful name of Our Lady, Christ's mother. It suits you well, *mademoiselle*.'

He doffs his hat to the ladies. 'I have heard that your journey across the Channel was most arduous, and I entreat you enjoy a good meal and rest this eve. Tomorrow we will off to Abbeville where my wife, the Dauphine Claude, and myself, shall entertain the new queen's court with a celebration ball.' He glances at Mary. 'I trust you all shall be in attendance.'

As the dauphin and his retinue ride off towards the town,

Mary's mind spins with confusing thoughts. Agnes looks over at her.

'Mary, are you well? You look feverish.'

Jane laughs. 'She is well. Her heart has been pierced with Cupid's arrow.'

Mary shakes her head, setting the linen lappets flapping. 'No. Never, Jane.'

'Mary, he is a prince, and a husband only newly married to Claude, Duchess of Brittany,' Agnes says. 'I urge you caution. Ladies of the court are but playthings to nobles and royalty. Your father has graced you with the gift of that fine pendant to remind you to maintain the honour of your family name. Do not cause the good name of Boleyn to fall into disgrace.'

Mary fingers the pearl pendant. 'I will do nothing to lower our good name, madam. I wish only to be a modest servant to our queen.'

Agnes nods. 'I am glad to hear it. Now, make yourself ready. We are nigh upon the town.'

Hôtel de Gruthuse, Abbeville, France
Two days later

Mary looks around from her seat amongst the English ladies-in-waiting at a long table in the great hall of the ancient Hôtel de Gruthuse castle. The servants are whipping away the remnants of the celebratory feast, and up in the gallery overlooking the hall, minstrels have embarked on a lively rollick of music on their harps, flutes, fiddles and drums. She presses the back of her hand against her mouth in a vain attempt to stifle a yawn.

'Mary, compose yourself,' Agnes admonishes is a loud whisper. 'It is not meet that you insult the hospitality of the dauphin and dauphine with a display of weariness.'

'I am sorry, milady. I have yet to recover from the journey from England. I have been sleeping ill, despite the comfort afforded by our lodgings.'

'Do you not credit that our own beloved mistress, the new Queen of France, is weary?' Agnes says. 'Regard her, Mary. See how she entertains her new husband, who is yet four and thirty years her senior, despite the prospect of a life chained to a man of such antiquity and far from her beloved England? She how she encourages his laughter, how she pays him the price of a kiss upon receipt of his betrothal jewels. See how she herself insists on filling his goblet with wine.' The duchess taps Mary's necklace. 'Remember who you are. Do yourself and your family honour. Do not give these French cause to disparage we good Englishwomen.'

Mary straightens up on the hard bench. 'Yes, milady. I shall take care.'

The minstrels commence a lively gavotte, and, with a nod from King Louis, the dauphin's noblemen and the dauphine's ladies hurry onto the stone floor under the soaring vaulted ceiling. Mary watches the French women flounce through the dance like colourful birds in their vibrant scarlet, green and blue silk dresses and their handsome hoods adorned with precious jewels. Dancing with them, the dauphin's handsome courtiers are only marginally less colourful than their partners in their short puff-sleeved velvet tunics and feathered hats. Mary runs her hand over the thick black velvet of her gown, embellished only with a modest application of gold embroidery along the square edge of its bodice. The gable hood sits like a stone on her head and she is conscious of the staidness of her appearance and that of the other English ladies-in-waiting.

So intent is she on her thoughts that she fails to notice the approach of the dauphin and his new wife, the small, plump, hunchbacked Dauphine Claude, who, at nearly fifteen, is the same age as Mary.

'My ladies, are you enjoying the festivities?' the dauphin asks.

'I have engaged the finest musicians in France to celebrate the occasion of my cousin's marriage to your lovely princess.'

Agnes rises from the bench and nods graciously at the royal pair. 'We are all most honoured to be in attendance at such a reception as this, on such a joyous occasion, Your Highness. Your hospitality is most welcome.'

Mary watches the dauphin's dark gaze scan the faces of the ladies-in-waiting until it comes to rest on her. She swallows as she feels the blood rise in her cheeks.

He smiles. 'And you, *Mademoiselle Marie de Boleyn*, I do not see you dancing. Is the music not to your liking?'

She glances at the young dauphine who smiles benignly back at her. 'No, Your Highness. I mean, yes, the music is most to my liking, but—'

'Yes? But? You may say, *Mademoiselle Marie*. I shall not be offended. I aspire only to be a munificent host.'

Mary swallows. 'Yes, Your Highness. It is that we have not been invited to dance.'

'Ah, of course.' He turns to the other ladies. 'An unforgiveable oversight on behalf of my court. I shall resolve the issue forthwith. I shall expect a dance with each of you myself once I accompany the dauphine back to her rooms. She speaks no English and prefers not to dance. It has been a long evening for her.'

As the royal couple leave the hall and the minstrels commence an energetic volte, Jane Popincourt takes a sip of the rich red wine. 'The dauphin is most handsome, is he not?' she says innocently. 'A pity he is shackled so to that poor little wife. Did you see how she limps?'

'Do not cast aspersions on our hostess, Jane,' Agnes admonishes. 'I have heard the dauphine is of a good moral and charitable character.'

Jan smirks. 'And she is Duchess of Brittany, which is coveted by both King Louis and the dauphin. The dauphin thinks only for himself. He has many mistresses. It is well that his wife has a charitable heart. She will need it with François as her husband.'

Mary adjusts her gable hood. 'I should be most honoured to dance with the dauphin.'

'I caution you again, Mary,' Agnes warns. 'I have observed how the dauphin regards you. You are yet but ten and five years old. Know that men harbour in their hearts many tricks to deceive. When they have had their wicked way, it will be as if nothing has happened. Trust no man in this court, most especially the dauphin.'

Chapter Fourteen

BRYHER & MARNIE

Los Angeles, California
June 2002

Marnie examines her fourteen-year-old reflection in the bedroom mirror, pulling her T-shirt tightly over her new push-up bra.

Her younger sister Bryher looks up from the book she's reading on the bed. 'Are you sure you want to wear that to the filming today? You look like Julia Roberts in *Pretty Woman*.'

'When you've got it, flaunt it, Mom says,' Marnie declares. 'She's the one who told me to wear it.'

'But you're supposed to be a ten-year-old in the commercial.'

Marnie shrugs as she dabs pink lip gloss on her lips. 'I can play ten.'

'Not looking like that you can't.' Bryher rolls off the bed and joins her sister in front of the mirror. 'I'm ten. Do you look like me?'

Marnie sweeps her turquoise eyes over her short, skinny sister, in her jeans and a well-worn Spice Girls T-shirt. Bryher's straight brown hair is tied back in a ponytail and she has a smudge of ink on her cheek.

'Only in my nightmares.'

Bryher pushes her sister's arm, causing her to smudge lip gloss over her cheek. 'You're mean.'

'And you're pathetic. I wish you'd never been born.'

Bryher's face crumbles. 'You don't mean that.'

Marnie smacks her lips together in the mirror. 'Oh, no? Mom and I don't need you. All you do is get in the way. If you'd never been born, I'd have this room and Mom all to myself. Instead, I've got to share everything with the world's most boring human. You're totally useless.'

'That's not true. I helped you learn your lines. I know them as well as you do.'

Marnie shoves past her sister and heads to the door. 'I don't need you. I only agreed to that because Mom told me to. See you later, Loser,' she says, slamming the door behind her.

Bryher flops onto her bed and buries her head in her arms.

I hate you, I hate you, I hate you, Marnie. I hope you die.

The bedroom door swings open. 'Bryher, what are you doing?' her mother barks. 'Get your jean jacket on. The sitter has cancelled. You'll have to come with us. Just sit in a corner and be quiet, okay? I don't want you ruining Marnie's first day on the Fresh Freddy's Burgers campaign. By this time next year, your sister will be a huge star.'

Bryher looks up from her perch on a wooden box beside the door to the dressing rooms, her science textbook open in her lap.

The producer slaps his baseball cap against his thigh and points at Marnie, who has had a growth spurt since her spring audition and is now a head taller than the other child actors.

'Is she wearing a push-up bra? I think she's wearing a friggin' push-up bra. F'Crissake. She's supposed to look like she's ten, not eighteen.'

'Marnie's only fourteen and she's a very good actress,' Kitty Finch says as she presses on Marnie's shoulder. 'She can play ten, can't you Marnie?'

Marnie nods as she bends her knees to appear shorter. 'I can play ten.'

The producer runs his hand over his gelled hair. 'This is crap. Serious crap.' He paces the set. 'This isn't gonna work.' He jabs his hand at Marnie. 'Look at her. She looks like she's off to the prom. The Fresh Freddy's Burgers execs are screaming at me in my office. They want an ordinary, all-American ten-year-old, not a teenage Marilyn Monroe. This campaign is supposed to run nationally for a year, with new billboards and commercials every month. At this rate, she'll look middle-aged in a year.'

Marnie grabs his arm. 'Please, Mr Kincaid, I can do it. I've been rehearsing for months. I'll take off the bra and scrunch right down.'

'Sorry, kid. It's not gonna happen. You're fired.' He looks at the other four children who are tossing a basketball around the playground set, and shoves his baseball hat back on his head. 'Now I gotta see if we can use one of these kids or the whole day's a write-off.'

'Wait, Mr Kincaid,' Kitty says. 'Maybe I can help you.' She beckons to Bryher. 'Bryher, come here. Hurry. Oh, for heaven's sake, don't dawdle. Put that book down and get over here.'

Bryher sets her science book down on the crate and hurries past the other kids, dodging the basketball as it flies towards her head. She joins her mother and the producer and glances at her sister, who is staring at her with a face contorted in horror. Kitty pushes Bryher in front of the producer.

'Mr Kincaid, this is my other daughter, Bryher. She's ten and she's been helping Marnie with her lines so she's word perfect. And she's as ordinary as you could possibly wish for.'

The producer scrutinises Bryher, who juts out her chin and folds her arms.

His face breaks into a toothy grin. 'Perfect! That attitude. I love it. She's short, she's plain. We'll draw on some freckles and she'll be perfect.' He looks at Kitty. 'You say she's ten?'

'Yes, I am,' Bryher interrupts. 'I'm ten and my name is Bryher Finch. I can do this.'

He laughs. 'Like I said. The kid's got attitude. I love it. Let me check with the execs and I'll be right back. In the meantime, take her over to costume and makeup and get her ready. I think you've just saved my ass.'

Bryher's gaze flicks back to Marnie, whose face looks like a red ballon about to burst.

Chapter Fifteen

MARY

Hôtel des Tournelles, Paris, France
November 1514

King Louis's courtiers and court ladies, who have assembled in a vast crowd around the roped-off list field in the Parc des Tournelles, cheer at the arrival of the beautiful new queen on the arm of King Louis XII. The old king, dressed in the finest velvets and furs, is bent and shuffling, and he is saved from the embarrassment of a stumble on the uneven earth only by the steadying grip of his young consort's hand. He waves at the cheering mass and greets the crowd with the smile of one who has discovered the joy of honey after a diet of insipid porridge.

Mary Boleyn glances at the row of armoured knights, their decorated lances held vertically as they sit astride powerful horses clad in full armour barding and gaily coloured silk caparisons. She and the other ladies-in-waiting follow the royal pair across the list field. On the far side, a covered, wooden viewing platform has been constructed and decorated with blue silk drapery festooned with the white *fleur de lys* of France. Mary sees the queen's head turn towards the jousters as they pass, and she follows the young queen's gaze to a jouster whose horse is bedecked in a caparison of the yellow rampant lions: the heraldic symbol of Charles Brandon, the Duke of Suffolk. The duke raises his visor and inclines his head as the queen passes; she acknowledges him with a slight tilt of her head.

'Did you see that, *Marie*?' Jane Popincourt whispers. 'I have heard that the Duke of Suffolk is the queen's lover.'

Mary jerks her head around. 'Really?'

'Ssh!' Agnes hisses. 'I will not abide such disrespectful tittle tattle. Pay attention. Attend to your queen and seat yourselves.'

King Louis climbs the two steps up to the platform and makes his way to a wooden settle dressed with silk cushions and fur throws, which he claims with an exhausted groan. The queen seats herself on an ornately carved wooden chair beside him, and Mary and Agnes hurry to arrange her lynx-lined cloak and her rich green velvet gown in elegant folds.

Mary then finds a place between Agnes and Jane on a bench beside the queen and scans the exhilarating scene before her. King Louis's trumpeters announce the commencement of the joust with a blare, and her heart beats wildly at the thrill of being part of the queen's coronation festivities. Ever since the queen's entourage arrived in Paris the previous week, following her coronation in the great abbey of St Denis, the days have been filled with processions, pageants, masques and balls. Mary is certain that not even her sister, in the Archduchess of Austria's court in Mechelen, could have experienced such a profuse display of abundance and joy. She fingers the golden 'B' of her pendant. If only her father could see her now, how proud he would be.

The knights part and the crowd gasps and cheers as the armoured figure of the Dauphin François, mounted on a black steed draped in the blue and white colours of France and clutching a long blue and white lance, gallops onto the list field. He halts in front of the prone king and his new queen and raises his visor.

'Your Majesties, I bid you welcome to the Field of Honour here today in celebration of our new queen's coronation. I shall, myself, engage in a joust with the Duke of Suffolk, to open the festivities. I entreat you …' His eyes wander over towards Mary and the other ladies-in-waiting. '… and your lovely English ladies, to enjoy the events of this joyous day.'

Mary's heart races as she watches him gallop to one side of the list field, while the Duke of Suffolk gallops to other, in readiness for the joust. Had the dauphin's gaze rested on her face just a moment longer than anyone else's? Had she seen his dark eyes flicker? She takes a deep breath to steady herself. She can hear her sister's voice in her head. *Don't be such a silly fool, Mary. He is heir to the throne of France. He could have any woman he desired. Why would he waste his time with a simple English girl such as you?'*

The crowd falls silent as the two men face off. Mary focuses her attention on the handsome figure of the dauphin. The air is rent with a blast of a trumpet and the two jousters charge. For a long moment, there is nothing but the sound of the horses' hooves pounding against the compacted earth. Then the crash of lances against shields and the thud as the Duke of Suffolk slams against the ground. The crowd roars and the queen is on her feet.

The duke raises his arm and waves as he stands up, and Mary sees the queen press her hand against her chest as the dauphin rides over to the fallen duke and offers his hand in assistance, which the duke accepts with a grateful nod. The crowd explodes into cheers of *'Vivre le dauphin! Vivre la France!'*

The dauphin gestures towards the king and queen, and the crowd's cries change. *'Vivre le Roi Louis! Vivre la Reine Marie!'* The queen responds with a gracious nod, though Mary observes that her gaze follows the duke as he remounts his horse and exits the list field to rejoin the knights.

She looks back at the dauphin only to see that he is watching her. This time his eyes linger on hers.

Perhaps she is not such a silly fool after all.

Chapter Sixteen

BRYHER

Puddleton, England
December 2024

Bryher holds up her phone as she wanders around Betty's house searching for a signal. Outside the rain is pelting down, and Betty has taken the only umbrella with her to her WI meeting, so there's no way Bryher's going outside to call Margot. She hesitates in front of Betty's bedroom door. It's probably pointless, she thinks, but she's tried everywhere else, even standing on top of the toilet seat. She must speak to Margot.

She opens the door and steps into Betty's bedroom, which is an explosion of pink and roses – with rose wallpaper, silky pink curtains and a rose-splattered carpet. Bijou looks up sleepily from the quilted pink bedcover.

'Sorry, Sneezeball,' Bryher says as she steps around the room, fruitlessly waving her phone. 'Just trying to find some reception.' She pulls out the chair at the dressing table and, after stepping on its seat, balances herself on the rickety legs.

'Bingo!' She taps on Margot's WhatsApp number. 'Margot, thank God you're there.'

'Hon, can't talk long. Lunch meeting with Julia and Sandra at Crossroads Kitchen in twenty minutes.'

'Fine, fine. I'll be fast.'

'Yes, Julian? Hold on, Bryher. What's that? Fabulous! You're a genius. Order a thousand of each and we'll hire some models to hand them out at the Lakers game.'

'Margot?'

'Hon, you'll want a "Team Bryher" T-shirt, I'm guessing?'

'What are you talking about?'

'Julian's started a "Team Bryher" versus "Team Jodie" internet thing. The likes are going through the roof. We're handing out T-shirts at the next Lakers game.'

'I'm not sure that's the kind of publicity I want. I want to be taken seriously as an actress.'

'Darling, it's exactly the kind of publicity you need. Get people on your side for a change.'

'Wait a minute. Didn't I just hear you tell Julian to order a thousand of each? Are you handing out "Team Jodie" T-shirts, too?'

'Bryher, darling, you can't have "Team Bryher" without "Team Jodie". People love to take sides. Besides, I've just signed Jodie.'

'What? You've signed the woman who's likely dumped me in this shit? Whose side are you on?'

'Let's just call me Switzerland. Hear me out, this is good for all of us. Hold on a sec. Yes, Julian? Team Jodie's jumped ahead? Right. Keep on it.'

'For crying out loud, Margot. I heard that.'

'Don't take it personally. It's just business. I'm raising both your profiles. What was it you wanted?'

Bryher wobbles on the chair and grabs for the wall to steady herself. 'I need you to send me more money. The trains here are extortionate and I need winter clothes. It's freezing in this country and I'm not going to wear a dead woman's kilt and twinset.'

'Darling, I'm sorry but it's taking some time getting the initial payment from the UK producers.'

'I've been working here over a month. What am I supposed to live on? Air? They need to pay.'

'They tried, but Jake's closed your joint account so the transaction didn't go through. They're asking for your bank account details.'

'Our joint account was the only bank account I had! Jake always took care of all our financial stuff. Everything I earned went into our joint account.'

Margot tuts. 'A woman should always have her own account. Just saying. I'll get Julian on to it. We'll get something sorted out.'

'I need money now. I've got financial responsibilities.'

'What responsibilities? Jake's taken over the debt on your joint credit cards by taking your name off them and you're living for free at your cousin's. If I were you, I'd be thanking both of them.'

Bryher teeters on the chair. 'You can't be serious. I had to borrow another bag of pound coins from Betty this week for train fare and my morning oat milk flat white from the train station kiosk. It's embarrassing.'

'Have you spoken to Jake? Maybe he can loan you some money—'

'Are you kidding me?' Bryher scratches at the rash that's flaring at her neck. 'I had no idea he was so vindictive. Anyway, I've already tried leaving him messages but he's ghosting me. I need a couple of thousand dollars quickly. I've got some ... family obligations.'

'I thought you didn't have any family.'

Shit. She's got no choice but to tell Margot. She needs her help.

'Margot, I—'

'Sorry, hon. Julian's waving at me. What's that, Julian? You've got Jodie Rogers on Fallon on Thursday? Amazing! Hon, I've got to go. I'll get Julian to wire another couple of hundred pounds to your local Western Union to tide you over until your pay comes through.'

'Marg—'

The call ends abruptly and Bryher huffs out an exasperated sigh. Two hundred pounds is nowhere near enough. She'll have to figure something else out. Maybe talk to Jeremy in the morning and see if she can get the producers to pay her what they owe her. Yes, that's what she'll do. She'll get them to pay the money into Margot's account and get Margot to wire her the money. She'll threaten to go on strike if they don't play ball. They can't afford to re-cast again, especially since a third of the mini-series has already been filmed.

She turns to step down, but the chair wobbles under her shifting weight. She flails in the air and lands hard on the carpet, knocking the wind out of her.

'Owwwww. Oww. Oww.'

Bijou meows from under the bed. Bryher turns her head to stare into the unblinking green eyes. The cat is sprawled beside what looks like an old red leather jewellery box.

'What have you got there, Sneezeball?'

She shoves the cat out of the way and slides the box out from under the bed. She sits cross-legged on the rose-splattered carpet and opens the lid. Inside is a jumble of garish necklaces, brooches and bracelets. She sifts through the costume jewellery until she spots a string of fat round pearls. She lifts the necklace out of the box. A gold 'B' hangs from the strand, three oval pearls dangling from its base. *Well, what do you know, Sneezeball? A copy of the Boleyn necklace.*

She scratches her itchy neck. What if she borrowed it, just until the film shoot is over? She'll have it back in the jewellery box before Betty knows it's gone. She weighs the necklace in her hands. It's a decent weight and the pearls have a lovely soft sheen. It's obviously a much better copy than the one at the studio. She'll try it out tomorrow. Fingers crossed, it works.

Chapter Seventeen

ANNE & MARY

Hôtel des Tournelles, Paris, France
February 1515

M ary tosses the embroidery she is working on to one side and rushes over to greet her sister.

'Anne! You have arrived!'

'Mary, take care!' Agnes admonishes. 'You are working a handkerchief for our mistress, the poor dowager queen. It is not meet to throw it onto the ground.'

Ignoring the elder lady-in-waiting, Mary embraces Anne, kissing her on both cheeks in the French fashion. 'How was your journey from England? We met with a terrible storm when we travelled here in October, such that I feared that I would end my days at the bottom of the English Channel.'

Anne's dark eyes sweep over the plush green velvet gown and fashionable French hood adorning her sister. 'We were fortunate not to have to endure such a drama, Mary. The sea was calm enough. Perhaps you are not well-suited to sea voyages.'

She moves past Mary and greets their step-grandmother, the duchess. 'Milady, I am well pleased to see you again. Are you well?'

Agnes kisses Anne's cheek. 'Very well, Anne. Heavens, you have grown into a lovely young woman. You were but a child when I saw you last. It is opportune that the Archduchess Margaret sent her English *filles d'honneur* back to England, and that your father arranged to have you join our poor Queen Mary's court here in France. She is in need of her countrywomen at this sad time.'

'I wish only to be of service to Queen Mary and be a credit to our family.'

Agnes nods and pats Anne on her cheek. 'That is well, child. Let me make your acquaintance with our poor widowed queen's ladies. King Louis's demise was such a shock to everyone not three months after their marriage. We are just this week released from the mourning seclusion at the Hôtel de Cluny and have been advised to prepare for King François's state entry into Paris three days hence.'

Choosing to ignore her sister's slight, Mary rejoins the women. 'It was a terrible blow for the queen. King Louis had been in good spirits through the Christmas festivities. Then to pass away so suddenly on the first day of the New Year—'

'They say it was caused by King Louis's marital exertions with his pretty young queen,' Jane Popincourt says.

'That is pure gossip put about by lazy tongues,' Agnes says sternly.

'And now the queen's English lover, the Duke of Suffolk, has arrived at court,' Jane continues, as she browses through a selection of colourful silk threads, ignoring the duchess's rebuke. 'The queen wishes to marry him, but King François wishes for her to marry a French noble.'

'Jane, where do you hear such drivel?' Agnes asks.

'Everybody is saying it,' Jane says with a shrug.

'That is quite enough,' Agnes admonishes. 'Ladies, we must remember that King Henry's sister is no longer the Queen of France. She is the dowager queen. The Dauphine Claude is now the Queen of France.'

She pats the chair beside her. 'Come, sit by me, Anne, and tell us of your time in the Archduchess Margaret's court. I shall have them bring us wine and sweetmeats.'

Mary returns to her chair and picks up her discarded embroidery. She watches as the women cluster around Anne, giggling and gasping as her sister regales them with tales of the court at Mechelen. She jabs the needle through the handkerchief's fine linen. *Popular Anne. Clever Anne. Anne the bluejay and Mary the wren.* What freedom she had felt, to have been spared the glare of Anne's sun for the past year. To have finally blossomed in the French court, to have attracted the admiration of none but King François himself. Mary glares at Anne. *Have you managed such a thing, sister? The admiration of a king?*

She observes her sister's slender figure in the stylish crimson velvet dress, her dark hair revealed by the equally fashionable French hood. Anne is not so very handsome, she thinks. Her complexion is olive and her face, though pleasant, does not have the delicate colouring she herself possesses. And Anne's eyes are dark, as is her hair, and her figure too slender. No, Anne does not have the fashionable beauty with which she, Mary, has been blessed. Her red-gold hair, flawless pale skin, clear blue eyes and rounded figure have always drawn admiration. Were an artist to select a model for Aphrodite, Anne would never be chosen.

The women gathered around her sister break out into peals of laughter. Mary frowns. Why is it that Anne commands such attention when her appearance is so ordinary? Had Anne not shown her little but contempt throughout their childhood, perhaps she would be as entranced as the others appear to be. How can they be so blind to Anne's calculating manner, to the charm that Anne has honed to serve her own desires?

Mary looks up as two maids enter, laden with trays of refreshments.

The duchess beckons the maids to approach. 'Ah, the wine and gingerbread has arrived. Let us enjoy a little repast. The dowager queen will no doubt require our services to prepare her for supper later.'

Three days later

'Look, the king is here!' Jane cranes her neck out of the window for a better view of the approaching parade of gaily clad nobles preceding the handsome figure of King François I astride a white horse draped with the blue and white colours of France.

Mary cannot suppress a smile of pride at the sight of her royal admirer as he waves at the cheering crowds on his approach to the Palais. 'Is the king not handsome?'

Jane casts her a sly smile. 'I imagine Queen Claude has much to occupy her in bed at night.'

Anne joins them at the window and scrutinises the French king. 'He is a handsome man, although I have heard he spends more time spilling his seed into mistresses than he does into his wife.'

Mary gasps. 'Anne! How can you say such a thing? I have only known the king to be an honourable man.'

Anne raises a fine dark eyebrow. 'Oh, you have "known" the king, Mary? In the biblical sense? I doubt our father's intentions were for you to become the king's mistress.'

Mary reddens. 'Of course not! Though I wonder as much of yourself.'

Anne's face hardens. 'I have no intention of giving away my best asset rashly, sister. I will not be forced into a loveless marriage to an impecunious country knight as punishment for gifting my maidenhood to a randy nobleman, or even yet a king.' She lowers her voice and whispers in Mary's ear, 'A whore is a whore.'

Mary gasps at her sister's vulgarity.

Anne laughs and taps the 'B' on Mary's pendant. 'You should remember yourself, Mary. You are a Boleyn. Do not trade your value lightly.'

'Well said, Anne,' Agnes says from her spot at the adjoining window. 'The men at court are naught but rutting stags playing at the games of chivalry. In the French court they are at their most licentious. Do not succumb to their sugared words.'

Mary watches the figure of the king pass beneath their window as the parade enters into the ancient Palais. She has done nothing wrong. In their brief encounters, King François has only ever treated her honourably, though his admiration has set her heart aflutter and reddened her cheeks. Besides, he is married to the good Queen Claude, who is beloved by the people for her virtuous and charitable nature, and who is yet with child – with the child everyone hopes will be the new Dauphin of France.

Oh, how she wishes she could love! Her heart is full. And in the slow days she spends sewing, singing, and playing cards with the dowager queen and her ladies, she dreams of little else but the kisses and embraces of a lover. In her nightly dreams, how often she has seen the face of King François! Were she able to turn her mind to other matters, she would do so in a thrice. Yet his face haunts her thoughts. In truth, she is happy for it, no matter what Anne says.

———————

The French king extends his hand to Mary as the minstrels commence a lively galliard.

'*Mademoiselle Marie*, you must do me the honour of accompanying me in a dance. I will brook no refusal.'

Mary glances at her sister, who stands beside her amongst the dowager queen's ladies in the Palais' grand hall. Ignoring Anne's raised eyebrow, Mary curtsies to the king and takes his hand. 'I should be most honoured, Your Majesty.'

She joins the king on the floor, conscious of the eyes of the court on the two of them. They fly through the energetic steps of the dance until she finds herself laughing at the faces the king pulls as he jumps and twirls around her. When the dance finishes, she curtsies again and thanks him. She is about to return to the ladies-in-waiting when he grabs her hand.

'Stay, *mademoiselle*. You cannot refuse the king the pleasure of your company for another dance.'

Mary glances at Anne who is watching her with the intensity of a cat at a mousehole. 'What of your queen, Your Majesty?'

'The queen has retired, wearied from the day's events. I, however, am as wakeful as one who has risen with the dawn. Come, *ma belle Marie*, do me the honour of your company in another dance.'

Mary looks into the king's dark eyes. Eyes that implore her capitulation to his will. She swallows. Does she dare to refuse the king when the eyes of all of his court are watching? Of course, she cannot.

She holds out her hand. 'It would be my pleasure, Your Majesty.'

Anne tosses and turns under the thick bedcover. She looks over at the empty space beside her where Mary should be asleep. Outside, the clock in the castle's tower strikes twelve, the gongs reverberating in the winter air. She feels her body tense with anger, with all she wishes to say to her sister.

How can you be so stupid, Mary? The king cares naught for you. You are nothing but a plaything in his eyes. Do not listen to his pretty words, or swoon at the loving gazes he casts upon you. Remember who you are!

You are a Boleyn! Do not ruin our good name with your silly, romantic notions. Think of your family. Think of me, Mary! If you lose your reputation on a careless liaison with the king, your tarnish cannot help but be visited upon me. I will not have it! I will never permit myself the weakness to become a man's plaything, whether he be a shepherd or a king. I will not be tarnished by your brush.

The chamber door creaks open and a sliver of light from the hallway torch slices into the room's gloom, where the embers of the dying fire cast a weak glow. Anne watches her sister gingerly shut the door and tiptoe over to the bed. She sits up against the pillow.

'Where have you been?'

'Anne! I did not know you were awake.'

'I have been awake since I first came to bed, waiting for you.'

Mary sits on the bed and slips off her shoes. 'The king wished to speak with me.'

'Speak with you? At this late hour? What could you possibly have to say that would interest a king?'

Mary removes her French hood and the linen coif which she sets on a table beside the bed. She runs her fingers through her hair and looks over at Anne. 'Anne, you needn't be cruel.'

'I have no desire to be cruel. I am simply stating a fact. King François is an educated man of great intelligence. You can barely write the Lord's Prayer in Latin. I am simply curious as to what you could possibly speak about.'

'Music. We spoke about music. And … and roses. He is fond of roses.'

Anne laughs. 'Ah, so the king is a minstrel and a gardener. He lowers the level of his conversation to meet the intellect of his companions.'

'You *are* cruel.'

Anne grabs Mary's arm. 'Have you lain with him?'

'Anne!' Mary pulls her arm away. 'We spoke. That is all.'

'He did not touch you?' Anne tilts her head as she scrutinises her sister. 'Kiss you?'

Mary runs her tongue over her lips. 'Anne, please.'

'Did he kiss you?'

Mary jumps up and pulls at the pins affixing the stiff silk-covered placard to her gown.

Anne climbs off the bed and pushes Mary's hands away from the delicate blue silk. She carefully pulls out the brass pins and drops them into her left palm. She lowers her voice. 'Mary, did the king kiss you?'

Mary chokes down a sob. 'Yes. But that is all. I … I left after that. I told him I could not.'

Anne nods. 'That is good.' She hands the pins and the placard to her sister and begins to unlace her sister's bodice. 'You must stay away from him.'

Mary weeps softly as Anne removes her gown. 'I know. I shall.'

'Good. I am glad of it. Now, step out of your kirtle and petticoat and come to bed. I am weary and I have need of rest.'

Chapter Eighteen

BRYHER

Elstree Studios, Borehamwood, England
December 2024

Bryher looks up from her Sudoku puzzle at the sound of Jeremy shouting out Dr Pieter de Beer's name. She watches the tall European head across the set of King Henry VIII's bedroom to join Jeremy and an irritated Archie Flanders, flamboyant in the embroidered and bejewelled costume of Henry VIII, in front of a fake leaded window.

'He is a handsome fellow, isn't he?'

Bryher looks over at Jennifer Foster who is perched on a bench, the skirts of her resplendent gown arranged carefully around her. 'Archie Flanders?'

Jennifer exhales a throaty laugh. 'Good heavens, no. Dr de Beer. If I were single, I would most definitely ensure that the handsome professor came into my sphere of influence.'

Bryher shrugs and flings the long black veil of her bejewelled French hood over her shoulder. Since their first meeting in her dressing room, Pieter has given no indication of any interest in her, which she finds slightly irritating. Since *Cop Town* had become a hit in the States, she's been used to surreptitious glances, appreciative smiles and gratifying flirtations from both men and women. Not that Pieter's indifference matters, of course. She's still married. She'll work everything out with Jake when she gets back to LA. Surely, Jake will have calmed down by then and they can have a reasonable discussion. You can't just stop loving someone overnight.

'He's probably married. Or gay,' Bryher says.

'He's not married, nor is he gay. He's quite famous over here, did you know?'

Bryher glances over at the tall historian. 'He is?'

'Oh, yes. He writes books and presents all sorts of programmes on telly about British history as well as advising on films and whatnot. He regularly tops the list of London's most eligible bachelors.'

'Really?'

'Yes, really. He worked on *Elizabeth and Essex* when I played Queen Elizabeth I, and from what I've observed, our Dr de Beer is rather a lone wolf. Women fall at his feet, and of course he's dated a few, but it never seems to last long. I think actresses bore him, which does him credit, in my view. Most of the thespians I've worked with bore me rigid. Shakespearean actors excepted, of course. Oh, the parties we used to have up at Stratford-upon-Avon during my days with the Royal Shakespeare Company.'

Bryher glances over at the three men, who are engaged in a heated discussion. 'He sounds like a player.'

'Oh, no, nothing so crude as that. He doesn't go out of his way to attract women. They simply flock to him. It's that Belgian charm. Like Hercule Poirot.'

Hercule Poirot? Who's Hercule Poirot? Bryher shrugs. 'I'm married.'

Jennifer raises a finely pencilled eyebrow. 'Oh. I thought—'

'You thought what?'

'Well, it's all over social media. You know …' Jennifer leans closer and whispers. 'The sex tape *ménage à trois*.'

Bryher groans. 'That stupid story is haunting me.'

'Darling, it's everywhere. I thought you and Jake had separated.'

'No. Well, kind of.' Bryher sighs heavily. 'We're on a break.'

Jennifer nods at Pieter. 'Then what better time than now to have a lovely fling? No strings attached. Perfect.'

'Jennifer!' Jeremy waves at the regal queen. 'Can we have you over here for a minute, please?'

'Duty calls.' Jennifer gathers her voluminous gown around her legs and launches herself off the bench. 'No doubt Archie wants to cut some of my lines to make himself look better. He really is an arse.'

'You were excellent in that scene,' Pieter says. 'Your accent has definitely improved.'

Bryher looks up at the historian and raises a dark eyebrow. 'Is that meant to be a compliment?'

'I'm sorry. I didn't mean any offence. Your English accent was always fine. It's just … better now. Like a native's.'

Bryher smiles. 'You can take your foot out of your mouth. Apology accepted.'

Pieter sits on a folding chair beside her. 'I see your neck is better. It must not have been the necklace after all.'

Bryher rubs the smooth skin on her neck above the gleaming pearls of Betty's 'B' necklace. 'Oh, it was the necklace. This one is Betty's. I borrowed it to see if I could wear it without breaking out in hives. It works perfectly. Not one itch. There's a problem with the clasp, though. It keeps coming loose. I'm afraid it's going to fall off in the middle of a scene.'

'May I take a look at it?'

'Sure.' She unfastens the faulty clasp and hands it to Pieter. He rubs a pearl against his teeth.

'What are you doing? Don't scratch them or Betty will kill me. She doesn't know I've borrowed it.'

Pieter laughs. 'Don't worry. I'm just checking to see if the pearls are real. If a pearl feels rough against your teeth, it's very likely real. These appear to be real. Cultured, I would imagine. Natural pearls are extremely rare now.'

He hands the necklace to Bryher. 'Go ahead. Try it.'

'Really?'

'It's fine. It won't harm the pearl.'

Bryher rubs a pearl against her front teeth, then hands it back to him. 'I can't feel anything. I have veneers.'

'Ah, it won't work, then.' He turns the necklace over in his hands. 'It's a good piece.' He looks at Bryher with an intense blue gaze. 'Before I became a historian, I trained as a jeweller with my father. Antwerp is one of the largest diamond centres in the world, with some of the best diamond cutters and jewellers. I grew up with it around me. Let me take it home tonight and I'll fix the clasp.'

Bryher shrugs. 'Sure, that'd be great. I'll need it back tomorrow morning, though. There's no way I'm going to wear that other cheap piece again. My neck can't take it.'

Pieter smiles. 'I shall guard it with my life.'

Pieter's London flat
Later that evening

Pieter places the necklace upside down on a linen handkerchief he has laid out on his desk. The pearls gleam in the low light of his desk lamp, almost throbbing with their rich, creamy lustre.

Picking up a magnifying glass, he leans over the tiny mark on the back of the gold pendant where a CH is stamped within a circle.

He sets down the glass and searches his bookshelves until he finds what he is seeking. He pulls an old leather-bound volume off the shelf. *Jewellers, Goldsmiths and Silversmiths of Tudor England.* He walks back to the desk and sits down in the chair.

The book's cover creaks as he opens it, and a silverfish falls onto the desk blotter. He watches the tiny insect wiggle across the green blotting paper for a moment, then squashes it with his thumb.

The stiff pages crackle as he turns them over to the Table of Contents. He runs his finger down the chapters until a name catches his attention. Cornelis Hayes.

He turns to the chapter.

Cornelis Hayes was a Flemish jeweller who settled in London in 1524. In 1526 he is named in the accounts of Sir Thomas Boleyn as having received a payment of £4, along with a notation itemising the amount of £3 12s 6d for 'Mistress Anne's bill'. In January 1527 he supplied a jewel with nineteen diamonds set in gold love knots to King Henry VIII for Anne Boleyn to wear on St Valentine's Day…

Pieter scans his finger past sketches of the jeweller's silver platework, until it rests on an illustration of Cornelis Hayes's mark. CH within a circle.

He sits back in his chair and stares at the pearls gleaming like a mermaid's treasure on his desk. His heart pounds. It is the real necklace. Not only that, it was made by his ancestor, Cornelis Hayes.

Chapter Nineteen

ANNE & MARY

Hôtel des Tournelles, Paris, France
February/March 1515

'Mary, fetch me my cloak. I am finding the hall chill this eve with the winter wind blowing through its cracks.' The young dowager queen smiles ruefully as she regards King François and Queen Claude at the head table. 'My new place at this lower table lacks the warmth and comforts I had become accustomed to as queen.'

Mary rises from the table. 'Certainly, ma'am. I shall be hasty.'

'Thank you, Mary. You are a credit to your good parents.'

Mary hurries past the courtiers and court ladies who are enjoying a light supper of rabbit and mutton pies and stewed venison. She exits through the main doorway to the courtyard and wraps her arms around herself as she is met with a blast of wintry wind. *Would that I had a fur-lined cloak,* she thinks as she rushes across the courtyard to the tower harbouring the chambers of the dowager queen and her ladies.

She is making her way back down the tower's curving stone staircase with the queen's cloak when she almost stumbles into the arms of a man climbing the stone steps.

'My lord! I mean, sire ... Your Majesty.' She curtsies awkwardly, teetering on the stairs. 'I am sorry. I did not expect another on these steps.'

King François smiles as he reaches out to steady her. '*Mademoiselle Marie*, it is I who must apologise. I have startled you. Do I have your forgiveness?'

Mary swallows as her heart thumps like a drum in her chest. The memory of his kiss flashes into her mind. 'It is I who should ask for forgiveness, Your Majesty. I should have watched where I was going, though I was in haste.' She wets her lips, all too aware of the warmth of the king's hand on her arm. 'I must return to the great hall. The dowager queen awaits her cloak.'

The king nods, the feather on his black velvet hat waving. 'Of course. Here, let me carry it. I credit that it is heavy.'

He takes the cloak from her before Mary can object.

She bobs her head. 'I thank you, Your Majesty. It was most awkward to carry on these narrow steps in such low light.'

'Then I shall be your guide, *mademoiselle*.' He tosses the cloak over his shoulder and offers Mary his hand.

She stares at his bejewelled fingers and then looks up at his face. His eyes shine like polished coals in the low evening light filtering in from a narrow window as he watches her. She takes hold of his hand. 'Thank you, Your Majesty. You are most kind.'

'Sire, please. Enough of "Your Majesty". It is so formal, don't you agree?' He squeezes her hand. 'Are we not friends, *ma chère Marie*?'

Mary feels her pulse thud in her throat and the colour rise in her cheeks. She looks down at the heavy cloak. 'I-I must away, Your Maj—sire. The dowager queen will be wondering what has become of me.'

The king smiles and releases her hand. 'Come then, *Marie de Boleyn*. We must not keep the dowager queen waiting.'

She follows him down the winding steps until they reach the door at the bottom. The wooden door rattles and groans from the pummelling of the February wind and Mary shivers. The king drapes the cloak around her shoulders.

'But this is the dowager queen's cloak. I cannot wear it.'

The king leans over and whispers into Mary's ear. 'I would not have your fair shoulders assaulted by the winter winds, *ma belle Marie*. Do your poor servant François the kindness of wearing the cloak until we reach the great hall.'

Mary stands still as the king ties the cloak's ribbon around her neck, her senses engulfed by the warm, musky scent of his presence, the promise she'd made to her sister forgotten as her heart quickens. He presses a kiss upon the skin of her neck and she shuts her eyes. His mouth follows the line of her neck, and her jaw, until it reaches her lips. He wraps his arms around her waist and presses her body against his. Her breath pushes out of her mouth in quick gasps as she enfolds him in her embrace.

'*Marie, ma belle ange*, my beautiful, beautiful angel,' he whispers.

The ringing of a bell in one of the palace's towers announcing the half hour shakes Mary from the rapture of the stolen moment. She pulls away.

'I must go, sire,' she says, her breath uneven. 'I … I promised I would make haste.'

François steps back. 'Of course. I shall let you precede me. I shall return in due course.'

Mary curtsies. 'Thank you, sire.' She reaches for the iron door handle but is stopped by his hand on hers.

'Come to me tonight, *Marie*.' He leans closer. 'I ache to have you in my bed. You have haunted my thoughts since I first saw you at Montreuil.'

Mary feels her cheeks flush and she swallows. 'I cannot, sire. My sister will query where I am going.'

François smiles. 'I shall arrange for your sister to be called to attend Queen Claude. You need not fear.'

Mary looks up into the king's black eyes. 'But I do fear, sire. I fear you.'

François threads his fingers through hers. 'Then let me allay your fears by being your servant this eve and many evenings hence, *ma belle*. You have infected my blood with love, and I am naught but a lowly servant in your presence.' He presses a kiss upon her lips. 'Say you will come to me, *Marie*.'

Mary feels the blood coursing through her body at the awakening of every fibre of her being. 'I will come, sire. I will come.'

One week later

Anne rifles through the messy jumble of her sister's stockings, linen shifts and nightgowns in the heavy wooden coffer at the foot of their bed. Surely Mary must have a spare coif in here somewhere. How bothersome that the servants have seen fit to take all her own underclothes to the laundry without her knowledge.

Her eyes catch a glimpse of a silk handkerchief embroidered with an unfamiliar initial. She takes it out of the chest and turns it over in her hands until the elaborate blue embroidery is upright. 'F'.

She sits back on her heels and holds the piece of delicate white silk up to her nose. Scented. The velvety floral scent of civet musk. The king's scent.

The door to the bedchamber opens and Mary enters, flushed

and holding her pendant. 'Anne, my necklace has come undone. Would you—what are you doing?'

Anne holds up the handkerchief. 'Why have you the king's handkerchief?'

Mary rushes forward and snatches the piece of silk from her sister's hand. 'It was a gift.'

Anne rises to her feet and brushes off the faint film of dust that clings to her silk kirtle where she has knelt. 'How came you by this gift?'

Mary drops the pendant onto the blue wool bedcover and tucks the handkerchief into her long sleeve. 'It is a private matter.' She slams down the coffer's lid. 'Why were you looking in my coffer? Is your own not sufficiently large for all your finery from the archduchess's court?'

'I was searching for a coif as mine have all been taken to the laundry.'

'You seek in the wrong location.' Mary walks over to a smaller coffer beside the bed and removes a simple linen coif. 'Here. Take this.'

Anne takes the coif and moves to stand before the polished metal mirror hanging upon the wall between the windows. She fits the linen cap over the plaits she has affixed across the crown of her head, then looks over at her sister.

'Mary, do not take me for a fool. I have seen much during my year in the archduchess's court. I am not a foolish child. You promised you would end this folly with the king.'

Mary's eyes widen in panic and Anne raises an eyebrow.

'The king gifted the handkerchief to me … as a keepsake,' Mary says. 'It means nothing.'

Anne's eyes narrow. 'Why would the king gift the dowager queen's lady-in-waiting with his own handkerchief? I can think only of one reason, and I scarce dare to utter it.'

Mary rushes over to her and grabs her hands. 'Anne, do not think badly of me. I can scarce contain my happiness.'

Anne frowns. 'What?'

Mary giggles. 'My heart has been pierced by Cupid's arrow. I am in love with King François, and he assures me that I am his.'

Anne jerks her hands away. 'Don't be a fool. You are not the king's. He is married to Queen Claude.'

'Yes, but the queen is always so poorly and not likely to last another winter.'

Anne laughs. 'Is this what he has told you? That you may be the next Queen of France?' She stops laughing. 'Mary, has he bedded you?'

Mary turns away from her sister.

Anne pulls at her shoulder forcing Mary to face her. 'Has he bedded you?'

'Yes!'

Anne stares at her sister. 'Then you are more of a fool than I would have credited.'

'You know nothing of it. King François loves me just as I love him.'

'Perhaps the king does love you, or perhaps he tells you he does so that he may obtain the favours he seeks – and which you share with him so loosely. But I assure you that once you are away from his sight, you vanish from his mind.'

'No! This is untrue.'

'Mary, you are not important. Not to the King of France, at least. You would do well to listen to me and protect yourself. You and I are at court by the good grace of the dowager queen and our father's efforts. We have but one master and that is our father. You must end this now before you find yourself with child.'

Anne picks up the pearl pendant from the bed. 'We are Boleyns. Do not disgrace our good name. Our father gave you this pendant to remind you of that. Do not forget it.'

———

Anne dips the quill into the ink jar and leans over the sheet of paper.

Sir,

I thank you for your letter and offer to you and my dear mother your humble daughter's best wishes. I am arrived safe at the French court in Paris and am now settled in the Hôtel des Tournelles, with the dowager queen and her ladies. There is talk of the dowager queen's impending betrothal to the Duke of Lorraine or the Duke of Savoy, as this is King François's desire, though the Duke of Suffolk is newly arrived at court charged by King Henry to escort his dear sister, the dowager queen, back to London. There is confusion yet as to where the dowager queen's future lies.

It is my desire to express my pleasure at my reunion with my dear sister Mary, however, it is with a heavy heart that I must instead advise you of her injudicious relations with King François. Mary has confided in me that she has become intimate with the king. I advised her to cease this behaviour with haste as it will do great harm to the reputation of the Boleyn name should this become common knowledge and cause the ruin of not only Mary, but of myself, her own chaste sister. The court has many eyes and ears, and the fall of an Englishwoman would cause delight amongst many here.

I entreat you, sir, to deliver Mary from the sins of her ways so that our good Boleyn name may remain unblemished for the secure future of us all. You may rest assured that I shall never act in such a rash manner and will honour our Boleyn name until the day of my last breath.

Written at Paris by your most humble and obedient daughter,

Anne

Chapter Twenty

BRYHER

Elstree Studios, Borehamwood, England
December 2024

In her dressing room, Bryher licks a finger and dampens down a stubborn hair which refuses to stay in place under the linen coif covering her hair, when there is a knock at the door.

'It's open!'

'Hello,' Pieter says as he enters.

'Finally! I've got to get to the costume department. We're filming a jousting scene somewhere today.'

'Apologies. The traffic coming up from London was terrible.' Pieter reaches into his pocket and takes out a small bundle wrapped in a fine white linen handkerchief. He carefully unwraps it and holds up the necklace. 'I've brought this back, as promised.'

Bryher pats the coif self-consciously. 'Great. Sorry you have to see me like this. I look like I'm wearing a diaper on my head.'

'They call them nappies in Britain.' He lays the necklace down on her dressing table and catches her eye in the mirror. 'But you do, rather.'

'You're not supposed to agree with me. You're supposed to say I look fabulous. I'm an actress. I have a sensitive ego.'

Pieter presses his hand against his chest and bows his head. 'I am a man of truth.'

'Oh, really?'

'I am an academic. I deal in facts. Truths.'

'Truths? You mean whatever white European men have written to suit their own purposes.'

He nods. 'Touché.'

She grimaces at her reflection as she smooths down the top of her linen shift.

'You look historically accurate,' Pieter offers, 'which is more to the point.'

'Oh, yeah, how could I forget? You're the history advisor keeping us all on our toes.' She holds the necklace up to her neck. 'Put this on me, would you, please?'

'Of course.' Pieter fastens the necklace around her neck. 'There. The clasp was quite badly dented. It should be fine now.'

Bryher pats the glittering 'B'. 'You've polished it up. It looks great for a cheap replica.'

'It's not a cheap replica. That's real gold and the pearls are definitely real as well. It shows expert craftsmanship. Whoever made this was a proper jeweller. Please assure me it will be kept in a safe place.'

Bryher winces as she remembers the tatty jewellery box under Betty's bed with Bijou on guard duty.

'Oh, yeah, sure. It's safe at Betty's.'

Pieter nods. 'Good. Though it really should be in a safe deposit box.'

'Right. Yes. I'll tell Betty.' *Like hell I'll tell her. Betty doesn't even know I've taken it.*

Peter clears his throat. 'Bryher ... I need to speak to you.'

Bryher's shoulders slump. *Here we go. He's heard about the scandal.* 'Uh, can it wait? I've got to get to the costume department.'

'All right. I have a meeting with the set designer in a few minutes myself. What if I were to take you to dinner in London tonight?'

'Dinner in London?' Bryher glances at Pieter. *What the hell? After all this time?*

'I thought you might like a break from the glorious Borehamwood highlife. Have you had a chance to see much of London?'

'No. Not really. I haven't had any time.'

'Well, then, there's no excuse not to come. London is very pretty at night.'

Bryher stares at Pieter in the mirror. She could use a break from Betty's cottage pie.

She smiles. 'Sure, why not? Somewhere that does vegetables that haven't been boiled to death would be nice. And it can't be too late. I'll need to catch the train back to Puddleton later.'

'That's fine.'

'And wine. Decent wine. I love Californian chardonnay.'

Pieter grimaces. 'Californian chardonnay? When all the great wines of Europe are on your doorstep? Sacrilege.'

She sighs. 'All right, then. I'll try something different. I'll need to get back to Betty's to change first, after today's shoot. How about I take the train into London and meet you at Victoria Station at eight?'

'Perfect. And should you wish to wear your coif to dinner, may I say that I find it quite charming.'

'Bryher? Bryher, dear,' Betty says over the phone. 'I'm sorry to ring you at work but could you stop by the Co-op on your way back and pick up some cat food for Bijou? I've run out and don't have any for her dinner. She'll be terribly cross with me. I would do it myself, but I have a bridge club meeting at the WI.'

'Sorry, Betty, one minute.' Bryher waves across the field where two knights on brightly-garbed horses wait for their cue. 'I'll be right there, Jeremy. Two minutes.' She returns to the call. 'Cat food, okay, fine—'

'Tuna is best. Bijou is very fussy.'

'Yes, sure, Betty. Listen, I've got to go, but one thing. I'm meeting Pieter de Beer for dinner in London later. I'll be back late so don't worry about me. I'll let myself in.'

'Oh, that lovely telly historian? I missed out on meeting him when I stopped by with the cakes. You must invite him to tea in Puddleton one evening. Wouldn't that be jolly? Oh, Marion Livesay would be green with envy.'

'Excuse me, Miss Finch? Could I get your autograph? My wife's a huge fan.'

Bryher turns around to see a balding, middle-aged man emerge from the crowd of bystanders holding out a piece of paper and a pen. *Great. Civilians. At least there aren't any—*

'Bryher! Bryher, luv! Gizz a smile, darlin'!'

Paparazzi.

'Betty, I've got to go. I'll get the cat food so Bijou doesn't die of starvation. Don't wait up.' She ends the call and sweeps around to face the photographers rushing towards her from where they've been parked along the country lane. Bryher faces them with her most enchanting smile.

'Miss Finch? The autograph?'

Bryher turns back to the autograph hunter. 'Sure, sorry.'

He hands her an envelope. 'You've been served.'

Bryher stares at the large white envelope. 'What? What are you talking about?' she says as the cameras flash. But the man has already disappeared into the crowd.

Chapter Twenty-One

ANNE & MARY

Hôtel des Tournelles, Paris, France
March 1515

Mary throws herself down upon the settle beside the window in the room she shares with her sister, her father's letter gripped in her hand.

'He is sending me away, Anne! I am to leave Paris to lodge in a place called Brie with a noble family called du Moulin – some distant relations of ours.' She holds up the letter. 'He says that I am to "attend a convent school to learn acceptable conduct until such time as a suitable marriage is arranged."' She flings the letter upon the floor. 'I am to be buried alive! How could you do this to me? You have betrayed my confidence to our own father.'

Anne continues her methodical peeling of the apple she is preparing to eat, angling the silver paring knife just so, so as to keep the peel from splitting. 'How could you think I would not, Mary? Your tumble into the French king's bed is not only foolhardy, but it endangers my own position at court. This I shall not tolerate. Nor will our father.'

'It is always about you, Anne, isn't it? What care you what I do?' Mary's blue eyes narrow. 'Or is it that you are jealous of the king's attention to me, even as he spares not a single glance towards you?'

Anne smiles as the apple peel curls into a perfect circle on the wooden table. 'I care not for the attention of a king who is wedded to another. I shall never be a man's mistress, no matter if he were the Emperor of the World.'

Mary laughs. 'Were a king to court you, say pretty things in your ear, press soft kisses to your lips, I assure you, Anne, you would capitulate. It is a wonderful thing to be the object of a king's desire. It marks you as a woman above all others.'

Anne slices off a piece of apple and balances it on the knife. 'I have no doubt it is a wonderful thing, Mary. Even so, I would not capitulate. I hold myself in higher esteem than you. I will make a good marriage to a man of means and power, of that you may be assured. You are now corrupted and are soiled in the eyes of any man of worth. Father is right to send you away until any whisper of your indiscretion has faded. You shall be forgot, and King François will soon find himself others with which to tarry. Of this I can assure you.'

Mary stares at her in despair. 'What of our bond as sisters, Anne? Do you not love me? I would never have betrayed your trust.'

Anne chews the apple slice and swallows. She slices off another piece and balances it on the knife. 'That we are sisters is a fact. We are bonded by blood, Mary. That you would not have betrayed my trust to save my reputation reflects poorly on you. That you, my own sister, would see me fall – and lose my name, and that of our family, my worth and my future – persuades me to keep my own counsel in affairs of the heart.'

'You are heartless, sister.'

Anne bites into the apple and watches Mary as she chews. 'I have as great a heart as any. It is simply that my heart is guided by my mind. You would do well to do the same.' She smiles as she slices off another piece of apple. 'Enjoy your stay in Brie. I have been invited to attend Queen Claude in Paris as one of her ladies. Father has arranged it.'

Chapter Twenty-Two

BRYHER

Co-op Convenience Store, Borehamwood, England
December 2024

Bryher tucks her phone under her chin and drops a package of Hobnobs into the shopping basket on top of some tins of luxury cat food and a tub of Ben & Jerry's Phish Food ice cream. Jake's voicemail kicks in.

'Jake, what's the meaning of serving me with divorce papers on set? I was papped! It's already all over the net—'

The message cuts off.

Bryher swears under her breath and grabs the phone. She speed-dials Jake's number again. 'Jake, call me. I told you nothing happened. I've been set up! Why don't you believe me? I'm not signing these papers until we've had a chance—'

The message cuts off again.

'Damn, damn, damn!' Again, Bryher redials. 'Look, please, have some compassion. Talk to me. It's not just me, I'm worried about Marnie—'

'Bry, it's me.'

'Jake, thank God. Look, half the money in our joint account was my money from *Cop Town*. I need it. I've managed to pay Marnie's residential home for the next two months with some money Margot sent me, but then I'm stuffed until I get another job.'

'That money was *ours*.'

'What are you talking about? What have you done with my money?'

'*Our* money, Bry. Investments. My new tequila line. A Korean-Mexican fusion restaurant in New York. Didn't you read the financial reports?'

'Financial reports? Seriously, who reads that stuff? You said you were happy to take care of all our finances.'

'And I did. It wasn't my fault you couldn't be bothered to read any of the reports I emailed you. If you'd been more on the ball, and been faithful, of course, you could've benefitted from all that. It's too late now.'

'Oh, my God. I can't believe this.'

She hears him sigh down the phone. 'Look, I won't see your sister out on the street, Bry. This has nothing to do with her. I'll pay for the care home and all Marnie's expenses. In fact, I'll do you a deal.'

Bryher leans against the ice cream freezer. 'What are you talking about, a deal?'

'I'll pay for Marnie forever. All you have to do is agree a quick, no contest divorce, on the grounds of your adultery. Oh, and no alimony. And don't forget I paid off your credit cards. Believe me, that was a shock. How does anyone spend five hundred dollars a month on nail extensions?'

Bryher rolls her eyes. 'I can't agree to that. It would be me admitting that the sex tape is real, and it isn't. I'm not the bad guy here.'

'And I am?'

'Well, it would be nice if you believed me. We were together for six years. How can you possibly believe that tape is real? What did Nick say about it? You must have spoken to him by now.'

There's a pause on the line. 'Nick said he met you at a party and you came on to him.'

'He what? No!'

Okay, so, she and Nick had been at a party where they'd gotten tipsy and … well, she can't exactly remember what had happened. They drank far too much Cristal champagne. She can't remember them making out or anything. All she remembers is Margot putting her in a cab home. Margot always has her back, which is a good thing because she pays her enough.

'He said he can't remember anything else, except that he woke up in a bed with that other woman in your threesome – the one in that sex tape,' Jake says. 'He doesn't even know her name.'

'What?'

'He said he got out of there as fast as he could and tried to forget it. Then the sex tape came out and you were in it with them.'

'I never—'

'How'd you do it, Bry? Did you spike his drink? Did you pay her? I just don't get it. Was it for the publicity? You know, the whole "There's no such thing as bad publicity" thing? Well, it worked. Your name's everywhere now.'

Bryher rubs her head where a headache is inching its way across her scalp. 'It wasn't me. I swear it. You've got to believe me.'

'We're done. I'd never be able to trust you now. I don't know you at all.'

Bryher slumps. Why won't he believe her? Is she such a shallow, fame-hungry person that Jake believes she's capable of something like that to further her career? Is that what he thinks she's become? Is that what she *has* become?

Well, I'm not going to go down without a fight, Jake Rogers. I'll show you what I'm made of.

She rolls her head to relieve the tension. 'What about the house?'

Jake laughs. 'We have a pre-nup, or did you forget? This is *my* house. Your name's not on the mortgage.'

'But I've been paying you half of the mortgage every month—'

'That's right, you've been paying *me*. You haven't been paying the bank. In effect, you were paying me rent. The house is in *my* name only.'

How could I have been so stupid? Why didn't I read the financials?

Bryher straightens up and stares at the display of chocolate Santas she's been leaning against. Realisation dawns on her. 'It's Juno, isn't it? You've fallen for Juno.'

Jake sighs. 'What can I say? You and I have had a good run, but it's over.'

'Wait, look. I want to figure out what's going on. I want to find out who's set me up. Not just me, either. Your brother, too. At least you're speaking to him, now.'

'Nick's blood. I'll be an uncle in a few months. We're sorting it out.'

'You're going to regret this. Juno's a gold digger. She wants in on your fame, and she wants your money.'

'I don't want to hear it, Bry. I'm going to marry her. Do yourself a favour and just sign the papers. And keep Juno out of this or Marnie will be out on the streets.'

Bryher watches the dull grey fields of mud and copses of denuded trees flash by through the train window. The late afternoon sky is dense with lead grey clouds, and rain spits at the dirty window. The screenplay sits heavy in her lap, and she flips through the curled edge of its top corner absentmindedly.

What has she done so wrong to find herself here? In a dead woman's awful coat on a cold, rattling train on her way to a pebbledash bungalow, as her life falls apart.

It's all Jake's fault. He refused to believe her and made her so desperate for money after she lost *Cop Town* that she had to take this stupid English mini-series. And Nick! Maybe … maybe Nick and Jodie planned this together! Or maybe it was Juno. Whoever it was must hate her, but why?

She rubs the headache throbbing at her temples. Why is this happening to her? What has she done to deserve this public humiliation? Now, she's homeless, virtually penniless and stuck in England working with people who think she's nothing but a talentless American TV actress. Her only way out is to agree to Jake's proposal. If there is a hell, the portal is in Puddleton, England.

Bryher sets the plastic bags full of biscuits, ice cream and cat food on the kitchen counter.

'Betty? Betty, are you home? Would you like me to boil the kettle?'

There's no response, but Betty's coat and umbrella are hanging in the hallway, so she knows she's home. Bryher puts the ice cream in the freezer and heads down the hallway to her room. She opens the door to see Betty sitting on her fold-out bed petting Bijou.

'Betty? What are you doing in here? I thought you said you had a bridge club meeting.'

Betty sets the cat down on the bed. She adjusts her yellow cardigan and folds her hands in her lap. 'I did but I cancelled it. Marion Livesay was none too pleased. She's had to drag Derek in to be the fourth at our table and he barely knows a trump from a rubber.'

'I hope you didn't cancel because of me. I said I was going into London tonight.'

Betty kisses Bijou on her head and sets her down on the nylon bedcover. 'As it happens, I did cancel on your account. Do you have something to tell me, Bryher?'

'Uh…' *Shit. The necklace.*

Betty frowns. 'Have you been in my bedroom? Should I start locking my door?'

'What … what are you talking about?'

'Here I thought you were a very nice young lady. With dubious taste in clothes and food preferences, but those things aside, a very nice young lady.'

Bryher chews her lip. 'Betty, I'm so sorry. I … I meant to tell you.'

'Ah, you meant to *tell* me. You hadn't thought to *ask* me. Why don't you tell me now?'

Bryher gestures to the bed and smiles weakly. 'May I sit?'

'As you wish.'

Bryher perches on the end of the bed and clears her throat.

'So, the other day I was looking for phone reception, and the only place I could find it was in your bedroom. I mean, I knew I could go outside, but it was pouring with rain. I tried everywhere else, I swear.'

'I see.'

'So, I was in your room standing on that chair—'

'You were standing on Mummy's antique Georgian chair? It's terribly delicate.'

'I'm sorry, I didn't think. Anyway, that's where I found reception.' She glances at Bijou and her eyes narrow. 'Bijou jumped up and scared me, and I lost my balance and fell—'

'Oh, dear! You fell off the chair? Were you all right?'

'A few bruises. I banged my knee pretty badly.'

'Oh, my.' Betty holds up the cat. 'Did you knock Bryher off

143

Mummy's chair? You naughty girl! No snackies for you tonight.' She settles Bijou into her lap. 'What happened then?'

'I, uh, I saw a jewellery box under your bed and … and I was curious. I couldn't help myself. I know I shouldn't have, but I took it out and had a look.'

'Indeed. And what did you find there?'

'Costume jewellery. A lot of it. And I found a 'B' necklace, just like the one Anne Boleyn was wearing in that picture we saw at Hever Castle.'

'The necklace that's no longer in my jewellery box.'

'Yes, well, the thing is, I'd been wearing one like it on set and it was giving me the worst rash. It must have had nickel in it. I'm allergic to nickel.'

'That is unfortunate.'

'So, I thought, why not borrow your necklace, just for the filming. I was going to give it back as soon as filming was over.'

'That's Mummy's necklace. You had no right to take it without asking me.'

Bryher nods. For the first time in a very long time she feels ashamed. Not even Jake's accusations made her feel this way.

'You're right. I'm sorry. I should have asked. It was thoughtless and I apologise.'

Betty inclines her head. 'Apology accepted. Where's the necklace now?'

Bryher reaches into her handbag and takes out the necklace. 'Here, I've got it. I never leave it at the studio. I've been taking good care of it. I've even had the clasp fixed. Take it. I'll wear the other one. It's fine.'

Betty takes the necklace from Bryher. 'Thank you, dear. It has sentimental value to me. It was Mummy's favourite necklace.'

She lays the necklace on the bed and tickles the cat under its chin. 'I remember Mummy wearing this at my eighteenth birthday party. She and Daddy had thrown a big party – that was before Daddy lost all his money investing in Betamax and he became a

bookkeeper. I don't think Mummy ever forgave him for that …
Anyway, it was held at Daddy's golf club in Surrey. He'd rented it
out for the whole weekend, which must have cost him a pretty
penny, indeed. Mummy looked marvellous, of course. She'd flown
us over to Paris and had Dior make us dresses, especially. Of
course, Mummy was so tall and slender – she was a fashion model
before she married Daddy, you know, back in the fifties. I think
Monsieur Dior was in despair when he saw short, plump little me.
I take after Daddy's side of the family.'

Bryher picks at a loose thread on the bedcover as she feels
another judder of empathy.

'I'm sure that's not true, Betty,' she says softly.

'That's sweet of you dear, but it is. Still, Mummy insisted Mr
Dior make me into a princess, and he did his very best. It was the
only time I felt she really noticed me.' Betty smiles wistfully. 'I
gave the dress away to the Salvation Army just last year. There
was no point keeping it. I'd never fit into it now. I hope it's found
a good home.'

The tough shell around Bryher's heart cracks a little at the
camaraderie she feels with Betty. The two of them growing up
plain, lonely little girls, living in the shadows of the bright stars
that were Betty's mother and her own sister, Marnie.

Chapter Twenty-Three

MARY

Chapel Royal, Placentia Palace, Greenwich, England
February 1520

Mary clutches the posy of pungent herbs her mother has given her – intended to fight off any evil spirits lurking within the palace – and steals a glance at her bridegroom. William Carey. It is a fine English name, she thinks. Does he require her to address him as William? She muses. Or will they become familiar enough for her to call him Will or Wills? She hopes the latter, since they will be husband and wife, though they are yet of small acquaintance. She will address him as 'Sir', she decides, until such time that the use of Christian names is appropriate.

She looks at the priest, who intones the wedding mass in monotonous Latin, and swallows to stifle a yawn, aware that William's distant cousin, King Henry VIII, her mother and several of the king's courtiers are all observing her. At least she has been spared the attendance of her father, who is still in France awaiting his diplomatic replacement, though she suspects he deliberately arranged this in order to absent himself from her wedding.

She feels the warmth of William's body beside her as he occasionally shifts his weight and the rich blue velvet of his doublet brushes against her silk sleeve. He is handsome, at least. A nice face, dark hair, and eyes the colour of the green sea. And young, only four years older than she. Mary is fortunate that her father has succeeded in making this match. Thomas Boleyn has reminded her of this several times since her return to Hever after five long years of exile in France. William is a man of good family, an intimate of the king in his role as one of the staff of the King's Privy Chamber, and, as her father wrote in his letters to her from France, is likely to rise to an influential position at court in the coming years.

Mary knows little of William's character, other than what she has been told and what she has observed in the three days of their acquaintance prior to the wedding. But what she has seen has been pleasant. She thanks God once again for her great fortune in this match, and for her release from the years of purgatory in Brie, far from the 'enticements' of the French court, in the household of Philippe du Moulin – King François's cup-bearer.

She bites her lip. *Enticements.* Her father's word. She had made a grave error in succumbing to the French king. King François had been so persuasive, so charming, so ... Oh, how she had loved him! But to be cast aside so cavalierly, after so brief a time, and thus thoroughly earn her sister's and her father's contempt at having yielded her maidenhood so readily ... Mary feels her cheeks redden at the humiliation.

Her father had deemed it imprudent for her to return to the English court, where rumours of her indiscretions may have preceded her, and, of course, her place at the French court had become untenable. She'd heard the whispers in the palace hallways – that she was the king's mule, an English whore. Her father had given her the choice – a convent or the cup-bearer's household, where she would stay until the gossipmongers had turned their tongues to other tales, and a good English husband could be found for her.

She has failed her family. She was meant to make a marriage to a high-ranking noble – an earl, or even a marquess. This had been her father's great hope. *She* had been her father's great hope. Now she is an inconvenience to be got rid of. All because she had given her love and her body to a man who had falsely professed his love to her.

Her sister had been right. She had been a fool to think King François would make her his queen. And now she sees Anne's status rise in her father's eyes. Anne has become the new favourite, their father's great hope to further the Boleyn honour.

Mary glances at William's fine, strong hands which he holds folded before him. Does he know of her disgrace? No, he could not. A man of such prospect, who enjoys the company of the king, would not deign to wed a woman whose reputation had been compromised. No, he could not know, and she will do everything to ensure he never knows.

Her life as Mary Boleyn is over. From this day forward, she is Mary Carey.

Chapter Twenty-Four

BRYHER

Raj Poot Restaurant, Shoreditch, London
December 2024

The Raj Poot restaurant is a din of chatter, the clink of utensils on plates, chair legs scraping on the wooden floor, and the shouts of the kitchen staff, which add a crescendo whenever the kitchen door swings open. Underneath it all, the recorded strains of an Indian singer weave through the noise like a hummingbird fluttering between flowers.

Bryher eyes the tiny restaurant's blood-red ceiling and its walls, which have been embellished with framed black and white photos of Bollywood stars. At the rear of the room, a bright green neon sign spells out 'BAR' over a counter beside the till.

'You know, I've never eaten curry before.'

'Then I'm sorry for you, Bryher. A good curry cures all ills. Did you know that chicken tikka masala is now considered Britain's national dish?'

'Really? I'm surprised Betty hasn't cooked it for me.'

Pieter smiles. 'I recommend it. It's quite delicious.'

They follow a young waiter to a small table and, after Pieter has run through the extensive menu of bhunas, pasandas, tikkas, baltis, biriyanis and dopiazas, Bryher settles on his recommendation – the chicken tikka masala – and, after some persuasion, a fruity German Gewürztraminer wine.

She smiles as the waiter makes an elaborate show of setting an ice bucket on a stand beside their table, uncorking the wine, setting the cork on the table in front of Pieter and pouring a small serving into Pieter's wine glass. Pieter swirls the yellow wine around the glass and, after taking a sniff, nods his approval. The waiter fills both of their glasses and disappears through the kitchen door.

Pieter offers his glass in a toast. 'To your first British curry in a proper curry house. Long may you remember it.'

Bryher clinks her glass to his. 'I'm sure I will.' She takes a sip and sets down her glass. 'I'm sorry about the paps. They're driving me crazy.'

Pieter shrugs. 'It's fine. They're opportunists. A lot of famous people film at Elstree.'

'Oh, right. Sure. I thought it was my agent doing it. She has them follow me all over LA. Keeping me in the media, and all that stuff. She says it's good for my career.'

'Is it? Good for your career?'

Bryher shrugs. 'Maybe. It's important to be famous in LA. Be seen in the right places.'

He sweeps his hand around the crowded restaurant. 'So, you never get to visit a place like the Raj Poot, I take it.'

She laughs. 'There's nothing like this where I live in Calabasas. Well, where I used to live with my soon-to-be ex-husband.' She takes a sip of wine. 'He had me served with divorce papers today.'

'Ah, I see.'

She takes another sip and looks across the table at Pieter. 'Don't pretend you haven't heard.'

'Heard what?'

'Come on. Seriously? You haven't googled my name?'

He smiles as he reaches for his wine glass. 'If I had, what would I have found?'

She looks down at her drink, and swirls the yellow wine around until it spirals. Has he really not searched her name on the net? 'Look, I don't know what you've read or heard, but all I'm going to say is that it's not true.'

'Fine.'

She raises her eyebrows. 'Fine? That's it? Don't you even want to know what I'm talking about?'

'I know what you're talking about.'

'Oh.'

He shrugs. 'I've been a victim of false rumours myself, Bryher. According to the British press, I'm the father of several illegitimate babies.'

She laughs. 'And are you?'

'Is your sex tape real?'

'No, but it's messed up my life. My husband's divorcing me, my finances are a mess, I lost my job on *Cop Town* and no one in Hollywood will touch me. I'm over here trying to escape the worst of the fallout.' She shakes her head. 'I don't know how they made the tape. They must've used AI or something. This scandal hasn't hurt my brother-in-law, though. If anything, Nick Rogers has benefitted. It's raised his profile, his wife's gone back to him, he's expecting twins and he's storming it at the international golf tournaments in South Africa. He's a pro golfer, and a really good one. I'll bet he gets some great sponsorship deal next. The paps there are all over him.' She sighs. 'I don't get it. Why am I treated like a pariah when Nick is the new golden boy?'

'Double standards. Modern society is very misogynistic.'

'Yeah. The patriarchy. It's shit … No offence.'

'None taken.'

The waiter arrives with their starters of onion bhajis and

vegetable samosas, several dishes of condiments, and a basket of complimentary poppadoms. Bryher helps herself to a bhaji and a spoonful of mango chutney and looks across the table at Pieter.

'So, now you know all about my tawdry life. Have I put you off?'

Pieter offers her a samosa, which she adds to her plate. 'Do you want to put me off?'

Bryher licks a drop of chutney off her finger. 'No.'

He takes a drink of his wine as he watches her chew the crispy bhaji. 'How is your onion bhaji?'

She nods as she swallows. 'Good. Really good.'

'Wonderful. Do you like the restaurant?'

Bryher scans the crimson room, the rushing waiters and the tables of animated diners. 'It wasn't what I was expecting, but I kinda do. It's unpretentious. And fun. I haven't had much fun lately.'

'Then enjoy yourself.' He helps himself to some naan bread. 'I'm enjoying myself.'

'You are? All I've done is complain about my ex and my disaster of a life.'

'Do you feel better?'

Bryher smiles. 'I do. I can't exactly talk to my cousin Betty about it, and my agent Margot is fed up of hearing about it.' She cracks a piece off the crispy poppadom and pops it into her mouth. 'What about you?'

'I'm not that interesting.'

'It's not what I heard.'

'Oh? What have you heard?'

'That you're a woman magnet.'

Pieter's blue eyes widen and he laughs. 'That's the first time I've heard that one.'

'So, you're not with anyone?'

'I'm here with you now.'

'You're being coy.'

'I'm single, if that's what you are asking.' He holds up his left hand. 'No wedding band.'

'A lot of men don't wear wedding bands.' Bryher sits back in her chair as the waiter clears their plates and arranges the main dishes they've ordered on their table. She scoops some of the steaming pilau rice onto a fresh plate. 'Were you ever married?'

Pieter pauses as he helps himself to the tarka dhal. 'Once. Briefly.'

'Briefly?'

He offers her the dhal. 'We were young. It was a long time ago.'

'I guess we both have baggage.' Bryher scoops some dhal onto her plate. She watches as Pieter spoons a dollop of mango chutney onto the side of his plate. He couldn't be more different from Jake, the quintessential sardonic American hero with all his rough edges. Pieter is smooth and, well, sophisticated. Where she'd always felt like a slightly clumsy girl around Jake, albeit, a lucky clumsy girl, she feels like a grown-up woman around Pieter. And she likes the feeling.

'You said this afternoon that you wanted to talk to me about something. What is it?'

'Yes. It's about the necklace.' He frowns. 'Where is it?'

She swallows a forkful of the mildly spiced lentil dish. 'I gave it back to Betty.'

He sets down his fork. 'What?'

'I gave it back to Betty. She was pretty upset that I took it without asking and I felt terrible. I'll just have to wear the cheap one from the costume department and dose myself up with antihistamine pi—what's wrong?'

Pieter pulls a pen out of his jacket pocket and grabs a paper napkin. He begins drawing. 'Betty's necklace. There was a maker's mark on the back of the "B". It's the initials CH inside a circle.' He pushes the napkin across the table to her. 'I've seen it before.'

Bryher frowns at the sketch. 'You've seen it before? Where?'

Pieter leans across the table. 'I have an ancestor named Cornelis Hayes. He was a jeweller from Antwerp who came to London and did work for King Henry VIII. He is known to have made jewellery for the nobles and royalty of the time. I have an old reference book of Tudor goldsmiths and jewellers. It's why I asked to borrow the necklace, to check the mark against the one known to be that of Cornelis Hayes.'

Bryher shakes her head. 'What are you saying? I don't understand.'

'In 1526, Anne Boleyn's father, Sir Thomas Boleyn, paid Cornelis four pounds for jewellery he had commissioned, so there is a documented connection between the Boleyns and one of King Henry VIII's jewellers. Perhaps it was for the "B" necklace.'

Bryher's eyes widen. 'You think Betty's necklace might be the real one?'

'I believe that is a possibility. If it is Anne Boleyn's necklace, it would be—'

Bryher presses her hand against her mouth. 'Oh, my God.'

'Don't get too excited.' Pieter reaches for the bottle to refill their glasses. 'There's the problem of provenance. The necklace would need to be able to be traced through history down to your cousin. How on earth would the Boleyn necklace have found its way into the hands of Betty …'

'Pilcher. Betty Pilcher.'

'Betty Pilcher.'

Bryher stares across the table at Pieter. 'I told you. I'm descended from Mary Boleyn and so is Betty.' She knew he hadn't been listening.

Pieter's leans closer. 'How do you know this?'

'Betty and I were just on a show called *Do You Know Who I Am?*'

'Yes, I know it.'

'Well, they filmed it at Hever Castle. They did a big thing

about unrolling a scroll and showing us how we're descended from Mary Boleyn, and possibly even King Henry VIII through Mary's daughter, Catherine Carey.'

Pieter sits back in his chair. 'This is very interesting.'

Bryher shrugs. 'The guide at the castle said a lot of people are descended from Mary Boleyn. Both her children had tons of kids.'

'That's true, but Catherine Carey was very likely the illegitimate daughter of Henry VIII. Cornelis Hayes was Henry VIII's jeweller and Betty has a necklace with Cornelis Hayes's mark on it. Not just any necklace, but a necklace identical to the one in Anne Boleyn's portrait.'

Bryher's eyes widen. 'You don't think …?'

'I don't know what to think. It's beyond imagining that it could be the real necklace. I need to see it again and have it examined by another specialist. Will you get it for me?'

'I … I don't know. I'll try.'

Betty will kill her if she finds it missing again. She'll just have to figure something out. This is too big of an opportunity to miss.

Several hours later, the restaurant has emptied. Bryher sips her gin and tonic, pleased that the slimline tonic isn't flat, the glass isn't hot from the dishwasher, there's more than one ice cube, and the bartender has slipped in a slice of lime rather than lemon. If she shuts her eyes and tunes out the eighties pop tunes, she could almost imagine herself in an LA bar.

'Are you enjoying yourself?'

She opens her eyes and smiles at Pieter. His face flickers in the shadows created by the candle guttering on their table. 'I am. Who would have thought the Raj Poot restaurant in … 'Where are we?'

'Shoreditch.'

'Right. Who would have thought the Raj Poot restaurant in Shoreditch would be my happy place?'

Pieter laughs. 'You need to get out more.'

'I guess. I haven't seen much of Britain, other than Puddleton and the studio. And Hever Castle, where I saw Anne Boleyn's portrait and the bed Henry VIII slept in when he visited the Boleyns.'

'What about the Tower of London, or Hampton Court, or the Clock Tower?'

'The Clock Tower?'

'Big Ben, which is actually the bell inside the Clock Tower.'

'Right. Like anyone knows that. I wouldn't mind seeing Big Ben before I go back to the States. And Buckingham Palace.'

'I'd be happy to show you around London, if you like.'

Bryher regards Pieter as she sips her drink. He is so unlike the actors she's met back in LA, who are all about tans and workouts and Botox and dietary restrictions. With his slightly off-beat blond good looks, and dressed in a tweed jacket, black shirt and jeans, he is a poster boy for the European man about the town.

He smiles, his blue eyes flashing in the candlelight. 'A penny for your thoughts.'

'Nothing.'

'You're not thinking about the necklace?'

'I was just thinking how European you are.'

He laughs. 'Well, I am a Belgian living in London, having studied at the Sorbonne in Paris.'

She swirls the ice around in her glass. 'You're very different to Jake.'

'Ah, the movie star.'

'Yeah.'

'How did you meet?'

'On a movie set. He was the big star and I had a couple of lines. It was a long time ago.' She sips her drink as she scans Pieter's face. *Maybe a good-looking European is exactly what I need right now.*

'You're shaking your head and looking at me most disapprovingly,' he says, amused.

'I was just thinking that I've probably missed my train to Puddleton.'

He glances at his watch. 'You have. Would you like me to call you a taxi?'

She feels a tingle run up her spine. 'Would you *like* to call me a taxi?'

He leans forward and his warm, musky scent engulfs her.

'Only if it's going to my flat.'

Chapter Twenty-Five

ANNE

Placentia Palace, Greenwich, England
4th March 1522

Anne looks up from the slim book she is reading and quickly slides it under a cushion on the window bench as her mother enters the chamber they have been assigned for the Shrove Tuesday festivities at York Palace in Whitehall.

'Good, you are ready,' Elizabeth says as she approaches Anne in a swish of forest green taffeta. She draws her fine auburn eyebrows together. 'What is that you are reading that you choose to hide it from your mother?'

'It is nothing of import …' Anne rises and crosses the room to regard her appearance in the polished bronze mirror. She smiles at her reflection and adjusts her bejewelled cap and the golden net over her dark hair. The fine white Milanese satin of her gown for the masque gleams in the light of the waning sun. She has been away at the French court for seven years, and for two years before that, at the court of the Archduchess Margaret. Years of exposure to the sophisticated European courts have polished the rough diamond that she'd once been to a glittering jewel. At almost twenty-two, Anne has learned to carry herself with grace, elevating her sharp chin to highlight the line of her swan-like neck. Her dark eyebrows arch pleasingly above her black eyes, which she now uses to great effect, to captivate, cajole, tease and persuade. Even her voice has changed, tempered by a soft French inflection.

'What is this?' Elizabeth says, waving the book at Anne. 'You are reading the Lord's prayers in French? This is forbidden, Anne. The Word of Our Lord must be read in Latin. This is blasphemy.'

Anne rushes over to her mother and grabs the book from her hands. 'Why should the Word of God be denied to those who have no understanding of Latin, Mother? Queen Claude believes passionately that the Lord's word should be readily available to all in their own languages. Faith is not to be found in miracles, rituals or pilgrimages, but in actions, in founding orphanages, financing schools, relieving the plight of the poor—'

'Miracles, rituals and pilgrimages form the foundation of our Catholic faith, Anne.' Elizabeth takes the book from Anne's hands and tosses it into the fire.

'Mother!'

'Were you to be found with that book, Anne, you would be burned at the stake for blasphemy.'

Anne huffs. 'But the French queen—'

'I care not for the French queen, nor the writings of these French evangelists. Take care, daughter. You are in England now, a good Catholic country. It is well you remember this. Now, it is time to fetch Mary and William and take the barge to York Place for the Shrove Tuesday festivities and your re-introduction into the English court. Deport yourself well so that you may secure a place in Queen Katherine's household and clear your mind of these radical ideas.'

Anne, Mary and six other ladies of the court, radiant in bejewelled caps, golden masks and glistening satin gowns, upon which their various virtues have been sewn in yellow silk – 'Kindness' for Mary and 'Perseverance' for Anne – laugh and shout from the three towers of an elaborate timber castle which King Henry's esteemed Cardinal Wolsey has erected in a vast room in his palace in Whitehall. Hundreds of candles light the room, throwing flickering shadows onto the vibrant tapestries. The Holy Roman Emperor Charles V's ambassadors, who are in London to discuss matters of foreign policy, appear to be suitably impressed by the festive display.

'Take yourselves away, sirs!' the women shout at the king and his posse of courtiers, clad in blue satin capes and golden hats, who assail the castle and its defenders of choirboys who are dressed as Indian maidens. 'We are pure maidens immune to your overtures!'

Henry launches a volley of dates at the defenders. 'We shall not be denied! We claim the Château Vert for King Amorous of England!'

The assailants dodge a barrage of twig arrows and fake shot from the defenders' bows and muskets as the women shower them with sweets and rose water.

Mary squeals as the defenders flee and the men climb the castle walls to capture the women. 'Anne, Anne! Beware! "Ardent Desire" approaches you from below!'

The handsome face of King Henry appears at the ramparts of Mary's tower. 'Ah, fair "Kindness",' he addresses her. 'You have been caught. And now you must spend the evening dancing with your king.'

Mary laughs. 'I am but a kind-hearted maid, King Amorous, and will gladly acquiesce, though I worry for the envy of the other maids.'

Henry leaps over the ramparts and joins Mary in the tower. He kisses her hand. 'I care naught for other maids, fair Mary. It is only you I seek.'

Anne watches the interaction between her sister and King Henry from the far tower. *Oh, Mary, take care. You have caught the king's eye, as you have done before. Do not make the same mistake again, or you will find yourself loved and cast away once more.*

She glances down at the crowd cheering on the entertainment. Mary's husband, William, stands alone by the great fire watching the king's flirtation with his wife. *Oh, William, I would not be you for all the gold in Wolsey's treasury.*

She looks back at the king. She has a role to play in this great country of England. This she has come to know in her heart. One day she will ensure King Henry will notice her, and when he does, he will never pursue another.

Chapter Twenty-Six

BRYHER

Elstree Studios, Borehamwood, England
December 2024

'And cut!'

Jeremy claps his hands together and hurries over from the monitor where he's been watching the scene. Once she has climbed down from her tower, he grabs hold of Bryher's hands. 'Darling, that was fabulous. The way you looked at Archie just now … Oh, it sent shivers up and down my spine.'

Bryher smiles, pulling her hands free of Jeremy's clammy grip. 'Thanks. I just went with what I was feeling.'

Archie Flanders puffs out an agitated breath. 'Seriously, Jeremy? You call that acting? You're not doing anything, Bryher. You're just standing there looking at me. I've seen more animation in a petri dish.'

'A petri dish, Archie?' Jennifer Foster, resplendent as Queen Katherine, joins Archie in front of the banquet table. 'I shudder to imagine in which circumstances you were observing the activities of a petri dish.'

'If you keep talking about petri dishes I'm going to heave,' says Cara Sweet, the actress playing Mary Boleyn. She rises from the bench and stretches out her arms as she yawns, the yellow silk letters of 'Kindness' stretching across the white satin of her gown. 'I've got to go for a wee.'

'I'll join you, darling,' Jennifer says as she swishes her costume. 'I need help with all these layers.'

'What an edifying conversation,' Jeremy says. 'Now, where were we?'

Archie waves a hand at Bryher. 'We were talking about how I'm having to act with a woman who can barely speak the King's English and who couldn't show a genuine emotion if it managed to find its way through her Botox and fillers.'

Bryher jabs her finger in Archie's face. 'You're a flippin' arse. How's that for the King's English? I've got more; you wanna hear 'em? I ride the train every day. It's very educational.'

Archie turns to Jeremy. 'She's a freaking liability, Jeremy. I didn't sign up to act with a Z-list American TV actress. Get her off the series, or I walk.'

Bryher and Jeremy watch as Archie stomps towards the dressing rooms.

'Shit. Should I be worried?' she asks the director.

'Darling, Archie's just throwing his toys out of the pram again. It's so utterly tedious. I'll go and massage his ego and it'll be fine. The truth is that he's merely adequate in the role and he knows it. I see what you're doing on camera. It's all in the eyes. Garbo had it. Garland had it. The divine Vivien Leigh had it. You have it. The camera loves you. Mark my words, you're going to be a big star.'

Chapter Twenty-Seven

MARY

Placentia Palace, Greenwich, England
March 1522

'Mistress Carey, will you do me the honour of permitting me to accompany you on your turn about the garden?'

Mary's heart jumps at the sound of King Henry's voice and she turns on the chalk path. The king approaches, tall and handsome in a broad-shouldered, fur-lined velvet box coat which swings around his muscular body. She curtsies. 'Your Majesty.'

He sucks in a deep breath and looks up at the blue sky, broken only by a scattering of clouds. 'What a fine day it is. I warrant such a day will awaken the sleepy heads of the daffodils and primroses. Come, shall we venture to the arbour? It is too early yet for the roses, but it is a pleasant place to rest.'

'As you wish, sire.'

Henry grins, his dark eyes glinting in the soft spring sun. 'Who is this "sire" you speak of, Mistress Carey? I see only a simple man entreating a lovely maid to accompany him on a pleasant walk.'

Mary focuses on the powdery white path. 'I am no maid, sire. I am a married woman.'

'Yet you venture out into the gardens on your own.'

'It is a fair day, as you say, and I wished to enjoy the air. My husband is busy with his duties. He prepares for a visit to Beaulieu to hire labourers for the house and the garden.'

The king gestures to the bench beneath the wooden arbour entwined with climbing roses in their first flush of green. 'I am pleased to hear it. Master Carey serves me well in the Privy Chamber. He will be a worthy steward of Beaulieu in my absence.'

Mary sits on the bench and arranges the heavy velvet of her gown around her legs. 'My husband is most gratified at your confidence in his abilities, sire.'

'And what of you, Mistress Carey?' Henry asks as he sits beside her. 'Are you most gratified?'

Mary looks over at the king who is watching her intently. 'I am, sire. You do my husband and myself a great honour with your patronage.'

Henry grunts. He leans forward and picks a yellow primrose which he presents to Mary. 'A posy for the fairest maid in England.'

Mary sucks in a quick breath and takes the flower. 'Thank you, sire.'

Henry takes hold of Mary's hand and rubs his thumb over her wrist. 'You do not wear my bracelet. Is it not to your liking?'

Mary shakes her head, the black veil of her gable hood waving over her shoulders. 'It is very much to my liking, sire.'

'Then I expect to see you wear it this eve at supper.'

Mary's fair eyebrows draw together.

Henry runs a finger over Mary's cheek. 'What is it, my dove. What disturbs you?'

'Sire, the bracelet features Your Majesty's likeness. The queen …' Her voice falters.

'Queen Katherine will dine in her chambers with her ladies as she does throughout Lent.'

Mary nods. 'I don't wish to—'

He grabs both of her hands, crushing the flower between Mary's fingers. 'Have you not read my letter? Have you not seen the words of one who loves purely? Mary, you have bewitched me with your beauty and your kind heart. I am naught but a besotted suitor who suffers at your indifference. Your sweet face haunts my every thought, so that I, the king of this great country, cares more for a kind word from Mary than for all the lands of France.'

Mary pulls her hands away. 'Sire, please, cease. I entreat you.'

Henry sits back. 'I see why the French king was so enamoured of you.'

Mary's heart thumps. 'Sire?'

Henry brushes the back of his bejewelled fingers across her cheek. 'You stir the blood with your refusals.'

Mary leaps to her feet. 'Sire, I must take my leave. My husband shall be wondering at my tardiness.'

Henry rises and bows his head. 'We mustn't keep Master Carey waiting, although we both know that the fawn will always fall to the hunter.'

———

My Dearest Fawn,

I gaze with the eyes of a besotted youth at the visage reflected in my window, imagining not myself but that it were your own sweet face who returns the look of love. How sweet the pangs of love, yet how I yearn for their satiation, as honey tames the hunger of a ravenous bear.

Did you not cast your eyes on the silver caparison draped on my horse at the tournament one week past, upon which I had the seamstresses embroider 'Elle mon Coeur a navera'? 'She has wounded my heart'. She, whom two days later was graced with the

role of 'Kindness' in the pageant of 'The Assault on the Castle of
Virtue' at Wolsey's house and danced so prettily with me before the
court and the ambassadors. She, whose name is Mary.

I surrender my heart to you, the angel of my imaginings, and
though the labours of my position currently necessitate my absence to
the palace at Eltham, thereby precluding me from meeting with my
love, which I so desire, I am sending this poor replacement, a bracelet
into which my picture has been set, to assure myself that I have a
place, as ever you do in mine, in your tender affections.

Your humble servant,
Henry R.

William Carey sets down his ledger and looks at his wife, who
sits reading the king's letter in her favourite chair by the casement
window in their two-room lodgings overlooking the activity on
the Thames.

'Another letter from him?'

'No, it is the one from the other day.'

'God rot him. I wish there was something I could do to take
you away from here, but I am a member of the King's Privy
Chamber. It is my duty to accompany the king wheresoever he
chooses.'

'You needn't harbour any concern.'

'No? What of the grant the king has just this past month
awarded me to oversee the expansion of his great house at
Beaulieu in Essex? What of the invitation for us to reside in that
house whensoever the king is elsewhere? What of my new offices
of bailiff of New Hall, Walkeford Hall and Hall End? I wish to
believe that my loyal service to the king has warranted me these
honours, but how can I not but harbour the thought that these are
gifts to persuade me to ignore his pursuit of you?'

Mary looks over at her husband, at the face so fine and

handsome, so little like the florid bluntness of his cousin, King Henry's. 'You have no cause to doubt that these honours are rewards for your loyalty and ability, William. That King Henry has chosen to grace me with the favour of his attention is the work of folly, and I have no intention to succumb. I am a married woman. He will tire of me soon enough when another of superior youth and beauty catches his eye.'

William smiles. 'Mary, there is none lovelier than you at court.'

Mary laughs. 'I have concern for your eyesight, sir. Anne is newly arrived at court and has already set tongues wagging with her French fashions and pretty dancing. I shall warn her to beware.'

William picks up his quill pen and dabs it into the ink pot. 'Anne may be a pretty dancer, but she cannot hold a candle to your beauty, Mary. Be well assured of that. It is no mystery to me why you have caught the king's eye. It is well he remembers you are a married woman.'

Mary gazes out the window and watches a barge laden with barrels bounce through the waves towards the city. She has made the mistake of capitulating to the will of a king before, and it nearly destroyed her. Though she is loath to admit it, her father's adroit manoeuvrings after her affair with the French king saved her reputation and enabled her to make the advantageous match with one of King Henry's trusted intimates. Although it wasn't the noble match her father had once envisaged for her, his eldest daughter – William's position as a second son meant he was without a landed estate of his own – his influence in the King's Privy Chamber as one of Henry's rumoured favourites had persuaded Thomas Boleyn to open his purse and bestow a substantial dowry on the Carey family.

Mary glances at her husband, who has returned his attention to their accounts. She is happy. She has made a good marriage to a good man. They are both in good health and, if God wills, she will carry the baby she conceives to term and all will be well. Let Anne enjoy the pleasures of court, as she so obviously does. Let her sister make the marriage her father had hoped for herself. She cares for none of that. While her union with William lacks the passion and excitement of her affair with the French king, she has come to love him for his kindness and solidity.

She slips the king's bracelet into the folds of the letter and joins William at the heavy oak table. She sets the letter and bracelet down in front of him.

'I wish for there to be no secrets between us, sir. I am your own good wife. I have no intention to indulge the king in his passing fancy. Now, it is nearly time for supper. Let us wash our hands and make our way to the great hall.'

Chapter Twenty-Eight

BRYHER

Pieter's Penthouse Flat, London
December 2024

Bryher awakens to the screech of gulls and a dull headache. The vestiges of a disturbing dream waft around her mind like feathers tossed about in the wind, but she can't grasp the teasing loops, and the illusive images fade to nothing. She opens her eyes and blinks in the dim light filtering in through the curtains in Pieter's bedroom. His body is warm beside hers. He shifts around and leans on his hand.

'Good morning.'

'You've got noisy birds out there.'

Pieter runs his fingers along Bryher's shoulder. 'They like being near the Thames.'

Bryher shuts her eyes and surrenders to Pieter's caresses. Maybe she shouldn't have let him persuade her to stay. Her life is complicated enough. She hasn't even signed the divorce papers yet. She smiles as he presses kisses along her neck. But what is so wrong with this? They are both unattached adults. Last night she was free in a way she's never felt before. Free of worries, free of responsibilities, free of guilt, free of inhibitions. She has never experienced a lover like Pieter, who explored every inch of her body until the pleasure had been almost – but not quite – too much to bear. Maybe Jennifer is right. Maybe a fling with a handsome European historian is just what she needs.

Bryher stretches and yawns. 'Betty's going to think I'm a scarlet woman when I rock up to the house wearing yesterday's clothes.'

Pieter kisses her shoulder. 'Or she will think you're just living up to your reputation.'

Bryher playfully pushes his arm and he falls back against the pillow. 'Where's your bathroom?'

He points at a wood-veneered door opposite the bedroom door. 'Through the dressing room.'

Bryher slides out of the bed and grabs Pieter's shirt from the pile of discarded clothes on the soft grey carpet. 'I'll be back in a minute,' she says as she slips on the shirt.

'I'm not going anywhere. Especially when you look like that.'

In the large, marble-tiled bathroom Bryher regards herself in the mirror and splashes cold water onto her face. She leans closer and presses at the tiny lines fanning out from the corners of her eyes. She grins into the mirror, watching the lines deepen. She raises her eyebrows and sees her forehead move. The Botox is wearing off. If Margot could see her, she'd book the first available appointment with a facialist. The funny thing is, she doesn't care. The person she'd been in LA is starting to feel like someone else altogether. The constant pressure to perfect one's appearance with the vile-tasting green drinks, Pilates classes, yoga classes, spin classes, Botox, fillers, dental veneers, and the diets – keto, detox, liquid, 5:2... From this distance, the unrelenting self-obsession seems vacuous and exhausting.

She looks out of the window at the view of the luxury

apartment buildings on the south side of the Thames, framed against the dull grey of the early morning December sky. She's actually starting to like the English greyness and the dewy moist air. It's like snuggling under a duvet cover, homely and comforting. So different from the brash, bright, hectic energy of LA. It surprises her that she doesn't miss it more.

She pads back across the carpet to the vast king-size bed and slips under the duvet. Pieter wraps an arm around her and pulls her against him.

'Your feet are cold,' he says.

'You'll just have to warm them up then, won't you?'

He pulls her on top of him. 'How do you suggest I do that?'

She smiles and looks down at him as she shrugs out of his shirt. 'I've got a few ideas.'

Bryher enters Pieter's open-plan kitchen/living room dressed in the previous night's clothes.

'That smells amazing.'

Pieter flips a pancake and smiles at her. 'Belgian pancakes. You haven't lived until you've had a Belgian pancake. They have a special ingredient.'

Bryher takes the mug of coffee he offers her. 'What's that?'

He makes a locking gesture in front of his lips. 'My lips are sealed.'

Bryher laughs as she wanders into the living room. 'You're like an onion, Pieter. You peel away one layer, and there's another underneath. Then, another and another.' She waves her hand in the air as if she's reading a theatre marquee. 'Dr Pieter de Beer, International Man of Mystery.'

'I'm not so mysterious.'

'Oh, no?' She runs her hand along the back of the charcoal grey leather sofa. 'You're an academic and a TV star. You're an historical advisor on movies. According to Jennifer you're one of London's top eligible bachelors. Then I find out you're a jeweller. And now you're cooking pancakes voluntarily. You probably climb mountains and heli-ski for fun. Am I right?'

Pieter flips a pancake onto a plate. 'That's pretty accurate.'

She stops in front of a cabinet exhibiting a collection of impressive jewellery. 'What's this? You're a jewellery collector, too? These look expensive.' She points to a necklace with a large blue diamond encircled by small sparkling white diamonds. 'Wait, I recognise that. Isn't that the Hope Diamond?'

Pieter joins her at the cabinet. 'I'm glad you think so. It's a copy, of course. They're all copies, using lesser stones like amethyst, tourmaline, zircon, freshwater pearls. When I studied jewellery-making, copying the masters was part of our assignments. I loved doing it. I wanted to see how close to the original I could get. It's become something of a hobby.'

He puts his coffee mug on a side table and retrieves a key from an engraved brass box. He unlocks a cabinet drawer and removes a red velvet box.

'What's that?'

'You'll see.' He opens the lid.

Bryher gasps. 'It's the Boleyn necklace.'

'Yes. Well, another copy. This one is quite valuable. I used good quality cultured pearls and eighteen carat gold. It's worth tens of thousands of pounds. It's why I keep it locked up, although I really should put it in a safe deposit box.'

'Do you really think Betty's is the original necklace?'

Pieter shrugs. 'I don't know. It would be an incredible find. Bryher, you need to find a way to borrow it from her so I can have it properly examined. Maybe offer to put it in a safe deposit box for her.'

Bryher looks down at the 'B' necklace. What if Betty's is the real necklace and she could get her hands on it? It would solve her financial problems and she wouldn't have to bow to Jake's blackmail. She'd be able to take care of Marnie and she wouldn't have to admit to adultery because of the sex tape. And the story … Margot could spin the story of the queen's necklace so that her face is everywhere. That'd show Jake. That'd show everyone.

'I'll see what I can do.'

'Wonderful.' Pieter shuts the lid and returns the box to the drawer, which he locks securely. 'Now, let's explore the delectable magic of Belgian pancakes.'

Chapter Twenty-Nine

ANNE & MARY

Placentia Palace, Greenwich, England
April 1522

Anne looks up from the annotations she is making in her *Book of Hours* with her quill as her sister enters the room.

'Mary, where have you been?' she asks. 'The queen was asking after you this afternoon. She wished to hear you sing "Farewell My Joy" as we were sewing. She says you have a pretty voice, though I do not credit it with being of particular remark. I have heard many sing better at Queen Claude's court in France.'

Mary removes her cloak and hangs it upon a hook by the door of Anne's room. 'I had errands. I have much to attend to with William's absence at Beaulieu.'

'Do you? I should have thought you would be happy to be relieved of the duties of a wife to that dull husband of yours.'

Mary sits down opposite her sister. 'That is not kind, Anne. William is a good husband.'

Anne raises a dark eyebrow. 'As good as King François?'

'Do not speak of that. It is well in the past.'

Anne shuts the prayer book and sets it in her lap. She smiles slyly at her sister. 'I, too, enjoyed the favours of a lover at the French court.'

'Anne! Does Father know?'

Anne tosses the book onto a table and rises. 'Of course not. Do not think me as silly a fool as you.' She fetches a bowl of ripe pears and a small knife. 'I have learned the art of discretion.'

Mary watches her sister cut a slice off a pear and slide it into her mouth. 'You surprise me, sister.'

Anne wipes away a dribble of pear juice from her chin. 'You above all should know not to be surprised by me. I am capable of much more than even our dear parents credit me for.'

She offers Mary a slice of pear which Mary happily accepts.

'But, Anne, were you not afraid of … of …'

Anne laughs. 'Of becoming with child? I took great care.' She chews on a slice of pear. 'There was a woman at the French court who was wise with the knowledge of herbs.' She eyes her sister. 'Why do you ask? Do you seek a wise woman here in the English court?'

'No! I am a married woman. I have no need of such things.'

Anne sets down the knife in the bowl. 'Are you certain?'

'Why do you ask such a thing?'

Anne shrugs as she wipes her hands on a fine linen handkerchief. 'I am not blind. I have seen the glances you and the king exchange at dinner in the great hall. You have been seen walking with King Henry in the garden. What might I make of this?'

'It is nothing. The king came upon me when I was out walking one morn and we exchanged pleasantries. Nothing more.'

Anne scrutinises her sister. 'All is well, then.'

Mary bites her lip as memories of the past week of 'accidental' encounters with the king flutter around her mind like a trapped bird. She has not slept and has eaten little, afraid of the passion which the king's ardour has stirred within the very core of her being.

'Anne … I …' She swallows and shuts her mouth.

'What is it?'

'It is nothing.'

Anne eyes her sister, taking in the blush that rises in Mary's fair cheeks. 'Mary, the queen has long suffered King Henry's wanderings. He has even acknowledged his bastard son by Bessie Blount. King Henry is, after all, a man like any other.' She smiles. 'Though handsomer than most. Tell me, which do you think handsomer? The English king or the French king?'

Panic pricks at Mary. 'Do not tease me, Anne. I have simply walked with the king in the gardens on a couple of occasions,' she lies. She worries at the heavy gold 'B' of the pendant necklace around her neck with her fingers.

Anne shakes her head, the black veil of her French hood waving against her shoulders. 'Oh, sweet, foolish sister. You ruined yourself with King François and our father saved your reputation so that you could be married to a dull young courtier. Do not ruin yourself with King Henry, who will only throw you over for another when he tires of you. What benefits did you receive from giving your virtue to the French king? Jewellery? Money? Title? Nothing. You received nothing. I would never make such an error.'

'I loved him. It was not about those things.'

'You are a fool. Have you not considered that King Henry's interest in you stems from his desire to possess the woman who was once the French king's mistress?'

'Poppycock. I cannot entertain this thought.'

'You are nothing to these men but a pretty plaything. It is well you have so dreary and sensible a husband. William would do nothing to compromise his position at court. Have you not considered that is why King Henry has sought you out? You have a pretty face and can dance and sing with some small skill, but there are many maids at court who outshine you. The issue is that they are unwed and likely to bear another bastard, which complicates the king's life. Better to have a married mistress, whose children will be acknowledged and raised by another man. It is much simpler all around.'

'You mock me, Anne.'

Anne claps her hands together and rises. 'I feel a thirst. The queen has gifted me with some fine Spanish wine. Care you for a draught?'

Mary regards her sister. How can Anne be so cold and unsympathetic when she, herself, is so full of warmth and emotion? Two sisters could not be more unlike. They do not even resemble each other. Had they not been born of the same parents, they would be strangers with little desire to make each other's acquaintance.

'Thank you, no. The afternoon draws on. I shall take my leave.'

Anne shrugs. 'As you wish. And Mary, you are no longer a Boleyn. You are a Carey now. Perhaps it is best you gift me with the Boleyn pendant. You have besmirched our good name with your liaison with the French king, and now you seek the attentions of another. You do not deserve to wear the pendant. If you are clever, the king will gift you with other jewels.'

Mary touches the 'B' of her pendant. 'I am born a Boleyn and I shall die a Boleyn. It is mine, Anne, and you shall not have it.'

Anne laughs as she pours herself a glass of the ruby wine. 'It will be mine one day, Mary. Of that you may be certain.'

———

King Henry looks up from a table stacked with books where he has been writing and flashes Mary a wide smile.

'You have come.'

Mary curtsies in the doorway of the king's private chambers.

'Yes, Your Majesty. The Countess of Oxford visited me with a message that you wished to see me.'

'The Countess of Oxford is a most able messenger.' He waves away an usher hovering by the door. 'Leave us,' he tells them. 'See that we are not disturbed.'

Mary's heart stutters as she hears the door shut behind her. She glances around the dark, wood-panelled room, which is dominated by a huge, intricately carved oak bed hung with embroidered curtains. Shelves of books line the wall behind the table at which the king sits, and a fire roars and snaps within a large stone fireplace. In the centre of the room, upon the floor, which has been strewn with fresh rushes, a second table groans with roasted meats, mounds of Spanish oranges, golden-crusted tarts, almond creams and jellies glistening like jewels in the candlelight. They are alone. Not for the first time in her life she feels akin to a hind trapped in a hunter's net.

'I shall not disturb you for long, Your Majesty.' She holds out her hand, revealing the king's signet ring, which her cousin, the Countess of Oxford, had given her when she'd delivered the king's message. 'I have come to return this.'

Henry rises from the table and approaches Mary, who feels the heat rise in her cheeks at the sight of the king's casual attire of a fine white linen shirt and black velvet hose, the simplicity of which only enhances his ruddy handsomeness.

He takes hold of Mary's hand as he collects the ring and raises it to his lips, pressing a warm kiss upon her skin. 'I thank you, my lovely English rose.' He pushes the ring onto a forefinger. 'Our benevolent Cardinal Wolsey would have been most vexed had my signet ring gone missing. No doubt he would have called for heads to roll.'

Mary swallows and curtsies again. 'With Your Majesty's permission, I shall take my leave.'

'Mistress Carey, I have before me a wondrous feast and I am disheartened at the prospect of supping with naught but my own company.' He pulls out a chair and gestures for her to sit. 'Please, do me the honour of supping with me this eve. And please, do not say you must attend to your husband. I know full well that he is in Beaulieu attending to his duties as my landlord there.'

Oh, blessed Lord. What am I meant to do? Mary glances at the door and back at the king who stands patiently awaiting her by the table. She presses a hand to her stomach. 'I ate much at dinner today, sire. I have a little appetite.'

'Wonderful. You admit to an appetite. Come, sit. Let me attend to your requirements.' He reaches for a plate and carves her a hearty slice of venison. He looks over at her and smiles. 'Come, Mistress Mary. Your appetite may be little, but mine is large. You would not have your Lord King starve, would you?'

Mary chews her lip. *There is nothing for it. I must sup with him. I will eat little, then I will leave.* 'No, sire, I would not have that.'

She takes a seat in the chair as Henry adds a slice of roast chicken to her plate. He offers her an ornate Italian glass full of rich, red wine, which she holds gingerly, fearful of breaking the fine glass.

'It is a good Gascon wine,' he says as he pours himself a glass. 'One may scorn the French for many things, but their wine is not one of them. I developed a liking for it when the French king had fountains running with it at the Field of the Cloth of Gold.'

Mary starts at the reference to King François. She eyes the king as he sits in the chair opposite her. Is it really the reason he pursues her, as Anne has suggested? Because she was once King François's lover?

Henry raises his glass in a toast. 'To the beautiful Mary, with whom I am most honoured to share this simple meal this eve.'

He takes a drink of the wine and sets the glass back on the table. Rising from his chair, he approaches Mary and offers her his hand. He kneels on one knee and presses her hand to the fine linen covering the warm flesh over his heart.

'Mary, I have yearned for this moment. I have imagined it a

thousand times in my dreams.' He threads his fingers through hers and raises their entwined hands to his lips. 'Mary, Mary, my heart aches for you. You are my own sweet angel, and holder of my poor, besotted heart.' He looks up at her. 'Tell me you want me. Tell me you want me as I want you or my heart will break, and you will have killed this unworthy king.'

Mary looks into Henry's beseeching blue eyes. Eyes that bore into her very core with the intensity of their gaze. Her heart beats a drum, and she struggles to breathe against the pressure of her whalebone busk. Why does her body betray her so? Why do the caresses of her husband not stir her blood like this until her body is aflame with desire?

Henry rises and pulls Mary to her feet. He presses his lips into the palms of her hands. 'Tell me you want me, Mary,' he says as he covers her fingers with kisses. 'Tell me you do not wish for my kisses on your lips, on your lovely long neck, on the flesh of your breasts. Tell me, and I will release you now and never trouble you again.'

Mary reaches up and pulls Henry's face to hers. She kisses him fully on his mouth. 'I want you, my lord,' she says kissing his lips, his cheeks, the fine red hair of his beard. 'I want you, Henry.'

Chapter Thirty

BRYHER & MARNIE

Los Angeles, California
March 2004

'Bry! Bry! Open the window.'

Bryher wades through the fog of sleep and opens her eyes to the sound of tapping on the window. She turns her head to see her sixteen-year-old sister, Marnie's, face through the glass. *Again? It must be way after midnight this time.*

She wriggles out from under the bedcovers and pads barefoot across the nylon carpet to the window. She pushes up the sash.

'Where've you been? It's late. Mom will throw a fit if she catches you.'

Marnie tosses her cowboy boots through the window and climbs into the room, her long wavy strawberry blonde hair falling in a tangle over her cropped T-shirt. She hikes up her tight, low-rise jeans and presses her finger against her smudged lip gloss.

'Ssh. Don't wake her up.'

Bryher flops back onto her bed. 'Don't worry. She's had half a bottle of gin tonight after finishing off a bottle of wine at supper. An earthquake wouldn't wake her.'

Marnie falls face first onto her bed fully clothed. Bryher looks over at her sister.

'Where were you? You missed the audition. Mom was furious.'

'None of your business and I don't care. I only got the audition because you're my sister. You're the only one Mom cares about now that you're the family star.'

Bryher sits up against the pillows and turns on the bedside lamp. 'That's not fair. I work hard on all those commercials. And I've got to study for my exams. You don't act or study and I know you cut most of your classes. What *do* you do all day?'

Marnie flips over on the bedspread. 'What do you care?'

'I'm your sister. I care.'

Marnie sits up on the edge of the bed and glares at Bryher. Her aquamarine eyes are bloodshot and smudged with mascara. 'You're not my sister.'

'What are you talking about?'

Marnie pulls open the drawer of the bedside table and takes out a pack of cigarettes and a lighter.

'Marnie, what are you talking about?'

She lights the cigarette and blows out a smoke ring as she regards Bryher. 'We don't have the same father.'

Bryher swings her legs over the side of the bed. 'That's not true! Take it back!'

Marnie crosses her legs and takes a long drag on the cigarette. 'It is. Ask Mom. Haven't you ever wondered why we don't look alike? Mom fucked some foreign guy and Dad threw himself off a bridge.'

'No! Dad was in a car accident.'

Marnie laughs. She jabs the glowing cigarette at Bryher. 'There wasn't any car accident. You killed my father,' she says, ash spilling down onto the sheets. '*My* father. Not yours. Your father was the foreign guy she fucked.'

Bryher jumps up from the bed and throws herself at Marnie. 'You're lying! You're lying!' she cries, flailing at her sister. 'I didn't kill anyone!'

Marnie pushes Bryher off her and stubs the cigarette out on the bedside table. She pulls on her boots. 'I wish you'd never been born. We were happy before you came along.' She slaps her chest. '*I* was the family star. I was the Sugarmilk kid, for fuck's sake. I was on Broadway!' She jabs her finger at Bryher. 'You ruined it for me, brat, stealing the Fresh Freddy's Burgers commercials. Those were mine and you stole them! It should be my face up on all those billboards!'

'That's not true!'

'It is! You're a thief and a murderer, Bryher Finch. And you're a little bastard. It's why Mom never loved you the way she loves me.' She shrugs. 'Now you're Mom's cash cow, but she still doesn't love you. If you'd never been born we would've been happy. My father wouldn't have killed himself and everything would have been fine. You ruined everything.'

Bryher shakes her head as tears stream down her cheeks. She throws herself at Marnie and pounds at her chest. 'You're lying! You're lying!'

Marnie pushes her away. 'Enjoy it while it lasts, because it won't. I know. As soon as you grow up, they'll dump you. Then you'll be a has-been, just like me.' She stomps across the room and swings her legs over the window sill.

Bryher rubs at her eyes. 'Wh-where are you going?'

'None of your business, brat. And don't tell Mom anything, or else.'

Bryher rushes over to the window and watches her sister run across the patch of grass in front of their rented house. She leans out of the window. 'Or else what?'

Marnie spins around laughing and gives Bryher the finger.

Chapter Thirty-One

ANNE & MARY

Placentia Palace, Greenwich, England
September 1523

Anne shuts the door to Mary and William's lodgings and eyes her sister. Mary, whose fair beauty she has always jealously admired, though she would scarce admit it to anyone, least of all to her sister, glows with loveliness. Mary's complexion gleams like fresh Devon cream, and a blush like the first kiss of pink on an apple blossom colours her cheeks. Her eyes shine as blue as the summer sky, and the pearls of the coveted 'B' pendant seem to reflect the lustre of her skin. Even her figure has ripened like a juicy peach, the curve of her breasts fighting against the tight placard of her gown's blue silk bodice.

'Mary, you are fair bursting out of your gown. I would forebear the honeyed fruits and marchpane, were I you.'

A cloud flits over Mary's face and she brushes her hands down her bodice. ''Tis true. My maid has had to loosen my lacings. It is a puzzle, as I eat no more than I ever did.'

Ignoring this, Anne helps herself to a handful of grapes from a bowl on a table and sits in a chair by the window overlooking the Thames. She watches the flow of barges, rowboats, single-masted crayers, and three-masted carracks laden with furs from the New World, spices from the Orient, Gascon wine, and carpets and silks from Italy. She spits out the grape pip and tosses it onto the floor rushes.

'I hear that your husband has been granted three of the former Essex manors of that traitor, the Duke of Buckingham,' she says as she chews another grape. She spits the pip onto the floor. 'King Henry favours Master Carey well. I wonder at the progress of a second son of a modest knight when there are many others at court of superior lineage and abilities.'

Mary retrieves a linen napkin from a coffer and thrusts it at her sister. 'My good husband has earned the grants the king has bestowed upon him through his diligent service,' she says frostily. 'Do not cast aspersions upon William's integrity.'

'Integrity?' Anne laughs. 'You are one to speak of integrity when you play Queen Katherine for a fool with the king.' Anne balls the napkin around the skeleton of the grape branch and drops it onto the table. 'Tell me, sister, do you not ever succumb to pangs of remorse? Of guilt?'

Mary presses her hand against her flushed cheek. 'Anne, please, cease this talk.'

Anne's dark eyebrows shoot upwards in amusement. 'You cannot believe the king loves you. The silly daughter of a lowly knight? Oh, Mary, you are far more a fool that I credited you for.'

Mary rises from her chair and grasps the table. She presses a hand against her mouth and stumbles across over to the chamber pot under the bed. Heaving, she pulls it out and vomits into the ceramic pot.

Anne approaches her sister and kneels beside her. She holds back the veil of Mary's headdress as her sister retches. 'My poor sister. Forgive me, you are not well. Here, let me remove your pendant so that you may not soil it.' She undoes the clasp and tucks the pendant into her bodice.

Mary staggers to her feet and allows Anne to guide her to her bed. 'I am sorry. I am sick.'

Anne stares at her sister. 'You are not sick. You are with child.'

Mary's blue eyes widen as the colour drains from her face. 'With child? How can that be?'

Anne chortles. 'It has something to do with visiting a man's bed. The question is, is the babe your husband's or the king's?'

Anne fixes the 'B' pendant around her neck and examines her reflection in Queen Katherine's gilded Spanish mirror. She pats the heavy gold 'B' and runs her fingers over the lustrous pearls. She was right to rescue it from her sister. Mary is a Carey now. She, Anne, is a Boleyn.

She smiles into the mirror. The king will tire of Mary, now that she is with child. Whether or not the babe is King Henry's, it will be acknowledged as a Carey. That spineless husband of Mary's can be relied upon not to make a fuss – he profits too much from the king's generosity. Besides, King Henry already has a royal bastard, Henry Fitzroy, by his previous mistress, Bessie Blount. What need is he of another, especially if it is a girl? Mary's day as King Henry's favourite is over.

Anne twirls one of the heavy oblong pearls hanging from the 'B' between her fingers. Now it is her time. She is no longer a carefree girl to be flattered into bed by any man, whether he be a humble knight or a powerful king. Her heart, once tender, has suffered grievously in the year past, when her relationship with the dynamic Harry Percy, heir to the lands and vast fortune of the Earl of Northumberland, was destroyed by the meddling Cardinal Wolsey. The scheming cardinal had taken Harry under his wing as a page in his own vast court, and had, with the old Earl, bludgeoned her lover into rejecting her and accepting a pre-arranged match with the simpering daughter of the Earl of Shrewsbury.

She will never forgive Wolsey for ruining her chance of happiness with the man to whom she had given her heart. Yet, in one regard, she must thank him. In the long months of her banishment to Hever Castle, far from court and the temptations of Harry Percy, she has felt a shell grow hard around her heart. She would never again allow herself to become a pawn in a man's game. She will show Wolsey, and the Earl of Northumberland, and Harry Percy, and any other man who seeks to move her around their chessboard for their own purposes, that she is a queen. And, in chess, the queen is the most powerful piece.

Chapter Thirty-Two

BRYHER

Puddleton, England
December 2024

'Betty?'

'Yes, dear?' Betty says as she shakes another dollop of brown sauce over her roast beef and Yorkshire pudding. She hands the bottle to Bryher. 'You really must try this. It's much better than ketchup in my view.'

Bryher politely refuses the offering. She lays down her fork and takes a sip of the cheap Merlot she'd bought from the local convenience store. She sets down the glass and looks across the dining table at her cousin.

'I've been thinking about your necklace, Betty. The copy of Anne Boleyn's necklace.'

'Have you? Why is that, dear?' Betty pushes the dish of horseradish sauce towards Bryher. 'If you're not having brown sauce, I insist you have some horseradish. Just a little, though. It's very strong.'

Bryher surrenders and dabs a small spoonful onto her plate. 'Pieter told me the other night that he thought it might be worth some money. It's not just cheap costume jewellery. He had a good look at it when he fixed the clasp. The pearls are real, you know, and the rest is real gold, not just brass-coated nickel. Have you insured it?'

'Oh, heavens, no. Insurance money is just money down the drain. Besides, I knew it wasn't a cheap copy. Mummy did like decent-quality costume jewellery, but no one wears that kind of jewellery anymore. It's all a bit …'

'OTT?'

'OTT?'

'Uh, over the top. Gaudy.'

Betty's blue eyes light up. 'Oh, yes. OTT. I'll have to remember that. I do enjoy learning the lingo of today's youth.'

Bryher chews on a mouthful of golden-crusted Yorkshire pudding. 'Pieter thought you should consider putting it in a safe deposit box. If you give it to me, I can sort that out for you.'

Betty shakes her head as she spoons a dab of horseradish sauce onto her plate. 'That's very kind of you, dear, but Puddleton is as safe as houses. We don't even lock our doors here.'

She gestures to Bryher's plate which is still half-full of roast beef, Yorkshire pudding, mashed potatoes, peas and carrots. 'Now, eat up. You mustn't let a good English Sunday lunch go to waste. I've made sticky toffee pudding and custard which we can have in front of the telly. I thought we could binge watch *Doc Martin*. It's so nice to have you home today. We're just like family.'

She looks over at Bijou who is sitting on the window ledge watching them eat. 'Isn't it lovely having Bryher here, Bijou? We're not alone in the world anymore.'

At Elstree Studios, the following day, Pieter enters Bryher's dressing room and shuts the door behind him. He crosses over to her and kisses her on the top of her linen coif.

'Do you have it?'

Bryher scratches at her inflamed neck under the costume department's 'B' necklace. 'If I had it, do you think I'd be wearing this cheap thing again?'

He squeezes her shoulder and looks at Bryher in the mirror. 'That's a shame. I really wanted to have my colleague look at it.'

'I know,' Bryher says as she applies mascara. 'Betty doesn't believe any of her mother's jewellery is valuable. It's not in a safe deposit box and she thinks insuring it is a waste of money.'

'That's not good. At least you said she keeps it in a safe place.'

'I did?'

'Yes, you did.' His eyes narrow as he regards her in the mirror. 'Where does she keep the necklace?'

Bryher bites her lip as she meets his blue gaze in the mirror. 'It's in an old jewellery box under her bed.'

Pieter slaps his forehead. '*Godverdomme!*' He spins around and paces the room. 'You have to get that necklace, do you understand?'

Bryher stares at him in the mirror. 'Uh …'

He turns back to Bryher and clutches the back of her chair. 'You have to get it from Betty? Promise me.'

Bryher turns in her chair and stares into Pieter's agitated face. She reaches out and brushes her hand against the rough beard on his cheek. 'Okay. I promise, Pieter.'

Chapter Thirty-Three

ANNE

Placentia Palace, Greenwich, England
March 1524

Anne retreats to the window where a dull grey light filters through the leaded glass. She breaks the wax seal on the letter and unfolds the thick paper.

Ah, finally. News from Mary. God willing, the babe is healthy.

My dear sister,

I write to you to share the joyous arrival of our precious daughter, Catherine, on the eighteenth day of March, the year of Our Lord 1524, whom we have named after our own beloved queen. Mother was in attendance and sends you her best wishes.

I so regret that you were unable to come to Beaulieu during my confinement. I was well attended by several ladies of the court who have experience in such matters. Catherine, or Cate as we have come to call her, is a jolly little sprite, with russet hair and large dark eyes much like your own. My dear husband William has visited from

London and is delighted that our child is robust and healthy, even though she is a girl rather than the son he wished for. I assured him that we are both young and we are likely to be blessed with a son in the future, if God wills. Mother will remain here with me until May Day after which William will accompany us back to court and she will return to Hever.

How fare you, Anne? Mother said that Cardinal Wolsey has proposed to the king that you marry Sir James Butler, the son of the Irish landowner who claims the Irish lands of our father's earldom of Ormond for himself. Mother says Father baulks at paying 'even one penny' of dowry to the man he says stole his rightful Irish lands. What think you of this marriage? It would take you far from court, which I know you would disfavour. It is well known that you are held in great estimation by Queen Katherine.

Anne, in all the activity of the past months, I have misplaced the Boleyn pendant. I cannot recall seeing it for some time and its loss distresses me most grievously. Would you look through our lodgings at Greenwich to see if it can be found? I have searched to no avail, but perhaps you will have more success. You know how dear the pendant is to me and I know how much you admired it.

Do come to Beaulieu if Queen Katherine permits. Despite our differences, you are my one sister and I do so wish for you to see your new niece.

Your sister,
Mary Carey

Anne folds the letter and looks out to the view of the wide grey Thames flowing sluggishly towards the sea. She reaches up and presses the gold 'B' of the pendant between her fingers and smiles.

It's mine, now, Mary. It is the Boleyn pendant and no one, not even a king, shall ever take my name away from me.

Chapter Thirty-Four

BRYHER

Puddleton, England
December 2024

Bryher tugs off the wellies she's borrowed from Betty and drops them onto the hallway tiles, almost clobbering Bijou who rubs against her damp jeans. Pieter helps her out of the tweed coat and hangs it, along with her handbag and his own raincoat, on a coat hook.

'Are you ready?'

Bryher nods. 'Ready as I'll ever be.'

'Bryher?' Betty calls out from the lounge. 'Is that you? Is someone with you?'

'No, it's a thief coming to rob you of all your worldly goods. Of course it's me. I've brought company.'

'Oh.' Betty looks up from the sofa and smiles as Bryher and Pieter enter the room. Her mother's jewellery is scattered across the coffee table. Bijou lumbers past them and jumps into Betty's lap.

'Betty, what are you doing?'

'Just having a good rummage through Mummy's jewellery. I'd quite forgotten Mummy had so much. All your talk about Mummy's necklace inspired me to sort it all out properly.'

Bryher gestures to Pieter. 'I hope you don't mind, but I've invited Pieter for some tea. Not supper tea, just tea tea. Pieter, this is my cousin, Betty Pilcher.'

Betty rises, clutching Bijou against her mint green twinset, and extends a hand to Pieter. 'Do come in, Dr de Beer. Bryher's told me all about you. I watch you on the telly all the time. I loved the series you did on that naughty Charles II and Nell Gwynn. Wasn't he a rake? I'm so sorry I missed you when I visited the set last month. I hope you managed to enjoy a slice of Charlotte Fennell's carrot cake before it was all gobbled up.'

'I did, thank you very much, Mrs Pilcher. Bryher saved me a piece.'

'Oh, it's Miss Pilcher. But, please, call me Betty.'

'And please call me Pieter.'

Betty smiles broadly, her cheek dimpling. 'Oh, yes, certainly.' She looks over at Bryher. 'I've just made a nice pot of Earl Grey, dear. The teapot's over there on the sideboard with some bourbon cream biscuits. Why don't you pour some tea for you and Dr de B … Pieter … and bring over a plate of bickies.'

She gestures to an overstuffed, chintz-covered chair. 'Have a seat, Pieter. That one by the electric fire is the comfiest. Just toss the cushions on the floor if they're a nuisance. Heaven knows, Marion Livesay, the president of our local WI, does whenever she's here.'

Pieter settles his tall frame amongst the lumpy needlework cushions and accepts a cup of tea from Bryher, who sits on the sofa beside Betty.

Bryher sets her teacup down on the coffee table, wincing at the sight of the 'B' necklace amongst the confusion of necklaces, brooches and bracelets.

'It's funny you have all your jewellery out today.' She picks up the 'B' necklace. 'Pieter thinks your copy of the "B" necklace might not be costume jewellery, after all.'

Betty looks over at Pieter. 'Really?'

Pieter leans forward. 'Yes, that's right. I trained as a jeweller many years ago, and I was able to examine it when Bryher gave it to me to fix the broken clasp. She may have told you that it's real gold and that the pearls are real, too. It's a beautifully made piece, and I believe it has some significant value.'

Betty smiles. 'Isn't that funny you should say that. I've just now decided to have it insured.'

The toilet in the guest loo in the hallway flushes.

Bryher glances towards the hall as she sets down the necklace. 'Is someone here?'

A man somewhere in his thirties with an air of permanent dishevelment enters the room.

'Oh, hello,' he says, approaching Bryher with his hand extended. 'Ollie Browne. Oliver, actually, but everyone calls me Ollie Browne. Better than Ollie Wood, right? Ollie Wood, "Hollywood", get it? Pleasure to meet you. Betty's been telling me all about you. You're Bryher Finch, the Hollywood actress.'

Bryher glances at Betty as she shakes his hand. 'I'm Betty's cousin.' She gestures to Pieter. 'Dr Pieter de Beer—'

'Sure, I recognise you. You're the history bloke from the telly.' Ollie holds out his hand to Pieter. 'Pleasure to meet you, Piet.'

Pieter smiles tightly as he shakes Ollie's hand. 'Pieter.'

'Sorry.' Ollie smiles back apologetically. '*Mea culpa*, Pieter.'

'Mr Browne is an insurance broker,' Betty says as Ollie makes himself comfortable in an overstuffed chair. 'Marion gave me his name. He comes highly recommended by her sister, Una, whose brother-in-law used his company for a claim when his new wife lost the diamond out of her engagement ring on the first day of their honeymoon. Twenty-eight years younger, she is. Una still isn't over the shock. Anyway, I invited Mr Browne here to have a look at Mummy's jewellery.'

Bryher exchanges glances with Pieter. 'I see.'

'It's all because of you, dear,' Betty says. 'You got me thinking with all that talk about safe deposit boxes and how you lock everything up in Los Angeles. I said Puddleton doesn't have any sort of crime, but Marion had a break-in last Wednesday, when she was out at the WI meeting, and someone took her telly and her VHS player. She was absolutely livid. She's had to donate her VHS tapes to charity and subscribe to Netflix on her new digital telly. That was a trial. She had to ask the paper boy to show her how to figure it all out. Why do they give you so many remote controls? In my day we'd just press one button on and off and Bob's your uncle. After that I thought to myself, best I have an expert take a look at Mummy's jewellery and see if I need to insure anything, just in case.'

Bryher frowns at the insurance man. *An insurance broker poking around? Seriously?*

'You should have mentioned something to me, Betty. Pieter's a jewellery expert. He can give it a proper examination to value it for you and you wouldn't have had to pay anything.'

'Yes,' Pieter says. 'Why don't you let me look at your jewellery? I'd be delighted to assess it for you, free of charge, of course.'

Ollie waves his hands. 'Oh no, you've got it all wrong.' He gets up and heads over to the sideboard. 'I don't charge for the visit,' he says, helping himself to a couple of biscuits. 'I get paid a commission on any deals I broker.' He takes a bite and heads back to his chair. 'You can have a look at my website,' he says as he chews. 'Conquest Insurance. It's all there.'

'That's right, dear,' Betty says. 'It's all there. He's advising me on the best insurance cover. He's assessing which pieces would benefit from a professional valuation.'

'Which will cost money,' Bryher says. 'Peter's offering to do it for free.'

Ollie takes a jeweller's loupe out of his breast pocket and holds the magnifying eyeglass up to his eye. 'I only use the best valuers, Betty, and they do it for a living.' He glances at Pieter. 'Not just as a hobby. I want what's best for my clients. You've got to protect yourself and your valuables from the greedy hands of those who disrespect the rights of ownership.'

'Oh, absolutely, Mr Browne,' Betty says. 'I couldn't agree more. Can I freshen your tea? Milk and three sugars, wasn't it?'

Ollie picks up a teacup from the bookshelf beside his chair and hands it across the coffee table to Betty. 'Most appreciated.'

'More bourbon creams?'

'Tea wouldn't be tea without a bickie I always say.'

'Pieter, more tea?'

'No, thank you.'

'Bry—'

'I'm fine.'

After refilling Ollie's teacup and adding two more bourbon creams to the saucer, Betty picks up Bijou and settles back onto the sofa beside Bryher. She gestures to the jewellery on the coffee table. 'What are your thoughts, Mr Browne? Any hidden treasures I should be calling *Antiques Roadshow* about?'

'There is something that caught my eye.' Ollie sets down his teacup and pushes aside a chunky red coral necklace and several art deco silver bangles. He picks up the 'B' necklace. 'This one looks very interesting.'

Bryher swallows. She is about to say something when Betty interjects.

'It's a copy of the famous Boleyn necklace. You know, Anne Bole—'

'Ah, yes. I knew I'd seen it somewhere before.' Ollie holds it up and inspects the gold 'B', turning it over and over in his hands.

He jiggles the pearls, then he rubs one of the oval pearls against his front teeth. He nods. 'Very nice. Real pearls and real gold.'

'It was one of Mummy's favourites.' Betty's blue eyes crinkle behind her glasses as she smiles at Bryher.

Bryher glances at Pieter who is watching Ollie like a cat at a mousehole. *I've got to get the necklace out of this Ollie Browne's hands.*

'Let me see it,' she says, standing up abruptly. Her teacup flies off her lap, spilling hot tea over Ollie's corduroy trousers. He drops the necklace onto the coffee table and jumps back with a yelp.

'Ow, shit!' he shouts. 'Sorry, I mean, ow, flippin' heck. Jeez!'

'Oh, my God,' Bryher says as she reaches for a paper napkin. 'I'm so sorry! That tea was hot. I must have really burned you. We'll have to get that looked at right away. Betty, call for a taxi to the hospital while I get him to the bathroom. Splash the burn with cold water, Mr Browne. Don't worry, we'll get you sorted right out.'

Chapter Thirty-Five

ANNE

Placentia Palace, Greenwich, England
Shrove Tuesday 1526

Anne looks across the top of the banquet table at the tumblers and jugglers shouting and weaving about the great hall in front of the carousing court. A riotous noise created by lutes, sackbuts, tambours and recorders bounces over the gaiety from the minstrels' gallery above the entrance doors. Anne spies Mary sitting beside their sister-in-law, Jane Boleyn, at a table of chattering matrons in a far corner of the great hall and wonders at Mary's lack of concern that she in now nothing more than a humble housewife to an insignificant courtier when she had once enjoyed the attentions of King Henry himself.

A roar and shouts of 'Huzzah!' rise from the revellers at the sight of King Henry, resplendent in a doublet and hose of gold silk embroidered with silver thread, entering the hall, followed by several high-ranking nobles carrying platters of roast beef, venison in pastry, scallops of veal and roast swan.

'Oh, how handsome the king looks,' Bess Darrell, the newest of Queen Katherine's ladies-in-waiting, whispers to Anne. She glances past Anne at the ageing queen, who sits at the banquet table smiling indulgently at her young husband. 'Would that I were the queen, so that I might take him to my bed this eve.'

Anne darts Bess a stern look. 'Ssh, Bess. Do not let the queen hear you say such things or you will be sent off to the kitchens to stew rabbits.'

Bess reaches for a hunk of bread. 'There is no chance of that. The knowledge I have of cookery would scarce fill a thimble. Both my former mistress, the Marchioness of Dorset, and our good Queen Katherine know their health would be imperilled were I to venture into a kitchen.'

Bess discards the crust and pops a soft mound of bread into her mouth. 'Did you see the symbol the king wore at the jousts today? It was most chivalrous. A heart gripped inside a press and surrounded by flames with the motto "Declare I dare not".' She shivers with excitement. 'To which maid in the court do you think he dares not declare himself?' She glances down the row of the queen's ladies at the table. 'Jane? Cecily? Margery?' She gasps and grabs Anne's arm. 'You don't think it's me, do you?' She presses a hand against the velvet placard of her bodice and reaches for a cup of wine.

'Don't be stupid, Bess. The king has eyes only for the queen, as it should be.'

Bess takes a drink of wine and wipes her mouth with the back of her hand. 'That's not what I heard.'

'Is that so? What did you hear?'

'Only that the king is in love with Elizabeth Amadas, the wife of the Master of the Jewel House. I've heard he's been sending her gifts.'

Anne's heart jolts. *Elizabeth Amadas? That bad-tempered hussy? Surely not.*

'I would not credit such loose talk,' she says. 'Compose yourself, Bess. The king approaches.'

King Henry makes an elegant bow before the queen, who acknowledges him with a nod. He makes a show of having the Marquis of Exeter place the platter of roast beef on the table in front of the queen and sends the other noblemen down the table to rest their platters of food before the queen's ladies.

'Look! He's carving the beef and serving the queen himself,' Bess says. 'How extraordinary.'

Anne nods. 'The king is an extraordinary man, else he wouldn't be the King of England.'

'Zounds! He comes our way.'

Just as she intended, Anne catches King Henry's eye as he approaches. His tall, muscular frame exudes the confidence of a man at the height of his power and virility, and the golden finery of his costume ensures that every eye in the great hall rests on no one but him.

He takes hold of Anne's hand and brushes his lips against the warm flesh. 'My lady Anne. I am most pleased to see you here this eve.'

Anne smiles. 'Where else would I be but here, Your Majesty? I wait upon the queen. Where Her Majesty ventures, I follow.'

The king nods, setting the peacock feather on his hat waving. 'Then, it is well that the queen is my own good wife, for I shall be assured of your company when she is about.'

Anne glances at Bess, who is twisting a ring on her finger as she listens to the conversation. 'As you will be assured of the company of all the queen's ladies, sire.'

The king laughs. 'Well said, my lady Anne.' He spreads out his arms. 'Now, for this eve only, I and my good noble lords will be your most humble servants. With which of our kitchen's delicacies may I tempt you?' He leans forward and whispers, 'I am partial to the venison myself.'

Anne stares into the king's deep blue eyes. 'Then venison is what I shall have.'

Chapter Thirty-Six

BRYHER & BETTY

Commercial Street, London, England
December 2024

B ryher eyes the nondescript brick building through the taxi window. Skewers of impaled, pressed meat hang behind the dirty glass windows of the shawarma takeaway at street level.

'What are we doing here, Betty? I thought we were going Christmas shopping.'

'We are, but I have a little errand to run here first. Let me pay the driver and I'll meet you on the pavement.'

Bryher pushes open the taxi door, recoiling at the smell of cooking oil and spices. Betty joins her, checks a business card she's taken out of her patent leather handbag, then approaches a door plastered with posters advertising a Jack the Ripper tour. She presses the dirty buzzer on one side of it.

Bryher looks nervously over her shoulder. 'Betty, what is this place?

'You'll see, dear.'

A woman's voice answers and instructs them to go to the top floor. The lift is broken so they make their way up the grubby staircase, past doors with yellowing signs for shipping companies and taxi services. A door with 'CONQUEST INSURANCE' painted on it in peeling gold letters has been left open and inside it they are greeted by a woman of indeterminate age with black-dyed hair and pink lipstick, wearing tight-fitting jeans, a Billy Idol T-shirt, and gold platform shoes.

'Sorry 'bout the lift, ladies. C'mon in,' she says in a heavy cockney accent.

Bryher looks at Betty and mouths, 'Conquest Insurance?' as they follow the woman into an office.

Betty smiles and nods, a streak of pink lipstick on her front tooth.

Oh, my God, Bryher thinks. *This is not good. If Ollie Browne gets his hands on Betty's necklace and shows it to a valuer who recognises the maker's mark, all hell will break loose. Betty will know the true value of her necklace, and I'll never get my hands on it to sell it and get myself out of my mess.*

'Ya want tea, coffee? Please say no, 'cause I'd 'ave ta go down ta the kebab shop ta get milk and my feet are already killin' me.'

'That's all right, dear,' Betty says. 'Bryher is treating me to lunch at Fortnum's later.'

'I am?'

Betty smiles at her. 'You'll love it. All the Americans do.'

Ollie Browne sticks his head around the office door. 'I thought I heard voices. Betty, lovely to see you again.' His eyes widen. 'And Ms Finch.' He steps forward and extends his hand to them both, shaking them vigorously one after the other. 'Wasn't expecting you, but the more the merrier as they say. Come on in.'

He takes a seat in the chair behind a desk on which papers and files are sprawled, and gestures to a pair of scratched and discoloured tulip chairs in front of it. 'Have a seat, ladies. Just don't move around too much in those chairs or you'll end up on the floor. Trust me, I've done it a thousand times.'

Bryher smiles tightly as she and Betty sit down. She glances around the office which is furnished in a motley collection of scuffed and worn mid-century modern furniture and grey filing cabinets.

'You found me okay, then, Betty?' Ollie retrieves a packet of Tic Tacs from his pocket and pops a mint into his mouth.

Betty waves the business card in the air. 'I did indeed. The taxi driver knew the address straight away.'

'I'm not surprised. Downstairs has the best kebabs in London. Cabbies love it. You oughta try one. I recommend the chicken shawarma.' He kisses the tips of his fingers. 'Fantastico.'

'What a lovely idea,' Betty says. 'Perhaps on our next trip into London. We're busy, busy, busy today. Christmas shopping and all that. Shall we get down to business, Mr Browne?'

He holds up a finger. 'Ollie.'

Betty grins broadly, her cheek dimpling. 'Of course. Ollie.' She opens the clasp on her handbag and removes a jumble of jewellery. Bryher's heart skips when she sees the 'B' necklace tangled amongst it. Betty sets the jewellery on top of a stack of papers on Ollie's desk.

Bryher coughs and clears her throat. 'Could I get a glass of water? My throat's a little dry.'

'Oh, sure,' Ollie says. 'No problem. Better than that, I'll get Chantelle to get us some Turkish coffees from the kebab shop as well. They're the best.'

'Oh, I don't think—'

Bryher grasps Betty's hand. 'That would be great, Mr Browne. Thank you. And water. With ice.'

As soon as Ollie leaves, Bryher frowns at her cousin. 'Betty, what's going on? You told me you'd decided to put your jewellery in a safe deposit box at your bank.'

'Oh, I know, but I had a good think about it, and, well, it's such a nuisance having to trot off to the bank every time I want to wear something … I thought having it insured and keeping it at home was the better option.'

'But you never wear the jewellery. Didn't we agree that it's all a bit gaudy?'

'OTT.'

'That's right. OTT.'

'Yes, but you never know, I might want to wear it one day and it's nice to know it's all close by.' She pats Bryher's arm with her gloved hand. 'I'm terribly grateful to you for looking out for me, dear. We're family and I know you care, which touches me, especially after I thought I was all alone in the world for so long.'

Bryher bites her lip. 'Yes, well—'

'You're the one who brought up the idea of insuring the jewellery in the first place, dear. I thought it was a silly idea at first, but what with Marion Livesay's telly getting stolen … well, one can never be too careful, even in Puddleton, can one?'

Ollie enters the office carrying a tray of cardboard coffee cups and a bottle of mineral water, which he sets on the desk. 'Betty's right, Ms Finch. Uh, are you sure you wouldn't rather to be called Bryher? We're all friends here.'

Bryher presses her lips together. 'Ms Finch works for me.'

'Sure,' Ollie says as he hands out the coffee. 'As I was saying, I agree with Betty. Insuring the jewellery is absolutely the right thing to do.' He unthreads the 'B' necklace from the jumble and holds it up. 'Especially this beauty.'

Bryher sets her face into a vision of calm as she watches him examine the necklace, even though her pulse is racing. He turns over the 'B' and squints at the gold. She swallows as she watches him take a jeweller's loupe out of a drawer and inspect the necklace under the magnifying glass.

It's a disaster.

'Hmm, interesting,' he says as he sets down the necklace and the loupe. 'It's definitely a good piece, just as I'd thought. I'd say you should insure it for, oh, £15,000. I'd get one of my valuers to look at it … but, yeah, I don't think we'd be far off £15,000.'

Betty claps her hands together. 'Fifteen thousand pounds! Did you hear that, Bryher? Oh, my goodness gracious. And to think that was sitting in a box under my bed all these years.'

'Are you sure about that, Betty?' Ollie asks.

'What do you mean?'

He dangles the necklace from his fingers. 'This isn't the same necklace I saw when I was at your house.'

Bryher's eyes widen. *What does he mean, it's not the same necklace?*

'What do you mean, it's not the same necklace?' Betty says out loud, echoing Bryher's thoughts.

'The one I saw at your house had a maker's mark. A circle with a CH in the middle. This one doesn't.'

'Are you sure about that? I mean, the maker's mark?' Bryher asks, her heart skipping erratically.

He shrugs. 'I suppose I could be mistaken. I only had a glimpse of it before the … tea incident …'

Bryher shifts in the chair. 'Right. Yes, I'm sorry about that. Are you okay?' She meets his gaze as he sets the necklace down on his desk.

'I'm fine. No permanent damage, which my future wife will be happy to know.'

'Perhaps you're confusing this necklace with another one … one you've examined recently, Ollie,' Betty suggests as she retrieves the necklace and slips it into her handbag. 'You must be looking at jewellery all the time.'

'That's true, but—'

'Have a look at these other pieces and let me know what you think,' she says. 'Maybe there's another hidden gem.' Betty giggles. 'Oh, that's a pun, isn't it? A hidden gem in the jewellery. Oh, isn't that funny?'

Bryher smiles tightly as Ollie sifts through the pile of costume jewellery. If this necklace doesn't have a marker's mark, that can only mean one thing. Pieter must have switched it at Betty's house and taken the original. Why would he switch the necklace and not tell her?

She wipes a bead of sweat off her forehead. There must be a good reason. Pieter's one of the good ones, isn't he? He wouldn't betray her. Or would he?

Chapter Thirty-Seven

ANNE

Hever Castle, Kent, England
June 1526

Anne wanders into the parlour reading the letter which has just been delivered to her.

Her mother, Elizabeth, looks up from her embroidery.

'Another letter from your royal suitor, Anne?'

'He is most persistent.' Anne holds up the bracelet which has been enclosed with the letter. 'He's sent me a bracelet with his portrait. If I wear this, people will believe I am the king's mistress. I shall not follow the same path as my sister, Mother. It did her no favours.'

'You are quite wrong. Mary's husband has benefitted greatly from the king's patronage. Just this spring, King Henry granted William the borough of Buckingham. Mary will be most reassured that a secure future has been provided for her children by His Majesty.'

Anne sits down on her father's ornately carved chair at the

head of the heavy oak dining table. 'That is well for William, as he would have been a knight of little consequence without the king's favours. I speak of Mary. She received little but a few trinkets for giving herself to the king.'

Elizabeth Boleyn frowns at her daughter. 'I caution you. Do not speak so about your own sister. It is not meet.'

Anne inspects the fruit bowl and wrinkles her nose at the offerings. 'I often wonder that Mary and I are sisters. We share naught in common but our name, but now that she is a Carey, not even that. She is content to play the country matron away from court. I cannot imagine a more soulless existence.'

'Yet you are here in the Kent countryside.'

'Not by choice, Mother. It is to stir the king's interest. My absence from court forces the king to pursue me in an effort to persuade my return. It is gratifying to know that he suffers in my absence. That he equates this'—she scans the letter—'*fervency*, yes, that's the word, that he equates this fervency with my absence is to my great benefit. He is forced to see my worth as more than a mistress.'

Elizabeth raises a fine auburn eyebrow. 'The king has a queen, Anne.'

'A queen who is past the age to bear the king a son.'

'He has a son in young Henry Fitzroy, upon whom he has granted the duchy of Richmond and Somerset.'

'Henry Fitzroy remains Bessie Blount's bastard.'

'Anne! Watch your tongue. You speak like a fishwife.'

Anne stares at the fireplace, unmoved by her mother's reprimand. 'The king is four and thirty. I have no doubt he wishes for his own legitimate son.'

'You wish Queen Katherine dead? This is treasonous talk. I urge you take care.'

'I wish no such thing. The queen is a pleasant mistress at court, though rather more pious than I feel entirely necessary. I am simply saying that I believe the king may consider ... another option.'

'I take it that you mean this option to be yourself.'

Anne smiles across the table. 'I am in no hurry. I am young. The longer I make the king wait, the older the queen becomes, and the more he may be persuaded to consider the sense of ... this other option.'

Elizabeth sets down her embroidery and regards her daughter. 'You are indeed your father's daughter. Were you a man, I imagine you would become the king's lead counsellor.'

'Yet, I am not a man and I am limited by my sex. The route to power for a woman is through a good marriage.'

Elizabeth laughs. 'You mean to marry the king? I must credit your imagination. When your father returns from London, I will speak to him about finding you a suitable match.'

Anne huffs. 'I had the love of Harry Percy, heir to the Earl of Northumberland, who wished to marry me and I him. Yet Father, despite all his efforts on my behalf, could not persuade that meddling Wolsey and the Earl to agree the match.' She rises from the table and collects the letter and the bracelet. 'I am uninterested in Father's matchmaking. I have found the man I intend to marry, and it is King Henry.'

'And once you achieve this dream, what then?'

Anne smiles as she hands her mother the apple. 'Then I will be Queen Anne, Mother, and I will help him rule England.'

Chapter Thirty-Eight

BRYHER

Pieter's Penthouse Flat, London
December 2024

'Bryher? I wasn't expecting you.'

Bryher pushes past Pieter and throws her coat and her collection of shopping bags onto the hallway bench. 'We need to talk.'

'Of course,' he says as he follows her into the living room. Outside the wall of windows, the lights of the high-rise flats on the south side of the river twinkle in the dark winter night. He holds up the crystal tumbler in his hand. 'I've just poured myself a scotch and water. Would you like one? It's a very good eighteen-year-old single malt.'

'Sure.'

Bryher stands in front of the windows, her arms folded, watching a brightly lit dining boat slide along the oil-black water. Now that she's here, she feels anger and betrayal swirling inside her. Pieter's treated her like a fool. Used her to get his hands on the necklace. He doesn't care about her. Why should he? No one's ever cared about her.

Pieter joins her and hands her the drink.

'Cheers.' She takes a sip and licks her lips.

He looks out the window. 'What did you want to talk to me so urgently about?'

She looks over at him. 'You seriously think I'm an idiot, don't you?'

He jerks his head around. 'What are you talking about?'

'The necklace. What else would I be talking about?' She heads over to the leather sofa and sits down. She looks back at him, tall and handsome against the night skyline. 'You're not the person I thought you were.'

He joins her on the sofa. 'What are you talking about?'

Bryher sets her drink on the marble coffee table. 'I was at Ollie Browne's office today with Betty. You remember him, don't you? Betty's insurance guy?'

Pieter nods and takes a drink. 'He didn't seem very competent to me. I was glad when you told me Betty had decided to put the necklace in a safe deposit box.'

'Yeah, well, she didn't. She set up a meeting with Mr Browne today and dragged me along. I thought we were going Christmas shopping. She's decided she wants to insure it instead and keep it in her house with her other jewellery.'

Pieter frowns and sets down his drink. He leans back against the sofa cushions. 'That's not good. If word gets out about that necklace possibly being the real one, Betty may become a target. It's not safe for her to have the necklace in her house.'

'Oh, I agree. The thing is, when he examined it today, he said it didn't have a maker's mark.'

Pieter's expression stiffens. 'Really?'

'Yes, really. The necklace Betty had today isn't her necklace. It's a good copy, he said. Worth around fifteen thousand pounds. He knew it wasn't the necklace he saw at Betty's.'

Pieter frowns. 'I see.'

'Betty was delighted though. Fifteen thousand pounds is a lot of money. She has no idea her necklace has been switched. Why did you switch it with your copy when we were at Betty's? Why didn't you tell me? How can I trust you?'

Pieter scrutinises Bryher for a long moment. 'I'm sorry, Bryher. Believe me, I had every intention of telling you. I was just waiting for the right time.'

She narrows her eyes. 'The time seems right to me now.'

Pieter sighs heavily and nods. 'Betty's necklace belongs in a museum.'

'A museum? Who are you to decide this kind of thing?'

'I'm a medieval jewellery expert. Betty's necklace *is* the real one. I know it. It shouldn't be in private hands. It should be on display for the world to see. Hiding it away is like hiding away the *Mona Lisa*.'

'It's not your call. It's Betty's necklace and I want it back.'

Pieter reaches over and brushes his fingers along Bryher's cheek. She turns her head away and he drops his hand. He picks up his drink and swirls the amber liquid around in the glass.

'Isn't it better this way? You said Betty is thrilled with the appraisal. Owning the real necklace would only be a burden to her. The replica she has is excellent, and you're right. It's the one I made. Identical in every way but for the maker's mark. I couldn't bring myself to copy that. It felt like a betrayal to my ancestor, Cornelis Hayes.'

'So you can't betray your ancestor, a dead guy, but you can betray me. And Betty.'

He swallows the last of his drink and sets down the empty glass. 'It's not like that. This is an exciting find. It's beyond you or me or Betty. Cornelis Hayes made that necklace for the Boleyns, and you and Betty are descendants of the Boleyns. Somehow, the necklace got passed down to Betty through all these centuries. I needed to borrow it to have it examined by another expert who values jewellery for the big auction houses. He agrees with me. He believes it's the real necklace, too.'

Bryher rises and walks over to the windows. *So Betty's necklace is the real thing. The actual Boleyn heirloom.* A shiver runs up her spine.

Keeping her expression impassive, Bryher turns to face Pieter. 'Where is it?'

'Where do you think?' He rises from the sofa and walks over to the display cabinet. After unlocking the drawer, he removes the red velvet box, then crosses the room and joins Bryher at the windows. 'Open it.'

Bryher lifts off the lid. Inside, the large creamy pearls and the gold 'B' of the pendant sit nestled upon a bed of white satin. She takes it out and hands it to Pieter.

'Put it on me.'

'Of course.'

She feels the smooth pearls and the heavy 'B' drape around her neck as he fastens the clasp. She presses her hand against the 'B' and inspects her reflection in the window. It is like looking at a ghost. A ghost of a lost queen.

Pieter comes up behind her and rests his hands on her shoulders. 'It looks like it was made for you.'

'I know. It's weird.'

He presses a soft kiss on her neck. 'I've had an idea.'

Bryher shuts her eyes, surrendering to the waves of pleasure spreading through her body. 'What idea?'

'What if you take the necklace back with you to the States?' he says as he traces her neck with his lips. 'Put it in a safe deposit box there. In a few months, you discover it in your late mother's belongings. You have it authenticated and valued. I can recommend some excellent people over there to do it. Then, I'll broker a handsome deal with a major museum where it will be put on display for the world to enjoy.' He turns her in his arms and his blue gaze sweeps over the contours of her face.

'Your money worries will be over and my ancestor will be recognised in history as the maker of the famous Boleyn necklace.'

'What about Betty?'

'Betty has the copy I made. A lovely necklace worth a considerable amount of money. She knows that you're a Boleyn descendant as well. When you "find" the real necklace, she'll accept the story that the necklace you discover in the US was your mother's.'

'Right.' She raises an eyebrow as she scrutinises him. 'What's in all this for you?'

'Seeing Cornelis Hayes acknowledged.'

'Sure, but I asked what's in it for *you*.'

He shrugs. 'I will have brokered a major deal for an iconic piece of history. I imagine I will have my pick of directorships of any major museum of my choosing.'

Bryher pushes away from his embrace and shakes her head. 'No, Pieter. We can't do this.'

'Why not? Surely, this is the best solution for everyone?'

'It's not our necklace. It's Betty's.'

She heads into the entrance hall and picks up her coat. She reaches into a pocket and takes out the replica necklace. 'Here you go,' she says as she lays it on the hall table. 'I'd say it's a fair trade.'

'Bryher, wait. Don't go like this. I'm sorry. I thought you'd understand. I thought it was the best solution for everyone. Don't you think the world should be able to see this necklace? We can work through this.'

He steps towards her and brushes a stray strand of hair away from her cheek. He leans closer. 'Don't go. Please. Stay. We'll figure something else out.'

Bryher feels her heart thrum as Pieter's warmth envelopes her, like a welcome gust of heat from an open door on a cold day. Maybe Pieter's right. Maybe she's misunderstood his intentions.

He'd just been trying to solve the situation with the necklace the best way for everyone.

She looks at his deep-set blue eyes watching her, pleading with her, and she feels like she is being seen for the first time in a very long time.

She nods. 'I'll stay, but on one condition.'

Pieter smiles, and it is like the sun breaking through a cloud. 'Absolutely.'

'You don't know my condition yet.'

'It doesn't matter.' He runs his fingers over the three heavy pearls at the base of the 'B'. 'You have me.'

'Make me some Belgian pancakes. I'm starving.'

Chapter Thirty-Nine

SIR THOMAS & ELIZABETH BOLEYN

Hever Castle, Kent, England
December 1526

'Nancy! Do not detain the king's post boy with your idle chatter. I have no doubt he has many stops yet to make.'

The servant takes the letters from the flush-faced rider and shuts the heavy wooden door. She curtsies to her mistress. 'I beg pardon, milady. He had a thirst and I asked if he wished a cup of ale.'

'He may take his ale at the alehouse when he changes horses. We are not a charity.'

'Yes, milady.'

Elizabeth sifts through the stack of sealed letters. 'Fetch a pitcher of cider from the kitchen and bring it to the parlour with two cups. Tread lightly. Your master is in a foul mood. He received the bill for Anne's dress and hood for the king's New Year revels yesterday and I fear that more bills have arrived today.'

Nancy curtsies again. 'Yes, milady.'

Elizabeth crosses the great hall and opens the door into the parlour. Sir Thomas sits in his chair at the head of the dining table, scowling as he scratches figures into a ledger.

'What is it? Can you not see that I am busy?'

'It is the eve of the New Year, Thomas. Can the accounts not rest until after Twelfth Night?'

'I would not need to be at the accounts at all were it not for the profligacy of my wife and daughter. It is well Mary is married and is her husband's burden now.'

Elizabeth sets all the letters on the table in front of her husband, but for one, which she waves in front of him. 'Mary has written.'

'Nothing from Anne or George?'

'Nothing, but they are both involved in the court revels.'

Sir Thomas grunts. 'For which they both might thank me. I have spoken many good words on their behalf into the ear of the king.'

Nancy knocks on the door and enters with a pitcher and two pewter cups which she silently sets on the table. When she has left, Elizabeth picks up a cup and fills it with golden cider. She hands the cup to Thomas and fills the second cup for herself.

'George has benefitted well from your efforts. His young wife Jane enjoys a good home at Grimston Manor in Norfolk and you did well to persuade the king to appoint him Royal Cup-bearer after that meddling Cardinal Wolsey cut him from serving the king in the Privy Chamber.'

'Wolsey sees the Boleyns as rivals for the king's favour.' He takes a drink of cider. 'It must curdle his blood to see our George at the king's side at every meal.'

Elizabeth sits in a chair by the leaded window and sets down her cup of cider on the ledge. 'I warrant Wolsey is not pleased with the attention the king has been bestowing on Anne. The more

Anne plays at resisting the king, the more he pursues her. She has confided in me that she intends to become the next queen.'

Sir Thomas laughs. 'I wonder what Queen Katherine would make of that.'

'The queen is beyond the years to bear a child and the king wishes for a legitimate son and heir. Were I the queen, I would take care. Anne could bend an oak to her will. She has decided on the king, and, mark my words, the king she shall have.'

She nods at the piles of letters. 'I noted a letter from the jeweller, Master Hayes. You may wish to pour another cup of cider before you open it.'

Sir Thomas reaches for the pitcher. 'Blasted girl. Anne will have me in the poorhouse.'

Elizabeth opens up Mary's letter. 'Ah, all is well with Mary. She regrets that she is kept at Greenwich over the holidays as William's new appointment as Keeper of Placentia Palace means he is much involved with the staging of the revels.' Elizabeth scans the letter. 'She says that the two children are well and healthy, and the king's daughter, Princess Mary, has taken it upon herself to take little Cate on walks around the palace gardens. She calls the child "her own dear little sister". What make you of that, Thomas?'

Sir Thomas frowns as he reads the jeweller's letter. 'It is but a figure of speech. It means nothing.'

'She says here of Anne that she has indeed captured the king's eye, but that she is deaf to Mary's pleas to tread carefully. Anne has made little effort to visit Mary since her return to court, and in Mary's view, Anne is far more concerned with bewitching the king than with playing the good aunt.'

Elizabeth sets down Mary's letter, and takes a sip of her cider. 'It seems our daughters are once again at odds. Two peas from the same pod could not be more different. Would you not agree, husband?'

'Three pounds, twelve shillings and sixpence for Mistress Anne's bill?' Sir Thomas reads. 'What in the name of Robin Goodfellow did Anne spend almost four pounds of my money on with Cornelis Hayes?'

Chapter Forty

BRYHER

Puddleton, England
Christmas Day 2024

Bryher sneezes awake. She raises her head from the pillow and squints across the bedcover at Bijou who is busy kneading her belly. She yawns and reaches out to tickle the cat's chin.

Bijou miaows and settles down on the covers in the indentation between Bryher's legs. Bryher lies back against the pillow as the cat purrs in the warm nest of the bedcovers. She looks around the bedroom where the plain furniture and Betty's doll collection look shabby in the weak winter sunshine filtering in through the venetian blind.

Bryher yawns. *So much for the white Christmas Betty's radio has been promising. Merry Christmas to me.* She stretches and debates getting up before she pulls the cover up to her chin and snuggles into the pillows. For the first time in a long time, she allows her mind to drift back to the Christmas she was six years old. She'd been obsessed with becoming a ballerina that year, had insisted on wearing her hair in a bun to school every day. She'd pestered her mother to enrol her in ballet classes at the local YWCA. Marnie had gone to a few lessons, too, before she'd got bored and taken up a hip-hop class instead.

More than anything, Bryher had wanted a tutu, in pale pink satin with a white tulle skirt. Just like her ballet teacher, Miss Hoff, had worn the evening they'd had their Easter recital.

Every time she'd mentioned the tutu to her mother in the months leading up to Christmas, the answer had been the same. 'Put it in your letter to Santa and be a good girl.'

So, Bryher did exactly that.

On Christmas Day she'd run down the stairs to the Christmas tree, knowing that Santa must have brought it.

She'd torn open her presents – a 'Lead Singer Barbie' complete with guitar and thigh-high black boots, a colouring book and coloured pencils, a Spice Girls T-shirt. But no tutu.

'Marnie, darling,' her mother had said after pulling out a box from behind the plastic tree. 'Here's one addressed to you from Santa.'

Marnie had pounced on the festively wrapped box like a mouse on cheese. Off came the reindeer paper, off came the red bow, off came the box lid, and the white tulle had erupted from the box like a blossoming flower.

'Oh, Mom!' Marnie had said as she'd held up the glorious ballet tutu. 'Look what Santa brought me! I love it! I'm going to put it on right now!'

'Isn't it lovely, dear? You must have been a very good girl.'

Bryher had burst into tears. 'But, Mom,' she'd cried. 'The tutu was at the top of *my* Santa's list. Marnie doesn't even like ballet.'

'Bryher,' her mother had said. 'When would you ever wear a tutu? You'll never be a ballerina. Ballerinas are beautiful, like your sister. She can wear it to parties. If you're nice to her, maybe she'll let you borrow it. Now go play with your Barbie and be thankful for your own gifts.'

That was the day Bryher stopped believing in Santa. She never went back to ballet class again. Thinking of it now, she feels the same aching disappointment she did that that Christmas.

A knock on her bedroom door is followed by Betty popping her head into the room.

'Merry Christmas, dear! Get up, sleepy head. I'm cooking up scrambled eggs and black pudding and Marion's brought over mince pies. I've even made coffee for you instead of tea. Real ground coffee, not instant. Oh my, it was dear! But it's Christmas, so never mind. Bijou! There you are. Come get some breakfast. I've got you fresh trout from the fishmongers. You'll like that, won't you, precious?'

Chapter Forty-One

ANNE

Placentia Palace, Greenwich
New Year's Day 1527

Anne stands with Queen Katherine's ladies-in-waiting in the King's Presence Chamber where trestle tables dressed with crimson cloth and laden with New Year's gifts for the king have been arranged around the wood-panelled room. Large tapestries depicting Henry's triumphs at Thérouanne and the Field of the Cloth of Gold hang from the walls, and fires warm the room from two immense stone fireplaces. She clutches her hands together within the folds of her flowing sleeves, worrying the rings on her fingers. Amongst the gifts is the one she has had commissioned from Cornelis Hayes, the jewelled silver-gilt pendant of a woman on a ship in a stormy sea.

She hides her nerves as she watches Henry pass along the tables, picking up an item to admire here, commenting about some impressive craftsmanship there. Her breath hitches, though, as he comes to her gift, which she has nestled amongst a bed of white satin. He picks up the jewel and examines it closely, smiling as he reads the white enamel words, '*Cherchant un refuge*' – 'In search of a refuge' – on the ship's hull. He glances over at her, his smile broad.

She looks to her right, where Queen Katherine stands observing the ritual. For a moment, their eyes meet, the queen's blue eyes as cold as the winter wind howling at the windows. Anne casts her gaze down and composes her face into a picture of propriety.

It has been a long year of playing cat-and-mouse with Henry, but Anne is ready to permit him to woo her in earnest to be his wife, and not simply as a plaything to be discarded. She will be his wife, his queen, the mother of his future heir, but she will not be his lover. He is her safe harbour in a stormy sea, if he is in earnest.

The next day a page slips a note to her as she is walking to her chambers after breakfast. She hurries to her room and rips open the seal which bears the king's signet.

Anne,

For so beautiful a gift, I thank you right cordially. The proofs of your affection are such that they constrain me ever truly to love, honour and serve you. Henceforth, my heart shall be dedicated to you alone, greatly desirous that my body could be as well, as God can bring it to pass if it pleaseth Him, whom I entreat once each day for the accomplishment thereof, trusting that at length my prayer will be heard.

Written with the hand of the secretary who in heart, body and will is your loyal and most ensured servant.

H autre ne cherche rien qu' AB

Anne laughs in delight and clutches the letter to her bosom. *Henry searches for no other than Anne Boleyn.* Around her initials he has drawn a heart.

She shall be Queen of England. And she shall have a voice.

Chapter Forty-Two

BRYHER & MARNIE

Los Angeles, California
April 2005

'Where is she? Where's my sister?'

Bryher looks across the ice-skating rink where she's filming a chewing gum commercial, to see Marnie push through the crowd of extras to the rink.

'Bryher! Bry!' Marnie shouts as she stumbles onto the ice. She's wearing thigh-high stiletto boots over her tight, low-rise jeans, a white patent leather jacket and sunglasses. And she is obviously drunk. 'Babe! It's my birthday! Aren't you gonna wish me happy birthday!'

'Cut!' the director yells. 'Will somebody get her off the ice?'

Bryher waves her hands. 'I've got it! Just give me a minute.'

'All right, everybody,' he shouts. 'Take five while we get this bozo out of here.'

'She's no bozo!' Bryher shouts back. 'She's my sister.'

The director holds up his hands. 'Whatever. Sort it out.' He taps his gold watch. 'Time is money.'

Bryher skates over to Marnie and pulls her to her feet. 'What are you doing here? I'm working.'

Marnie loops her arm over Bryher's slender shoulders. 'You should be in school, babe. You're only thirteen. Don't mess up like I did.'

Bryher shuffles off the ice with her sister and shoves her into a spectator's seat. 'I'm not messing up. I'm doing home schooling now.'

Marnie laughs. 'What? Mom's teaching you at home? She knows nothing about anything, except how to exploit her kids and dump them when they stop making her money.'

'Don't talk about Mom like that. I have a tutor.'

'Ooh, a tutor. Look at you.' Marnie reaches into her jacket pocket and takes out a spliff. 'Got a light?'

Bryher takes the spliff and stuffs it into the jacket of her puffer jacket. 'You can't smoke that here.'

'Look at you being a goody-two-shoes. I've seen you smoke.'

'Yes, well, not when I'm working.' Bryher looks over her shoulder at the crowd of extras who are watching them like rubberneckers at a car crash. She takes hold of Marnie's arm. 'Come on. Let's go outside.'

She staggers to the exit, Marnie leaning heavily on her shoulder. Once they're outside, Marnie props herself against the building's brick wall and gestures at Bryher.

'Give it back. It's my birthday and I can smoke weed if I want to.'

'Not here you can't. I'll give it back when you leave.'

'I've got nowhere to go.'

'What are you talking about? Weren't you seeing that guy?'

'Sure, I was seeing that guy, and that other guy, and …' Marnie grunts. 'Who cares? They're all the same. They just want sex.'

'Stop. I don't want to hear about this stuff.'

'Oh, come on. Don't tell me you're still a virgin, after all the parties you've gone to with me and Mom.'

'I'm only thirteen. I'm still a kid.'

Marnie sighs. 'Yeah, well, enjoy it while it lasts, because being an adult sucks.'

'You're not even an adult yet, you're seventeen, Marnie.'

'Seventeen going on forty.' She looks at Bryher with her beautiful eyes. 'Do you have any idea what it's like being a has-been at seventeen?'

'Don't talk like that. If you clean yourself up, you can start going on auditions again.'

'Yeah? Why would I want to go on auditions, only to be humiliated by someone like you?'

'They're just commercials. You could study acting and go for parts on TV and in the movies. You're good enough.' Bryher scrutinises her sister, taking in the dishevelled golden hair and the dark circles under Marnie's eyes. 'You just need to stop the drinking and the drugs and start over.'

'Babe, the drinking and the drugs and the guys are what keep me going.' Marnie holds out her hand. 'Come on, give me the spliff. I'm going. I don't want to disturb the big star. I'm surprised Mom's not here watching her cash cow.'

'She's at home. She wasn't feeling well.' There's no way she's telling Marnie that their mother is sleeping off another gin bender. Bryher hands her sister the spliff, and Marnie pockets it.

'Happy birthday, Marnie.'

'Thanks, babe.'

'Where are you going?'

'Don't worry about me. I'm sure I'll find a party somewhere to celebrate.'

Chapter Forty-Three

ANNE

Placentia Palace, Greenwich, England
May 1527

I t is a fine May afternoon, and the garden at Placentia Palace is alive with birdsong and the sweet scent of lilac and early-flowering roses. Anne strolls down the gravel path towards a bench shadowed by a rose arch, smiling as she rereads the king's January letter.

> *… Henceforth, my heart shall be dedicated to you alone, greatly desirous that my body could be as well, as God can bring it to pass if it pleaseth Him, whom I entreat once each day for the accomplishment thereof, trusting that at length my prayer will be heard.*

She folds the letter and slips it into the embroidered silk bag hanging from her gilt girdle. Picking a red rose off the winding shoots the gardener has tied to the wooden arch, she holds it up to her nose and breathes in its heady perfume. Life is good. The king has just this past month elevated her father to the peerage as the Viscount Rochford and asked him to lead the English delegation in the signing of the treaty with France, promising King Henry's daughter, the Princess Mary, in marriage to the French king's second son. The Boleyns' star is rising, and Anne has no doubt that she is the impetus to her family's growing fortunes.

'My lady Anne! Oh, happy day that I chance upon you in such a pretty place.'

Anne looks up to see the handsome figure of thirty-five-year-old King Henry striding down the path, his face flushed and his leather boots dusty from a recent ride in the park.

'Your Majesty,' she says as she curtsies.

The king takes hold of her hand and draws her to her feet. His gaze traces her face as he smiles. He holds up her hand to his lips and kisses the soft pale skin. 'How can it be that even the rose's beauty pales against the fairness of my own sweet lady?'

Anne looks down coyly. 'Your Majesty does the rose a great injustice.'

Henry places his fingers under Anne's chin and raises her face until their gaze meets. 'The rose, as am I, is but a servant to the grace of my lady Anne. Come, sit with this poor king for a moment. I am weary of the company of men and wish to bask in the warmth of your smile.'

Anne joins the king on the bench. 'Did you enjoy a good ride in the park this morn, sire?'

'I did. Your brother George bagged a deer which will be on the table for dinner tomorrow.'

'George has always enjoyed the hunt. When we were children, he was forever bringing home rabbits and pigeons he had caught in the forest around Hever.'

'The Boleyns are a family of great heart.' Henry brushes his fingers along Anne's cheek. 'And none more so than you, fair Anne. How I long for the day that I call you my wife,' he lowers his voice to a whisper, 'and take you to my bed to worship you as you deserve.'

'Sire, I wish this, too.' She wipes a bead of sweat from Henry's brow. 'How goes your conversations with Cardinal Wolsey on the subject of the annulment of your marriage to Queen Katherine?'

Henry sits back against the wooden bench and sighs. 'It progresses. I have expressed to the cardinal my doubts of the validity of my marriage to my late brother's widow. He is arranging a church court to test the lawfulness of this marriage a fortnight hence. My argument is that I am in fact related to the queen through her marriage to my late brother and we should never have been wed. The difficulty is establishing whether the queen's marriage to my brother Arthur had been consummated. If, as the queen declares, she was untouched when Arthur died, my argument fails and I shall have to find another route to the annulment.'

Anne wafts the rose under her nose. 'Then I shall pray for the church court to judge favourably in this regard.'

'That is well, my heart.' He takes the rose from Anne and tucks it into a slit in his crimson velvet doublet. 'How fare you for the revels tomorrow eve after the jousts? Master Holbein has painted the ceiling of the temporary banqueting hall with all the stars and planets of the heavens, and crafted a triumphal arch depicting the Battle of the Spurs at the entrance to the theatre. I have a thought to commission him to paint my portrait.'

Anne strokes Henry's hand with her own. 'I look forward to playing one of the fair damsels awaiting rescue from the rugged mountain in the masque, sire. It promises to be a jolly eve. I wish only that we could sup together, but that is the role of your queen.' She sighs. 'I shall be sat amongst the chattering ladies and forced to turn a sympathetic ear to my sister as she recounts yet another tale of my nephew's adventures with mashed carrots.'

Henry grasps Anne's hands. 'Though we may not sup together, I shall dance with none other but you, Anne.'

'The queen will be displeased.'

'The queen finds pleasure in displeasure.'

'The court will talk.'

'I care not what the idle tongues at court witter about. I am the king and above such janglings.'

'Yet I am not protected by the cloak of monarchy.'

Henry's gaze grows serious. 'Anne, should any person speak ill of you, they will have my wrath rained upon their heads. Be certain about it.'

Mary's eyes alight on the shining golden 'B' of the pendant hanging from Anne's neck as her sister enters the banqueting hall.

'I can't believe my eyes.'

Her husband, William, looks up from the timings he has scribbled beside his list of the evening's events. 'What can't you believe?'

'Anne. She wears my pendant though she had sworn upon Robin Goodfellow's grave that she had no knowledge of its whereabouts after I lost it.'

'Perhaps you left it at Hever and she found it there.'

Mary's blue eyes narrow as she watches her sister flirt with the courtiers on her way to the table where Queen Katherine's ladies-in-waiting are seated. 'She did not find it at Hever. Both she and I know how she came to have it.' Mary tosses her napkin onto the table and rises from the bench. 'Excuse me, William, I shall return shortly.'

Mary hurries past the guests streaming into the hall and catches up to her sister. She grabs Anne by the arm. 'Anne, wait.'

Anne spins around and stares in surprise at Mary. 'Mary? What ails you?'

Mary's fine eyebrows rise. 'What ails me, sister?' She nods at the pendant around Anne's neck. 'You are wearing my pendant, though you'd sworn to me you had no knowledge of its whereabouts.'

Anne rolls her eyes. 'It is the family pendant, Mary. I have as much right to wear it as you.'

'Our father gave it to me before I left for the French court. It is *my* pendant and I demand its return.'

'Mary, you are embarrassing yourself. I entreat you to return to your good husband. Look, the queen observes us. Father would be most displeased if word were to reach him of your gracelessness in the queen's presence.'

Mary glances at the head table where Queen Katherine is, indeed, watching them with a look of opprobrium. She sets her jaw and looks back at her sister.

'I shall return to my husband, but this matter is not closed. It is my pendant and I expect its prompt return, else I shall raise the issue with our father who knows full well for whom he had it crafted.'

From atop the painted wood and plaster mountain, Anne, along with the other court ladies, waves at the courtiers clothed in cloth of gold who are scaling the rough-hewn boulders. She has dismissed the tiff with her sister from her mind; instead she shouts encouragement to her brother, George, who is climbing, as agile as a goat, towards the squealing Madge Shelton, despite the thunderous look directed at him by his young wife, Jane, on the opposite mountain peak.

An arm reaches out to grab Anne and she screams in delight as she is lifted from her perch. The rugged, bearded face of the king's trusted friend, Sir Henry Norris, breaks into a laugh. 'Mistress Anne, I have come to rescue you on the king's order. I entreat you to come with me, else I will end my days headless on Tower Hill at the king's pleasure.'

'Oh, good sir, I would not have that,' Anne says as she loops her arms around the courtier's shoulders. 'You have a fine head which sits well upon your shoulders.'

Norris grasps Anne's waist and begins edging his way down the craggy plaster cliff. 'That is well, for upon my shoulders I prefer my head to rest.'

At the bottom of the mountain, the courtier delivers Anne to King Henry and, doffing his ostrich-feathered golden cap, he bows before making a prudent retreat.

Henry leads Anne away from the clamour of the masque's participants towards the table of the queen's ladies-in-waiting. She smiles like a smug cat as she takes in the raised eyebrows and whispers of the court at the king's open attention to her.

'Sire, it appears we have caught the attention of the court. It is well that the queen has retired to her chambers.'

Henry squeezes Anne's hand. 'I care not. It is time for all to know the true nature of my heart's desire.'

Anne casts him a flirtatious glance. 'And what is the true nature of His Majesty's heart's desire?'

Henry leans in and whispers, 'To make you my own true wife and queen of all of England.'

Chapter Forty-Four

BRYHER & MARNIE

Los Angeles, California
October 2006

Someone is shaking her awake.

'Bryher! Wake up!'

Bryher opens her eyes to see her mother's bloated and flushed face looming over her. She sits up. 'Mom? What is it?'

'It's Marnie,' her mother says, her breath stale with beer and gin. 'The police have just been here. She's in the hospital.'

'What? What happened?'

Kitty heads towards the door. 'Get dressed.'

Bryher climbs out of bed and heads to the closet. 'But Mom, what happened?'

Kitty turns to Bryher, her hand on the doorknob. 'Overdose. They found her in an alley in Hollywood.'

Bryher stands at the foot of the hospital bed, oblivious to her mother's dramatic wails as the doctor discusses Marnie's condition. Marnie lies under a white sheet, seemingly as lifeless as a mannequin. A mannequin with tubes sprouting out of it, like the shoots of an old potato. Someone has washed her face, and, without the layers of blush, eye shadow, lip gloss and mascara, Marnie looks so much younger than eighteen. Bryher cocks her head as she studies her sister's face. A bruise is growing on Marnie's left cheek and her top lip is cut and swollen. *You'll look like a chipmunk when your cheek swells, Marnie. You'll be bummed about that when you wake up.*

Every now and then the words of one of the doctor's filter through to Bryher. 'Coma … non-responsive … cocaine … heroin … overdose …'

She swallows down the lump that's formed in her throat. *I didn't mean it, Marnie. When I woke up last night to find you going through my purse, I lost it. Trying to steal from me? From your sister? Just to get high?* Bryher rubs away the tears running down her cheeks. *I didn't mean it, Marnie. I don't want you to die.*

Bryher steps away from the bed and grabs onto the back of a chair as she looks at her sister. Anger suddenly flares inside her like dry leaves catching fire. *How could you, Marnie? You had everything I'd ever wanted. Beauty, talent, charisma, Mom's love, and you threw it all away. You stupid, self-pitying idiot. How could you do this to Mom?*

She stares at her sister lying still under the sheet. *How could you do this to me?*

Chapter Forty-Five

ANNE & MARY

Beaulieu Palace, Essex, England
July 1527

The ornately carved oak door to King Henry's private chambers swings open and Queen Katherine sweeps into the room, the silks of her black gown and gable-hooded veil billowing like black sails on a stormy sea. She stops short when she sees Anne seated at the table sharing a dinner of roasted quail, guinea fowl, almond creams and Gascon wine with the king.

The queen glares at Anne with frosty blue eyes. 'My lord, I came to dine with you as a wife with her husband, yet I see my seat has been usurped by your harlot.'

Henry raises up his golden goblet and gestures to an empty seat at the table. 'Come, Katherine, wash your hands at the basin and join us. We shall make a merry trio.'

Anne glances sideways at the king as she sips the ruby wine. She looks back at the queen, whose pale complexion, stamped with the lines of age around her eyes and across her forehead, grows pink with fury. Why the queen insisted on accompanying Henry on his visit to the vastly expanded Beaulieu Palace, where he is meeting with his councillors, her own father amongst them, to discuss the king's divorce, is beyond fathoming. Anne sets down her goblet and brushes her fingers along the pearls and 'B' of the pendant, taking care that the light visibly catches all angles of the emerald ring on her finger – crafted by Cornelis Hayes – that the king had given her as a gift earlier that day. She is no harlot. Though the king entreats her at every juncture, she is resolved. She will be Henry's queen, and only then will she lie with him in his bed.

She smiles slyly at the queen. 'Please, Your Majesty, do join us. The almond creams are delicious.'

Katherine huffs, turns her back on Anne and addresses Henry. 'Sire … Husband … I have heard rumours that I am to be sent to a nunnery.' Her voice breaks and she takes a breath to steady herself. She approaches Henry and grips his arm. 'I am your true and legitimate wife. It is not true that our marriage violates the first degree of affinity through my marriage to your brother, Arthur, for he departed this earth before the marriage was consummated. I was pure when I came to you as your bride.' She glares at Anne who juts out her chin defiantly. 'I am your true and legitimate wife and I will not see my place as your queen usurped by this guinea hen.'

A cloud darkens Henry's face. 'Do not speak of Mistress Boleyn in this manner. I will not permit it.' His eyes narrow as he glowers at his wife. 'Is that understood?'

The queen bites her lip, refusing to respond.

Henry rises and slams his hand upon the table, almost spilling his wine. 'Katherine, is that understood?'

'I shall leave you to your entertainment, husband. My appetite has abandoned me.' Casting Anne a glare, the queen gathers up the voluminous silk of her gown and heads towards the door, slamming it loudly behind her.

Anne looks over at Henry. 'We would do well not to underestimate the queen, my love. She is determined to stand her ground in the matter of your divorce.'

Henry pushes away his plate of guinea fowl bones. 'She fights a losing battle. I should never have been persuaded to marry my brother's widow. Leviticus states in the Bible that "If a man shall take his brother's wife, it is an unclean thing and they shall be childless". This is a divine law, Anne. The pope had no power to waive Leviticus's injunction when Katherine and I married. The marriage is unlawful, and it shall be annulled.'

'Yet, you are not childless, sire.'

Henry takes a drink of his wine as he frowns. 'A girl. My daughter is no heir to the Crown of England.' Henry sighs. 'I love my daughter, for she is my flesh and blood, yet she bears the brand of illegitimacy through my unlawful marriage to Katherine.' He reaches for Anne and runs his fingers along her cheek. 'You shall be my queen, Anne, and our son shall be my heir. Be assured that no one shall stand in our way in this matter. Not even the pope himself.'

Henry leans over and presses his lips against Anne's. He traces the line of her jaw with hot kisses and whispers as he grasps her hand against the velvet his doublet. 'Come lie with me, my heart. I yearn for your kisses and the feel of your sweet body against mine. Do not torture me with your reserve.'

Anne pulls away. 'I cannot, my love. When I am your wife and your queen, then we shall enjoy all the pleasures of Eden, this is my true promise to you.'

Henry sucks in a deep breath and sits back on his chair. 'You cause my blood to run as thick as honey. It is a sweet torture to have you by me, yet not possess you.'

Anne rests her hand upon his and rubs his bejewelled fingers with her thumb. 'I shall not tarnish God's plans for us by laying with you when you are yet wed to another. I wish our marriage to be right and good in His eyes so that no one may say otherwise.

We must ensure that our son's legitimacy as your heir is incontestable.'

Henry smiles. 'You speak the truth, my heart, as much as I regret the delay.'

He rises and walks over to an enormous linen-fold coffer emblazoned with his coat of arms. He removes a small red velvet box and brings it over to Anne. 'For you, my love, to remind you of our enduring connection.'

'Another gift?' She lifts her finger, on which the emerald sparkles. 'It is not yet one day that I have enjoyed the adornment of this lovely ring.'

Henry persists. He holds out the velvet box. 'But Master Hayes has surpassed himself with this endeavour.'

Anne smiles in concession. She opens the box and gasps at the sight of a pearl necklace from which a heavy gold pendant set with rubies and diamonds forms the entwined initials H and A. She lifts the necklace from the box. 'Oh, my love. This is a beautiful thing.'

'It is time for you to retire your pretty Boleyn pendant. You are the king's great love, and I entreat you to wear this in my honour so that all shall know that we are united forever and all time.'

'Mary! Good,' Anne greets her sister the following day. 'William said I would find you out in the gardens with the children.'

Mary Boleyn squints against the sun at the fashionable figure of her sister approaching her through the palace's new rose garden. She hands the Batholomew doll to three-year-old Cate, instructing her to play with her younger brother, and rises from the clipped lawn.

'Anne? I thought you would be out hunting with the king as is your custom.'

'Not today. I wished to speak to you.'

'Did you? That is a surprise. I thought you had no time for anyone but the king.' Mary brushes grass clippings off the blue silk of her kirtle. 'Our father is very well pleased with you. He serves you up to me as an ideal which I failed to achieve when I had the chance.'

Anne gestures to the grand structure of the renovated palace. 'You have done well enough for yourself. When you are not in residence at Placentia Palace, you enjoy the privilege of living in Beaulieu Palace as the wife of its keeper.'

'The wife of the palace's keeper is not good enough in the eyes of our father. You know that as well as I. Now that I am William's wife, he ignores me and devotes all his attention to you and George.'

'Oh, poor Mary. I would feel sorry for you, yet I don't. You have had all the advantages I have had and more. You were always the beauty of the family, the eldest daughter of a respected royal courtier and ambassador. You attracted the notice of both the French and English kings, long before I came onto the scene. What I would have done had I been blessed with all your advantages! And yet, here am I, betrothed to the King of England, and you, the wife of a simple courtier.' Anne shrugs. 'It is a wonder to me how the wheels of fate turn.'

Little Henry Carey tumbles over onto the gravel and bellows out a wail. Mary hurries over and hugs him, distracting him with a soothing melody. She looks over at her sister as the toddler settles.

'What is it that you wished to speak to me about? It is time for the children's supper. I don't wish to tarry much longer.'

Anne unties a black velvet pouch hanging from her gilt girdle. She holds it out to Mary. 'I thought you might wish to have this. I no longer have use of it.'

Mary kisses her son on his head and, rising, takes the pouch from Anne. She opens it and pulls out the pendant.

'The Boleyn pendant? You have finally seen fit to return it to me, its rightful owner?' Her eyes flick to the new pendant around Anne's neck. 'Ah, I see. H and A. Of course, you no longer have need of this modest pendant.'

'You speak the truth. The king gifts me with jewels and houses and gowns such that I have no wants. Have your pendant back. Keep it for little Cate, if you wish, for I have no further need of it.'

Mary threads her fingers through the lustrous pearls. 'Indeed. I shall keep it for Cate. It is well that she knows that Boleyn blood courses through her veins ... along with the king's.'

Anne's eyes flash. 'You are never to say such a thing again. If anyone suspects that Cate is the king's daughter, my relationship with Henry will be labelled incestuous and all our father's and my efforts will be for naught. Cate is and has always been a Carey, is that understood? Never speak such a slur against the king again, else ... else ...'

Mary's blue eyes grow icy. 'Else what? I speak the truth. Cate is the king's daughter, just as is the Princess Mary. Take care how you treat me, else the truth will out.'

She picks up Henry and takes her daughter by the hand. 'Now, I must bid you farewell. The children are hungry, and I am weary of this conversation.'

Chapter Forty-Six

BRYHER

Borehamwood, England
January 2025

Bryher scans her loyalty card at the Costa coffee counter in the train station. After grabbing the large oat milk skinny latte, she heads through the morning crush of London-bound commuters up Shenley Road towards the film studios. Except for a few cafés and sandwich shops catering to the early morning crowd, the jumble of clothing stores, restaurants, opticians, pubs and convenience stores that line the road are still closed. She glances at the time on her phone – a quarter past seven already and another fifteen minutes before she reaches the studios. Half an hour late. Another morning facing the wrath of Jeremy.

Her phone rings. 'Margot? It's past midnight there. What are you doing calling so late?'

'Working in bed, hon. No rest for the weary.'

'You're not calling me about Jodie's social media post about her spread with Nick in *Hello!* magazine, are you? Both wearing

"Team Jodie" T-shirts? Did you see the size of the nursery? It's bigger than Betty's house.'

'You've seen that already? Oh, Julian is good. He's taken over Jodie's account and is getting her so much coverage. I've got offers coming in left, right and centre for her.'

'Whose side are you on? You're supposed to be *my* agent. Where are my offers?'

'They'll come, hon. Give it time. Look, what are you doing the sixteenth of February?'

'February? Lying on a beach in Mexico, I hope.'

'That'll have to wait. The producers have to extend the shoot for an extra month so Archie Flanders can fit in his part in the next *Mission Impossible* movie. He couldn't say no to Tom Cruise, could he?'

Bryher groans. 'I hope Tom makes Archie jump out of a plane. He gets nauseous just sitting on a horse.' She sits on a bench and balances the coffee on the wooden seat slats. 'What's the scoop? What's happening in February?'

'I've got you two tickets to the BAFTAs ceremony at the Royal Festival Hall in London.'

'The BAFTAs?

'The British Academy Awards. Why don't you take that dishy historian?'

'Yeah, well, we'll see.'

'Come on, hon, you'd look fab walking down the red carpet with him on your arm. The paps will love it. I can work with that. They want you to present the award for … Wait a minute … here it is. Best Sound Editing.'

Bryher screws up her face. 'Best Sound Editing? What even is that?'

'It's the best I could do at short notice. Your connection to Anne Boleyn is all everyone's talking about since *Do You Know Who I Am?* hit US TV. The producers on *Henry and Anne* managed to get you the BAFTAs gig on the back of it all. They see it as a big

PR opportunity. Hon, it *is* a great PR opportunity. The sex tape thing will be old news, though you've got to admit it's raised the familiarity factor of your Q rating. We just need to work on your popularity factor to get your Q rating up there with Jake and the other A-listers.'

'Jake's back on the A-list already? Really?'

'Well, he was yesterday. Things move fast in Hollywood. He's Captain Tyro, after all. You, I've got to work on. This BAFTAs gig is important.'

Bryher takes a sip of her coffee. 'All right. Fine.'

'Good. Those pictures of you in costume with your darling cousin on set showed up in *People* magazine last week. You're the spitting image of Anne Boleyn when you're in costume and wearing that necklace. The public's lapping it up. They're loving this Bryher-and-Bertha family fest.'

'You mean Betty.'

'Whatever. And those pictures of you and that sexy professor out and about in London – *oo la la*. Forget Jake. Everyone's talking about you and Dr de Beer.'

'Speaking of that, the paps are driving me crazy. You've got to call them off.'

'It's the price of fame, hon. Now, when you're at the BAFTAs you'll be rubbing shoulders with all the British big names. Kate Winslet, Hugh Grant, Helen Mirren, Emily Blunt and Ralph what's-his-name. You'll need something amazing to wear. I'll text you the contact details of the stylist all the British actresses use. He's got Stella McCartney and Victoria Beckham on speed dial.'

'Who's paying for that? I mean, thanks for sending the money to Betty's account earlier, but I've had some big expenses. I've dropped a bomb on clothes at Primark and Zara which are the only places to shop in Puddleton. Don't even get me started about the train fare.'

'Hon, I'll send Betty some more money and I'll get the

production company to reimburse you for your BAFTAs dress. And shoes, you need amazing shoes. Keep the receipts.'

'Louboutins?'

'Louboutins, Blahniks, Choos, whatever your little heart desires.'

Bryher watches a stream of early morning commuters in their black puffer jackets and grey coats rush past her towards the train station. She takes a sip of the tepid coffee and sighs. 'I guess I'm going to the BAFTAs, then.'

'Wonderful! Now hear me out. I've had a brilliant idea. Remember you told me that Betty has one of these copies of Anne Boleyn's necklace? Why don't you wear it when you're presenting?'

'What? Why?'

'I'm going to leak that it's the real Boleyn necklace.'

'What! No!'

'Hon, calm down. Listen to me. Everyone knows from *Do You Know Who I Am?* that you and Betty are descendants of the Boleyns, so everybody will believe it *is* the real necklace. Imagine it: *"Bryher Finch to wear Anne Boleyn's iconic necklace to BAFTAs."* Your picture will be everywhere. You play this right, and I'll have Tarantino and Scorsese knocking down my door for you.'

An image of her waving at the crowd as she makes her way up the red carpet wearing a gorgeous gown and the Boleyn necklace flashes into Bryher's mind. Margot's got a point. It's her chance to step into the international spotlight. Finally. It's what she's always wanted. Isn't it?

'I … I … It's a great idea, but what about the security? What if someone tries to steal it, thinking it's the real necklace?'

'What does that matter? It's just a cheap knock-off, right? Who cares if it gets stolen?'

Bryher winces. *But it's not a knock-off. I'd actually be wearing the real necklace. Why couldn't I have kept my big mouth shut?*

'Betty would care. It's her necklace.'

'So? I'll get the producers to stump up for a replacement. It's not a problem.'

Bryher chews her lip. Pieter would be horrified. 'It was Betty's mother's favourite necklace. Betty's quite attached to it.'

'Then talk to her, hon. Make her say yes. It's going to be amazing, darling.'

Bryher sighs. 'Okay. I'll do my best.' She takes another sip of coffee and glances at her watch. 'Have you heard anything from Jake? He's all over the internet. I didn't know Juno was married.'

'Apparently neither did Jake, until Juno's husband sent some goons around to his place and trashed his car with baseball bats.'

'Oh, my God! Tell me it wasn't the Maybach. I love that car.'

'Who cares about the car? Now Juno's saying she's pregnant with Jake's child.'

'You've got to be kidding.'

'News broke this morning on *TMZ*. I've been fielding calls all day from advertisers dropping Jake's deals. So much for his Q rating. It's been in freefall since the news hit. Like I said things happen fast in Hollywood. A-list today, Z-list tomorrow.'

'They'll come crawling back. Like you said, he's *the* Jake Rogers. He's a multiverse hero.'

'Yeah. Jake does seem to be untouchable, which is a good thing for my bank account. Hon, I've got to go. God knows I need my beauty sleep. Call Rodolpho or Armando or whatever his name is to find you a gown. We want fuckable but not slutty.'

Bryher switches off the call and slides the phone back into her shoulder bag. This would be so much easier if she hadn't slipped the real necklace back into Betty's jewellery box. Now, she'll have to convince Betty to loan it to her for the BATFAs.

I'll break the internet. My name will be everywhere. I'll be the star I was always meant to be. That's a good thing, right?

Chapter Forty-Seven

ANNE & MARY

Hever Castle, Kent
June 1528

A nne shifts aside the *Book of Hours* prayer book she has been reading, and settles down on the bench by the leaded glass window in her bedchamber with the king's latest letter. She has been back at Hever but a week, since the sweating sickness had broken out in London. She'd been sent home on the king's instructions from his palace at Waltham, where he had retreated with the queen and a few of his most trusted courtiers, amongst them her brother George, in an effort to escape the pestilence. She would be with him still if her own silly maid had not taken ill.

Anne gazes out through the leaded glass to the view of sheep grazing on the green fields. Why could the queen not have been sent somewhere else? To another of the king's palaces, or even to a convent? She feels her face flush as the ire at her own exile from the king burns inside her like a stoked fire. *It is not fair! I should be with the king! I am his beloved, not her.*

She breaks the seal on the letter and unfolds the stiff parchment. She smiles as she scans the letter, his worry over her health, his relief that she has shown no signs of illness, but it is the final paragraph that pleases her best.

> ... *I beg you, my entirely beloved, not to frighten yourself nor be too uneasy at our absence; for wherever I am, I am yours, and yet we must sometimes submit to our misfortunes ... comfort yourself, and take courage and avoid the pestilence as much as you can, for I hope shortly to make you sing for joy of your return. I wish you in my arms, that I might a little dispel your unreasonable thoughts.*
>
> *Written by the hand of him who is and always will be yours,*
>
> *Im-H.R.-mutable*

Anne smiles. *The immutable King Henry.* She wipes at the perspiration on her forehead with the back of her hand. Not for the first time she rues the discomfort of her clothing in the heat of the summer. She pulls off her French hood and the linen coif and shakes her head in the stagnant air. She stands and pulls at the brass pins in the silk placard as she staggers to the door.

No! It cannot be. Please, dear Lord, don't let this happen now.

She pulls at the latch and leans against the panelled wall. 'Mother!' she cries out. 'Mother! Help me!'

She collapses onto the wooden floor, her tears mixing with the sweat streaming down her cheeks. *Why now? Why me? Please, sweet Jesus, save me.*

Two days later, Mary enters her lodgings at Placentia Palace laden down with warm white manchet bread, a chunk of buttery Cheshire cheese and a leather bottle of ale. William smiles at her from the bed, where he sits buckling his shoes as the yeasty scent of bread wafts into the room.

'Ah, well done, Mary. My stomach has begun to rumble.'

She sets the food and ale onto the table by the leaded window, where the early morning sun thrusts a bright light over the room's heavy wooden furniture. 'Mine as well, William. It was fair torture to resist the urge to take a bite of bread on the way up from the kitchens.'

He joins her at the table and, picking up a knife, slices through the bread. He chews at the crusty slice as he gazes out at the river which is empty of its normal chaotic stream of boats and ferries. 'Have you had word of your sister and your father at Hever?'

'Mother has written to say the king has sent his own physician to attend to them. It is most concerning. Anne seems to have caught the sweating sickness when they were in the king's party at Waltham Abbey after they fled the disease in London. I thank Our Lord that George has made a recovery, though many are yet succumbing.'

William sits down and pours out a tanker of ale. 'This sweating sickness is a cursed affliction. The king has now shut himself in the tower at Hunsdon House for fear of infection, and dismisses us all from his service. I swear he fears illness more than death itself.'

He slices off two chunks of the cheese and hands one to Mary. 'I rue that we sent Cate and Henry to Hever owing to this pestilence in London now that Anne and your father are there ill with the sweat. May God protect them all.'

Mary fingers the rosary she has looped through the brass chains of her girdle. 'I pray to our Holy Mother Mary every hour for their safety. It is of some small succour that the disease appears to disdain children for those who are strong and fit.' She pours herself a small draught of ale. 'I am worried for the health of Anne and my father, to be sure. It is a fearsome sickness. One can be in full health in the morning and on one's deathbed by mid-day so quickly does it extinguish one's breath.'

William finishes his bread and slaps the crumbs from his hands. 'All the more reason to enjoy life while one is still breathing.' He stands and stumbles against the table.

'William? Take care or you will upset the ale bottle.'

He nods. 'I partook of the ale too swiftly. My head swims.' He takes a deep breath and exhales. 'There. Better. The day is fair, and I am of a mind to go for a hunt in the park. The deer are plentiful this year.'

'Are you certain that is wise? We have been advised to stay within the palace until the sickness passes.'

'The sickness is all but over, Mary. What harm can a day hunting in the fresh air do? I fear I will die of boredom if I stay inside these walls much longer.' He leans over and gives Mary a peck on her cheek. 'I shall be back for supper and I shall have a great hunger for both food and my wife, but not necessarily in that order.'

Mary laughs. 'I shall ensure my presence and a supper fit for our king, my love.'

Williams blows her a kiss from the doorway. 'Wear your Boleyn pendant so that I may remove it and kiss the flesh upon which it rests.'

'Mistress Carey! Open the door! Mary, please, quick!'

Mary drops her needlepoint onto the table and rushes across the room. She opens the latch and jumps aside as Thomas Heneage, a member of the King's Privy Chamber, bursts into the room dragging William.

'William?'

'He took ill during the hunt.'

'Quickly, put him on the bed.'

She rushes ahead of the courtier and pulls open the velvet bed hangings on the large four-poster bed. The burly courtier, one of William's favourite hunting companions, lays William on the bedcover. She feels William's sweat-soaked forehead. 'What's happened? Has he fallen?'

Thomas backs away from the bed and lifts his arm to cover his nose. 'It's the sweat. He was full well until one hour past, and then became convulsed with shivering. He complained of dizziness and said that his head throbbed like he was being hit by an iron. I took him upon my horse and he was overcome by a great exhaustion such that I feared he would unseat us both.'

Mary stares into the terrified eyes of the courtier. 'How can it be? He was full well this morn.'

Thomas shakes his head as he backs away further. 'I will pray to God that he survives the eve. You would be well to leave him and save yourself.'

The door slams. Mary stands in the middle of the room staring blindly at the door's dark wooden planks.

A groan from the bed. 'Mary?'

She sets her face into a smile and turns. 'Yes, my love. I'm coming.'

Mary sits down in the chair by the window where her husband had just that morning enjoyed his final breakfast. Outside, the fine summer day has faded into an inky blackness upon which the slender waning crescent of the moon hangs like a gleaming brooch. She pulls the candlestick with its spitting tallow candle across the table's grooves and indentations and picks at a hardening drip of wax.

William is dead. At twenty-nine she is a widow with two fatherless children. She turns in the chair and looks over at the gentle rise of William's body under the shroud of bedcovers. She fingers the smooth pearls at her neck and takes a deep breath. She shuts her eyes and prays.

Dear Lord, please look kindly upon the soul of my good husband, William Carey, and save me from this terrible sickness so that I may now be both mother and father to our poor, sweet children. Give me the strength to move forward in this life and please, Lord, show your mercy to my father and my sister, Anne, so that they, too, may live to see another day. Amen.

Chapter Forty-Eight

BRYHER

Puddleton, England
January 2025

Betty sets the dish of steaming shepherd's pie on the table and hands Bryher a serving spoon.

'Help yourself, dear. Do you want any brown sauce or sliced bread with that?'

Bryher eyes the mound of mashed potatoes jiggling and plopping on top of the bubbling minced lamb and vegetables, glad for the forgiving stretch jeans she'd bought from the local Primark. She'll just have to treble her Pilates classes when she's back in LA.

She digs out a scoop of the pie. 'You don't happen to have any ketchup, do you?'

'Coming right up, dear, though I fail to understand you Americans and your obsession with ketchup when brown sauce is so much tastier.'

Bryher takes a sip of tap water as Betty returns from the

kitchen carrying bottles of ketchup and brown sauce. Betty settles down on her chair and serves herself a healthy portion of the shepherd's pie. She lays a paper napkin over her tweed skirt and looks across the table at Bryher. 'Go ahead, dear. You mustn't let it go cold on my account.'

Bryher squirts a dollop of ketchup over the mash and sets the bottle back on the table. *Please let her say yes. It's now or never.*

'Betty, uh, I … I had a call from Margot in LA this morning. I've been invited to present an award at the BAFTAs next month, can you believe it?'

'The BAFTAs? Oh, that's marvellous, Bryher. Well done!' Betty frowns over the top of her eyeglasses. 'Oh, dear. You've got a spot of ketchup on your top. Let me clean that up for you.'

Bryher looks down at the miniscule drop of ketchup. 'It's fine, Betty. It's nothing.'

Betty returns with a damp tea towel and dabs at the spot. 'There, much better. We can't have you running about in soiled clothes again, can we?' She sits down in her chair and tosses the tea towel onto the serving trolley.

Bryher pulls the wet cotton away from her chest. 'Thanks.' She picks her fork and digs it into the steaming mound of lamb mince and potatoes. 'You must be looking forward to getting the spare room back once I'm gone.'

Betty helps herself to the brown sauce and squirts the condiment over her meal. 'Dear, you may stay as long as you wish. You're family. I've become used to sewing in the lounge, although I think I may need to increase my eyeglass prescription. The light isn't quite as good as in your room.'

Bryher takes a bite of food and watches Betty enjoying her supper with relish. She takes another sip of water. *Here goes nothing.*

'Margot told me to glam it up for the publicity.' She clears her throat. 'She wants me to wear your "B" necklace, because of me being Anne Boleyn in the mini-series and all that. She thinks it will be good PR.'

Betty butters herself a slice of bread. 'Does she, now?'

Bryher clears her throat again. 'Yes, and it would be. Great PR, I mean.'

'I see, dear.'

'Right, well, you know things haven't been great for me since, well—'

'We don't need to talk about that.'

'I'm … I'm really counting on this mini-series to turn things around for me. The publicity I'd get by wearing your necklace would be a huge help.'

She watches Betty scoop a forkful of the mash onto the bread and take a bite. *Why are you making this so hard, Betty?*

'Do you think I could borrow it … your necklace? Just for the BAFTAs?'

Betty sets down her fork and knife and regards Bryher over the condiment bottles. 'Of course, dear. I think it's a marvellous idea. Mummy would be delighted. Her necklace at the BAFTAs for all the movie stars and telly stars to see! You don't suppose Martin Clunes will be there, do you? That would be the cherry on the cake.'

'Really? Oh, Betty, thank you!' Bryher feels a surge of affection for her cousin. Inspiration hits her like a wave. 'Of course, you're going to need to choose a necklace for yourself,' she says.

'Whatever for?'

'How do you feel about being my date for the BAFTAs?' *Margot will love this.*

Betty presses her hand against her turquoise cardigan. 'Me? Oh, Bryher, oh, yes! Oh, this will be such fun! Wait till I tell the girls at the WI. They will be simply spitting with envy.'

'And cut!' Jeremy calls out the following day at Hampton Court Palace Gardens. 'Great job, ladies. Go grab yourselves some lunch. Someone get the kids, will you? And get that doll away from the girl. It's an expensive prop, not a toy. You're done for the day, Bryher. I need you on set at Elstree tomorrow, at nine sharp, in full costume.' He taps his watch. 'Nine. Not nine-thirty.'

'I got it. I can't help it if the trains keep getting cancelled, can I? Today they said it was due to lack of a driver. I mean, seriously? These are scheduled trains. Don't they have back-ups?'

'Welcome to Britain, Bryher,' Cara Sweet – in costume as Mary Boleyn – intones, as she brushes crumbs from the candy bar she's eating off the blue silk bodice of her gown. 'We live in a constant state of resigned acceptance, that anything that can go wrong, will go wrong at the worst possible time … while it's raining and you've forgotten your umbrella.'

'Bryher, can I talk to you?'

Bryher looks over to see Pieter standing on the path by a giant yew tree.

Cara leans over to Bryher. 'Looks like you've got an admirer, lucky girl. See you at the food van. I'll grab you a sarnie. Tuna or egg mayo?'

'Thanks, Cara. Egg is fine.'

Bryher approaches Pieter. 'Hi. Long time no see.'

He leans forward and presses a kiss on her lips. 'All of twenty-four hours. Did you miss me?'

Bryher laughs. 'More to the point, did you miss me?'

Pieter smiles and hugs her. 'Always.' He stands back and runs his hand through his dark blond hair. 'I need to talk to you.'

'Yes?'

He points to a bench. 'Let's sit down for a moment.'

Bryher shrugs. 'Okay.'

They sit on the bench and Bryher watches the crew deconstruct the fake summer flowers, the arbour, the cameras and the lighting equipment. She looks at Pieter. 'What's up?'

'I've been thinking a lot about Betty's necklace.'

'You and me both.'

'Yes, well. I've got to get this off my chest.'

'Sure. What is it?'

Pieter's eyes sweep over Bryher's face, and a line creases his forehead. 'I was out of line about my museum plan. I should never have presumed to take the matter into my own hands. I … I got carried away. You probably thought I was crazy.'

Bryher tosses the veil of her French hood over her shoulder. 'Yeah, just a little.'

'I didn't mean it that way. I'd just got so excited when I realised I was holding my ancestor's necklace in my hands.'

Bryher laughs. 'How do you think I feel when I wear it? Feel it around my neck? Anne Boleyn's necklace. It's like it resonates with her energy. But that's not a reason to hatch a plan to steal it from Betty.'

'I know. But I hope you understand why I feel it should be in a museum where everyone can admire it. It's a piece of history.'

'You have a good point.' She shrugs. 'Maybe we should tell Betty the truth and let her decide.'

Pieter shakes his head. 'No, it's better that she doesn't know. She might lock it away for good, or give it away to some charity … I don't know. It's too much for someone like her to handle.'

'Someone like her? What do you mean?'

'Betty's an ordinary woman living a simple, contented life. Do you think she really wants the attention and disruption that being known as the owner of the Boleyn necklace would bring? She'd be the target of the press, and the security would be a nightmare for her. She would never be able to wear it or even look at it, because it would need to be kept in a very secure safe in a very secure building. And the insurance policy she'd have to take out on it would be outrageous.'

'Right. I see.' She hadn't thought about these things. Pieter's right. If Betty knew the necklace was the real one, it would ruin her life.

Pieter shifts on the bench. 'I've been thinking about this, about how telling Betty would affect her. I wracked my brain about how to ensure the security of the necklace. That's how I came up with the plan of switching it for the necklace I made. I thought it was the best way to keep both the real necklace and Betty safe.'

'And have the pick of directorships at a major museum.'

'Yes, yes, I know. Like I said, I got carried away. It isn't about that. I want to see the necklace in a museum and, yes, I want to see Cornelis Hayes recognised as the jeweller who made it. That's all.'

He reaches out and rests his hand over hers. 'Bryher, I don't think I'm wrong in wanting this, but I understand if you think I went about it the wrong way.' He threads his fingers through hers. 'I don't want to jeopardise what we have. I want you to know how sorry I am.'

Bryher brushes a brown leaf off her long, embroidered silk sleeve as she swallows a lump in her throat. She's lucky to have a man like Pieter walk into her life just when she'd thought she'd lost everything. She's been holding back from him, she knows it. Enjoying their time together, but not thinking beyond the end of February. But now, with his blue gaze penetrating her as if he's trying to read her mind, she thinks maybe she could fall for him. Maybe it's time to believe in love again.

She leans forward and kisses him. 'Thanks, Pieter.' She stands up and, taking hold of his hand, pulls him to his feet. 'I've got a date with an egg sandwich at the food van. How about joining me and I'll spring for the tuna and sweetcorn I know you love.'

Pieter smiles and loops her arm through is. 'That sounds like an offer I can't refuse.'

Chapter Forty-Nine

THE BOLEYNS

Hever Castle, England
July 1528

'Another letter from Mary, Thomas.'

'Yet again? Has she nothing better to do than waste ink and paper?' Thomas Boleyn says as he frowns over his ledger at the dining room table.

'Shall I read it?'

'As you wish. It will save me the effort.'

Elizabeth Boleyn breaks the red wax seal on Mary's letter and settles on a bench by the leaded window in the dining room.

Sir,

I write to you again as your own humble daughter, Mary, and appeal to your goodness to aid me and my two poor fatherless children in our hour of need. I am yet of your blood, and through me, the blood of the Boleyns runs through the veins of Cate and Henry, your own grandchildren. The situation since my last letter has worsened. I must leave the courtier lodgings at Placentia Palace and William's creditors pursue me for payment of his debts. I have but a lowly income from the small rents from my late husband's Essex manor and the annuity from Tynemouth Priory upon which to support myself and my children, and we shall shortly be homeless.

Please, good sir, I entreat you to extend your kindness to your own good family and invite us to retreat to Hever Castle until such time as circumstances improve.

I remain your loving daughter,
Mary

Elizabeth Boleyn tosses Mary's letter down on the dining table in front of her husband. 'It is shameful that you continue to ignore her pleas for aid.'

Sir Thomas looks up from his ledger and regards his wife's flashing dark eyes and indignant expression. 'Mary has had both the French king and the English king in her power and has failed to benefit from either attachment. It is only from my own judicious arrangements that I secured her, soiled as she was, a marriage to an honest man of good family, although it was hardly the noble marriage I had envisaged for my eldest daughter. That her husband has succumbed to the sweating sickness and left her in a compromised state is an apt punishment for her youthful promiscuity.'

Elizabeth winces at his ruthlessness.

'And yet you condone Anne's relationship with the king.'

'Anne is not Mary. She will ensure that she benefits from the king's affections in material ways.'

Elizabeth tuts. 'In ways which will be to your own benefit, I warrant.'

He picks up his quill and dips it into a pot of black ink. 'Were I you, I would not complain, wife. My benefit is your benefit.'

Elizabeth raises her fine auburn eyebrows. 'I am Mary's

mother and grandmother to her children. Their welfare is of the utmost concern to me. Would you have your own flesh and blood out on the streets of London, begging? Is it that you see no further use in Mary now that you believe her to be past the age to secure a worthy husband? In truth, I believe your affection for your children lasts only as long as they are useful to you and your ambition.'

'I shall not have an impoverished weeping widow casting a shadow on this estate. Mary will need to find her own solutions to her problems.'

Elizabeth straightens her slender back and folds her hands against the black velvet of her richly embroidered gown. 'I wonder that you can sleep at night, husband, for you have the soul of the Devil himself.'

Elizabeth dips her white quill into the pot of black ink and bends over the sheet of parchment at her bedroom table.

Anne,

I write as the concerned mother of your sister, Mary, whom, with the departing of the soul of her husband, William, has fallen upon difficult times. She must leave her lodgings at the palace and has appealed to her father for succour for herself and her children here at Hever. Her father is resolute in his determination to cast Mary and the babes to the winds of Fate, which I, as Mary's mother and grandmother to her children, cannot abide.

I entreat you, as Mary's only sister and blood of her blood, to speak to the king as I know of his affection for you. Entreat His Majesty to persuade your father to honour his responsibilities to Mary and her children. I would not be so presumptuous to ask, but the situation has become untenable, and your father's intractability reflects badly upon the Boleyn name.

Your loving mother

Windsor Castle
July 1528

Anne bites into a fat green apple, then licks the tart juice off her lips and gazes out the open window in the king's apartments towards the view of the River Thames below. She leans into the sunlight streaming into the room, wipes her hands on a cloth, and picks up the letter she has just written to Mary.

Sister,

Oh, Mary. How is it that Boleyn blood courses through your veins? Our brother George enjoys the king's attention as a Gentleman of the Privy Chamber, and George's wife Jane is happily settled into the king's gift of Grimston Manor in Norfolk. I myself have secured the affections of King Henry and enjoy his attentions in full view of the court. What of our sister Mary, who once held the affections of two of the most powerful men in this world? Mary, who now finds herself a homeless widow on reduced income? I beseech you, sister, wear our family pendant and know who you are.

Mother has written me of all your many misfortunes. I am not so hard-hearted as our father. I do have sympathy for your position. The world is not made for women. We can find ourselves tossed about like corks on a stormy sea through no error of our own. It would not be seemly for my own sister to become a homeless pauper, even if that is God's own will. I have, therefore, spoken to the king about your

circumstances. He has promised to write to our father to impress
upon him the obligations he has to you in your extreme necessity.

I remain your affectionate sister,
Anne

She folds the letter and lays it beside her, then leans against the dark oak panelling to watch two swifts sweep through the blue summer sky. *Mary, you had every advantage – beauty, a good family, places in the courts of Europe and England, the attention of two monarchs – and you have let all your advantages run through your fingers like water. I do not wonder that our father turns away from shouldering the embarrassment of your fall. Were you not my sister, I would care little for your situation. But you are my sister, and I am but a hair's breadth away from becoming Queen of England. I will see you settled, but there will be a price to pay for my having to plead to the king for his aid in this private family matter.*

Anne tosses her apple core out the window onto the wooden terrace below, narrowly missing a guardsman stationed at the foot of the stairs up to the king's apartment. She laughs when the guard turns to look up at the culprit, and retreats back into the room. She fetches the letter and, taking up the Boleyns' bull's head seal which she carries on a silver fob at her waist, presses the signet into the hot wax.

Chapter Fifty

BETTY & BRYHER

Puddleton, England
January 2025

Betty yawns and blinks into the gloom of the bedroom. She leans over and squints at her alarm clock – 3:17am. She's had a terrible time sleeping since the streetlight outside her house went out just before Christmas. There was something comforting about the dull yellow light that would creep into her room through the gaps in the curtains. She hates the dark, especially since her eyesight has become so bad. She'll have to send another letter to the council about the streetlight. She'll mark it URGENT this time. That should get their attention.

She switches on her bedside lamp and throws back the covers. She slides her feet into slippers and pulls on her flannelette dressing gown. Now that she's awake, she may as well have a wee and make herself a cup of cocoa. She needs her sleep if she's to meet with Marion at Tealicious to discuss the WI's winter jamboree in the morning.

She's stirring the pot of simmering milk when she hears a thump in Bryher's bedroom. *That's odd. Bryher's out at her boyfriend's place in London tonight.* She tuts. *Oh, Bijou, what have you knocked over now?*

She turns off the heat on the milk and pads down the hallway.

'Bijou? Are you on Bryher's bed again, you naughty girl?'

She opens the door and stares into the dark room at the hulking figure dumping out drawers onto Bryher's bed. She gasps.

'Who on earth—?'

A gloved hand covers her mouth, and a searing pain shoots across the back of her head. Her knees buckle. Then … nothing.

'Betty Pilcher,' Bryher says to the nurse on the ward desk as she attempts to control the panic spinning inside her like a fairground waltzer. She glances at Pieter beside her, then back to the nurse. 'She was brought in last night. They told me at the reception desk she's on this floor. I'm her … family. Where is she?'

The nurse looks up the information and points down the corridor. 'Ward C, turn left down the corridor. It's at the end of the hall on the right.'

Bryher pushes away from the nurse's station and heads towards the ward.

'Bryher, wait.' Pieter grabs her arm. 'Do you want me to come with you?'

She shakes her head. 'No. Wait here and get me a coffee, would you? There must be a machine around here somewhere. My nerves are shot. Who would beat up a harmless woman in her own home? It's crazy.'

'I know. It's awful,' he says gently, 'but at least she's all right.'

'She's not *all right*, Pieter. Marion said she's got a concussion.

Thank God she found Betty this morning. I should have been home last night. This never would have happened.'

'If you'd been there last night, it might be you here in the hospital. She was found in the guest room – your room.'

'I should have been there.'

Pieter slaps his gloves against the palm of his hand. 'Look, I'm sorry, Bryher, but I have an important meeting I have to get to. You'll be all right, won't you? Betty's in good hands here.'

'A meeting? Right. Fine.'

'I'm sorry. I could stay …' He shakes his head. 'What am I thinking? I *will* stay.'

'No, it's okay. You're right. Betty's in good hands here in the hospital. Go to your meeting.'

Pieter kisses her on her cheek. 'You're sure?'

'I'm sure.'

'Call me later.'

'I will.'

Bryher pulls open the curtain around Betty's hospital bed and sets her face into a mask of calm to hide her shock. Betty's head is wrapped in a white gauze bandage and her eyes are ringed with deep purple bruises.

'Betty, good grief.'

Betty winces as she attempts a smile. 'Bryher, dear. I'm awfully sorry. I'm a bit of a mess today.'

Bryher tugs the curtain closed and sits on a blue plastic chair by the bed. 'What happened? Marion found my number on your fridge and called me. She said she'd found you this morning when you didn't meet her for tea at Tealicious. The police said you'd interrupted a robbery.'

'Yes, dear. The fellow was rooting around in your room. I'm afraid it's a bit topsy turvy.'

'Don't worry about that.' Bryher reaches across the bed and grips Betty's hand. 'How are you feeling? Marion said they're going to keep you in here for a few days to check you're okay.'

'Don't worry about me. I'll be fine. Where's Bijou? I hope she hasn't run off with all the commotion. She's not much of a people person.'

'Marion has her.'

'Oh, good. I'll have to bake Marion one of my lemon drizzle cakes once I'm home. She's a good stick.' Betty points to a button on the side of the bed. 'Would you press that, dear? I'd like to sit up. They never give you enough pillows in the hospital.'

Bryher presses the button until the head of the bed rises to Betty's satisfaction. Betty exhales an exhausted sigh. 'That's better. There's nothing to see lying down except for the holes in the ceiling tiles.' She points to the tile directly over her head. 'There are seventy-four holes in that tile. I've had quite a fascinating morning.'

'The police want me to report back to them if anything's been stolen.'

'That's good of you to check, dear,' Betty winces as she attempts a frown, 'but there's nothing of any value for them to steal. I put all Mummy's jewellery in a safe deposit box, just like you advised me to do, and I've insured Mummy's 'B' necklace with Mr Browne's company. I'm so glad I did. It seems that Puddleton is becoming a crime hotspot. What is the world coming to?'

Bryher exhales a relieved sigh. *That's a relief. The necklace is safe.* 'Yes, well, you can't be too careful these days.'

Betty reaches over and pats Bryher's hand. 'You were right all along. I was just being a stubborn old stick. I couldn't imagine that Mummy's old jewellery was worth anything. I used to play dressing-up with it when I was a little girl. Then, when Mr Browne said her "B" necklace was worth fifteen thousand pounds, well, I changed my mind and toddled off to the bank with all her jewellery.' She points to the acoustic-tiled ceiling. 'Somebody up there is looking out for Betty Pilcher.'

'It sure looks like it.' Bryher glances at her watch. 'I've got to go, Betty. I've got to let the police know if anything's missing.'

'Of course, dear. If the robber has taken the telly, that's all to the good. I'll replace it with a new flatscreen telly on my house insurance. I may even splurge on a subscription or two. Marion is quite taken by Netflix, although nothing can take the place of *Doc Martin* in my view. I think that Martin Clunes is adorable.'

Bryher pushes open the door to Betty's bedroom and gasps at the chaos of clothing, shoes, hats, makeup, dolls and women's magazines strewn over the bed and floor. The wardrobe doors yawn open like an empty mouth, and drawers lie upended over the furniture.

She heads down the hallway to her room. It's the same mess of clothes and ransacked furniture, but the expensive new laptop she'd just bought from the local tech shop is still where she'd left it on top of the dressing table.

Why did the thief leave behind Betty's TV and my laptop? Wouldn't they have just grabbed anything they could get their hands on and run? This was no opportunist thief. Whoever hurt Betty knew exactly what they were looking for. The necklace.

Other than herself and Betty, only two other people know that Betty has the Boleyn necklace. Pieter and Ollie Browne.

One of them wants the necklace for themselves. Badly enough to attack Betty.

Chapter Fifty-One

MARY

Placentia Palace, Greenwich, England
July 1528

Mary is packing the children's clothes into a basket with the help of four-year-old Cate as the toddler, Henry, attacks a plate of mashed apple at his high chair. She rises to her feet with a groan to answer a knock on the lodgings' door. Her eyes widen at the sight of a king's page who hands her a sealed document.

Mary stares at the document. 'What's this?'

'From Mistress Boleyn at Windsor Castle.'

'Another letter? She is making good use of the king's pages.'

The page, whose face is marked by the angry skin of youth, shrugs.

She smiles as the boy shifts on his feet impatiently. 'It is no doubt a response to my letter of thanks. Thank you, sir.'

Turning back into the room, she shuts the door behind her and breaks the familiar red seal.

Mary,

I am well pleased that our father has responded to the king's bidding and that you and the children will be shortly returning to Hever Castle. However this is not the matter upon which I write to you.

I have, by the grace of His Majesty, been granted the wardship of my nephew Henry Carey through which I shall be responsible for the custody of the lands inherited by your son upon the death of his father William. In relation to this, I shall have the right to the income from said lands until Henry reaches the age of one and twenty at which time the lands shall revert to him.

In return for taking on the responsibility of the guardianship of my nephew, it shall be my sole responsibility to maintain these estates and provide for Henry's care and education, and arrange a suitable marriage for him at his majority.

I trust you shall be relieved to be unburdened of these responsibilities, and know that your son's secure future will be assured under my guidance. Your own welfare, as well as that of my niece Cate, are now the responsibility of our father, with grateful thanks to our good King Henry.

Anne

Mary's presses her hand against her tight bodice as she gasps for breath. Anne is taking her son from her? She looks over at the young child, who is happily slapping at the apple mash on the pewter plate. She rushes over to Henry and, grabbing him from the high chair, presses him against her, unconcerned about the apple staining her silk gown. She kisses her son's strawberry blond curls. *Henry, my dear sweet boy. How can she do this to us? Has she no heart?*

Cate looks up from the floor where she is playing with her gaily dressed Bartholomew doll. 'Mama, what's the matter?'

Mary smiles weakly at her daughter. 'Nothing, Cate, my love.

I'm sad to leave our little home, but you will have a lovely big garden to play in at Grandpapa's house.'

'With flowers?'

'Yes, my dove. With flowers. Grandmama has a pretty flower garden.' She sets Henry down beside her daughter. 'Play with Henry for a little, Cate. Mama has some work to do.'

Mary sits down and stares at the grooves on the wooden tabletop. By taking away her access to the revenue from her husband's lands, meagre though it may be, Anne has deprived her of any income whatsoever. She and her daughter are paupers in bondage to her estranged father. A heat rises in Mary, sweeping over her like a flood of lava. *How dare you, Anne? How dare you rob me of my son and my dignity? How dare you cast me and my daughter on the mercy of an unloving father? I will NOT be beaten. I will NOT be left penniless.*

She hurries over to a large wooden coffer at the foot of the bed and raises the lid. She lifts out a red leather box and sets it on the bedcover. Opening the lid, she carefully lays out each piece of jewellery on the crimson silk bedcover. Finally, she removes the Boleyn pendant from the jewellery box and spreads it out on the bed. The pearls gleam softly in the afternoon light and the golden 'B' presses its indentation into the soft silk.

She runs her fingers over the lustrous pearls. *What good is jewellery on a pauper's dress? I will not be left penniless, Anne. By you, by Father, by anyone.*

Chapter Fifty-Two

BRYHER

Puddleton, England
February 2025

Bryher jolts awake. She blinks as her eyes adjust to the gloom of the room. Her mouth is as dry as a desert and her tongue feels like sandpaper. Bijou raises her head from the nest she's made in the duvet and stares at her.

'What are you looking at?' Bryher eyes the cat. 'Go back to sleep.'

She grabs the glass from the night table and takes a drink of the cold water. Shivering, she snuggles back under the duvet as the memory of the dream wafts through her mind.

She was at a nightclub in some city with her mother and Marnie. The club was heaving with a mass of people dancing and drinking. A giant mirror ball spun above their heads sending flickering reflections like stars over the room and the dancers' writhing bodies. Coloured lights flashed to the music, and Bryher watched, fascinated, as the bodies jerked and twitched around her.

Someone pulled Marnie up onto a platform and she joined them in a suggestive dance, careful not to spill the rum and Coke she'd been drinking over her tight T-shirt and jeans. Bryher watched Marnie toss her long red-gold hair around as she gyrated to the music. She felt something cold being pressed into her hand.

'Here, sweetheart,' her mother said. 'It's Coke with a splash of rum. You're a big girl, now. Why don't you get up there with Marnie? You don't want her to have all the attention, do you? Don't tell me you're still a little brown mouse?'

Bryher looked down at the drink and over at Marnie. She turned back to her mother, who is laughing as a man's arms snaked around her. 'But, Mom, I'm only twelve …'

Bryher turns over and picks up her phone from the night table. She checks the time: 3:23am. She drops the phone back on the table and flops against the pillows.

It wasn't a dream. She remembers that night as clear as yesterday. One of many, many nights Mom took her out partying with Marnie. Her first rum and Coke at twelve. Her first spliff at thirteen. Cocaine at fourteen. It had all seemed normal, because her mother made it seem that way. It had all seemed normal until the night Marnie had overdosed.

Pieter bursts into Bryher's dressing room at Elstree Studios waving several tabloid newspapers. 'What's going on, Bryher? You're all over the tabloids' front pages.'

Bryher cleans the last of the heavy makeup off her face and tosses the wipe into a bin. 'It's probably just some more pap shots. I've even been papped buying coffee at Borehamwood train station.'

Pieter holds up a newspaper. '"*Bryher to Wear Boleyn Bling to*

BAFTAs!"' He tosses the newspapers onto a table. 'You can't be serious. The BAFTAs? The biggest media event in Britain? You can be sure the jewel thieves out there are salivating. What are you going to say when the reporters ask you where you found it?'

'Calm down, Pieter. I've spoken to Margot about this. I'm not going to say anything specific. Everyone knows from *Do You Know Who I Am?* that Betty and I are descendants of the Boleyns. It's not a stretch to think we could have the necklace.'

'What about your talk about Betty's safety? This is going to bring out all the crazies. She won't be able to stay in her house. Somebody's already broken in.'

'Yes, but they didn't know she had the necklace.' Her eyes narrow in the mirror. 'Or did they?'

'What are you talking about? No one knows she has the necklace. But they'll know soon enough, when you show up wearing it at the BAFTAs.'

She turns around in her chair. 'That's not really true, is it, Pieter? I know and you know.'

Pieter shakes his head as he paces the small area of floor that's not covered with shoes and bags of prawn cocktail crisps. 'What are you saying? Are you accusing me of hiring someone to break into Betty's house, rough her up and steal the necklace?'

They stare at each other for a long moment, then Bryher turns back to the mirror and picks up the brush. 'You're right. I'm sorry.' She pulls the brush through her hair. 'This whole necklace thing is stressing me out. But somebody else does know about the necklace.'

Pieter frowns until a realisation comes over him. 'Oliver Browne.'

'Exactly. I've been to his office. Let's just say he doesn't look like he's swimming in in a sea of money.'

Pieter leans against the makeup table. 'We've got to get the necklace out of Betty's hands. It's not safe, especially now that all these stories are coming out in the media.'

'Yeah. Margot is brilliant at her job. By the end of the day, everyone's going to know I'm wearing it to the BAFTAs.'

'Listen to me. Why don't we switch the necklace at the BAFTAs with the one I made? I'll be there presenting an award too. I'll put it in the locked drawer in my flat. It will be safe there until we figure out what to do.'

'Switch it at the BAFTAs? We'll be surrounded by people and everyone will be looking at my neck.'

'We'll do it backstage after you make the presentation. I'll be waiting in the wings. You complain about the clasp being loose and I'll offer to fix it. I'll do the switch then.'

'Are you sure? There'll be security guards everywhere watching the necklace like hawks.'

'I know. It's not ideal, but it's our best chance before you get whisked away by your agent for interviews.'

Bryher nods. 'Okay. Then what?'

'Once the show is over, experts will want to examine the necklace and, when they do, they'll see that it's the replica that I made. The same one that Oliver Browne valued and that Betty insured. The press will lose interest and Betty will have a valuable copy in her safe deposit box. You'll take the real necklace back to the States and "find" it in your late mother's effects in a few months' time. Bryher, it's the only way to protect Betty.'

Bryher stares at her reflection in the mirror. Maybe Pieter's right. It's not safe for Betty to keep it. And, after all, she's as much of a Boleyn as Betty is. She has as much right to the necklace as Betty does. It's in Betty's best interest for her to switch it with Pieter's necklace. Then she'll sell it to a museum where everyone can see it.

'Okay, Pieter. Let's do it.'

Chapter Fifty-Three

ANNE & MARY

Windsor Castle
August 1528

Cornelis Hayes strides through the castle courtyard, oblivious of the admiring glances of a cluster of Queen Katherine's ladies-in-waiting. He makes his way through an arched tunnel and out into the herb garden where he spies the king's favourite sitting on a bench under a rose arbour with several other ladies of the court.

'Mistress Boleyn, if I might humbly beseech a word.'

Anne looks up and bestows an artful smile on the jeweller. 'Master Hayes. Of course. Has my good father advised you of the new commission I wish to discuss with you for my dear mother's birthday?'

'Yes.' He glances at the other ladies and inclines his head in greeting. 'It is another matter I wish to speak to you about. Perhaps we might take a turn around the garden? The day is pleasant and not overly hot.'

'Of course. Ladies, linger well behind us if you would.'

Cornelis eyes the women doubtfully. 'The matter is of a sensitive nature, milady. Might we be afforded some privacy?'

Anne smiles, and her dark eyes flash with humour. 'My good Master Hayes, it is best that I stay within sight of the ladies, else my good lord, His Majesty, may take umbrage at the news that I had met privately with a gentleman that my ladies deem "a fine and handsome creature".'

Cornelis smiles awkwardly. He gestures towards the vine-covered pergola in the near distance. 'I am your humble servant.'

They stroll past the rose garden, which is heady with the scent of sweet English roses, lavender and rosemary, the ladies lagging a respectful distance behind.

'I trust you are well recovered from the sweating sickness, milady? I was aggrieved to hear of your illness and that of your father.'

'My brother, George, was afflicted as well. Yes, we are all well recovered.'

'I am pleased to hear it.'

'You were fortunate enough to escape the sickness, Master Hayes?'

The jeweller nods. 'I was, I thank God, as was my dear wife.'

'I am glad to hear it. My dear brother-in-law, Mr Carey, was not so fortunate.'

'Yes, I am aware of this.'

They walk together in silence.

'My commission for King Henry's New Year's gift is progressing well?' Anne asks, breaking the silence.

'Yes, milady. Very well. It shall be completed in good time.'

Anne picks a rose and, after inhaling its perfume, holds it carefully between her fingers. 'What, then, is this urgent business of yours?'

Cornelis glances over his shoulder, reassured that the court ladies are some distance behind them, before reaching into the leather pouch attached to his belt and retrieving an item. Careful to hide it from view of any watchful eyes, he shows it to Anne.

'The Boleyn pendant?'

'It is the very same, milady. Your sister has entrusted it to me to pawn.'

'My sister is pawning her jewellery?'

'I thought it would be wise to advise you of this.'

Anne hands the jeweller the rose and, taking the pendant, runs the smooth pearls between her fingers. The perfect rounds are cool against her skin, and the gold 'B' with its three oval pearls sits heavy in her palm.

'Our father gifted this to Mary on the occasion of her fifteenth birthday. I am loath to admit my envy at the time. Mary said that our father told her, "I gift you this as a reminder of your family and your duty to honour your name wheresoever life chooses to take you." Would that she had heeded him.'

'I know this necklace well, milady. I made it with mine own hands. I purchased these pearls from the Americas from a Spanish trader in Paris.'

'It is well you brought this to me. I will see to it that you are repaid the monies you extended to Mary.'

The jeweller inclines his head. 'Thank you, milady.'

'Has she brought you any other pieces?'

'A few, yes. Not so grand as this.' He pats the leather pouch. 'I have them here with me.'

'How much money did you extend to my sister for all of these?'

'It is something over twelve pounds, milady. Twelve pounds, nine shillings and sixpence.'

'Twelve pounds! Mary shall do well for some time with that amount.' Anne hands the pendant back to the jeweller. 'Put this in the pouch. I shall take ownership of all these items. I am a Boleyn, too, and these jewels belong to our family.'

Cornelis offers the leather pouch to Anne who tucks it under her long sleeve. 'I thank you for bringing this to my attention, Master Hayes. I am in your debt. I do not wish for my sister to become subject to idle talk amongst the court. The Boleyn name must not be sullied by my sister's misfortunes, which I venture have been caused her by her own imprudent actions. I have seen her settled at our father's house in Kent. She must learn to remain there if only to ensure the prevention of any future embarrassment to the Boleyn name.'

———————

A week later, Anne arrives at Hever Castle and enters the parlour, which is newly furnished with rich tapestries from Flanders and ornately carved oak furniture. Mary sets down the embroidery frame on the dining table and rises to greet her sister.

'Anne. Mother told me you were coming to visit. You have missed Father. He has gone back to London to meet with the French ambassador.'

'No matter. I shall see him when I return to London.'

'I trust your journey from Windsor was uneventful?'

Anne kisses Mary on both her cheeks in the French fashion. 'It was. The king loaned me a good Barbary mare. My groom has taken her to the stables with his own horse. We shall rest one day and leave the day after morrow. I have already spoken to Mother and been to my room to refresh myself.'

Mary scans her sister's exquisite sky-blue silk gown and the matching French hood studded with gems. 'Such a short visit? What is so pressing that you must return to London with such haste?' She picks up her embroidery and recommences her work on an intricate red rose. 'Oh, of course. You must be fearful that the king's eye might be caught by another in your absence. I have heard whispers of a babe with the blue eyes and russet hair of the king born this past June to one of the palace's laundresses.'

Anne glares at her sister as she settles into a new oak armchair carved with the Boleyn crest. 'If anyone would be accustomed to the whispers of others, it would be you, sister.'

Mary raises a fine blonde eyebrow. 'I suspect you shall outdo me in this regard before long. You have always been one to seek the attention of others, while I have not.'

Anne picks a purple grape off a bunch in a bowl on the table. 'Truly? That is not my perception.'

'Why? What have you heard?' Mary asks. 'I have endeavoured to be circumspect in my behaviour since William's passing, despite being stripped of my home, my income and even my own son.'

Anne spits out the grape pip into her hand. 'Your son is with you yet and shall be until he is of the age to be schooled. I am not about to take a babe away from his mother's breast.'

'That is of some small comfort, but by persuading the king to grant you my son's wardship, you have stripped me of any income whatsoever.'

'It was a necessity, Mary. It is the king's responsibility to make provision for fatherless heirs to estates. As William's estate is small, I simply suggested to His Majesty that I, as the boy's aunt, be named my nephew's guardian in this matter, to which he was agreeable. It is common knowledge in our family that you lack judgement and the ability to manage things.'

Mary grimaces at the slur. 'Father agreed to this? To taking away my right to manage my son's estate?'

'Father suggested it.'

Mary laughs mirthlessly. 'So I am in to be penned up at Hever Castle like one of the king's lions in the Tower?'

Anne sighs as she glances around the room, taking in the new furnishings. 'I am truly sorry for your plight. William was a good man, though a simple one, and unlikely to have distinguished himself at court but for the favours bestowed upon him by King Henry.' She gestures to the expensive tapestries and the solid silver candlesticks on the table. 'I cannot imagine that you would have ever found yourself living amongst such luxuries as plain Mary Carey. I am ensuring, as your son's aunt and guardian, that monies from the estate are being set aside for Henry's education and well-being, and to ensure that the estate is managed properly.'

'So, I am not to have any influence upon my own son's life.'

'You are his mother. Of course you have influence. You simply don't have authority.'

'And Cate?'

Anne shrugs. 'Cate is a girl and of no consequence until she is of the age to marry. You may have as much authority over her as you wish until then.'

'And if it were known that my daughter is the king's child? What then, Anne?'

Anne's dark eyes flash. 'Your daughter is and always shall be a Carey. Is that understood?' At Mary's silence, Anne slams her hand against the arm of her chair. 'Is that understood, Mary?'

Mary bites her lip and regards her sister. At twenty-eight, Anne is like a swan at the peak of its beauty. The full crimson foresleeves of her dress and the ropes of pearls hanging from her slender neck enhance her dark, elegant beauty, and her jewel-studded French hood frames her oval face, bringing attention to Anne's best feature – her intense, coal-black eyes. Though it is true there are others in the court whose features sit more regularly, and who, like Mary herself, are graced with the fair hair and blue eyes considered the epitome of feminine beauty, it is Anne, always Anne, who holds a room with her bewitching charm.

'Everything has come easily to you, hasn't it, Anne?'

'What do you mean?'

'You have always been Father's favourite. He secured you a place at Archduchess Margaret of Austria's court a full year before Mother pushed him to find me a place at the French court. I am the elder sister. I should have been given a place at court first.'

'If only you could have seen yourself through my eyes all the years of our childhood at Hever. You were Father's favourite then. His golden child, his pretty, sweet Mary. He and Mother had such plans for you. Many times, I overheard them speak of your future as the wife of a grand nobleman.'

'Yet it was you who Father placed at court first.'

Anne shrugs. 'Yes, in the Archduchess of Austria's court, not in the glorious French court. The Archduchess Margaret is known to enjoy intellectual pursuits. Perhaps, when she invited him to send one of his daughters to her court, our father believed I was more suited as one her ladies because of my intellect. In that regard, you cannot disagree that he was right. More likely, he was waiting to place you in the French court, where your talents for singing and dancing would bring you to the attention of a well-placed future husband. Yet you dallied with King François and ruined your reputation. Furthermore, you have disgraced yourself at any court in which you have been in attendance.'

'If only you knew the truth of it.'

'I know enough.' Anne sighs. 'I have not made this journey to argue with you. It fatigues me greatly.' She unties a small leather bag from her girdle and extracts the pearl 'B' pendant. She holds in up and dangles it in front of Mary. 'I had a visit from Master Hayes.'

Mary's face blanches. 'You left me with little choice. I had no option but to look to anything I had of worth and seek recompense for it.'

'I don't begrudge you divesting yourself of the other jewels. They of are of no interest to me.' Anne's voice rises. 'But this one? This is the Boleyn pendant. It is not your place to cast it aside like a valueless trinket. Master Hayes informed me that he had made it by his own hands at our father's request.' She returns the pendant to the leather bag. 'I shall take ownership of it now and keep it where it belongs, in the Boleyn family.'

Mary's throat tightens. 'My own family has cast me adrift. Even our brother's wife refused to have me and my children stay at Grimston Manor. I had little choice but to exchange my jewellery for money.'

'You should have come to me. I was *not* best pleased to hear from the mouth of an outsider like Master Hayes that you have been pawning your jewellery. This is a private family matter and should remain as such. How would it have been received by the court if my sister's plight had become common knowledge? It would have reflected poorly on *me*, and this I *shall not* permit, not when I am so close to becoming queen.'

Mary's heart hardens at the selfishness of her sister's words. 'Sister. I didn't wish to trouble you when you have been having such difficulties with Cardinal Wolsey amid the king's desire to annul his marriage to the queen.'

Anne's eyes narrow. 'And how do you know of this?'

'You forget, I was living at Placentia Palace with my husband in the midst of the English court. The king's desire to have his marriage annulled in order to marry you has been the fuel of much speculation amongst the court for some time.'

'What is the mood of the court in light of these janglings?'

Mary shrugs. 'That you are English-born is seen as favourable by some.'

Anne pops another grape into her mouth. 'Good.'

'Though many call you a whore, a harlot—'

Anne rises abruptly. 'When I am queen, they shall rue their words.'

'Take care. You speak treason against Queen Katherine.'

'I care not for that sour-faced Spaniard, and nor does the king. Her time as the Queen of England is nearing its end. I will see myself on the throne by the king's side, Mary. Mark my words.'

'And then what? What will you do then?'

Anne stares in surprise at her sister. 'Well then, God willing, I shall be a good queen to the English people.'

'And how do you intend to do that?'

Anne's dark eyes flash. 'I have read much on the subject of

church reform from the pens of the French humanists, whose writings were introduced to me by the Archduchess Margaret. I share their belief that the people should read and hear the Word of God in their own language rather than in Latin, a language that only the educated can understand. I believe the wealth of the monasteries should be shared amongst the poor to better their earthly lives, and that I have a role to play in the future of England. I shall bear Henry's heir. I believe with all my heart that God has put me on this earth for a reason. Because of me, the Boleyn blood will course through the veins of England's monarchs and our name will live on until the Day of Judgement.'

'You do not ask much of God.'

Anne glares at Mary. 'For good or ill you are my sister. I shall not see you out on the streets. At my request, the king has agreed to assign you an annuity of one hundred pounds. Now, I am much fatigued from the journey and will sup in my room. Please extend my apologies to our mother. I shall be away to Stone Castle tomorrow to visit the Wingfields and ride out at dawn for London the next morn. I shall say my farewells to you now, as we shall not meet again on this visit.'

Chapter Fifty-Four

BRYHER & BETTY

BAFTA Awards Night, Puddleton, England
February 2025

Bryher pulls aside the lacy nylon net curtain at the lounge window and sees a shiny black Mercedes Benz parked on the road outside Betty's house, as incongruous as caviar at a car park picnic. She hurries down the hall as quickly as her gold strapped Prada shoes permit.

She knocks on Betty's door. 'Betty, are you ready? Our car's here.'

'Come in, dear! I need your help.'

Bryher enters the rooms and stops short at the sight of her cousin, who is resplendent in a fuchsia, sequinned dress with matching satin shoes, a pink feathered fascinator and white opera gloves. A black patent leather handbag is looped over one arm, and across Betty's shoulders sits a fake fur stole; she is also wearing large clip-on diamante earrings.

Betty touches the earrings. 'I wasn't certain about which of

Mummy's earrings to wear with my new dress. What do you think of these?'

'Uh, they're lovely.' She frowns as her eyes fix on the 'B' necklace around Betty's neck. 'You're wearing the "B" necklace? I thought you were going to lend it to me. That was the plan, remember? It's all over the media that I'll be wearing the necklace.'

'Oh, I know, dear. I subscribe to the *Daily Mail*. Everyone thinks it's the real Boleyn necklace, isn't that silly?'

Bryher gulps down the lump forming in her throat. 'It's publicity, Betty. It's supposed to help promote the mini-series and help me revive my career. I really need to wear it.'

Betty reaches out and pats Bryher's bare arm. 'Don't worry. I've got that all taken care of.' She picks up a black velvet bag on her dressing table and hands it to Bryher. 'Here, dear. Open this.'

Bryher eyes the velvet bag. 'What is this?'

'You'll see. Open it.'

Bryher unties the gold drawstring and takes out a grey box imprinted with HEVER CASTLE in silver serif font.

'Hever Castle?'

Betty nods, the fuchsia feathers in her fascinator bobbing with her. Bryher sets down the velvet bag and opens the box. Nestled on a bed of white satin is a replica 'B' necklace.

'You remember that lovely guide, Malcolm, whom we met there when we were at Hever Castle, dear? Well, I rang up the castle and they found him for me. I asked him to send me the best copy of the necklace they had in stock for a very important event. It was only sixty-five pounds, so don't worry about reimbursing me. I'll wear Mummy's and you can wear the Hever necklace. We'll be twins!'

Bryher holds up the necklace and frowns. 'The whole idea is for everyone to think the necklace I'm wearing is the real one. It'll be confusing if you're wearing a "B" necklace, too.'

Betty waves her gloved hand at Bryher as Bijou pads into the room and circles around her legs. 'Don't be silly, dear. Two is better than one. Those paparazzi people will love seeing us both wearing Boleyn necklaces, don't you think? We're both Boleyns, after all. I was in *Do You Know Who I Am?* as well, don't forget. I get stopped on the street in Puddleton all the time by people asking for selfies.' She picks up the cat and rubs her nose into Bijou's fur. 'Isn't that right, Bijou? We're Puddleton celebrities, aren't we?'

Bryher smiles weakly. *Why couldn't Betty just follow the plan? This is all going to explode in my face. So much for my career revival.*

'This is the most exciting thing to happen to me in … oh, forever, really,' Betty says as she takes the necklace from Bryher. 'Turn around, dear.'

Bryher's stomach drops as she watches in the mirror as Betty fixes the Hever necklace around her neck. *This is a disaster.*

'Marion and I took the train and the bus to Brent Cross Shopping Centre especially to go shopping for my BAFTA dress, did I tell you?' Betty says as she fumbles with the clasp with her gloved fingers. 'The choice there is so much better than in Puddleton.' She looks down at her fuchsia satin pumps. 'You don't think the shoes are OTT? I thought black patent leather might be better, to match the handbag, but Marion was adamant that my shoes should match my dress. You don't think it's too mother-of-the-bride, do you?'

Bryher smiles weakly. 'They're perfect.'

Betty picks up Bijou and stands beside Bryher in the mirror. 'Don't we look wonderful! We're ready to show London how the Boleyn girls do glam. Mummy would be so proud.'

Chapter Fifty-Five

ANNE

Holbein Gate, Whitehall Palace, London
25th January 1533

Anne enters the small turret room at the top of the new gatehouse at Whitehall Palace on the arm of her father, safely away from the prying eyes of the court at Greenwich. Behind her, her sister Mary carries the train of the pale pink gown that she herself has intricately embroidered with gold on the stiff bodice and the long, flowing sleeves. A long lace veil trails over Anne's shoulders from the white satin French hood, which is liberally strewn with pearls. In front of Anne, illuminated by the torches affixed to the stone walls to dispel the pre-dawn gloom, Henry awaits her, formidable and handsome in his gold brocade gown, his ermine-trimmed crimson velvet mantle, and his favourite feathered, black velvet cap, which is richly studded with diamonds and rubies.

Finally, finally, the day has come. Finally, Anne will become

Henry's wife, and soon, once his divorce from Katherine is finalised, and she has been crowned, she will be Queen of England and mother of the king's heir.

She meets Henry's gaze, and sees a smile tease his sombre expression. Since she told him that she is with child, he has treated her with such tenderness as to fill her heart with a joy so bountiful that she fears at times it will burst. It is not the wedding she imagined, but it is enough. Katherine has been banished from Henry's court these past two years, and Anne has taken Katherine's place at court, joining Henry at his table in the great hall, and, since November, in his bed. It was time.

For six long years Anne made the king wait, and in that time he has proven his love for her. He has broken with the Catholic Church and progressed with the divorce from Katherine. He has secured their marriage licence, and together they planned to celebrate a grand wedding upon receipt of the papal bulls granting the annulment of Henry and Katherine's marriage. Unfortunately, these were not expected for another three months or even longer, but when she'd told him she was with child, the king had determined to marry her without delay so that the child would be born in wedlock. Her child – their child – will be Henry's long-awaited Prince of Wales.

They've had to step carefully, hence the secrecy around their wedding in the early hours of this winter morning. There were those at court who sympathised with Katherine's plight and who would be eager to cast doubt upon the validity of their marriage were they to marry before the papal approval had arrived. If that were to occur, the legitimacy of their son would be called into question.

Anne catches her mother's eye. Never has she seen her parents so happy. They have been given rooms, along with her brother, George, and his wife, Jane, here in Whitehall Palace and are revelling in their status as the new queen's family. Anne may even appoint Mary as one of her ladies-in-waiting and release her from her exile to Hever Castle, though she is yet undecided on the matter.

She joins Henry before the chaplain and rests her hand upon his.

Chapter Fifty-Six

BRYHER

Skylon Bar, Royal Festival Hall, London
February 2025

Bryher sweeps her gaze over the celebrities crowded into the plush mid-century modern interior of the Skylon Bar at the top of the Royal Festival Hall on the south bank of the Thames. Betty has gone off to the bar in search of a sweet sherry, and Bryher is searching for Margot to tell her the disastrous news about the necklace.

She spies her agent's elegant presence in front of the window wall behind which the lights of London's north bank glitter along the Thames, and weaves through the crowd towards her. She taps Margot on her black-gloved arm. 'I've been looking all over for you.'

'Darling.' Margot leans in to air kiss Bryher and excuses herself from a conversation with the handsome young star of a surprise British hit film. She leads Bryher past the champagne waiter like a black-feathered swan, grabbing two long flutes of the fizzy champagne, and steers them into a corner. Margot hands a glass to Bryher, her gaze sweeping over Bryher's gold silk gown with its ethereal tulle skirt. 'Armando has outdone himself. You look stunning, and the necklace is perfection.'

'You're very glam yourself. You look like a blackbird. Who are you wearing?'

Margot runs her gloved hand over the figure-hugging black feathers that gleam like spilled petrol as she moves. 'A fabulous new designer that Carine Roitfeld told me about when I was in Paris for the couture shows.'

'It sure makes a statement. Especially the headdress. Kinda Cher, circa 1986.' Bryher takes a sip of champagne. 'Margot, I've got to tell you something—'

'Darling, don't worry. I know you haven't done this kind of thing before, presenting in front of all these A-listers, but you'll be fabulous. There's nothing to worry about. Just remember, they're all dying to see you and this amazing necklace.'

'That's exactly what I want to talk to you—'

'I've arranged an interview with *Vogue* for you, to talk about the necklace. Julian's over at the glam cam now discussing your twirl. Practise the twirl before they film it. You need to keep your eyes focused on the camera and just slowly swish around. The camera does all the work. You'll look fab, hon.'

'Hold on—'

'And I've got a big surprise for you later. I'm just such a genius. Tonight is going to be explosive. Tomorrow morning your name will be on everyone's lips. Get ready for your new career, because Tarantino, Scorsese, the Coens, Gerwig … everyone will be after you.'

'That's amazing, Margot, but the thing is—'

Margot waves at someone in the crowd. 'Hon, I've got to go. I've just seen someone I need to speak to.' She taps the diamond Cartier watch over her black satin glove. '*Vogue* journalist on the red carpet by the glam cam in fifteen minutes. Don't be late.'

Bryher watches Margot disappear into the crowd and grunts in frustration. A hand grabs her waist and a familiar musky scent wafts to her nose. She turns around and sees Pieter, dressed for the occasion in a bespoke dinner suit.

'Wow, you look great.'

He leans in to kiss her cheek. 'As do you.'

Bryher laughs. 'You like the dress? It's a new young designer Armando found.' She twirls around, the gold tulle floating like a cloud.

'You look amazing.' He grabs her hand and heads towards the door. 'Come with me.'

'Where are we going?'

'We won't be long.'

He leads her into the hallway and through a nondescript door onto a deserted service staircase. He presses her against his body and nuzzles her neck. 'I missed you.'

She loops her arms around his neck and opens her mouth to his insistent kisses as a warmth spreads through her belly. 'Are you ready for tonight?'

They hear footsteps on the concrete stairs and pull apart as a waitress carrying a tray of canapés comes into view. The woman passes them with an incurious glance and exits through the door.

'We're acting like teenagers making out in the school stairwell.'

Pieter brushes a wayward strand of dark hair behind Bryher's ear. He rubs the 'B' of the necklace between his fingers and frowns. 'What's this? Where's the real necklace?'

Bryher huffs. 'Betty's wearing it. She surprised me with this one from the Hever Castle shop when we were getting dressed. She said we'd look like twins.'

'No, no, no. This is not good. You have to switch them.'

'I know. I've got to go have an interview with a journalist from *Vogue* on the red carpet in a few minutes and do a twirl for the glam cam. I'll find a way to get Betty to switch necklaces after that.'

Pieter shakes his head. 'No. You need to wear the real necklace for the interview. They'll know this one's a cheap copy. You'll be called out on the red carpet in front of the world. You'll be a laughing stock, and Betty—'

'Betty will be a target.'

'Exactly. You can be sure there are jewel thieves here watching both of you.'

'Shit. This is bad.'

'It is. Very bad.'

Bryher nods. 'I'll find a way to do the switch now. Just be sure to meet me backstage as soon as I've presented the award, just like we planned. We won't have much time.'

'Oh, I'll be there. You can be sure about that.'

'Bryher, dear, look who I found!'

Bryher enters the Skylon Bar to see Betty, sherry in hand, approaching her accompanied by Ollie Browne who is holding a pint of ale.

What the—? Bryher fixes on a practised smile. 'Mr Browne? I didn't take you for a movie fan.'

He scans the glamorous crowd. 'I'm not. I've been hired to keep an eye on some jewellery that Swarovski has loaned to a TOWIE actress.'

'TOWIE?'

'*The Only Way is Essex,*' Betty says. 'It's a British reality show.'

'Exactly,' Ollie says after gulping down some ale. 'It's kind of like the British Kardashians, only without the private jets and megabucks.'

'It's very good,' Betty says as she sips her sherry. 'I haven't missed an episode in years.'

Ollie smiles at Bryher as he eyes her necklace. 'Nice necklace,

Ms Finch.' He looks over at Betty. 'Two of them. That's very interesting.'

Betty runs her gloved fingers over the 'B' of the necklace she's wearing. 'I thought I'd wear Mummy's necklace to help Bryher promote her mini-series. Bryher's wearing one from Hever Castle.'

'Is that right?' Ollie looks at Bryher. 'So, *you're* wearing the Hever necklace? Interesting. That's not what the papers are saying. In fact, they're saying—'

Inspiration strikes in the form of Betty's crush, Doc Martin himself, over on the other side of the room, and Bryher grabs Betty's arm. 'If you'll excuse us, Mr Browne, I've just seen Martin Clunes.'

Betty's eyes widen behind her glasses. 'Martin Clunes? Really?'

'Just over by that waitress with the canapé tray. Let's see if we can get a selfie.' She waves at the insurance broker. 'Nice to see you, Mr Browne. Enjoy the show.'

Ollie toasts her with his pint glass. 'I'm sure I will.'

Bryher pushes Betty behind a large plant when they return from their chat with Martin Clunes.

'Betty, I need to talk to you.'

'My goodness, dear,' Betty says as she smooths the fuchsia sequinned sleeve of her dress. 'Whatever is the matter?'

'It's the necklace. I've got to do an interview for *Vogue* on the red carpet in a few minutes. I need to wear your necklace. I can't wear this copy.'

Betty presses her hand against her necklace. 'But Mummy's is a copy, too.'

'Yes, but a very expensive one, with real pearls and gold. It's just for a few hours, Betty. I'll give it back to you as soon as the

BAFTAs are over. You don't want me to be humiliated on a live-streamed interview if they find out I'm wearing a cheap copy, do you? I'll be called a liar, a ... a publicity whore—'

'Oh, Bryher!'

'Yes. And worse. My career will be finished. My reputation ruined. Your reputation, too.'

'Mine?'

'Yes. Don't you see? You're part of all of this. You're my cousin. We're both Boleyn descendants. They'll say we were planning some kind of scam. You don't want that to happen, do you? What would the ladies at the WI say?'

Betty fans her face and swallows to catch her breath. 'Oh, no, dear. That would be terrible. Marion Livesay will never put me forward for vice-president of our local chapter if that happens.'

'Exactly.'

Betty sighs. 'All right.' She hands Bryher her sherry glass and unclasps the necklace. 'Just for tonight.'

'That's great, Betty. That's the right decision. You've just saved both our lives.'

'Bryher!' the crowd of photographers and ticket-less onlookers shout as she steps onto the red carpet. 'We love you, Bryher!' 'Bryher, love, over here!' 'Show Jake what he's missing, Bryher!'

Bryher smiles her most winning smile, her heart thumping wildly with exhilaration. Margot gives her a thumbs-up from the sidelines, while Julian, as slender and nervy in his bell-bottomed navy velvet dinner suit as a young, red-haired David Bowie, gets ready to film the interview on his smartphone. Margot was right. The story about Anne Boleyn's necklace seems to have buried the sex tape scandal for good. Everybody loves her again, and it feels amazing.

Bryher waves at the crowd, provoking a roar of approval.

Mom and Marnie, if only you could see me now. I'm not the little mouse you thought I was. I've worked hard all my life. I deserve this.

Karina Carr, *Vogue*'s editor-at-large, greets Bryher on the red carpet in front of the glam cam operator.

'Bryher, you look amazing tonight. Tell me who you're wearing. The embroidery on the bodice is simply stunning. The detail is exquisite.'

Bryher runs her fingers over the intricate embroidery of red and white roses twining around white falcons on the bodice of her gown. 'Isn't it, Karina? It's Georgina Brink Couture. The roses and the white falcon were Anne Boleyn's symbols after she married King Henry VIII. Anne loved fashion and was quite a trendsetter. Georgina was adamant that the dress had to pay homage to Anne's love of fashion.'

'So you brought Anne Boleyn with you to the red carpet tonight.'

'I did.' She scans the crowd, smiling broadly. 'And let me say I'm so thrilled to be here in beautiful London. It's such an amazing city. I absolutely love it here.'

Another scream from the crowd, even louder than before. Bryher spots Julian recording the interview on his phone while Margot stands beside him talking into her headset.

'Well, that's not surprising,' Karina says. 'You're descended from Anne Boleyn's sister, Mary, as we all know from *Do You Know Who I Am?* How has your life changed since that show was aired?'

'Oh, incredibly, Karina. I've been over here filming a mini-series, *Henry and Anne*, all about Henry VIII and Anne Boleyn, which will be out on Netflix later this year.' Bryher turns to the crowd. 'Be sure to watch it, everyone!'

More shouts. 'We will! We will! We love you, Bryher!'

Karina gestures to the necklace. 'Tell me about the necklace. It's absolutely gorgeous. Can I touch it?'

'Sure.'

Karina runs her fingers over the three oval pearls hanging from the gold 'B'. 'Lovely. They're heavier than they look, and such an unusual shape. Is it truly Anne Boleyn's necklace?'

Bryher traces the outline of the 'B' with her fingertip. 'Allegedly.' She gestures to a pair of heavyset men in dinner suits and earpieces. 'I appreciate these security guards everywhere. I'm very honoured to be wearing it tonight. It feels like a piece of history.'

Karina gestures for the cameraman to zoom in on the gleaming pearls and large gold 'B'.

'Tell me, how did you find it? It's been lost for centuries,' she asks.

'That's a long story for another day, Karina. Suffice to say, it was handed down from Mary Boleyn's children to their descendants until it ended up here'—she taps the pearls—'around my neck.'

The cameras flash in an explosion of white light, and Bryher blinks, momentarily blinded, as Karina takes her elbow and guides her towards the glam cam.

'Are you ready, Bryher? On the count of three, give us a twirl in that lovely dress.'

Bryher nods.

'One, two, three!'

She starts to spin and is mid-twirl when someone steps into the shot and lands a punch on her nose. The glam cam records it all in ultra-slow motion as the crowd gasps.

'What the—' Bryher winces in pain as she holds her throbbing nose and stares at the heavily pregnant blonde woman in front of her.

'Jodie?'

Jodie Rogers, her belly straining against the green satin of her couture gown, is practically panting with anger. 'You're a lying, cheating bitch, Bryher Finch. Nick didn't stand a chance once you got your claws into him, you selfish, self-centred homewrecker.

You don't care about anyone except yourself. The best thing Jake ever did was dump you.'

Bryher stares at Jodie's agitated green bulk and flailing arms. 'Jodie, no!' she hears herself shouting. 'It's not true!'

'The hell it isn't. Oh, my Go—' Jodie breaks off to clutch her belly as water puddles around her shoes. 'Dammit. My waters just broke!'

Chapter Fifty-Seven

MARY

London
May–June 1533

'Oh, my word, Mary! Have you ever in your life seen such a fantastical display?' asks her pretty blue-eyed cousin, Madge Shelton. 'I hear they have organised six of these pageants along the new queen's coronation route.'

Mary gasps as a model of a white falcon swoops down a wire from a castle façade constructed by the royal carpenters and alights on a papier mâché tree, releasing a cloud of red and white roses into the air over the heads of the bystanders.

'It is beyond incredulity,' she says to Madge – who is also one of Anne's ladies-in-waiting – as a gilded chariot, emblazoned with the entwined H and A of the new royal cipher, rumbles over the recently laid gravel.

Ahead of them, in front of six of her ladies, who are garbed in scarlet velvet and sit astride white horses, a heavily pregnant Anne acknowledges the shouts of the spectators from her cushioned litter with a gentle wave of her hand. Her long dark hair ripples out from beneath a gold coif decorated with gemstones. Anne is resplendent in a white, cloth-of-gold gown and a mantle lined with ermine. Four barons hold a canopy of golden cloth over her head.

Madge laughs and claps her hands in delight. 'Oh, look, an angel is sliding down another wire … it's setting a crown on the falcon's head!'

'It is indeed marvellous,' Madge's mother, Anne Shelton, says as she flaps at a drifting rose petal. 'It appears the king has emptied the royal coffers to pay for your sister's coronation, Mary. This procession alone is said to be a mile long.'

Mary glances at her aunt. 'Anne wouldn't have it any other way. This is what she has dreamed of since she first caught the king's eye. I warrant she fancies herself the Cleopatra of England.'

Her aunt grunts. 'Hubris will be Anne's downfall if she does not take care. Have you not noted how many of our countrymen and women refuse to doff their caps or call out "God Save the Queen" as she passes by? Even the new HA cipher of the king's and queen's initials is being met with cries of "Ha! Ha!"'

Mary nods. 'I have noted this. There are many who still support Queen Katherine and despise the manner in which that pious queen was deposed. King Henry has cast such slurs upon Queen Katherine's character and branded their marriage unlawful, their daughter illegitimate, and Anne is deemed responsible for bewitching him away from an honest, pure woman. Have you not heard the names she has been called this very day? They do not bear repeating.'

Her aunt nods towards the six ladies-in-waiting riding ahead. 'I wonder that you are not riding ahead with your sister's favoured ladies, Mary. Your mother and your sister-in-law are included, yet you, her own sister, is not.'

Mary laughs. 'I am no favourite of my sister's. We have barely spoken since my banishment to Hever Castle after my husband's death. I was only included in her wedding party because of our mother's pleas. It is a surprise to me to be included in the coronation at all.'

Their chariot rumbles by a white marble fountain gushing with free wine where Londoners squabble as they dip everything from cups to shoes into the cascades to secure a drink.

Mary sighs. 'Ah well. It is good to be away from the bondage of Hever, if only for a few days. For this brief respite, I thank my sister.'

Coronation Banquet, Westminster Hall
1st June 1533

Mary stares up at the spectacular oak hammerbeam roof and carved angels of Westminster Hall, and around the room at the walls hung with rich Arras tapestries. At the far end, on a raised dais canopied in gold cloth, Anne wears the new jewelled crown made for her by King Henry's goldsmith, Cornelis Hayes. Anne sups with the Archbishop of Canterbury, served by several nobles of the court. The king is nowhere to be seen, having retreated to a hidden alcove with the French and Venetian ambassadors to observe the banquet privately, so as not to deflect attention away from the new queen's coronation celebrations.

Melodious serenades waft over the festive diners from the minstrels' gallery as each new course's entry is trumpeted. Mary's cousin squeals as the banquet's organiser, the Duke of Suffolk, resplendent in a crimson velvet doublet glistening with pearls, rides by on his horse.

She spies her father sitting beside the Lord Chancellor at the table of nobles where he is engrossed in conversation. Since her arrival in London where her father now spends most of his time, he has made no effort to meet with her. Her brother George is absent, having been sent on an embassy to France, and her mother has seated herself at the head of the table of the court's women and appears intent on currying favour with Anne's noble ladies-in-waiting.

Mary picks up a morsel of roasted swan and chews the gamey meat as she listens to Madge and her aunt assess the fashions of the court ladies. She glances back at her sister. Around her neck, Anne wears a gold pendant upon which the initials H and A, encrusted in rubies, are entwined like vines on an arbour.

Oh, how the Boleyns revel in your rise, Anne. Our father is now the Earl of Wiltshire and the Earl of Ormond, and our brother has become Viscount Rochford. Even you rose to the peerage as the Marquess of Pembroke before your marriage to the king. Yet I am nothing but a poor banished creature sent to rot away at Hever far from the curious eyes of the court for fear they might remember me there as the king's mistress.

An arm clad in the crimson velvet of one of the courtiers, who have been called upon to act as servitors at the banquette, reaches past Mary and takes hold of her empty silver cup.

'More wine, Mistress Carey? I cannot have you expiring of thirst on such a grand occasion.'

Mary looks into the face of a swarthy young man at least ten years her junior with eyes the colour of warm earth. He smiles and his blunt features transform into an appealing handsomeness.

'Yes, thank you. I indeed have a thirst.'

He smiles as he pours out a generous portion of ruby Gascon wine from a pewter jug. 'Are you enjoying the festivities? I warrant the king himself didn't enjoy such lavish celebrations upon his own coronation.'

Mary smiles politely as she takes the cup. 'It is a fine change from my quiet life in Kent. I haven't enjoyed the pleasures of the court for some years.' She draws her eyebrows together. 'How do you know my name? I do not recall making your acquaintance.'

The courtier's gaze rests upon Mary's face. 'I noted you amongst the ladies on the queen's barge during the flotilla on the first day of the celebrations, and again the day after on a chariot in the procession. I asked of you and was told you were the queen's sister, Mistress Carey.'

'You asked of me? I am naught but a lowly widow and mother of two children. You are a youth yet and could have no interest in one such as myself.'

The courtier leans closer and whispers into Mary's ear, 'And yet I do.'

'Stafford!' a bishop shouts from the nobles' table. 'Stafford! Cease your flirtations and fill my cup, fellow, before I perish of thirst!'

The courtier smiles at Mary. 'I must attend to the bishop before he sets the Duke of Suffolk and his horse upon me.'

Mary smiles. 'Your name is Stafford, then.'

He presses his hand against the crimson velvet of his embroidered doublet. 'I am your servant, William Stafford, Mistress Carey. With your permission, I shall find you later and feed you marchpane and sweet wine, and we shall learn all about each other.'

Chapter Fifty-Eight

BRYHER

The BAFTA Awards, Royal Festival Hall, London
February 2025

Margot bars the door to the ladies' toilets as Betty hands Bryher a wad of toilet paper to staunch her nose bleed. 'It's occupied!' she shouts as someone pushes against the door. She huffs. 'Honestly, Julian has to be the world's worst sentry. Guard the door, I said. Tell them the toilets are broken, I said. Useless, just useless.'

'Oh, dear, Bryher,' Betty says. 'You've got blood on Mummy's necklace. Let me take it and clean it off. You can't go on stage like this.'

'It's a disaster,' Bryher moans, as Betty unclasps the necklace. Bryher staggers to a cubicle to grab more toilet paper.

A knock on the door.

'Go away!' Margot shouts.

Julian pushes the door open a crack and pops his pale, angular face around the door. He hands Margot a napkin stuffed with ice and his smartphone. 'You need to see this. The glam cam shot's gone viral.'

Margot grabs napkin and the phone from Julian and presses start on the Instagram story. There, in perfect slow motion, Jodie raises her fist and punches Bryher squarely on the nose, sending her spinning in a whirl of gold tulle.

'Oh, wow. She really got you good there, hon. Twenty-seven thousand likes? Julian's not kidding. This really is going viral.' Margot kisses the phone. 'I'm a genius.'

Bryher comes out of a cubicle and Margot hands her the icy napkin. She sniffles as she presses it against her nose in the mirror. 'What do you mean, you're a genius? Did you have something do to with Jodie being here?'

Margot thrusts the phone at Bryher. 'Take a look. It's brilliant, hon. You and Jodie duking it out in slow motion. You both look amazing. I had to pay megabucks to rent a private plane to fly Jodie here, but it was so worth it. She's a much better actress than I thought she was.'

The blood drains from Bryher's face. 'You organised this? It was staged?'

'Bryher, darling. The world will be talking about both of you tomorrow. The offers will be rolling in. Hold on, hon'—she taps at her Bluetooth headset—'call coming in from Fallon's people. I've got to take it.'

Bryher's stomach heaves and, dropping the napkin into the sink, she stumbles back into the toilet cubicle.

Betty knocks on the door. 'Bryher, are you all right, dear?'

'No.'

'It's not that bad, really. Come out and let me help you clean up. Heaven knows I have enough experience dealing with Bijou spitting up hairballs.'

The cubicle door opens and Bryher staggers to a sink. She looks in the mirror. Her mascara is smudged, her nose is swelling, there are flecks of blood dotted amongst the embroidered roses, and a few of the white falcons look like they've been stabbed. She groans. 'I'm a mess, Betty. How am I supposed to go on stage looking like this?'

Betty brushes Bryher's dishevelled dark hair over her shoulder and drapes the necklace around her neck. She fixes the clasp and pats Bryher's shoulders as they look at each other in the mirror.

'Not to worry, dear. We'll fix you up as good as new. A little powder on your nose and Bob's your uncle. I know you're feeling humiliated, but you mustn't let that stop you from going out there and holding your head up high. You're a Boleyn, just as Anne was and her sister, Mary, and our great queen, Elizabeth I. What did they all have in common? Fortitude. Find your fortitude, dear. Go out there and be proud of who you are.'

Chapter Fifty-Nine

ANNE & MARY

Placentia Palace, Greenwich, England
September 1534

The solid silver cradle, studded with gemstones the colour of berries which the king had commissioned from Cornelis Hayes, sits shrouded in shadows in a corner of the abandoned nursery. Anne stands silently in the centre of the room as she turns her gaze from the empty cradle to the figures of Adam and Eve painted on yellow ochre walls by the king's artist, Holbein, and a neatly folded stack of baby clothes.

She is now four and thirty years of age. She has given the king a daughter and a stillborn son, and her failure to give her husband the son he so sorely desires weighs heavily on her heart. She walks over to a polished bronze mirror which hangs on the wall and stares at her face in the rippling metal. She runs her fingers over her cheek and chin and down the long curve of her neck. She is young yet. Perhaps her cheek has lost the freshness it had carried when the king had first begun to court her almost nine years before, but she is still handsome, if only too aware of the presence of court beauties who dart the king pretty glances and tease him with flirtatious quips when they believe her back is turned.

The door swings open and Henry's bear-like frame fills the doorway. 'Anne, there you are. I have come to tell you that your sister has arrived and is causing tongues to wag. I have sent instructions for her to retire to your chambers to await you.'

'Mary? She did not apprise me of her visit.'

He shuts the door and enters the room. 'Why are you alone here in this gloom? It is not meet for you to torture yourself with thoughts of what might have been. I will have these items removed so that you are not tempted to punish yourself with sorrowful musings.'

Anne shakes her head. 'No, please, sire.' She rubs the black silk of her kirtle over her flat belly. 'I shall have another child and it will be a healthy, strong boy. I know it in my bones, my love.'

Henry gazes around the room. 'If God wills.'

Anne grabs Henry's hands. 'God does will, Henry. Has He not guided us through many years of difficulties to bring us together as husband and wife, as King and Queen of England? Why would the Lord bring us to this place if not for us to create a great Tudor dynasty with you at its head? I will have a son, my love. It *is* God's will.'

Henry scans his wife's slender figure. 'By your age, Katherine's child-bearing years had ceased.'

Anne's face hardens and she pulls her hands away. 'I am not the Spaniard. My womb is yet fruitful.' She steps back and scrutinises her richly garbed husband, whose palate for Gascon wine and rich food has added bulk to his once-athletic frame. He is handsome yet, she thinks. Handsome and powerful. There is no combination more intoxicating for a woman. This she knows full well. She has noted the whispers broken off upon her approach, the surreptitious glances, the guarded words of her most loyal ladies-in-waiting when she asks of the king's whereabouts.

Her dark eyes narrow. 'You have been absent from my bed this fortnight past. I have seen how you gaze at the Seymour girl. Or perhaps it is sweet Mary Zouche who caught your eye during my months carrying your child? I am not a fool, sire. I have heard the talk of the "imperial lady" who assures your illegitimate daughter, Mary, that her tribulations will end sooner than expected. What can that mean but that this "lady" aims to replace me in your affections and reinstate the Spaniard's daughter as your heir over our own daughter Elizabeth?'

Henry's brow furrows and his eyes flash. 'Do not test me, Anne. Shut your eyes and endure such as those better than you have done before you. I can cast you down as quickly as I raised you up.'

Anne's blood rises in a surge. 'You dare speak to your wife like this? The woman you have pledged your very life and body to? The woman whom you said you would love above all others for all eternity? Are you as false as any knave in the street?'

Henry raises his hand to strike, but turns away in rage. 'Do not vex me, wife! I am the king and I shall do as I please. Go attend to your sister. She is fruitful yet, though by whom is the question. It seems I have erred greatly and chosen the wrong sister.'

Anne enters her chambers to see Mary staring out of the window.

'Mary, I was not expecting you at court. What brings you to London?'

Mary turns around, her pregnancy curtained by the loose folds of her green velvet kirtle and black woollen mantle.

Anne lets out a breath. 'It is true, you are with child. How came you like this? And how have I just found out?'

Mary runs her hands over her belly. 'I am no longer at Hever. I have not been there since this summer past. I have been living in Hertfordshire with my husband.'

Anne's eyes widen. 'Your husband?'

Mary smiles. 'Yes. William Stafford, whom I met at your coronation.'

Anne rubs at the headache forming at her temple. 'Who is this Stafford? I have not heard of him.'

'He is a soldier, lately stationed at the king's garrison in Calais. He is a good man, Anne. He loves me with all his heart, and I reciprocate that love.'

Anne reaches for a green glass bottle of Gascon wine and splashes some into a silver cup. 'Love? You married a simple soldier for love? Father gave his blessing for this?'

'No. We married in secret. Our parents have disowned me. They swore never to utter nor write my name again, which is why you have not heard of this. They told me I do not exist for them. They thanked God that you have had the foresight to take Cate into the household of your daughter, the Princess Elizabeth, at Hatfield Place, and have sent my son to be educated at Syon Abbey.' Mary sighs heavily. 'Anne, my life these six years past at Hever has been a misery of despair and loneliness. When William offered me a chance of a life with a loving husband, I could not refuse.'

Anne glares at her sister as she paces the floor. 'What have you done? You should have come to me about this marriage. *I* am the head of the Boleyn family now by virtue of my queenship. As my sister, you were required to ask my permission before embarking on this ill-advised union.'

'I am the elder sister, Anne. I have no cause to seek your permission, queen or no.'

Anne stamps her foot. 'You have made a simple soldier the brother-in-law of the King of England! How do you think King Henry will respond to that?' She slaps her chest. 'And what of me? There are many who speak against me. Did you not consider how this will reflect on my reputation? To have a wanton sister, the king's past mistress, clearly with child out of wedlock?'

'I am married. I bear no shame here.'

Anne huffs. 'You look like a mare about to drop her foal. When is the child expected?'

Mary rubs her belly. 'In November.'

'And yet you say you married this … this solider in the summer. Anyone who can count will know that the babe was conceived out of wedlock.'

Mary sits down on a chair carved with the entwined initials of Henry and Anne. 'I know we should have waited until we were wed to share a bed, but William has spent the past months travelling from Calais to England, at great expense, to see me.'

'To see you? Where? I scarce credit our parents welcoming him into Hever Castle.'

Mary sighs wearily. 'It is of no import. It … it … Anne, I love him. With all my heart and body, I love him. You must know how that feels? King Henry annulled his marriage to the queen for the love of you.'

'*I* am the queen. There is no other.'

Mary's shoulders sag. 'I am truly sorry that you cannot see my happiness for your own ire.'

'An ire that is well-warranted.' Anne folds her arms as she regards her sister. 'Why came you to Greenwich? You could have written to me and spared both yourself the journey and myself the embarrassment.'

Mary wets her lips. 'I came … I came to request the Boleyn pendant.'

Anne laughs. 'The Boleyn pendant? Whatever for?'

'It is rightly mine, Anne.' Mary plays with her fingers as she rests her hands on her belly. 'And the truth is that William's income is little … I … I thought to pawn it until my annuity comes in January and I can redeem it and keep it for Cate. It is my thought to give it to her upon her sixteenth birthday.'

Anne laughs coldly. 'Do you think I would release the family pendant to you to be pawned again? What's more, do you think the king will continue the payment of your annuity now that you are married? The monies were to aid your upkeep and that of your children in your widowhood. The children are both now under my care. You are now the responsibility of this William Stafford and in no need of an annuity. You would do well to return to your soldier and live out your days as simple Mrs Stafford.'

'Anne, please—'

Anne walks to the door and unlatches the handle. 'Your queen requests your departure. You have shamed our family. You are forbidden to return so long as I sit upon the throne. Do not trouble me again.'

Chapter Sixty

BRYHER

The BAFTA Awards, Royal Festival Hall, London
February 2025

Out on the stage at the BAFTAs, the MC is reeling off weak jokes that provoke polite titters from the crowd. Bryher shifts on her feet and bites her lip as she does the breathing exercises she'd learned in yoga class.

Breathe in, breathe out. From the belly, Bryher. That's right. Breathe in, breathe out. You're a Boleyn. You're a Boleyn. You've got this. You've got this. Breathe in, breathe out.

She glances across the stage to the wings and spots Pieter. There's no way she can get to him. Margot's clinging to her like chewing gum on a shoe. There isn't any time, anyway. She's up next. She just has to hope the necklace switch goes smoothly once she's done the presentation.

'Okay, we're on standby,' the stage manager is saying. 'I'll count down and you and your co-presenter will enter the stage together.'

Bryher jerks her head around. 'Co-presenter?' She looks at Margot. 'You never told me I'd be co-presenting.'

'Bry? Margot, you've got to be fucking kidding me.'

Bryher spins around. 'Jake? Oh, my God. You can't be serious.'

Margot ends her phone call and spreads her hands. 'Surprise!'

'What's going on?' Jake says.

'Yes, Margot,' Bryher jabs a finger at Jake. 'What the hell is he doing here?'

'It's just for the night,' Margot says, ignoring the stage manager who is beginning to panic. 'Think about the publicity for the two of you!'

Bryher presses her fingers to her forehead. 'I can't believe you did this. And the Jodie thing, too? I think I'm going to have to reconsider our relationship when this is over.'

'The night?' Jake says. 'The whole night?' He jabs his thumb at Bryher. 'With her?'

Margot picks an imaginary fluff of lint off Jake's tuxedo jacket. 'A few minutes, darling. Five minutes. Ten max.'

'Margot—'

'*Ssshh!*' Margot raises her finger and shushes Bryher. 'Darling, everything I do is for your own good. You want to be a star, don't you? Well, don't you?'

'Yes. Yes, fine. I do.'

'Well then, trust me. I know what I'm doing. Jake is in London doing a press tour for *The Twin Universe: Seven*. It was too good a chance for me to pass up.'

Bryher shoots daggers at her agent. 'Five minutes on stage and not one second more, do you understand?'

Margot nods, setting her feathered headdress fluttering like a flapping turkey. 'Absolutely, hon.'

Bryher glares at Jake. 'You had no idea about this?'

'Not a clue,' he says. 'You think I would have agreed to it if I did?'

'Darlings, can't you see? This is going to be huge,' Margot says, waving her arms dramatically. 'Jake Rogers and Bryher Finch reunited! Bryjake rides again! Trust me on this. Your careers have both been in a slump. Jake, I haven't been able to book you another job since *The Twin Universe: Seven* wrapped months ago. I know the audience loves you, but producers, not so much right now. And Bryher, the only job I could get you was a low-budget mini-series in a foreign country. What do people love more than a break-up? A reunion! Now, go out there and kiss and make up.'

Breathe, Bryher, breathe.

She narrows her eyes at her ex. 'Five minutes, Jake. We're actors. It's time for an Oscar-winning performance.'

A nerve twitches under Jake's left eye. 'This better work, Margot, or you're fired.'

'Darling, when have I ever failed you?'

The stage manager shoves the envelope with the winner's name into Bryher's hand and begins the countdown.

'I'll be batting away offers for you both in the morning. Mark my words.' Margot gives Bryher a spontaneously awkward hug. 'You go, girl. Be the star you are.'

Bryher takes another deep breath and tosses her artfully tousled hair over her shoulder. She's going to kill Margot later, or, at the very least, call up all of Margot's facialists and nail technicians and cancel all her appointments. She glances over at Jake who is staring straight ahead, the nerve under his eye now twitching under his skin like a Mexican jumping bean. At least she's not the only one suffering through this.

Setting her mouth into a megawatt smile, she strides out onto the stage with Jake, the gold tulle skirt of her gown floating around her like a soft sunlit mist. The audience gasps as they appear, and cameras flash like fireworks going off. She waves at the clapping audience, casually brushing the necklace with her hand, lingering on the golden 'B'. Someone in the audience whoops and she blows a kiss in their direction.

'Enjoy it while you can, Bry,' Jake whispers under his breath as he flashes a white smile and waves at the audience. 'You're finished in this industry.'

'I've heard *The Twin Universe: Seven* is going straight to streaming,' she whispers back. 'Looks like your movie star days are over.'

She steps up to the plexiglass lectern and pauses to take in the moment as the audience quietens down. Every hint of nervousness, every prick of irritation at Jake, melts away like ice in April. She feels the eyes of the audience and the warmth of the spotlight on her, and energy zips through her body like electricity. *This is where I belong.*

'Good evening, ladies and—'

'Gentlemen,' Jake says, leaning into the mic.

'Good evening to you, too, Jake,' Bryher says, irked at his interruption. *So that's how it's going to be.* She glances at the teleprompter and fixes a smile on her soon-to-be ex. 'How are things up on The Twin Universe's moon?'

Jake grins at the audience as he reads his line. 'Still waiting for my golf drive to land.'

The audience laughs.

'I wouldn't worry,' Bryher says, reading her lines off the teleprompter. 'I know you're used to digging the ball out of sand traps. You'll be a pro up there.'

The audience groans.

'How about you, Bry? Missing the old US of A?'

'Sure, but England's been amazing. And the rain! So good for the skin. It's English Botox.'

'That'll be all the LA facialists crying in their coffees.'

Bryher smiles at the audience. 'You would know, Jake.'

Laughter rumbles through the auditorium.

Jakes looks at the teleprompter and holds up his hands. 'Wait. I can't do this.'

Bryher jerks her head around, her smile still fixed. 'What are you doing?'

'I can't do this. This is all fake, folks.' The room falls as silent as a cemetery. 'We're standing here lying to you. Doesn't anyone want the truth? I know I do. There's nothing honest about Bryher and me being together here. It's all a PR stunt.'

A murmur rolls through the theatre.

'Jake,' Bryher whispers. 'What are you doing? Are you crazy?'

Jake gestures to Bryher. 'Bryher's just asked if I'm crazy. I don't know. Maybe I am. All I know is I can't pretend that we're a couple, because we're not. I'm not in love with Bryher.' He waves his hand at her. 'In fact, I don't even like you, Bryher. You're as fake as they come. Your teeth, your hair, your nose, your boobs, even your stupid necklace. They're all totally fake.'

Bryher stares at Jake as her stomach drops. She grasps the lectern and swallows to regain her composure as the orchestra springs into action. *I'm not going to let this happen. I'm not going to take this public humiliation anymore. I have a voice and I'm going to use it.*

She looks over at Jake, the ferocity of her expression causing the audience to fall silent. 'You know what, Jake? You should be ashamed of yourself, speaking to me like that.' She turns back to the audience. 'In fact, you all should be ashamed of yourselves. Does posting all those memes and awful, repulsive gossip about me on your social media make you feel good? Not one of you has listened to me. All you care about is tearing me down. And, boy, do you love tearing people down. Well, I've got a voice and now you're going to listen.'

Jake tugs at her arm. 'What are you doing?' he hisses.

Bryher pulls her arm away. 'Stop it, Jake. And you stop it, too!' she shouts at the orchestra. The music comes to a clanging halt.

She stares out at the sea of faces. 'I'm Bryher Finch. I'm an actor, a woman and a human being. I have feelings. Cut me and I bleed. For the past four months I've been ridiculed, denounced, castigated and humiliated in the press, on television and on social media. And not once have I been asked for my side of the story. Shame on you. Shame on all of you.

'I've done nothing wrong. It's not me in that tape. You can believe me or not, I don't care. And you know what, even if it were me,' she shrugs, 'how is it any of your business? My private life is my private life. I haven't broken any laws. I haven't been arrested. What's happened to me is a lot worse. I've been judged and found guilty by the internet where everyone is anonymous. I hope none of you ever have to go through what I've been through, because it's hell.'

She juts out her chin in defiance. 'I'm proud of myself. I have nothing to hide.'

The silence is deafening. Then one person begins to clap, followed by another, and another. Soon the whole auditorium is thunderous with applause.

Bryher's heart races as the humiliation she has been carrying since the scandal broke washes away like dirt down a drain.

Jake steps up to the mic and, pointing at the necklace, looks at the audience. 'You don't really think that thing is real, do you? It's a total con.' He looks at Bryher. 'Isn't it, Bry? It's all a big con. I'll even prove it.'

He moves forward to grab the necklace just as the theatre suddenly plunges into darkness. Somebody screams. Then, just as suddenly, the lights come back on.

Bryher grasps at her neck. 'It's gone!' she shouts as she struggles to stand. 'It's gone! Where's the necklace, Jake? What have you done with it?'

As security guards and stage crew rush onto the stage, someone grabs her.

'It's me,' Pieter says. 'Are you all right?'

Bryher presses a hand to the back of her neck. 'My neck. The clasp gashed me when they yanked it off.'

'Here, take this.' Pieter pulls a handkerchief from the breast pocket of his dinner jacket and helps her to her feet. She presses the cloth against the cut on her neck and points a finger at Jake, who looks disorientated. 'He's got the necklace.'

Pieter grabs Jake by his arms as the security guards swarm around them. 'Where is it? What have you done with the necklace?'

Jake scowls at Pieter. 'Get off me! I haven't got it! Why would I want a cheap piece of shit like that?'

'Pieter.' Bryher moves towards him as Jake is bundled off stage. 'I saw Ollie Browne in the bar earlier. I'll bet he's been watching me and Betty all evening. He probably saw us switch the necklaces in the bar.'

'*Godverdomme*! That bastard! He won't get away with this. Bryher, go and find Betty. I'll call you as soon as I find him.'

Chapter Sixty-One

ANNE

Placentia Palace, Greenwich, England
January 1536

The noble spectators rise to their feet and cheer as King Henry – his bear-like physique suited in polished and gilded armour and a surcoat bearing his coat of arms – enters the jousting list at Greenwich. He is astride a black Barbary destrier, which is draped in a blue silk caparison embroidered with red and yellow crosses over its heavy armour. Anne cranes her neck to watch her husband as he takes his place at the near end of the field while his opponent, his courtier, Sir Henry Norris, readies himself at the far end. She acknowledges his salute to her with a nod of her head and rests her hands on the gentle swell of her belly.

The Christmas season had been one of joyful celebration. The difficult years following the king's excommunication from the Catholic Church after declaring his right to be God's head on earth of the new Church of England are over. Anne credits herself for being her husband's strength and support against the opposition of the pope and the Catholic bishops, and is of no doubt that the king would have wavered in his resolve had it not been for her persuasive arguments to break with Rome. Now the monasteries are being dissolved and she must persuade the king to use that vast wealth to build schools and colleges instead of pouring it into the treasury and lining the pockets of Henry's grasping and ambitious minister, Thomas Cromwell. And she will work to persuade the king of the benefits of holding the mass in English so that all the people of England can hear God's words for themselves.

But more than all of that, she is with child again. What joy it had been to relay the news to the king on Christmas Day! How he had embraced her and covered her face with kisses! After the difficult months following her miscarriage and the embarrassment of her sister's injudicious marriage, her own influence in Henry's court is rising once again.

She smiles. And now the Spanish queen is dead this past fortnight. What a blessed year this New Year shall be. The shadow of the old queen laid to rest and a new prince for King Henry to bounce on his knee. Finally, all is well.

A trumpet blasts and the two jousters lower their lances and spur their steeds onward. The damp winter earth of the list field is thrown up into great clods as the horses' hooves pound against the ground. As the king's horse charges towards Norris and his chestnut charger, it wobbles in a patch of mud. Henry's lance hits Norris's saddle, throwing the king onto the field with a crash of metal, his great horse falling on top of him.

Anne rises to her feet as the crowd gasps. The king lies motionless as Norris clambers off his horse and hurries to the monarch's side. Several courtiers break through the barriers to the field and rush to the king's aid. Anne sucks in air as her knees sway beneath her. She reaches out to grasp for the wooden railing of the viewing stand, and then, nothing.

Five days later, Anne wakens to the sight of Henry leaning heavily on a crutch beside her bed, as he observes her with a face heavy with sorrow.

She reaches out for him. 'Henry? My lord? What has happened?'

'You have lost my son.'

Anne presses her hands against her belly. The budding roundness is gone and the trauma of losing yet another baby is fresh. 'It was the shock of seeing you fall, my love. But you recovered and, though I fainted … I was well. Until … until …' A sob rises in her throat. 'God cannot be this cruel.'

'I see that God will not give me a prince.'

She reaches out to him again, but he makes no effort to comfort her. 'We can try again, my lord. I am yet young. I am yet fertile.'

'You bewitched me to win my affections.'

'I did not! My affections for you are true.'

'I was a foolish slave to your enchantments. It is incredulous to me that I was once in such thrall to you. You who are nothing more than an ordinary woman.'

Anne pushes herself up against the pillows. 'Henry, my love. How can you say such things to me?'

'You have failed to give me the healthy son that you promised.'

Panic rises in Anne's chest. 'There is time, my lord.'

'Were you truly with child, or was it a ploy to keep me close?'

Anne feels a prick of anger. 'How can cast such a slur upon me? I carried your son, even as you whispered pretty things to that whore, Jane Seymour, over dinner at Wolf Hall this September past!'

Henry's face flushes and he leans over Anne's bed. 'Do not castigate me for a harmless dalliance when you and your ladies entertain an army of courtiers in your chambers. I should have known when I first tupped you and you did not bleed that you were not to be trusted. A virgin? I think not. I believe you were corrupted in France just as was your wanton sister.'

Anne lets out a frustrated scream. 'Do not compare me to Mary! I am nothing like her!' She pounds the white linen shift covering her body. 'I am your queen, Henry! You are my one great love. You are disappointed, as am I, but we can try again. We will have a son and he will be such a prince that you shall rue the day you spoke so ill to me.'

Henry regards Anne, his face impassive. 'Do not address me by my Christian name. I am your king. Forget this at your peril.'

Chapter Sixty-Two

BRYHER

The BAFTA Awards, Royal Festival Hall, London
February 2025

The concourse outside the Royal Festival Hall is a confusion of celebrities, police and paparazzi. Bryher shields her eyes from the flash of cameras as she follows Margot, Julian and Betty out into the crowd.

'Bryher! Bryher! Over here!' a photographer shouts.

'Bravo, Bryher! Great speech!'

'Who do you think took the necklace, Bryher?'

'Is it Anne Boleyn's real necklace? How did it feel to wear it around your neck?'

Betty grips Bryher's arm. 'Good heavens. Is this all for you, dear?'

A reporter thrusts a microphone into Bryher's face. 'Was the theft all a PR stunt? What do you say to that now that you've found your voice?'

Margot steps in. 'I'm Bryher's agent, Margot Chen, and we

categorically refute these allegations. My client has just been physically assaulted and robbed on live television. Can't you see she's injured and traumatised? Please, have some consideration.'

Julian leads them over to concrete steps behind a barrier set up by the police. He drapes his velvet dinner jacket around Bryher's shoulders and offers her a bottle of water. She glances at Margot, who is speaking to the press through her headset.

A camera flash goes off, then another. Bryher presses Pieter's handkerchief against the wound on her neck with one hand and holds up the other to shield her face.

Why can't they just leave me the fuck alone?

'Don't worry, Ms Finch,' Julian says. 'I'll deal with them.'

'Thanks, Julian.'

Betty takes Pieter's soiled handkerchief from Bryher and retrieves a clean, lacy one from her handbag. She takes a small bottle of water out of her handbag and pours a few drops on the cloth before handing it to Bryher.

'Take this, dear, and wipe that nasty gash on your neck. You don't want it to get infected. They really did yank off the necklace, didn't they?'

Bryher nods. The past few hours have been like a surreal dream culminating in a nightmare. She presses the handkerchief against her neck.

'I'm so sorry, Betty. It was your mother's necklace. I had no right to wear it, and now it's gone.'

Betty pats Bryher's shoulder. 'I'm just glad you're all right, dear. It's just a silly bit of sparkle on a string. It's nothing.'

Bryher chokes down a sob. 'It's so not nothing, Betty. If you only—' She wads up the damp handkerchief. 'I'm so sorry. You've been so good to me, and I've let you down.'

Betty hitches up her dress and joins Bryher on the step. She takes the handkerchief from Bryher and dabs at the mascara'd tears running down her cheeks. 'Don't be silly. You're much more important. We're family, after all.'

Bryher licks a salty tear off her lips. 'Are we? Really?'

'Of course! We're cousins. We both thought we were alone in the world, and now we're not. Isn't that lovely?'

Bryher relaxes into Betty's hug. She isn't really alone. There's Marnie. But, Marnie … No, she's never had a family. Not really. Not like this. Not with someone who really cares about her. 'It is.'

Betty smiles. 'Anyway, dear, you told me to be careful with the necklace. You warned me about dangerous people. I should have left it in the safe deposit box.' She shrugs, the fuchsia sequins glittering under the streetlights. 'At least I had it insured, and that's all because of you, dear. I won't be out of pocket. Fifteen thousand pounds is quite a windfall for me and Bijou.'

Bryher takes the handkerchief from Betty and blows her nose. She stuffs it into her clutch bag and looks over at the police ushering away the paparazzi. Then she spots Ollie Browne and leaps to her feet.

'It's him! He's the one who took it! Stop him!' She points at Ollie as she shouts at the police. 'Stop him! He's the thief! He stole the necklace!'

Two burly policemen grab hold of Ollie, and Bryher gathers up her tulle skirt and rushes across the concourse like a boat at full throttle, Betty, Margot and Julian trailing in her wake.

'You!' she says, jabbing her finger. 'I should have known it was you all along.'

Ollie holds up his arms as one of the policemen frisks him. 'You've got the wrong end of the stick, Ms Finch.'

'You've been coveting that necklace since the first day you saw it at Betty's, haven't you? You tried to steal it from her house and left Betty in the hospital. That was you, wasn't it?'

He rolls his eyes. 'You're delusional. I knew the necklace that I saw at Betty's was one of a kind, but I would never have hurt anyone to steal it. I'm an insurance broker, not a thief.'

The policeman steps away. 'He's clear.'

Ollie smiles at the police as he brushes down his jacket. 'Thank you, officers. I know you were only doing your job.'

'It had to be you,' Bryher says. 'Only three people other than Betty knew it was in her house. You, me and …'

He cocks an eyebrow. 'And? Why can't you say it? I know it's on the tip of your tongue.'

Bryher rubs her forehead. 'Yes, Pieter knew, too. But he wouldn't have stolen it. I know him.'

'Is that right? So, where is the sterling Dr de Beer now?' Ollie looks around at the crowd. 'I'll tell you where. He's on some plane with that necklace. Face it, you've been had.'

Chapter Sixty-Three

ANNE

Placentia Palace, Greenwich, England
2nd May 1536

Anne leaps to her feet and claps her hands, calling out *'Well done!'* as the tennis player she has bet upon smashes a volley past his opponent. She smiles down at her twelve-year-old niece, Cate Carey, whose forehead is furrowed in concentration.

'It is well, Cate. My champion has won the set.'

Cate looks up at her aunt with her dark brown eyes and shrugs. 'It is most difficult to follow the rules of real tennis, Aunt Anne. The ball jumps all over the floor and walls so quickly that I can't keep it in my sight.'

Anne laughs, amused by the forthright tongue of her niece, a recent addition to her ladies-in-waiting. She tucks a stray strand of Cate's auburn hair under her bejewelled French hood. 'No matter, Cate. It becomes easier when you have watched many matches.'

She leans past her niece and beckons the courtier who is taking bets from the spectators seated on the viewing platform.

One of her senior ladies-in-waiting tuts. 'It is not meet that the Queen of England bets upon sporting events like a commoner. If you must place a bet, ma'am, you should arrange to have a page do this on your behalf. This kind of behaviour does you no favours amongst the populace who yet mourn the death of Queen Katherine.'

Anne shakes out coins from the embroidered purse she carries on her golden girdle. 'The Spaniard is dead and cold in her grave. As for the English people, let them grumble, for this is how it shall be.'

There is a commotion at the doors to the viewing gallery and she looks up from counting out coins to see one of the king's guards striding purposefully towards her.

'Sir?' she asks when the guard stops in front of her.

'Your Majesty, you are ordered at the king's command to appear before the King's Council.'

Cate grasps hold of Anne's silk sleeve. 'What's happening, Aunt Anne? Why must you go? The tennis match has just started. Can they not wait? You are the queen, after all.'

Anne cups her niece's face with her slender hand. 'It is simply the king playing a prank to test me, Cate. Stay here and I shall return soon.' Anne leans forward and whispers in Cate's ear, 'Be certain to collect my winnings.'

Then she rises, and smiles at the guard's impassive face. 'You may walk behind me, sir, for I know the way.'

Later that afternoon, Anne sits under the shadow of the cloth-of-gold canopy on her own royal barge, on which she had last sat on the day of her coronation, three years before. She grasps her hands as she runs the events of the past few incredulous hours through her mind.

She'd been met by her uncle, the Duke of Norfolk, along with that duplicitous chancellor, Cromwell, as well as a handful of other councillors, and had been subjected to a barrage of questions such as she, even in her darkest of dreams, could never have imagined.

Had she entertained the lowly musician, Mark Smeaton, alone in her chambers on the 15th of May the previous year? Had she been paying said Smeaton for his services to her as her lover? Does she admit that she spoke treasonously of the king's death in a conversation with another of her lovers, the king's courtier, Henry Norris, this Friday past – as reported by her own sister-in-law, Jane Boleyn, Lady Rochford? Had she taken her own brother, George, to her bed on more than one occasion? What explanation does she have for her evil behaviour?

How could she have done anything but laugh in the face of such inanities? All through the interrogation her own uncle had stood there, tut-tutting like a sanctimonious prig. And then, to be told by him that she was being formally accused of adultery and treason!

She had denied it. Of course she had. Yes, she may have been indiscreet in some of her private conversations, she may have cast a smile in the direction of a witty courtier – but adultery? How could she not laugh in the face of such an unjust accusation? 'I am your queen,' she had said, 'who loves my husband well, and who would never compromise the sanctity of our marriage, such as you accuse me of.'

Her uncle had tut-tutted, that viper Cromwell had smirked, and shortly thereafter three more councillors had entered the chamber with a warrant for her arrest, signed by the king himself.

Now, she is here, sitting on a barge painted in her colours, with her coat of arms emblazoned on its sides, propelled by rowers accompanied by the beat of a drum. She is alone, bereft of her ladies, deaf to the roar of insults from the crowds gathering along the shoreline of the Thames, as news of her arrest has quickly travelled. For nigh on two hours she has sat here as the rowers fight the currents of the tide, asking herself over and over, *Where did it all go wrong?*

She reaches up and presses the gold 'B' of the Boleyn pendant against the exposed skin above the neckline of her richly embroidered blue silk gown, until she feels the metal imprint itself upon her skin like a brand. She is a Boleyn. She will convince Henry of his grave error. She has garnered his displeasure because of her failure to provide him with the son he so longs for. This can be remedied. She will send her husband a note and beg for his forgiveness for being the cause of his great disappointment. She will tell him of her love, assure him of her loyalty and render void any doubts he may harbour of her fidelity.

The barge jolts as the rowers steer it towards the gate into the great Tower of London. The last time she was here she was readying herself for her coronation. Now she must ready herself for the battle of her life.

Chapter Sixty-Four

PIETER

Heathrow Airport, London
February 2025

Pieter settles into a first-class seat on the late-night flight to Abu Dhabi. His heart is pounding. It had all gone so smoothly. He couldn't have planned it better himself if he'd tried.

Bryher's ex-husband showing up like that! He bites his lip as he stifles a laugh. Perfect! It was absolutely perfect. With Bryher trying to keep her composure while Jake Rogers dragged her reputation through the mud on live television, and Bryher's agent distracted with the PR disaster unfolding on the BAFTA stage, he'd seen his moment delivered to him like a gift on a golden plate, directly into his hands by Bryher herself.

You would have loved the drama, wouldn't you, Bryher? All eyes on you, isn't that what you wanted more than anything? I did you a favour. Poor Bryher, victim of a nasty theft in front of the world. Play that sympathy card and watch the job offers roll in. I know you will. You're just another vain, self-centred, fame-hungry actress. You're two a penny, Bryher Finch.

There'd been no need to fumble with switching the necklaces backstage. No need to use his back-up plan, had they not managed to make the switch backstage, to have Bryher mugged outside the theatre and the real necklace stolen from her. Instead, he'd paid the thug extra to get the lights switched off, whatever it took. He didn't like dealing with people like that, but needs must. It had got rather messy with Betty. She wasn't meant to have been hurt. All he'd wanted was the real necklace. If the stupid woman had just stayed in bed asleep, she would have been fine.

It had been tempting to leave with both necklaces, but he knows it was best to sacrifice his replica. They'll find it when they search the theatre, and everyone will think it's the necklace Bryher had been wearing. Not the real necklace, of course, just a very, very good copy. He now has the real necklace to do with whatever he wishes. Bryher will know by now, of course, but what does he care? No one will believe her and he'll be long gone.

'Sir, would you like to put your briefcase in the overhead locker?'

Pieter smiles at the attractive flight attendant. 'I'd prefer to keep it with me, thank you.'

'Are you sure, sir?' she asks in a soft Welsh lilt. 'You'll have more room to stretch your legs. It will be much more comfortable.'

Pieter's smile tightens. 'I'm fine. Thank you. May I trouble you for a cold glass of your best champagne? I have had some good news on the work front, and I feel like celebrating.'

'Certainly, sir. I'll right back.'

Pieter watches the flight attendant walk down the aisle and disappear behind a curtain. He sets the briefcase on the fold-up table and turns the dials on the lock. It releases with a click and he opens the case. There, on top of two starched shirts, sits the necklace.

Finally, it's his. *Sorry, Bryher. This necklace was made by my ancestor, Cornelis Hayes. If anyone has a claim on it, it's me.*

He removes the necklace from the briefcase. He weighs it in his hands and frowns. Something's wrong. It feels … He turns over the gold 'B'. There's no maker's mark. He presses a pearl against his teeth and rubs. It's as smooth as a polished stone. The pearls are fake. His heart races as he examines the 'B'.

It's a cheap copy! Somebody has switched it.

Bryher.

He stuffs the necklace back into the briefcase and slams down the lid.

'Here you go, sir. A glass of Lanson Noble Brut 2005—'

He tucks the briefcase under his arm. 'I have to get off. I have an emergency.'

'I'm sorry, sir. The doors have closed. I have to ask you to take your seat as the pilot is preparing for take-off. And please put your briefcase under the seat.'

'You don't understand.' Pieter stands and makes to push past the flight attendant. 'I have to get off this plane. I have to get off now!'

'Sir, please. The doors are closed. You have to sit down. We're leaving for Abu Dhabi.'

Pieter slumps into the seat and waves away the glass of champagne as all his careful plans crumble to dust. He stares blindly out of the window as the plane reverses and taxis out to the runway, two words jolting around his brain at every bounce of the wheels on the tarmac.

Bryher Finch. Bryher Finch. Bryher Finch.

Chapter Sixty-Five

ANNE

The Tower of London
19th May 1536

Before Dawn

Anne fiddles with the pearls of her pendant as she paces the stone floor in her chambers in the Tower, while her priest murmurs prayers for her soul on a chair in the glow cast by the flickering candles. The four ladies-in-waiting she has been assigned during her internment, none of them sympathetic to her situation, and whom, she suspects, have been chosen to act as Cromwell's spies, are long asleep in the adjoining room. Her young niece, Cate, is her only friend amongst her attendants, having delivered herself to her aunt upon word of Anne's incarceration in the Tower, her presence permitted, no doubt, owing to her extreme youth and innocence.

A deep fatigue engulfs her. She has slept little in the past two days, and has spent the long dark nights in prayer; at times asking for the king's forgiveness and begging for a reprieve of her sentence to death for treason, adultery and worse – incest with her poor brother, George, executed two days past with five other innocents – and at other times, when despair overwhelms her, for God's mercy and a swift, painless deliverance from this life.

She cups her bare head with her hands and rubs at the dull headache that throbs at her temples. How has it all come to this?

Not three years before she had been preparing for her coronation, secure in the love and devotion of her new husband, King Henry VIII. She had revelled in the knowledge that she would be in a position to influence the king on matters of religious reform, education and charitable causes. She can see now how Cromwell's jealousy of her influence on the king, on her insistence that the wealth of the monasteries be used for the people rather than to aid the growth of Cromwell's own riches, has led Henry's most trusted advisor to become the orchestrator of her fall.

She has never been unfaithful to the king. The injustice she feels at the heinous lies cast upon her wounds her to her very core. How can Henry, who once declared to her his undying love, cause this travesty to be visited upon her? Perhaps her greatest defect was in failing to give Henry the heir he'd so desired, and for this he has judged her wanting. And replaceable.

Though she knows this may be so, in truth, she knows also that her pride has delivered her to this fate. She was so confident in Henry's love that perhaps she became careless in the company she kept, and the impolitic witticisms she shared with intimates like her brother, George, and the king's courtier, Sir Henry Norris, another victim of the king's wrath. In this regard she is entirely culpable. Her pride made her believe she was untouchable, invincible. That she had a mark to make in this world. Her pride, combined with Cromwell's treacherous ambition and Henry's disappointment at her inability to give him an heir, has led her to this day. The day she will die.

'Aunt Anne? Why are you yet awake?'

Anne looks up to see Cate, dressed in a linen nightgown, approach her from the ladies' chamber.

'Cate, you should be in bed. Do not trouble yourself with your aunt's worries.'

'I cannot help but be troubled by your worries. Come, lie with me on the bed and rest ere you collapse from fatigue.'

Anne expels an exhausted sigh and, joining her niece, lays down on the fine silk damask bedcover.

'Better?'

Anne smiles at her niece. 'Better. You are thoughtful, Cate. Like your mother. She has always been the kinder of us two sisters.' She brushes her niece's soft round cheek with her hand. 'How fares your mother in Calais? Is she content with her life there?'

'She is well. She expects another child soon. She wishes for a girl to be a companion to the babe Edward.'

Anne nods. 'I am happy for it. She, of all of the Boleyns, has escaped the intrigues of these past weeks. I should never have banished her from court for marrying a man I considered beneath her status as the queen's sister. My pride was pricked. Mary was always true to me, yet I treated her poorly. It is a great regret of mine. At least I am happy she is out of harm's way.'

'My mother loves you yet, Aunt Anne. She always asks me to pray for your happiness in her letters.'

'That is well like her.' Anne sighs. 'And now my poor brother is dead, my father plays judge to the other men who have been executed and trips along to Cromwell's bidding, and my own uncle, the Duke of Norfolk, has delivered me my death sentence. I hear nothing from my mother at Hever, whom, I suspect, has been ordered by my father and my uncle to distance herself from me. Only you, Cate, and God Himself, offer me comfort in this time of great distress.'

A tear runs down Cate's cheek and she begins to sob.

Anne embraces her niece and hugs her close. 'Do not cry, my sweet. I await my meeting with God this morn with the knowledge that I am innocent of the accusations against me. I am content in the knowledge that the Boleyn blood runs in the veins of my own sweet daughter, Elizabeth, who, if God wills, shall one day sit upon the throne of England. You share that blood, through my sister and through the king himself.'

Cate frowns. 'What mean you by that?'

'My good, sweet Cate. King Henry is your father. Elizabeth is your half-sister.'

'But my father was William Carey.'

'Indeed, William Carey was your true father in every way a father should be. But the king was your sire. You carry royal blood. Be good to your sweet sister, Elizabeth. She will need a friend when I am gone.'

Anne sits up against the pillows and unclasps the 'B' pendant from around her neck. She presses it into her niece's hands.

'Take this, Cate. Keep it safe and hide it from prying eyes. I hear that the king has confiscated my belongings. I do not wish this to fall into the hands of another. It is the Boleyn pendant. Royal blood may course through your veins, but you are also a Boleyn. When one day it is safe for you and your descendants to wear it, I will look upon you from Heaven and smile.'

Chapter Sixty-Six

BRYHER, BETTY & OLLIE

Puddleton, England
February 2025

Betty enters the living room from the kitchen and looks over at Bryher and Ollie Browne, who are dunking chocolate Hobnobs into their tea.

'Well, that was quite a surprise,' she says.

Bryher wipes a soggy crumb from her lip. 'Who was that on the phone?'

'The police. They found Mummy's necklace buried in a plant in the bar at the Royal Festival Hall. They've asked me to come and collect it.'

Bryher teacup rattles on the saucer. 'They found it?'

'Careful, dear, or you'll spill your tea and I'll have no end of bother getting the stain out of the slipcover. They've had an expert examine it. It's a very good copy, just as Ollie said.'

Bryher's heart sinks. *You thought this all out didn't you, Pieter?*

Now you've got the real necklace and no one but me knows. She forces a smile. 'That's great, Betty. I'm really happy for you.'

'Well, well, well,' Ollie says, as he scoops the documents he'd laid out on the coffee table back into his briefcase. 'It looks like I won't be paying you out your insurance money after all, Betty. I can't tell you how happy that makes me.'

'You can't put a price on Mummy's necklace. It has sentimental value.'

Ollie helps himself to another Hobnob. 'Promise me you'll keep it in a safe deposit box. It'll save me from having to write you a cheque if it goes missing.'

Betty sits down on the sofa beside Bryher and picks up her teacup. 'Believe you me, I've learned my lesson. One can't be too careful these days. Marion Livesay has just had a security system installed, and I'm thinking of doing the same. I'm afraid Puddleton isn't the place it used to be. Munkittrick's Sweetshop just had its window broken and all the black liquorice stolen. I mean, that doesn't bother me in the least as I detest black liquorice, but somebody out there likes it enough to steal it. It's very good for the digestion, apparently. Gets the bowels moving. Maybe the thief had constipation.'

The phone rings in the kitchen.

'Oh my, I'm popular today. Excuse me for a moment.'

Ollie Browne wipes his mouth with a paper napkin and sucks a crumb from his teeth. 'So, Ms Finch. I'm curious about something.'

Bryher eyes him over the rim of her teacup. 'What's that?'

He leans across the coffee table. 'What happened to the real necklace?'

Bryher swallows and reaches into her acting arsenal to compose herself. 'I have no idea what you're talking about.'

He laughs. 'Sure you do. That first day we met here, remember that? I was looking at Betty's jewellery and I saw this amazing "B" necklace.'

'The one the police have just found.'

'No, the one I saw had a maker's mark. I told you that when you and Betty dropped into my office, remember?' He takes a notebook out of his jacket pocket and flips the pages until he finds what he's looking for. 'Here. I even made a sketch. I remember it like it was yesterday.'

Bryher glances at the crude drawing and shrugs. 'You must be thinking about somebody else's necklace. Betty's necklace doesn't have a maker's mark. You examined it yourself when we were in your office.'

'You're absolutely right. The necklace I valued didn't have a maker's mark, but the one I saw first definitely did.' He taps his forehead. 'I have a memory like an elephant. I did a little research.' He chuckles. 'Who am I kidding? I did a lot of research and I found out that the CH mark was used by a jeweller named Cornelis Hayes who was one of Henry VIII's jewellers.' He leans back against the overstuffed chintz chair. 'Funny that.'

She raises an eyebrow. 'So?'

'So, I think that first necklace I saw could be the real Boleyn necklace, that's what I think.'

Bryher laughs. 'Wouldn't that be wild? You have a great imagination. You know what I think?'

'No, enlighten me.'

'You saw the necklace, which didn't have a maker's mark. Then, you probably dreamed about it and got confused.'

'I know what I saw.'

She glances at her watch and rises from the sofa. 'Sorry I can't be of any help, Mr Browne. I've got a car coming for the airport in half an hour. I've got to finish packing.'

Ollie jumps to his feet and extends his hand. 'I never thought I'd see the day where I got to meet a real Hollywood movie star, Ms Finch. I've gotta say, you're a great actress.'

Bryher shakes his hand. 'Bryher. We're friends now, after all, Ollie. Aren't we?'

Bryher tucks her phone under her chin as she locks her new silver suitcase. 'Margot? What is it? The taxi's going to be here any minute.'

'Hon, I've got great news. I've got you booked on Fallon, Kimmel and *Saturday Night Live*. You're hotter than hot.'

Bryher sits on the bed and takes hold of the phone. 'You're kidding. I thought that Jodie incident at the BAFTAs was *it* for me, not to mention the sex tape. I still can't figure out how they did that.'

'Body doubles, dark lighting and a hooker, darling. It's obvious.'

'But how would they have known about my tattoo? The only people who know about that are Jake and—' Bryher gasps. 'You did it? You made the sex tape?'

'Bryher, hon, I had to do something. *Cop Town* had already told me they were killing you off at the end of the season. They said they wanted "fresh blood". I had to do something to make everyone sit up and take notice of you. You've got to admit it worked.'

'I can't believe you did that to me. And Nick? What about him. You almost destroyed his marriage as well as mine.'

'Yes, well. He and Jodie were in on it. There's no such thing as bad publicity, right?'

'My marriage tanked, but sure.'

'Be serious, hon. Your marriage was already over as soon as Juno came on the scene. You know that as well as I do.'

Bryher grinds her teeth. 'I'm seriously pissed off at you. You have no idea what you put me through.'

'Come on, it wasn't so bad, was it? You've got a mini-series under your belt, a lovely new cousin you never knew about, offers flooding my desk, and your face about to appear on the cover of *People* magazine.'

'What? I'm on the cover of *People*? Really?'

'I'm talking to *Variety* and *Vogue* as well. Bryher, you're a star. Your life will never be the same. Say "Thank you, Margot. You're the most brilliant agent in Hollywood".'

'Let me think about it.'

'You love me. I know you do. Hold on. Yes, Julian? Gerwig's on the line? Hon, got to go. Busy, busy, busy.'

Bijou jumps onto the bed and curls up beside Bryher.

'There you are, Bijou,' Betty says from the doorway. 'You know you make Bryher sneeze. Off the bed, you naughty girl.'

Bryher tickles Bijou's chin. 'It's okay. I'm getting used to her.'

'You're all ready to go?'

Bryher looks over at Betty, who is holding a small gift bag tied with gold and red ribbons. 'All ready.'

Betty sits on the bed beside Bijou and hands Bryher the gift bag. 'A little going-away present.'

'You didn't need to do that.'

'I wanted to, dear.' She rubs the cat under its chin until it purrs. 'I'll be sorry to see you go. We both will, won't we, Bijou? You've become part of our family here.'

'I feel the same way. My world was falling apart when I came here. You helped me start putting it back together.'

'Well, you're always welcome here, dear. You're not alone in the world anymore and neither am I.'

Bryher knows she's not alone. She's never been alone. There's Marnie. Maybe … maybe it's time to tell Betty.

'Betty, I … I have a sister. Her name's Marnie.'

'A sister? Really? Why didn't you say?'

Bryher shrugs. 'Marnie's … not well. She was a child actress – a very successful one. Everybody loved Marnie Starr. That was her stage name. Marnie Starr. No one knew she was my sister. She was the kind of person who lit up a room like a sparkler. A rare quality, Betty. I don't have it, as much as I wish I did. Marnie was a star from the day she was born. That's why Mom called her Marnie Starr.'

Betty picks up Bijou and settles her in her lap. 'What happened? You said she's unwell.'

Bryher's voice breaks. 'Yeah. I blame myself.'

'You mustn't do that. Guilt is a terrible burden to carry.'

'I do blame myself, though.' Bryher presses her hand against her mouth to suppress a sob, and Betty pats her shoulder.

'It's all right, dear. You don't have to say anything else.'

'I do.' Bryher hesitates. 'I've never been able to tell anybody about this. Not even Jake. He knew about Marnie … but he didn't know the details.' She wipes at a tear tracing down her cheek.

'One night when Marnie was eighteen we had a terrible argument. I caught her trying to steal money out of my purse. I called her horrible names. I told her … I told her I hated her and I wished she'd die.' Bryher swallows. 'She had an overdose that night, Betty. She almost died. Maybe it would have been better if she *had* died.'

'Don't say that. She's your sister.'

'Marnie never recovered. She was in a coma for a long time. Her brain was damaged.'

'Oh, that's sad,' Betty says softly.

'I stopped studying and kept working … commercials, theatre, game shows, you name it. I lived at home and gave Mom all my money to take care of Marnie. When Mom died of a stroke a few years ago, I found Marnie a good residential facility just outside of San Francisco not far from where we grew up.'

'You're a good sister.'

'I'm not. I'm a terrible sister. I paid for Marnie, but I never visited her. Not once. I couldn't bear it.' A sob slips through her lips. 'I feel so bad.'

'But why? It wasn't your fault.'

'It was! When I was ten I cheated Marnie out of a national

campaign for a huge fast-food chain. There were going to be TV commercials, magazine ads and billboards all over the country, and Marnie had won the role after a long audition process. Then there were delays and the first commercial wasn't filmed until five months later. Mom dragged me along to the filming because she didn't want to pay for a babysitter. The thing was, Marnie had … matured over the summer. She was fourteen and she was so pretty – strawberry blonde hair and beautiful blue eyes – but she looked seventeen. The fast-food execs were shocked. They wanted an ordinary, all-American kid, not a hot teenager. So, Marnie was out. Mom was so desperate, she pushed me in front of the execs to audition, in place of Marnie. They drew some freckles on me, tied my hair in pigtails and I auditioned and I got the part. Marnie was furious. Suddenly, I was Mom's golden girl, and I loved it. For a few years I got all sorts of commercials. Marnie was used to being the chosen child and she spiralled, badly. She got into drugs and stuff.'

Bryher heaves an almighty sigh. 'If I hadn't stolen that commercial from her, maybe none of that would have happened. Maybe she'd be the big star today, not me.'

'Oh, Bryher. Those were your sister's issues, not yours.' Betty takes hold of Bryher's hand and squeezes. 'It wasn't your fault. Say it. Say "It wasn't my fault".'

Bryher bites her shaking lip. 'It wasn't my fault.'

'That's right. Keep remembering that. All right, dear?'

'I'll try.'

'Good.'

Betty shoos Bijou off her lap and rises. 'Now, put my little gift in your suitcase and open it when you get back to Los Angeles. It's just a little something to remember us by.'

A few hours later, Bryher settles into her first-class seat and opens her Chanel shoulder bag. She takes out the gift bag and examines the silver and gold paper and the tumble of ribbons that Betty has obviously made an effort to curl with scissors. Bryher has never been good at waiting to open presents. Jake always called her an 'Immediate Gratification Girl'.

She tears into the paper and pulls out a small grey box stamped with 'HEVER CASTLE' in silver. She smiles and opens the box. Inside, on a bed of white satin, sits a 'B' necklace.

There is a small note tucked into the box with her name written on it with a flourish in blue ink. She unfolds it and reads:

For Bryher,

Because we are both Boleyns.

Love, Betty

Chapter Sixty-Seven

ANNE & CATE

The Tower of London
19th May 1536

Anne stands in the centre of the chamber, still and calm, her *Book of Hours* clutched in her hands. Cate smooths out the folds of the grey silk damask gown around her aunt's slender figure as the other ladies prepare Anne for her final hours. The room is silent except for the rustling of silk and the sound of the women's shoes upon the stone floor as they drape a short mantel lined with ermine about Anne's shoulders.

Anne has requested the windows be thrown open to the beautiful May morning, and a soft breeze drifts into the room. One of the Tower's ravens caws outside and Anne smiles, though her eyes are focused on a place far from the rich trappings of the regal chambers. In truth, Cate has never seen her aunt look so lovely. Her face exudes a serenity far removed from the agitations of the previous days, and an air of tranquillity envelopes her, such that her whole self appears transformed.

As the ladies tie up Anne's lustrous dark hair, Cate retrieves her aunt's favourite jewel-studded French hood. But Anne smiles and shakes her head.

'Not that one, Cate. On this day of all others I shall wear a good English gable hood, for I am a good Englishwoman.'

Once the dressing is completed, Anne walks over to a polished metal mirror and examines her reflection. She runs her hand over her cheek and down her slender neck.

'I heard say the executioner is very good, and I have a little neck.' She laughs, stopping abruptly at the sound of a knock on the door.

With a final glance into the mirror, she turns to greet the constable to the Tower of London. 'Master Kingston, I wish you a good morn.'

The elderly courtier bows his head. 'The hour has come, milady.'

Anne takes a deep breath. 'Let me go hither to die, for soon my pain shall be over.'

Cate's body shakes and the sobs she has been trying so hard to suppress explode from her very core like a dam bursting. She throws herself into her aunt's arms. 'Don't go, Aunt Anne. The king is kind. He will not permit this.'

Anne brushes away a wet tendril of auburn hair from her niece's cheek. 'The king *is* kind, Cate. A gentler nor more merciful prince was there never. Yet I have been judged by the law to die and I will speak nothing against it, though I am a good woman and free of guilt for the crimes against which I have been judged.'

She presses her *Book of Hours* into Cate's hands. 'Guard this well. I have found much succour in its pages over the years. I pray you remember me fondly. You have been a brave, good companion in these last days. Remember me to my sister, your mother, and be a friend to my sweet child Elizabeth in all the days of her life.'

Cate stands at the window in the Tower clutching both the *Book of Hours* and the 'B' pendant in her hands. Outside, the sky is as blue as the forget-me-nots scattered over the grass by the moat, like specks of blue paint. Somewhere, a robin sings and a gull swoops by. Suddenly, the peace is rattled by the eruption of cannon fire along the nearby Thames.

Cate shuts her eyes and presses her aunt's gifts against her as the tears run down her cheeks.

Chapter Sixty-Eight

BRYHER

Los Angeles, California
March 2025

Bryher unlocks the padlock on the metal roll-up door and heaves at the rusty handle until the door jerks and judders into its overhead slot. She coughs and waves a hand at the dust cloud rising from the stack of boxes and old suitcases.

She slides her new Loewe raffia bag over her head and takes out the Hever Castle gift box Betty had given her. She opens the lid and runs a finger over the gleaming pearls of the Boleyn sisters' 'B' necklace. She smiles as she turns over the B and sees the CH inside a circle.

You knew all along, Betty, didn't you? No wonder you didn't want me to wear it at the BAFTAs. No one would have ever thought that the queen's necklace was in an old box under ex-teacher Betty Pilcher's bed in Puddleton, England. I don't know how you pulled off the switch. You're a far better actress than I am. You had us all fooled.

She glances into the yawning gloom of the lock-up. A soulless storage unit in the suburbs of Los Angeles seems a sad resting place for Anne Boleyn's necklace, but who would ever think to look for it here?

Bryher shuts the lid and slides the box into her hoodie pocket. But first, she wants to find something. She shifts aside the boxes marked 'Xmas Decorations', 'Tax Files', and 'Photo Albums', restacking them as she burrows towards the rear of the unit. *There it is.* The box she'd stuffed her late mother's bank statements, utility bills and rental agreements into. Paperwork that had been too overwhelming to deal with when sorting out a place for Marnie had been the priority.

She heaves the cardboard box out into the hall and kneels on the concrete floor. She yanks off the packing tape and opens the box. Maybe, just maybe it's here. She riffles through the papers until she finds an envelope with her mother's miniscule handwriting.

Important Papers.

Tearing open the envelope, she slides out the documents. She unfolds them one by one. Her parents' marriage licence, her father's will, Marnie's birth certificate. She opens the fourth document.

City and County of San Francisco
Live Birth California

This Child:	*Bryher Catherine Finch*
Sex:	*Female*
Date of Birth:	*8/6/1992*
Place of Birth:	*San Francisco General Hospital,*
	San Francisco, California
Father of Child:	*Rodrigo Suarez*
Mother of Child:	*Catherine Mary Farnsworth Finch*

Bryher's hand shakes as she rereads the birth certificate. She'd only ever seen her short form birth certificate, without her parents' names on it. Her mother had organised her first passport years ago when they'd had a commercial shoot in Jamaica. Bryher had just renewed it over the years, so she'd never seen her full birth certificate. Marnie *was* telling the truth. Robert Finch wasn't her father. It was some man named Rodrigo Suarez.

She reaches into the envelope. There's one more document, folded into a small square. She slides it out and unfolds the well-worn paper. Robert Finch's death certificate. Cause of death: Suicide.

A sob wrenches her body, shaking and jolting her like an earthquake. Marnie was telling the truth the whole time.

San Francisco, California
Several days later

Bryher sits in her car in the parking lot of a large, red-bricked Victorian building surrounded by an expanse of clipped green lawn and flowerbeds flush with daffodils and early-flowering tulips. Beside the paved walkway to the house, a large sign advertises 'Green Oaks Adult Residential Facility'. She's only ever been here once, the day she checked Marnie in after their mother died. Four years now, almost five. *Time flies.*

Bryher expels a deep breath and gets out of the car. *It's time to change that, Marnie. We're family.*

Inside the building, Bryher talks to the receptionist, and is then led by a nurse down a quiet, lino-floored hallway to a room on the second floor at the corner of the building.

'Marnie, dear, you have a visitor,' the nurse says. 'It's your sister, isn't that nice?'

Bryher swallows as she sees Marnie siting up against two fat pillows, picking at the cotton sheet as she stares into space.

'Thank you,' Bryher says to the nurse. 'I'll only be a little while.'

'Take as long as you like, Ms Finch. She's not going anywhere.'

Bryher walks over to the bed and pulls up a yellow plastic chair. Marnie is thinner than she remembers, and her cheeks have lost their youthful fullness, but her hair is still a lustrous red-gold and her eyes the turquoise blue that won her so many commercials in her childhood.

Bryher clears her throat and shuffles the chair closer.

'Hi, Marnie. It's me. Bryher. You remember me, don't you? Your sister.'

She watches Marnie for any reaction, but there is no flicker of recognition. Nothing but the staring and the constant picking at the sheet.

'So, uh, Marnie. It looks like they're taking good care of you here. I made sure to find you a nice place.' She turns her head to look out of the sash window which has been fixed to open just a few inches. 'You have a lovely view. There's a field across the road and I can see some black and white cows. I think they're called Holsteins. There's a big oak tree just out on the lawn and the daffodils are coming up.'

She looks back at her sister and takes hold of the restless hand. Marnie's fingers close around hers and Bryher rubs her thumb over Marnie's fingers.

'I've just finished filming a mini-series over in England. You know who I played? Anne Boleyn, Henry VIII's second wife. The one he loved most of all. The one who was the mother of Elizabeth I. It's quite the story.'

She brushes a strand of golden hair out of Marnie's eyes. 'I met a lovely lady over in England. She's a cousin of ours. Her name's Betty Pilcher. We were on a TV show together and we found out we're both descendants of Anne Boleyn's sister, Mary. Isn't that something? Some people even say that through Mary, we're descended from one of Henry VIII's illegitimate children. We might have royal blood. Isn't that wild?'

She releases Marnie's hand. 'I've brought you something.' She reaches into the pocket of her hoodie. 'You're the oldest sister, so this really belongs to you.' She holds up the 'B' necklace Betty had given her. She rubs her fingers over the maker's mark on the back of the gold initial.

She smiles at Marnie and fastens it around her sister's slender neck.

'There. It's where it belongs.'

'How are you doing in here?' the nurse asks as she enters the room. 'I brought you a nice hot cup of coffee.'

Bryher rises. 'Thank you, but I'm on my way.'

'Already? Did you have a nice visit?'

'Yes.' She glances at Marnie and smiles. 'Yes, we did.'

'Oh, isn't that a pretty necklace you've given her.'

'It is, isn't it? It's just a cheap necklace I picked up in London. Brass and plastic pearls. I thought it would look pretty on Marnie. A "B" to remind her of her sister Bryher.'

'That's very good of you, Ms Finch. Such a lovely thought.'

She smiles at the nurse. 'I wouldn't want it to get lost. Sentimental reasons, you know?'

'Of course, I entirely understand. Every room has a small safe, just like in a hotel. I'll be sure to put it in there whenever Marnie's not wearing it.'

'Thanks very much. I'd appreciate that.'

'Shall I see you out?'

'I know my way. I'll come again next week. In fact, I'll come every week. We'll take the necklace out of the safe and she can wear it then. Let's get her outside in a wheelchair when it gets warmer. Would that be okay?'

'I know our Marnie would love that. She's lucky to have a sister like you.'

Epilogue

BETTY

Puddleton, England
April 2025

Betty sets down her cup of milky tea on the coffee table along with a plate of Hobnobs. She picks up the remote for her new flatscreen TV and sifts through the channels until she finds *Doc Martin*.

'Bijou! Bijou, sweetie,' she calls out to the hallway. 'Our favourite show is on! I've got bickies.'

The cat pads down the hallway and across the lounge's green carpet. She leaps up onto the chintz-covered sofa and settles down beside Betty.

'There's a good girl,' Betty says as she strokes the cat's fluffy grey fur. Her fingers jiggle the large gold 'B' of the pearl necklace around Bijou's neck. 'Aren't you a pretty girl, Bijou, with your new collar? It was such a shame to hide it away in a safe deposit box, wasn't it? It's so much nicer to see it worn, don't you think?'

She breaks off a piece of a biscuit and feeds it to the cat. She is pleased with herself. Everything has worked out perfectly. Even better than she'd hoped. She'd even ended up with a lovely, valuable copy of her mother's necklace. How that had happened is indeed a mystery, but who is she to question providence?

She'd been so worried about Bryher wearing her mother's necklace to the BAFTAs after the break-in. What if someone were to try to hurt Bryher just to get their hands on it, just like they'd hurt her? She'd thought she'd got away with it, buying the Hever necklace for Bryher to wear instead. But then Bryher had insisted on switching it for Mummy's necklace for that silly interview. That had made her terribly nervous. When that kerfuffle with Bryher's sister-in-law happened, Betty had seen her chance to switch the necklaces back in the ladies' toilets, and that's just what she'd done.

Whoever stole Bryher's necklace would have found themselves with a sixty-five-pound Hever copy. Betty laughs at the thought. She would have loved to have seen their face! No one would have noticed little Betty Pilcher wearing the real Boleyn necklace. Silly people. The Boleyn necklace was hiding in plain sight the whole time.

Now, Bryher has the real necklace, as she should, and she's getting on so well since she's returned to America, what with her new role in the next Greta Gerwig movie and *Henry and Anne* about to be broadcast on Netflix. Luck has changed direction for Bryher, and Betty couldn't be happier for her.

Giving the necklace to her in a Hever gift box was their little inside joke. Of course, she would have left it to Bryher in her will, but why wait? She's as healthy as an ox, and it was hardly the kind of thing to wear to the WI Christmas ball. No, it was time to pass it on to the next generation. One day she'll tell Bryher the whole story about how the queen's necklace came to be in the hands of Betty Pilcher. It's a very good story.

She picks Bijou up and settles the cat in her lap. 'There we go, Bijou. Just in time for *Doc Martin* and that lovely Martin Clunes.'

A Note About The Boleyn Sisters' Ages

No record has been found of the birthdays of Mary and Anne Boleyn, so I have relied on the extensive research of Alison Weir in her biography *Mary Boleyn* (Vintage Books 2011) and John Guy and Julia Fox in *Hunting the Falcon: Henry VIII, Anne Boleyn and the Marriage that Shook Europe* (Bloomsbury Circus 2023). The general consensus is that Mary was the elder sister by a year or two, with her birth likely in 1498 or 1499, and Anne's in 1500 or 1501. It is thought that their brother, George, followed in 1503 or 1504 (see pages 24 and 25 in Alison Weir's book and page 34 in John Guy and Julia Fox's).

In *The Queen's Necklace*, I have set Mary Boleyn's birth in 1499 and Anne's in 1500.

Acknowledgments

A few years ago I was in Newfoundland researching *The English Wife*. My main base was at my cousin Jennifer's in St John's, who is the daughter of my half-uncle, Gus Edwards, and his English wife Stephanie. Gus and Stephanie had met during WWII in England when Gus was stationed there with the Newfoundland infantry. They fell in love, married, and Stephanie moved to Newfoundland as a war bride (as did my main character Ellie in *The English Wife*).

After busy days researching and writing, I'd spend the evenings playing killer games of Settlers of Catan with Jennifer and her husband Rob (we're a game-playing family and we take no prisoners). During one of these evenings we were talking about family history, and Jennifer casually mentioned that her English uncle, Gavin, had traced their family back to Mary Boleyn via Mary's eldest daughter. Catherine Carey. Well, my ears pricked up. It turned out that Jennifer had all of her uncle's notes and the family tree that he had meticulously drawn out. Gavin had been a headmaster in a boys' school in England and was a dab hand at research.

That evening was enough to light a spark in my mind, which, over the next few years, fizzed and sputtered and refused to go out even as I researched and wrote the first three books of the Fry Sisters series. Then, in London in 2023, I visited a Hans Holbein exhibition of his evocative portrait drawings of the Tudor court, and I suddenly just *had* to write this book. I decided it would be a book about sisters – Mary and Anne, along with contemporary sisters Bryher and Marnie. And what would connect these two stories, the historical and the contemporary? An object… What object? Something iconic. Something recognisable. Of course! The 'B' necklace that appears in several of Anne's portraits. And that's how *The Queen's Necklace* was born, over my cousin's kitchen table in St John's, Newfoundland, during a break from playing Settlers of Catan. Thank you, Jennifer!

I could not have written *The Queen's Necklace* without the support of the research undertaken by Alison Weir in her book, *Mary Boleyn*, and John Guy and Julia Fox for *Hunting the Falcon: Henry VIII, Anne Boleyn and the Marriage that Shook Europe*. The breadth of their research, and the skill with which they have brought to life the lives of Mary and Anne Boleyn and the members of the Tudor court, helped me greatly in my attempt to recreate the environments in which the Boleyn sisters lived.

Thanks, as ever, go to my sister, Carolyn Chinn, for reading an early draft and being such a great beta reader. She always helps me make the book better.

It takes a team to produce a book like *The Queen's Necklace*, and I owe a debt of gratitude to my publisher, Charlotte Ledger, at One More Chapter, and to my editor, Helen Williams, and her team of sub-editors, Emily Thomas, Dushi Horti, Janet Marie Adkins and Laura McCallen, who all contributed so much to tightening and polishing my early drafts into this finished novel. Thanks as well to designer Ellie Game for the lovely and evocative cover, and my agent, Joanna Swainson for her continued support.

I hope you enjoy reading it as much as I enjoyed writing it.

HAVE YOU READ THE FRY SISTERS SERIES?

In 1913, in a quiet corner of London, the three Fry sisters are coming of age, dreaming of all the possibilities the bright future offers. But when war erupts their innocence is shattered and a new era of uncertainty begins.

As the three sisters embark on journeys they never could have imagined, their mother Christina worries about the harsh new realities they face, and what their exposure to the wider world means for the secrets she's been keeping…

Available now in paperback, ebook and audio!

The Fry sisters enter the Roaring Twenties forever changed by
their experiences during the Great War. Now, as each of their lives
unfold in different corners of the globe, they come to realise that
the most important bond is that of family.

Available now in paperback, ebook and audio!

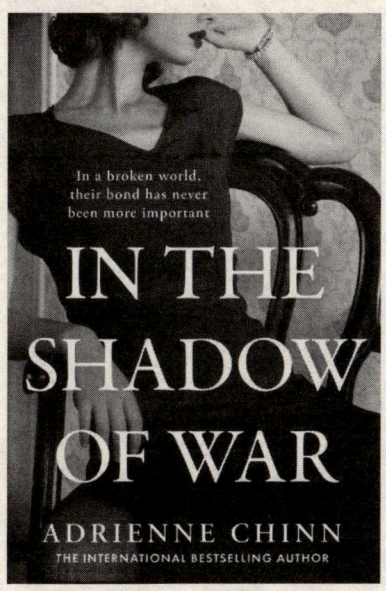

ONE MORE CHAPTER

YOUR NUMBER ONE STOP

FOR PAGETURNING BOOKS

The author and One More Chapter would like to thank everyone who contributed to the publication of this story...

Analytics
Imogen Wolstencroft

Audio
Fionnuala Barrett
Ciara Briggs

Contracts
Laura Amos
Inigo Vyvyan

Design
Lucy Bennett
Fiona Greenway
Liane Payne
Dean Russell

Digital Sales
Laura Daley
Lydia Grainge
Hannah Lismore

eCommerce
Laura Carpenter
Madeline ODonovan
Charlotte Stevens
Christina Storey
Jo Surman
Rachel Ward

Editorial
Janet Marie Adkins
Kara Daniel
Charlotte Ledger
Laura McCallen
Jennie Rothwell
Sofia Salazar Studer
Emily Thomas
Helen Williams

Harper360
Emily Gerbner
Ariana Juarez
Jean Marie Kelly
emma sullivan
Sophia Wilhelm

International Sales
Peter Borcsok
Ruth Burrow
Bethan Moore
Colleen Simpson

Inventory
Sarah Callaghan
Kirsty Norman

Marketing & Publicity
Chloe Cummings
Grace Edwards
Katie Sadler

Operations
Melissa Okusanya
Hannah Stamp

Production
Denis Manson
Simon Moore
Francesca Tuzzeo

Rights
Ashton Mucha
Alisah Saghir
Zoe Shine
Aisling Smyth
Lucy Vanderbilt

Trade Marketing
Ben Hurd
Eleanor Slater

**The HarperCollins
Distribution Team**

**The HarperCollins
Finance & Royalties
Team**

**The HarperCollins
Legal Team**

**The HarperCollins
Technology Team**

UK Sales
Isabel Coburn
Jay Cochrane
Sabina Lewis
Holly Martin
Harriet Williams
Leah Woods

**And every other
essential link in the
chain from delivery
drivers to booksellers
to librarians and
beyond!**

YOUR NUMBER ONE STOP

ONE MORE CHAPTER

FOR PAGETURNING BOOKS

One More Chapter is an
award-winning global
division of HarperCollins.

Subscribe to our newsletter to get our
latest eBook deals and stay up to date
with all our new releases!

signup.harpercollins.co.uk/
join/signup-omc

Meet the team at
www.onemorechapter.com

Follow us!

@onemorechapterhc

Do you write unputdownable fiction?
We love to hear from new voices.
Find out how to submit your novel at
www.onemorechapter.com/submissions